MYS
CON

Ingram

BRUSHBACK

NOVELS BY K.C. CONSTANTINE

K.C. CONSTANTINE

BRUSHBACK

THE MYSTERIOUS PRESS

Published by Warner Books

A Time Warner Company

Mysterious Press books are published by Warner Books, Inc.,
1271 Avenue of the Americas, New York, NY 10020

Visit our Web site at http://warnerbooks.com

 A Time Warner Company

The Mysterious Press name and logo are registered trademarks of Warner Books, Inc.

Printed in the United States of America

First printing: March 1998

10 9 8 7 6 5 4 3 2 1

Library of Congress Cataloging-in-Publication Data

Constantine, K. C.
    Brushback / K.C. Constantine.
        p.   cm.
    ISBN 0-89296-646-7
    I. Title.
    PS 3553.O524B78   1998
    813'.54—dc21   97-10130
                                                                 CIP

Author's Note

The great Boston Red Sox hitter Ted Williams is portrayed herein as having participated in events which occurred solely in my imagination. My apology to Mr. Williams for having used him thusly without seeking his permission. I hope my fictional portrait is not inconsistent with his actual ability and character.

BRUSHBACK

The admissions clerk was short, thick through the middle, and had lips so thin Carlucci couldn't tell she had a mouth until she started shouting at him. He usually had no problem empathizing with people doing anything remotely connected to emergency work, because he thought he'd seen just about every kind of stress they routinely had to deal with and so he tended to overlook rudeness in the name of efficiency. But he'd been in Conemaugh General Hospital's ER three nights out of the last four, and each time, within seconds after he'd appeared at her window, this admissions clerk was shouting at him for no reason that he could imagine.

Up to now, he hadn't otherwise identified himself except as the son of the patient, that is, the bearer of the insurance identity card. So far, his only concern had been getting medical attention for his mother. He didn't know whether she was having heart attacks or anxiety attacks, even though two different doctors on the first two nights both came down clearly on the side of anxi-

I

ety. Carlucci wasn't reassured because, of course, his mother wasn't reassured. While it seemed to him that she wanted to believe the doctors who'd told her the symptoms they were observing did not indicate coronary artery disease, everything she said and did showed her raging disbelief. Every time one of the heart unit nurses attached the leads from an ECG monitor to Mrs. Carlucci and checked her vital signs while asking for her symptoms, Mrs. Carlucci protested loudly that she didn't want to talk to any goddamn female nurse, she wanted to see a goddamn male doctor, anybody ever know a nurse yet that knew as much as a doctor? "You go to medical school or something? Hell no! Get a doctor in here!"

Carlucci rolled his eyes and sighed and shrugged apologetically at the nurses who'd been the targets of his mother's tirades, but they didn't seem too impressed that Carlucci was on their side. Without exception, if they were not necessarily overflowing with bedside optimism, they were all professionally calm and courteous, no matter how abrupt and abrasive Mrs. Carlucci was or how apologetic he was. As far as Carlucci could tell, to the nurses his mother's fearful, angry outbursts were just one more symptom to be observed.

The admissions clerk was another story. Her piercing looks and shrill orders kept banging into Carlucci's consciousness while he watched his mother being attended to by the assistant director of the ER, a tall, fortyish, curly-haired son of blond Italians. The man seemed to put Mrs. Carlucci at ease just by touching her forearm after he took her blood pressure himself, not because he didn't believe the nurses' readings but apparently because he saw it as an opportunity to touch Mrs. Carlucci. He kept his hand on her forearm while he talked to her, patting her in time with his words and holding her hand after he'd taken her pulse and looking at her so unwaveringly that Carlucci could see his mother's breathing slowing down. He admired how the doctor could so quickly put his mother at ease, and envied it.

Fact was, he couldn't touch his mother except when she demanded his help getting in or out of his Chevy or when she occasionally asked him to sit next to her on the couch and watch TV and she'd forget herself and pick up his hand and hold it between both of hers. Otherwise, every time he tried to touch her she pushed him away, and she'd been doing that for so long he'd stopped thinking of trying to touch her except when she thought of it first.

Even while caught up in his envy for the doctor's touch, Carlucci knew it was wasted emotion. It was useless to think his mother would let him back into her life the way he'd been before the army and Vietnam and his father's accident and death. Carlucci considered himself lucky to be able to watch this doctor with his mother and to appreciate it and envy it and yet still have the sense to know it was beyond him. All he could do for his mother was what he thought any good son was supposed to do, which amounted to what she would permit him to do—in addition to everything she required, whether she appreciated that her requirements were being met or not. Most of the time, she did not.

Every time he helped her up or down steps, for example, which he had to do because her knees and hips were ravaged with arthritis, she invariably bitched at him for always being on the wrong side. "Not that side! The other side! You never know what side you're supposed to be on, honest to God."

After the doctor finished telling Mrs. Carlucci that nothing she was describing or nothing he was observing led him to conclude she was having anything but a "mean old nasty attack of the nerves," he told her he was going to prescribe a very mild tranquilizer for her. Then he leaned close to her and smiled and made her promise she would take one the moment she felt "one of these mean old nasty episodes coming on." He gave her hand another squeeze and motioned for Carlucci to follow him into an-

other part of the ER, well out of Mrs. Carlucci's hearing. He was
carrying a metal clipboard with him, reading as he walked.

When they were some distance from Mrs. Carlucci, the
doctor, still reading, said, "What's this, uh, the third night now?
Out of the last four?"

"Three out of four, yeah. Sorry, man. I mean, she says it's her
heart, she's grabbin' her chest, what am I, am I s'posed to argue
with her, tell her it ain't? What kind of heartless prick would I
be—'specially since I don't know what I'm talkin' about. So hey,
you know, I get her up here, fast as I can, what am I s'posed to do,
you know? We get here, you guys say it's somethin' else. I hate
botherin' you people in here, but there's no way I can't bother you,
you know?"

"Well don't worry about that. Uh, she under a lot of stress
lately? Or more than usual? Death in the family, problems with
relatives, neighbors, the furnace break, hot water tank, anything
like that?"

"No, nah, none of that stuff. It's me—well not me exactly,
it's my job. It's, uh, I'm, uh, I'm actin' chief of police."

"You are?" The doctor couldn't help himself. His eyebrows
went up in disbelief as he gave Carlucci the once-over.

"Yeah, yeah, I know, everybody thinks I got delusions of
grandeur, I know—"

"No no, I didn't mean anything, I'm sorry, that was, uh—"

"It's okay, it's all right, nobody believes me when I tell 'em.
But that's the thing, see. The mayor and his cronies on the council, I don't know what they're waitin' for, they want me to be chief,
they don't want me to be chief, somebody wants to put somebody
else in there, you know, there's all this politickin' goin' on, it's been
goin' on for months now, and meantime, I'm tryin' to get the department offa paper and onto computers, and I'm puttin' in a
lotta hours and my mother's gettin' really pissed. I mean more
pissed than usual. I don't know what else to tell ya. You're askin'

for stress, that's the stress. That's the thing that's changed. The only thing."

"Uh-huh, okay. Well first you have to know I'm not a cardiologist and if she wants to see one, if she's not happy with my diagnosis—but from reading her chart I can see I'm not alone here. So if you think that's what she wants, I can recommend a couple of very good heart guys, both here and in Pittsburgh, Allegheny General. But unless I'm missing something very small— and I don't want to tell you I know more than I do, I mean if you think she needs to see one, if you think she'd be more comfortable seeing one, if it would be more reassuring to her, then by all means, let me give you a couple of names—"

"No, nah, I mean, Jeez, you're the third guy looked at her now, and you all say the same thing, I mean, what the hell. Three of you all come to the same conclusion, right? Anxiety, right? I mean, I'm convinced. I mean, who ain't anxious? Some of us a lot more'n others. Problem is, what do I tell her—'cause she doesn't believe me about this. So how do I convince her you guys're right? My problem's not with you guys. It's when it's eleven o'clock at night and she's rubbin' her chest and she's startin' to hyperventilate, what do I say then?"

"The other two times, uh, did it happen around the same time?"

"Time of day? Yeah. Right around eleven, yeah."

"Happened every time around eleven? What's going on at eleven?"

"The news, that's all I can think of."

"Sorry? The news? What do you mean?"

Carlucci hung his head. "See, I don't, uh, I don't watch the news. Can't stand TV mostly about anything, but, uh, especially I can't watch the news. Somethin' happened to me a long time ago. When I came back from Nam. I just, uh . . . I don't know, I just can't watch it."

"And this is a problem between you and her?"

"Oh yeah. Big problem. Big. Most of the time, you know, she doesn't say anything—not anymore. But she used to really get on me about it. But every once in a while, you know, here it comes, off the wall, or from behind the pillows on the couch, I don't know where it comes from, but all of a sudden she can't stand it anymore. Starts talkin' how it ain't normal, how I'm not normal, which is all just a variation on the noise she used to throw at me about how if I didn't go in the army . . . if I didn't enlist and, uh, wind up in Vietnam . . . my father'd still be alive—I know, I know, don't look at me like that, it doesn't make any sense to me either. Never did. But it does to her."

Carlucci had been sighing and looking everywhere but at the doctor. He stopped sighing and fixed his gaze on the doctor's eyes and held out his right hand. "My name's Carlucci. Ruggiero. Most people call me Rugs. Some people think it's 'cause they can walk on me. Unfortunately, my mother's one of those people."

"Marino. Joe. No relation to the quarterback for the Dolphins. My father calls me Doc, but my mother's still calling me what she used to call me when I was in kindergarten, you know, 'My beautiful baby Joey.'" He smiled and shook Carlucci's hand warmly.

"So, uh, what do I tell her? How do I keep her convinced she's okay? I mean, hey, she's gettin' up there, you know? I mean, she grabs her chest and she says she's havin' one and I say no you're not and it turns out she's havin' one, you know, I'm gonna have one hell of a time livin' with myself afterward—or with her. You see the predicament?"

"Course I do. Look, I've prescribed a tranquilizer. Very mild. She can take four a day. One every four hours while she's awake. Does she drink?"

"No, Jesus, don't even say beer around her, uh-uh. Sometimes I wish she did."

"Well, that's okay, 'cause then there's no problem she could mix the two and forget how many tranquilizers she took or when she took the last one. You just remind her they're there for her to take, okay? Just temporarily. Get her over the rough spots, that's all, it's not a permanent thing."

"Oh yeah, absolutely. I'll tell the ladies that watch her. They'll make sure."

"More important, I think it would be better all around for you to get her some counseling."

"Whatta ya mean, 'all around'?"

"Just what I said. Sounds to me like you and she have some problems."

"You mean the both of us?"

"Yeah. From what you just said, I think it could help you both. But definitely she needs to talk to somebody. And if the thought of a counselor scares her, then maybe a priest—"

Carlucci shook his head and snorted. "Hey, she ain't goin' for no priest, that's out."

"Well, somebody else then. 'Cause she can be helped about this. I think you both can. Excuse me, did you say you have somebody watching her? Why's that?"

"Well, the reason I have somebody there, uh, you know, watchin' her is, uh, she, uh—how do I say this? She just hasn't been right since my father died."

"Uh-huh, I see. So about the priest, what? She's not a believer then, is that what you're saying?"

"Oh she's a believer. Just no priests, that's all. Watches church on TV. Especially black church, you know? Loves that music. Gets up and dances with it. It's practically the only exercise she gets. But otherwise, nah, she quit goin' to church after my dad died. Couldn't make up her mind whether it was my fault or the pope's. It was neck and neck there for a while. Lately, last couple years, the Vatican's takin' the heat. But that's subject to change at any second, you know? Depends how much overtime I'm workin'—which if I didn't work, I couldn't pay the women who watch her, know what I mean? I'm sorta screwed no matter which way I go."

"Well do you think you could get her to a psychologist? I know a couple of good ones. And if money's a problem, I'm sure they'd be happy to work something out with you."

"Listen, the more I think about this, the more antsy I'm gettin', I mean, I can hear it now—'Hey, Ma, whatta ya say I take you to see this guy, you talk to him a little bit every week, an hour maybe, you know, you talk to him about what's botherin' you, you know, doesn't matter what it is, all you have to do is, you just sit there and talk to him, okay? And maybe I'll talk to him too. Maybe we'll both talk to him.' Shit, I'd have to be wearin' Kevlar, man. Vest and helmet both.

"I'll tell ya what," Carlucci went on. "How about you go try it, huh? You tell her she needs to talk to somebody, that's why she's been in here three times since Monday, ain't nothin' wrong with her heart, it's all in her head. Go 'head, *you* say that, okay? I'll watch. But lemme warn ya, she went fuckin' nuts when I suggested it, you know? Just *asked* her one time what she thought about goin' in the county home. I mean she fucking flipped out when I brought that up, so you figure out how she's gonna react to what you're gonna say."

"All right, sure," Dr. Marino said. "Be glad to. I know there's a lot of resistance at first. There always is. Nobody wants to think they need any help—especially not that kind. Why do you think it's so easy for most people to transfer their emotional problems into physical ones? It's a lot easier to deal with the physical ones, you know? You take a pill same time every day, get an operation, everything's fine. For some people that's way easier than admitting they've got things wrong they can't deal with. And for people in your mother's generation, it's especially difficult to see any connection between what's wrong physically—or what they think or hope is wrong physically—and what's going on in another part of their life. But that's what I think she really needs—to find out what's going on in the rest of her life. I'll just write her a prescription and hand it to her."

"I thought you were writin' her one for a tranquilizer."

"I did. I'll just write her another one to see a psychologist. I'll give her two names."

Carlucci laughed and sighed and shook his head. "Just like that, huh? Hey, you can write her anything you want, it doesn't matter what you put on the pad there, 'cause what I wanna see is you tellin' her, right to her face, what that prescription's all about. And who's gotta get her there, that's what I wanna hear, 'cause that's gonna be me. I'm gonna be who has to try to get her in the car every time. But you go 'head, I'm right behind ya—but one second. Before I forget, I gotta register a complaint about the admissions clerk."

"The admissions clerk? What about her?"

"Every time I've brought my mother in here, all three times now, that woman's yellin' at me, that clerk. I just can't get it through my head—I mean, this is the way she was trained to handle people? When they come in here all stressed-out?"

"Well, in her behalf, I have to say she usually acts that way to get people to come to the point, 'cause a lot of people sort of hem and haw around, and her job is to get things moving as quickly and efficiently as possible—"

"Excuse me, but I can't accept that."

"Why not?"

"I've been a cop for twenty-two years, almost twenty-three, more than half that I've been a detective. Last ten years I've been a sergeant, now I'm actin' chief. Fact is, I couldn't tell ya on a bet how many times I've been in this ER, and the only people who have ever raised their voice at me—up to now—were the ones I had to restrain, or arrest, or both. I know how to give information, I know how to get information, I know not to waste people's time when they're doin' their jobs, but three times now I bring my mother in here, and three times this woman is screamin' at me. You say you're the assistant director, right?"

"Right, yes I am."

"So unless there's somebody else in here who's over you right now, you're the man, right?"

"Right again."

"Well I'm tellin' ya right now. I ever have to come up here in an official capacity and that woman's workin' and she screams at me? Soon as I'm done doin' what I came for, I'm gonna make sure she finds out that jail food is a whole lot worse than hospital food. And she's also gonna find out how much fun it is to make bond, I guarantee it. So if you don't want that to happen, you go tell her to figure out some other way to get things movin' quickly and efficiently—is that what you said?"

"Yes, that's what I said."

"I mean it. I'll bust her for interferin' with a police officer in the performance of his duty and anything else I can think of."

"Well I think I can understand your problem, I don't think I'd like anybody screaming at me if I was in your situation, but, uh, if you don't mind, I would prefer if you'd let me talk to her, okay?"

"No, uh-uh, I do mind. You go talk to my mother, you go tell her you're gonna prescribe some visits to a shrink and it's gonna be my job to get her there. And I'll listen to you do that and see if I can pick up some, uh, pointers on how to talk to her, 'cause it's obvious she thinks you're the cherry on top of this sundae here. And then when you're done with that, you can come with me while I talk to the lady out front, okay?"

Before they could make a move, a pager went off and they both automatically reached for their belts.

Carlucci got to his first. "It's mine. Lemme go see what it is before you talk to my mother, okay?"

"Whatever, that's fine."

"Okay to use one of your phones or do I gotta use a pay phone?"

"Use one of ours, that's alright."

Carlucci hurried to the many-sided desk in the center of the ER, Dr. Marino trailing behind, and picked up a phone and called his station. A nurse tried to tell him that the phone was for official use only but Marino waved her off, saying Carlucci was a cop.

"Rocksburg Police, Nowicki speakin'. How may I help you?"

"Carlucci. You page me?"

"Yeah. Fischetti got waved over when he was makin' a pass through the Flats after the football game, and some guys, old teenagers, they were drinkin' beer in an alley? Found a body, all beat to shit and back. Hold on to somethin'."

"Do what?"

"Hold on to somethin'. Fish says it's Bobby Blasco."

"Get out—huh? Is he sure?"

"Yeah. Fish collared him enough times, he oughta know him. Found him like only two doors down from his apartment, or row house I guess it is."

"Yeah, well, you're right, he oughta know him. He's sure it's him, no doubt?"

"Says it's him, man."

"Jesus Christ. What's it look like?"

"Fish says he's all busted up. Somebody really worked him over."

"Busted up? Possible he coulda got hit by a car?"

"No, uh-uh. 'Cause the water authority's workin' on a line at one end of the alley, and they got horses up on both ends and it's been like that for at least two days, so no way a car came through there."

"Fish called 'em? The water authority?"

"No, I called 'em. He said the horses were up when he got there. Had to move 'em to get in. Then he backed out and put 'em back up. Authority told me how long they been there."

"So you called everybody, right?"

"Yeah, except the coroner ain't answerin' his pager. But I'll get him."

"So who's down there with Fish?"

"Just one state cop. Don't ask me how come he showed up so fast. But he told Fish it's gonna be a while before their evidence truck gets there, maybe never."

"Why's that?"

"Apparently they got a murder-suicide up around New Kensington. You want me to see if the county's free?"

"Hey, you know me, I'd rather have the state guys any day of the week. But let me get down there and find out what's happenin', I'll let you know, okay? Bobby Blasco, no shit."

"Yeah, no shit."

"Okay. Keep tryin' the coroner. I'm in the ER with my mother."

"Again?"

"Yeah again. So I'm gonna be here for a little while yet, at least a couple more minutes, I gotta hear what the doc's gonna say to her. Then I gotta take her home—aw shit I can't take her home. But if they don't wanna keep her—and she wants to go home, aw fuck—I don't know what's goin' on, it's all screwed up, I gotta go."

Carlucci hung up and stood there for a moment shaking his head, thinking, Jesus Christ, Bobby Blasco. He picked up the phone again, dialed the station again, and told Nowicki, "I hope you didn't tell any reporters about this, right?"

"Nobody called from the paper yet tonight."

"Nobody? Hell, by now usually they woulda called twice."

"Yeah, I thought it was strange too, but you know, it's Friday night, maybe they're all doin' football shit."

"Yeah, well when they call, it hasn't happened yet, you hear? And you call Fish and tell him to tell everybody down there to shut up about it. Tell him keep the scene locked up as tight as he can—nobody in who doesn't live there, got it?"

"Fish knows that, man, but you know somebody from down there's gonna be callin' the papers, or the TV stations, c'mon."

"Tell him anyway. Keep it as clean as he can for as long as he can. Every jock sniffer and his brother's gonna be down there.

Man, we're not ready for this. Hold it—one more thing. The auxiliaries that were workin' the football game, they all gone?"

"Oh, I'm sure, yeah. Sure, they were probably gone an hour
ago."

"Shit. We could use 'em—listen, if there's just the three of
us down there, we're gonna need help. You might have to call 'em
back."

"Whatever. I'm here till seven."

Carlucci hung up again and told Dr. Marino he was ready.
Marino peered at Carlucci and asked if he was all right.

"Why?"

" 'Cause you look a little pale all of a sudden."

Carlucci dismissed that by saying, "Look, soon as we get
finished here—soon as you get finished—with my mother, uh,
how about you keep her here tonight, okay? I got a real problem,
I mean, I never had to handle anything like this, so I can't really
take the time to take my mother home and get somebody in to
watch her, you know? What I'm sayin' is, you know, even if it
doesn't look like she should be here, like you don't have any reason to keep her here, you know? Make something up, okay? I
mean it, I'm in a squeeze here. I really gotta take care of somethin' and I can't be thinkin' about her right now, especially since
you say she's all right, you know what I mean?"

"Well, I think a lot will depend on how she reacts to what
I say. But there'd be no physical problem about keeping her. I'm
sure we've got the beds. Don't know how your insurance company's gonna like that—you have any idea how much it costs to
stay in this hotel?"

"Hey, you have any idea what kinda hassle I'm gonna have
tryin' to find somebody to watch her—at this time of night?
C'mon, man, you gotta help me out here."

"What if she doesn't want to stay? It is her choice, you
know? Patients have rights, you know? Statutory rights. Patient's
bill of rights, you ever hear of that?"

"C'mon, Doc, just tell her you wanna watch her overnight, that's all. Forget about my insurance company, forget about her rights. Right now, there's something—I don't wanna say it's more important than her, you know? But it is—especially since you say she's okay. But at this fucking moment, I don't have any choice, okay? Listen, I'll make ya a deal. You help me out here, I'll let your admissions clerk alone, how's that?"

Dr. Marino thought that was very funny. "Let's see now. I put your mother under, uh, observation, under questionable circumstances to say the least, and in return for this you agree not to threaten another hospital employee with arrest, is that the deal? This is gonna cost your insurance company, which is to say you, because they're not gonna pay it, I can tell you that right now—this is gonna cost you upwards of six hundred bucks at least—are you aware of that? Do you understand what I just said? Six hundred dollars? Probably more. If you understand what I just said, okay, then let's go talk to her. But if she says she wants to go home, there is no legal or ethical way, based on my diagnosis, that I can force her to stay here, I don't care what kind of a hassle that creates for you, do you understand me?"

"Yeah, I understand you. Do you understand me? Huh? Ever hear of Bobby Blasco?"

"No. Should I?"

"See, he's my problem. Some kids just found him dead. You maybe never heard of him, but around here, especially in the Flats, Bobby Blasco was a really big deal, probably the greatest jock ever come out of this town. One of those all-everything guys, football, basketball, baseball, especially baseball. Only guy ever come outta the Flats—that I know of—made it to the major leagues. You never heard of him?"

Dr. Marino shook his head. "I just moved here last year. Hasn't even been a year. Ten months. I'm from Philadelphia."

"Well trust me. When word gets out, you're gonna know who he is. Was. And I gotta keep a lid on it before that mob starts trampin' all over the scene, get it? You understand what I'm talkin' about, I know you do. You know—clean and sterile above the table, dirty and unsterile below the table, right, ain't that what you guys say?"

"Yes. Right."

"Okay. Same thing with a crime scene. Except the whole thing's clean. And it's also dirty. The trick is keepin' the dirt that's there there and doin' everything you can do to keep new dirt from comin' in, okay? It's not possible, but you gotta try, and I need to go help my patrolman do that, okay? 'Cause when the creeps find out who this is, they're gonna be trampin' all over that place lookin' for souvenirs. Two cops ain't gonna be able to keep it clean. In fact, I can't even stay to listen to you talk to my mother. You know she's all right, I know she's all right, I mean I trust what you said about her, it ain't her heart, it's anxiety, so, Doc, I can't stay, believe me. You have to keep her here, I can't be worryin' about what it's gonna cost. 'Cause I don't do this thing right, it won't be just my mother I'm worryin' about, you follow me?"

Ten minutes later, Carlucci was in the Flats, on the south side of the Conemaugh River, trying to pull into the alley between Seneca and Washington streets. Along with the Rocksburg Water Authority horses, Fischetti's black-and-white was blocking the alley on the southern end and a state police cruiser was blocking the other end. Their light bars had brought everybody out; both ends of the alley were jammed with people trying to edge the horses forward so they could get a closer look. Some of them were pressed against the yellow tape Fischetti had hung across the alley above the horses. Carlucci called Nowicki and told him to get anybody he could, auxiliaries, volunteer firemen, anybody, to come and work crowd control.

Carlucci put his portable light on the roof and turned it on and got out with his flashlight on and started to put it in people's eyes to move them back. He pulled his collar up as a stiff cold breeze blew in off the river, carrying with it the strong chemical smell of the sewage treatment plant on the north shore. "Okay, people, listen up, please. I don't want anybody tryin' to get in this alley. Anybody comes on the other side of that tape without being asked specifically by a police officer will be arrested and prosecuted for disorderly conduct and interference with the police in the performance of their duty. You get one warning, people, and that was it."

He hustled down the alley until he came up beside Patrolman Larry Fischetti and a state police trooper he didn't recognize.

"Yo, Rugs," Fischetti said, down on his haunches, shining his flash on blood spatters on the bottom of a battered plastic garbage can.

"Where is he?"

"Right over there." Fischetti turned his flashlight on the body lying on its back, right leg doubled at the knee under the left, left arm across the stomach, right arm across the throat. Bobby Blasco was wearing a sleeveless white undershirt and dark trousers and nothing else.

"What shouldn't I be steppin' in?" Carlucci said.

"Fuck, man, it don't matter where you step, blood's everywhere. We're all steppin' in it. How you s'posed to not step in it, huh? Hey, Nowicki said he was gonna call the DA's evidence truck. He do it? State guys're out on somethin' forty miles from here, murder-suicide, somethin', ain't that what you said, Trooper? This is Actin' Chief Carlucci by the way. That's Trooper Dulac."

Carlucci shook hands with Dulac and said, "I told Nowicki to wait and see till I got here. Okay, so I'll go tell him. You hear whether he got the coroner yet?"

"I haven't talked to him since I called it in, man. And I hope you called somebody for crowd control, man, these people been trampin' all over here. Fuckin' mess we got."

"Yeah, I told him. You talked to anybody yet?"

BRUSHBACK 17

"Just the dudes that found him. But nobody else, not yet. Right after I got here, till Dulac showed up, it was everything I could do just to keep the vultures out."

"What'd the kids say? Are they kids, guys, what?"

"They're adults, you know, eighteen, nineteen. Fuckin' kids to me. They say they just found him, that's all. They were down at the football field after the game, juicin' and screwin' around. They ran outta beer, so they decide to come borrow some from one of their uncles, lives three doors down from Bobby B., and they practically tripped over him. They didn't have any lights, so they just thought he was passed out, drunk, you know, till one of 'em decides to check it out, so he puts a Bic lighter in his face and practically has a heart attack. Or so he says. That would be, uh, Zupanc, James. Personally, I think he's a scavenger."

"Why you sayin' that?"

"'Cause I caught a glimpse of red around his nails on his right hand. I didn't say anything about it, but you need to check him out."

"Okay. I will. What else?"

"I just happened to be cruisin' Seneca Street after the game, you know, it got a little nasty right at the end of the game—maybe you didn't hear about that, and while I'm at it I wanna make an appointment to talk to you about those fuckin' auxiliaries, man, they're a waste, no shit, they're worse than useless—"

"Yeah yeah, I know all about them—forget about them, what'd the kids say?"

"Hey, they just come runnin' outta the north end of the alley, you know, hollerin', wavin' their arms. And here we are."

"What time?"

"Twenty-three seventeen when I first spotted him. Blasco. So they waved me down around two minutes, tops, before that. I called Nowicki, he called Troop A, then he called you. I got twenty-three forty-nine now, how about you?"

"Yeah, me too," Dulac said.

Carlucci said he was a minute slow. "Okay, lemme go call Nowicki, get the DA's truck down here. Trooper, no way your guys're gonna get back here any time soon, right? 'Cause believe me, I'd much rather have your guys."

Dulac shook his head. "From what I understand, they just got started around twenty-two hundred. Not likely they're gonna be done till tomorrow, oh six hundred maybe, but I wouldn't hold my breath. They got at least three deceased. Husband, who was apparently the shooter, and the wife and one kid. Last I heard they were still not sure if there was only the one kid. So, uh, how you wanna break this down? You want me to take the crowd down the north end there?"

"Fine," Carlucci said. "I wanna take a look at him, then I'm gonna get my camera, do a sweep of both sides of the alley here after I get him pictured up—where is he in relation to his place? Nowicki said two doors down, is that right?"

"Yeah, more or less," Fischetti said. "And before you ask, I don't know who lives there. They ain't answerin' the door. That was the only door I tried. But far as I can tell, the blood starts up by his door, right in front—which was open by the way. But no lights on inside. TV was on, I could hear it. Maybe more than one."

"You didn't go in?"

"No. 'Cause people were already startin' in the alley from both ends and I had to clear 'em out and get the tape up and, uh, till Dulac here showed up, you know, I was just tryin' to take in as much as I could."

"I gotta go call Nowicki, get my cameras," Carlucci said. "I'll be right back. Go 'head, Trooper, don't wait on me. Those kids still here?"

"Yeah, they're still here," Fischetti said, turning back to the garbage can he'd been studying before. "And if you have to squeeze 'em, they're all underage."

Carlucci nodded, then went walking quickly back to his

Chevy, cringing that he was probably trampling evidence with every step. He called Nowicki again and told him to call the DA to authorize the use of their evidence truck and crime scene technicians. Then he got his Polaroid and Nikon cameras out of the trunk, checked them for film and batteries, and went quickly back north in the alley again.

Trooper Dulac had stopped about ten yards beyond the body and was focusing his flashlight on a garbage can against the row houses on the eastern side of the alley. He was calling for Carlucci to join him.

When Carlucci got there, Dulac said, "Think I found the weapon. Look at that."

Carlucci shone his own light on the dented aluminum can, its lid askew because of the handle of something tan and covered with blood which was sticking up, preventing the lid from fitting. "I think we can rule out a master criminal here," Dulac said dryly. He handed his flash to Carlucci and, stretching his rubber gloves back over his wrist, picked up the lid by the edges of the handle. He set it on the bricks beside the can while Carlucci bent over the can and shone his light into it.

It was a Ted Williams model Louisville Slugger baseball bat, streaked with blood down to the handle. There were only two spaces, about the width of two hands, about four or five inches up the handle that were relatively free of blood. Carlucci could see flesh and hair matted to the barrel of the bat above the trademark. He took half a dozen pictures, two each of the can, the contents, and the back of the building.

"Okay," Carlucci said. "We know which way he, she, or they went, and we know from that mob down there, that's about where the trail's gonna end, so until the DA's crew gets here, I think the best thing you can do is work that crowd down there, see what you can get, and I'll get the pictures. Man, how about this, huh? All the people he hit with a baseball, fuckin' bat gets him."

"What? I don't follow."

"You don't know this guy, do ya?"

Dulac shook his head. "The patrolman said he was some famous baseball player, but he was before my time, I never heard of him."

"Oh he was famous alright. Pitcher. Went to the major leagues. He's a really big deal around here—was. Not with everybody, just some people. Also famous for throwin' at guys' heads. But some people around here, they act like he was Jesus Christ come down off the cross, let him get away with all kinda shit, just 'cause he could do all these tricks with balls. Baseballs, footballs, basketballs. Didn't last too long in the majors. Only pitched a couple games. Then supposedly he slips in the shower horsin' around, cracks his elbow, the end. Been livin' on his rep ever since. And believe me, his rep, man, I don't know how many times I got called to his place—places. His saloons, his houses, his apartments, fuckin' guy was just bad news. Ever see that movie, *The Bad News Bears*? 'Bout a buncha cute little misfits on a baseball team?"

"Yeah, I've seen that," Dulac said. "Thought there was a couple of those movies."

"Probably was. Well that was the original, right there," Carlucci said, nodding toward Blasco's body. "Except the last thing that fucker was was cute. Tell ya the truth I can't understand how he lasted this long. I thought he woulda got dusted, man, a long time ago."

"Nobody liked him, everybody hated him, what?"

"It was more like he couldn't stand for anybody to like him. He made it hard. He was tough to take, man. Many times as I had to arrest him, you know, I'd always be lookin' for a way not to take him to jail, you know? He was a real hard-ass, but there was somethin' about him, I don't know, you just felt sorry for him. But then he'd finally figure a way to piss ya off, so you'd have to put him in the car. Anyway, let's go to work."

Carlucci took pictures of the body from both sides, then

close-ups of the head from all sides and directly above and then from the bottoms of the feet up. Then he worked his way north in the alley, first taking a shot of the back of the row house, then a shot of the alley floor until he had photographed overlapping shots of every inch of the entire block of the alley, stopping every so often to make an entry of the time and his position in his notebook, just to corroborate the time and date that would be on the backs of the photos.

Then he went back to Blasco's row house door and shot the stoop, the door, and the door frame. Then he shone his flash around on the wall inside the door until he saw the light switch, turned it on with the edge of his Nikon, and checked out the door and everything he could see from the outside. Then, working as methodically as he had in the alley, he photographed the hall leading from the alley into the kitchen, just about four feet from the alley door. He turned on every overhead light he could find, using the edge of his Nikon to trip the wall switches, looking at the floor every time he moved his feet, making sure he wasn't stepping on anything he could see that might pertain to what had happened.

By the time he'd photographed every room on both floors of the entire apartment—kitchen, dining room, and living room on the first floor, two bedrooms and a bath on the second—he was confident that whatever had been done to Bobby Blasco had started either in the back doorway or out on the stoop. There was nothing inside the row house that indicated to Carlucci in any way that the first blow had been struck inside. There was no blood that Carlucci could see, and nothing looked obviously out of place, though that was a large assumption because the place looked like it hadn't been cleaned in weeks, maybe longer. The most obvious thing that caught Carlucci's eye was that there were three TVs in the place, one in the living room, another in one of the bedrooms, and the third in the bathroom, and they were all on and all tuned to the Discovery Channel.

He returned to the back-door frame and examined it from the inside, shining his flash on every inch of it, but saw nothing unusual. Then he hunkered down and started going over the floor just inside the door and the stoop beyond it, which consisted of one step made of a single block of sandstone. Again, nothing caught his attention. He started shuffling forward on his haunches, south toward the body, when he spotted the first drops of blood. He was just getting out his tape measure when he heard the siren from the district attorney's office crime scene truck. Before he could say anything, he saw Fischetti hurrying south. Fischetti called over his shoulder, "Hey, Rugs, they're probably gonna want you to move your car, man."

"Aw don't let them in!" Carlucci shouted, but Fischetti didn't respond. "Ah shit," Carlucci muttered, hustling after Fischetti. When Carlucci reached the truck, Fischetti was already in his black-and-white with the motor running, waiting for Carlucci to move his Chevy.

"Shut it off, Fish," Carlucci said on his way to the driver-side door of the van. "Hey, guys, you can't bring this thing in here. The whole alley's the scene, you gotta start this end and work clear to the other end. Whoever did it coulda come in either end, but I'm pretty sure he went north when he left. The weapon's between the body and the north end, but no matter, the truck gotta stay here. You can't bring the truck in—hey! Ho? Anybody listenin' to me?" He was talking to the backside of the driver, who was fiddling with something on the floor between the seats.

"Hey, Carlucci," the driver said, turning around with a heavy expulsion of air. "Fuck you, tiny asshole, don't tell us how to work a fuckin' scene. Learn how to collect prints, then you can pop off, ya little fuck."

"Aw man," Carlucci said. "Why'd I know it was gonna be you, Emrich, huh?"

Carlucci recoiled as Crime Scene Tech Howie Emrich leaned

down and said, "The fuck you think it was gonna be, huh, genius?" blowing a geyser of beery breath into Carlucci's face.

"You jagoff you, you're drunk! Huh? Holy shit, man, I can smell you from a yard away, Jesus Christ."

"Hey, asshole, it's Friday night, what'd you expect? It's high school football in western Pennsylvania, it's Miller time, this Bud's for you, it don't get any better'n this. Durin' the game, you drain your Thermos, after the game you haul ass down to Evanko's, get a fish, warm your body, fill your soul with all the killer hits you just saw, know what I'm sayin'? Whatta ya think, Jack? Think he knows what I'm talkin' about, huh? Fuck he does, he don't have a fuckin' clue. Guys like him don't know what America's all about. America's all about football, tiny asshole—which you don't understand. 'Cause they made you play with the girls when you were in high school. Stop lookin' at me like 'at, I ain't drunk, get outta my way. You want the work done right, you send in the pros. You called for the pros, the pros have arrived. Now move your bony ass, get outta the way."

"Hold it, Emrich, don't get out, I'm tellin' ya."

"Ho, listen to him, don't get outta the truck—get the fuck outta the way, ya little prick."

"Who's with you? Who's that in there? Is that you, Turner?"

"Yeah it's me, Rugs. Jack."

"Hey, Jack. Tell your partner stay where he is or I'm gonna arrest him, I'm not jokin'."

"You're gonna what? You're gonna do what now? Arrest me? Fuck you," Emrich said, snorting and trying to move Carlucci aside with his left foot, a combination shove, sweep, and kick.

Carlucci darted aside to slip the full impact of the sweep-shove-kick and instinctively jabbed the end of his flashlight as hard as he could into the side of Emrich's knee.

"Ow, man, ow! You fucker you! What'd you do, you little prick?" Emrich started howling and nearly fell out of the truck trying to clutch his knee.

"Last warnin', Emrich," Carlucci said. "I'm tellin' ya, stay in the truck. You try to come outta the truck again, you're goin' in the back of that car with cuffs on. Fish! C'mere! Now! You listenin' to me, Emrich? I promise. I'll charge you with everything I can think of, and I can think of plenty right now, startin' with drunk and disorderly. How fast you wanna lose your job, huh? You so drunk you don't have sense enough to tell your boss you can't respond to the call? And you, Jack, no shit, you let this guy drive? I'm surprised at you, man. Nothin' this jagoff does surprises me, but you, man, I'm really surprised at you."

Turner shrugged at Carlucci and said, "Hey, he had the keys, what was I supposed to do, huh?"

"I'll tell ya what you better do, you want him to hold on to his job, huh? You got any respect for him at all, you better handcuff him to the steerin' wheel, the jagoff, I'm not jokin', 'cause he gets out? And messes up my crime scene, I'll bust ya both, I mean it, Jack."

"Aw c'mon, Rugs, Jesus," Turner said.

"Little fucker you, son of a bitch," Emrich growled, still clutching his knee, grunting through his teeth from the pain.

"Listen up, Emrich. You get outta this truck, you're under arrest, D and D, interference with a police officer, A and B on a police officer—that's a felony, jagoff—remember felony, huh? I got two witnesses plus all these civilians standin' around saw you try to kick me outta the way. All I did was respond, defend myself."

"Kick you! Fuck you! You're dreamin'. You're the one did the A and B with that, uh, whatever ya used, ya little prick! Anybody needs to be arrested it's you!"

"You been told, Emrich. Let's go, Jack, we wasted enough time already, c'mon, we got lotsa work here." Turner stepped into the back of the van, came out with his two kits, evidence and fingerprint, leaned close to Emrich and whispered in his ear for a long moment, with Emrich grumbling the whole time. Then

Turner got out the other side and followed Carlucci north in the alley after Carlucci told Fischetti to canvass the crowd and to start the canvass of the row houses from the south end of the block. "And if that jagoff gets out of the truck and you see him outta the truck? I'm orderin' you to arrest him, cuff him, put him in the back of your vehicle, you understand me?"

"Yes sir, actin' chief sir," Fischetti said indignantly, shaking his head. "Just remember he's a big dude, Rugs, okay? He gets out, I'm gonna need help, man. And I really don't feature bustin' anybody works in the DA's office, you know? I know I know, you're orderin' me to do it, but if I have to do it, I wanna know you have it in writin' somewhere, know what I mean? So make a very careful note about it, okay? Write it down, man, 'cause I'm writin' it down, right now. I'm serious. I want my ass covered if I have to do this. Bad enough I get beat up, I don't wanna lose my job on top of it, understand?"

"You're covered, don't worry, there's gonna be lots of paper about that asshole. Drunk fucker. He's why I wanted to wait for the state guys. Thinks 'cause he was a state cop for thirty years he knows every fuckin' thing. And this ain't the first time he showed up drunk. First time I was too scared to do anything about it, but not this time, no way. He gives you any shit, just holler. Okay, let's get started—oh. Gimme those kids' names, the ones that found him."

Fischetti stopped writing and turned back a couple of pages in his notebook. "Uh, Zupanc, James, age eighteen, 227 Washington Street; then, uh, Seslo, Robert, nineteen, 235 Washington; and Filopovich, Albert, also nineteen, 239 Washington. I'm pretty sure they'd all flunk a breath test, if you needed 'em to."

"Well, maybe we will. Which one did you say you thought got in his pockets?"

"Zupanc, yeah. James."

"And you saw blood on his fingers, is that it?"

"I think so. I'm not sure now, so don't hold me to it, but yeah."

"Okay, let's do it."

Carlucci hurried to Trooper Dulac's side, pulled him back from the crowd at the north end of the alley, and gave him the three names Fischetti had just given him. "I'll take Zupanc, you take Seslo, then whoever gets done first takes the last one, huh, this Filopovich? Bring 'em in the alley, whatta ya think? About maybe three, four steps from the body? Turn 'em around so they're looking at it?"

Dulac chewed his lower lip while listening, nodded, then approached the crowd, calling out, "Mister Zupanc? Mister Seslo? James Zupanc, Robert Seslo, you gentlemen here? Mister Zupanc, you wanna step in here with the chief? Go with him, please. That's it. Mister Seslo, you come with me, please."

James Zupanc shuffled out of the crowd, hands in the pockets of his blue jeans, his breath steaming red, blue, and white as he sidled around the state police cruiser.

Carlucci led Zupanc down the alley toward the body, stopping about five yards from it and turning his back so that Zupanc had to face the body. Then Carlucci flashed his light from both sides, left first, on Zupanc's face, searching for anything that would indicate Zupanc had been involved in more than just finding the body. "Hold out your hands, please."

"Huh? What for?"

"Just hold out your hands, please, right in front of you."

Zupanc muttered and bobbed his head from side to side, but he took his hands out of his pockets and held them out reluctantly, waist-high.

"Okay. Turn 'em over, I wanna see the backs of 'em."

"Hey, what, you think I did somethin'? Huh? I didn't do nothin'. Just screwin' around, that's all, after the game. We come in the alley, there he was, you know? The cop was drivin' by, just happened to be drivin' by, we hollered at him to stop—"

"How old are you, Mr. Zupanc?"

"Huh? Me? Eighteen. Why?"

"I can smell beer on you from three feet away. You know the legal age for consumption as well as I do. To purchase and consume alcoholic beverages under the age of twenty-one is a misdemeanor, you know that. And if I wanted to see your wallet now, would I be findin' a phony ID, huh? Got somethin' that says you're twenty-one when you ain't, that's another problem—would you be havin' that problem?"

"Huh? No. I don't have no phony ID, I didn't buy anything—"

"Then there's the problem of theft from a corpse, that's also a misdemeanor—dependin' of course on how much you took."

"Huh? Hold it, man. What theft—I didn't steal nothin'! C'mon, man, what's goin' on? I'm the one said we better call the cops, ask them other guys—"

"Before you found out who it was. When you thought it was just some drunk passed out, right. Then you found out who it was and then you started goin' through his pockets, don't try to bullshit me now, there's blood around the cuticles of your right index finger and your right middle finger, I can see it with just this flashlight here. Hold your right hand up again, take a look yourself. Get it up there, see for yourself what I'm talkin' about."

Zupanc shivered and tried to put his hands behind him and then brought them around and jammed them into the front pockets of his jeans.

"I'm gonna tell ya once more. Take your right hand outta your pocket and hold it up there so I can put a light on it. I want you to see for yourself what I'm talkin' about. Do it!"

"Aw shit, man, I didn't do nothin', I was just, you know . . . aw man, what the fuck." He scowled and licked his lips and slowly drew his right hand out of his pocket and held it up.

"Look at it," Carlucci said, shining his light on it.

"Aw man, this sucks, man, I didn't do nothin'."

"Look at your hand! Look at the first two fingers. At the cuticles there. You see that red stuff, huh? You gonna tell me you chewed a hangnail off, huh? That man is covered with blood, it's all over his pants. You put your hands in his pockets. What're you, some kind of pervert, huh? You get off feelin' up a corpse, huh?"

"Aw come on, man, Jesus—"

"Or were you lookin' for some quick cash? Which?"

Zupanc began to shuffle around, his head bobbing, shoulders hitching and jerking. "Hey, I'm no fuckin' pervert, let's get that straight right now, okay? I ain't no fuckin' fag, okay?"

"You listen to me," Carlucci said, inventing everything he said next, making it up as he went. "If you touched any part of him, you know? His genitals? We can tell that. Simple little DNA test, you know? You know where we find DNA, huh? It's in your sweat, among other places. And your fingers sweat, James. If you touched him, you know? Touched his dick, huh? If you did, we'll know that, takes like about fifteen minutes, that test, that's all. And don't think about washin' your hands, 'cause that won't work. Your DNA? That stays with you, man. DNA is forever. And it stays on him, too. So why you wanna lie about it now? To me? That's stupid. Are you stupid? Huh? You don't look stupid. Why you wanna act stupid?"

Zupanc was looking at the bricks, at his shoes, anywhere but at Carlucci.

"Look at me, James. Look at me, goddammit! Why you actin' stupid? You went in the guy's pockets, yes or no?"

"Aw man—"

"Yes or no! Answer me!"

"Aw man, what the fuck. I thought he was drunk, you know, passed out, I was just lookin' for a little change, that's all, Jesus Christ, I ain't no fuckin' pervert, Jesus Christ, that makes me gag—"

"Wonder what your friends're gonna say when I ask 'em—"

"Ask 'em what? What? Fuck you gonna ask 'em, huh?"

"What you like to do. Maybe they'll tell me somethin' else—"

"Aw shit, man, you can't ask 'em 'at, Jesus Christ, c'mon, man, you can't say nothin' like 'at, c'mon. Okay, so I was lookin' through his pants, Jesus, I wasn't coppin' no feels, holy fuck, man, don't ask them guys 'at, ho Jesus, please. Look. Here." Zupanc dug deep into his left front pocket. "Look look, here. Seven bucks, that's it, man. That's all he had on him. I took it, okay? I confess. Here it is. Take it, man, I don't want it, no shit, I shouldn'ta took it, I'm sorry I took it, honest to God, I shoulda never did that. Here. Take it. C'mon."

"Stay right here, James," Carlucci said, turning and going to Jack Turner's side. Turner was bent over, working his way around the body with a flashlight.

"Hey, Jack, give me some evidence bags, okay? You got some?"

"Yeah, in my kit. What, you didn't bring any?"

"I'm drivin' my personal car. All my stuff's in the city car."

"Help yourself. Hey, Rugs?"

"Yeah?" Carlucci said, looking through Turner's evidence collection kit until he found the kinds of paper bags he was looking for.

"You really gonna write him up?"

"Emrich? Fuck you think, huh? I'm tired of bein' called a tiny asshole. You know what he used to do to me, huh? When he was with the state? Used to sing that Elton John song, remember? 'Tiny Dancer'? Remember that? He used to sing, 'Tiny asshole.' Every time he saw me."

"C'mon, Rugs. I'm talkin' about now. Everybody gets drunk once in a while."

"I don't believe you said that, Jack. What, you some kinda stimulation freak? You get off ridin' with drunk drivers? Huh? Get some thrill outta that?"

"You know what I mean."

"Spell it out for me, man, 'cause I don't know what you mean. Am I s'posed to be worryin' about his job or somethin'? Somebody in his family got some fuckin' terminal disease he can't get insurance for? Fuck him. Comes to him my heart's harder'n these bricks we're standin' on. There's a guy murdered his wife last year, he's walkin' around 'cause that asshole back in that truck—your partner back there—he fucked up every piece of blood evidence he collected at that scene. Every fuckin' one. You were sick or somethin', vacation maybe. But nothin' he collected stood up. Know why? 'Cause he was drunk. He mismarked every fuckin' one. I didn't say a fuckin' word. Not to the DA, not to the judge, not to anybody, not to your boss. I ate it. Fuckin' near choked on it, but I ate it. But you think I'm gonna watch him fuck up another one while he's callin' me names 'cause he's drunk, then you don't know me, Jack. Once? Yeah. Twice? Never fucking happen."

"His wife's sick, Rugs. Real sick."

"Hey, then I'm sorry for her. But I'm sorry for anybody married to him, sick or healthy. But she ain't who screwed my case and she wasn't drivin' that truck tonight and far as I know, she doesn't call me names. And I'm surprised you don't have your own key for that truck. That's stretchin' the hell outta friendship, you ask me. Thanks for the bags. "

"Okay, Rugs, had to ask, you know. I been workin' with the guy for a couple years now, you know?"

"Then I'm as sorry for you as I am for his wife."

Carlucci returned to James Zupanc's side and told him to put the seven dollars into the paper bag he held open for him. Carlucci used his felt marker to note the time, date, and temporary case name, BlascoRPD, and then noted that the money was received from Zupanc.

"Okay, James, anything else you wanna tell me? Keepin' in mind you're up for two misdemeanors here."

"Like what? Like what're you talkin' about, I ain't got nothin' to tell you. I'm tellin' ya, man, we were comin' back to see Albert's uncle. We were gonna get some beer, that's all."

"Albert who?"

"Filopovich, man. His Uncle Joe. Right there on Washington Street. We was just takin' a shortcut through the alley here, that's all, I swear to God, man. I had no fuckin' idea who that was."

"Would that have made a difference?"

"Huh?"

"Who it was? Are you sayin' if you knew it was Bobby B., you wouldn't've been in his pockets? Or you sayin' that's why you were in his pockets, 'cause you knew it was him. Which?"

"Aw no, wait wait wait, you're tryin' to get me all fucked up here. Say that again? If I knew it was him or if I didn't know it was him—I woulda done what now again? I ain't followin' you."

"When did you know who it was? First place, did you know Bobby Blasco? Did you know him or did you just know who he was?"

"Yeah. Course. Everybody knows him around here. Who don't know him? He owns Bobby B's."

"That's the only way you know him?"

"How else'm I s'posed to know him?"

"That he was a famous pitcher?"

"Famous what?"

"Pitcher, you know," Carlucci said, holding up his right hand with the thumb and his first two fingers curled around an imaginary baseball.

"Oh. Nah. You mean like I'm supposed to think he was somethin' special 'cause he was some kinda old-time pitcher or somethin'?"

"That didn't mean anything to you, huh?"

"Like what? What would I care? Baseball ain't no-fuckin'-where, man. 'Less you wanna go to sleep. Hockey's where it's at, man, you kiddin'? Somebody got me four tickets to the Pirates I don't know when it was, man, like last July. I lose big-time on them fuckers. Stood outside Three Rivers Stadium, man, only way I could get rid of 'em was to go for less than they were goin' for at the gate. Yeah. You think I'm shittin' ya, huh? But that's the truth. But you get me four tickets to the Penguins, man, I'll make a hundred percent, you kiddin'? Their top's like forty-somethin'? I'll get a hundred easy. No problem. Two minutes, guaranteed. But you could stand outside Three Rivers Stadium till the fifth inning with them Pirate tickets. Ain't that when they open the gates, let everybody in?"

"I didn't know they did that."

"Maybe they don't, I don't know. My old man's always talkin' how they used to do at Forbes Field. Or maybe it was the seventh inning, I forget. I'm just sayin', you go to sleep with them, the Pirates, that's all. Baseball. Fuckin' borrr-ing, man."

"Get back to Bobby Blasco. You didn't know him otherwise?"

"Otherwise? Like how? He was just, you know, the guy owned that joint by the bridge. I heard people say it used to be pretty nice at one time, like it was the only good restaurant ever down here. But I mean, how good could it be? Who the fuck'd put a nice restaurant down there? On Helen Street? You gotta be wacked-out to do somethin' that stupid. Who's gonna eat there? Nobody from around here."

"So you were never in his place, you never bought beer there, you never gambled there?"

"Gambled? In his place? I look like a gambler? Shees."

"You never had anything to do with Bobby Blasco? Nothin'. Until tonight."

"Like what, man? I mean, I see him around, so what? I don't know anything about him. I don't do anything with him, I don't go in his joint, I don't buy anything from him, I mean what're you talkin' about, I don't get this. Just 'cause I tried to make a little score there, c'mon, like what're you sayin', I used to do somethin'

with him or somethin'? Like what? Huh? Forget that other shit—
no way. I took the money, I shouldn'ta done that, I gave the
money back—to you. Didn't give it back to him—you know what
I mean."

"Okay, okay. So did you hear anything?"

"What? You mean tonight?"

"Yeah tonight, sure, but anytime. You hear anything at any
time about him? Like anybody especially pissed off at him, anything like that?"

"Like what, man, I don't get it. He's like, shit, he's older'n my
old man. We don't talk about him—me, my friends. We're talkin'
Mario Lemieux, Jaromir Jagr, Ulf Samuelsson, man, Penguins, we
don't talk baseball. You wanna talk baseball, go talk to my old
man—if you can find him. My old man's the one always talkin'
about Bobby what's-his-face, not me. I'm tellin' ya, all we did was
find him, man, we come through the alley, we find him, man, I swear
to you, that's all we did, practically tripped over him, swear to God."

"Okay," Carlucci said. "Okay. Now listen up. I don't want
you to go anywhere, I want you to stay right here, I don't want you
goin' home, I want you right where I can see you at all times, understand?"

"Aw Jeez, what for—didn't do nothin', come on!"

"Because I don't have anybody here to take you down the
station right now, and I am gonna take you down there—"

"What for? Jesus Christ I told you everything I did—"

" 'Cause you found the body, okay? 'Cause I have to take a
statement from you to that effect and I need you to sign it, okay,
and I can't do that here, so just be quiet and don't go anywhere.
Just do what I tell ya and everything'll be cool. Just back up and
lean against the back of that house and don't say anything."

Zupanc backed up, muttering and cursing under his breath.
Carlucci went over to Trooper Dulac, who was writing in his notebook.

"I talked to both of them, Seslo and Filopovich," Dulac

said. "They say they were drinking in somebody's car after the game, they ran out of beer, they were heading for Filopovich's uncle's place, they were either gonna raid his refrigerator or his wallet, whichever came first, and they took a shortcut through the alley and they nearly tripped over the body. If they made this one up, they're good at it, 'cause there's enough discrepancy to make it sound right."

"Check 'em for bruises, scratches, blood, ripped clothes?"

"I was comin' to that. Nothin' that I could see. Course I think we oughta be lookin' at them in good light somewhere. I told them not to go anywhere."

"Good. 'Cause when we finish, I'm gonna do just that. Uh, either one say anything about takin' anything from the body?"

"Yeah. Both of 'em, unsolicited. Said it was your guy, Zupanc, who took the money out of his pockets. They swear they never touched him. Said it was his idea, his act."

"Uh-huh. Okay. So, you wanna work the crowd? I'll go around the front and start workin' south on the door-to-door. Okay with you?"

"Whatever," Dulac said. He headed for people pressing against the yellow tape at the end of the alley as Carlucci sidled through the people and turned left and headed for the row houses fronting on Washington Street.

In less than fifteen minutes, Carlucci met Fischetti coming from the other end of the block of Washington Street. Either people were asleep and weren't answering the knocks, or they were old or frightened or hard of hearing and hadn't heard anything, or they were already milling around the ends of the alley. Twenty minutes later, they had the same result from a canvass of the row houses in the same block of Seneca Street.

"What'd you get in the crowd, anything?"

"Nothin'," Fischetti said. "Hey, Rugs, why're we even talkin' to these people? I know it's SOP, man, but, Jesus, you know who it's gonna be."

"Oh yeah? Who?"

"Gotta be somebody—I don't mean you know exactly who it's gonna be, but Jesus, there's about three PFAs outstanding—"

"Two."

"Hell, he got two ex-wives and they both got one out on him—"

"Just the one has. The other one dropped it after it expired."

"Well then there's his girlfriends, I know at least one of them for sure has one outstanding. We just got it, it's not even a week old. Plus I think one of his father-in-laws, he's still alive, and Christ knows how many brother-in-laws—I mean, how many times we get called, huh? This guy's sheet for domestic disturbance, hey, you gotta know it better'n I do, man, come on. Fuckin' judges been lettin' him skate for years, so why we even talkin' to strangers? It's a waste."

"What would be a bigger waste would be me explainin' to you why we're doin' what we're doin'. 'Cause if you don't know by now why we're doin' it, you need to get into another line of work, Fish, I mean seriously, man. One thing at a time, okay? One place at a time, one person at a time, one interview at a time. You can't do everything at once, okay? That make any sense to you? Yeah I know about the PFAs, I know about all the threats that've been made, I know about all the judges that let him skate. But what're we supposed to do, huh? Not talk to these people here? Sometimes I don't believe you, man, long as you been on the job? C'mon, I gotta call Nowicki, see if he ever got anybody from the coroner's office yet. You sure you didn't get anything from anybody at the south end of the alley?"

"Ah that was just creepshow time, that's all. More fun than TV. And if you wanted to get rid of 'em, man, best thing you could do is, I'm tellin' ya, I been thinkin' about this. I'm serious, man. I think you should carry a TV camera, and every time you run into a mob of ghouls like this, you know? You should take their picture and tell 'em if they go home they'll see themselves on TV."

"That's not bad, Fish, except you're forgettin' a coupla little things. Like money and time."

"I'm not forgettin' nothin', man. I thought it out—"

"Fish, stop right there, okay? We don't have money to waste on a TV camera, number one, and if we did, number two, local news only comes on like three times a day, you know? Noon, five or six, and eleven, right?"

"Yeah. So? You get a phony name tag, you know, or a jacket, says you're from one of the stations in Pittsburgh, they all got trucks roamin' around lookin' for creepshow stuff. That's all the fuck they put on there anymore, you know that."

"Fish, Fish, listen to me. Say somethin' happens at seven-thirty, so say you do fake 'em out, take their pictures then, you know? You think they're gonna run right home and get in front of the tube till the news comes on at eleven? Especially since they're not gonna see me drivin' off anyplace, you know, to get the film processed, huh?"

"Well, you could hire somebody, you know?"

"What?" Carlucci said, snorting and laughing. "Like what, a buncha actors, you mean? A pretend TV crew? Just to break up the ghoul mobs? Fish, you're beautiful man, honest to God. Where exactly you think we're gonna get the money to do that, huh? Hire a coupla actors, rent a camera and microphones, rent a truck, Jesus man, what? We keep 'em on a twenty-four-hour clock, huh? It's good you're a cop, Fish. 'Cause as a con man, I mean, as a hustler, you'd be on welfare in a week. And not a half an hour ago, you're writin' down an order I gave you and tellin' me to write it down 'cause you don't wanna get sued, you want your ass covered if you have to arrest that jagoff Emrich, and now here ya are, talkin' this goofy shit. And you're serious, too, man, don't try to deny it, you should see your face. C'mon, let's see if Dulac found anything. Or Turner."

"I ain't gonna deny it. Why would I deny it? I just forgot about the time, that's all."

"And the money. Little thing like money. 'Cause somebody'd have to go to the mayor with it. And council. I think I'll let you handle that, okay? See what it feels like. That's a trip you haven't taken yet, goin' to council, beggin' for money. You shoulda heard the shit they gave me when I asked 'em for the computers. Really. But next time, you're invited. No shit. I want you to hear all the fucked-up questions they ask you. Really, man, you'll get a whole new perspective on law enforcement. Serious. Think you'd like that?"

"Hey, Rugs, quit bustin' my balls, okay? So it wasn't such a great idea, you made your point, what the fuck."

"No, man, I'm serious, I really want you to go with me the next time I have to ask council for money. I want you to hear what goes on."

"Yeah. Right. We'll see."

Jack Turner asked Carlucci to help roll the body at twelve thirty-five. They found no surprises, just more blood, more contusions, more abrasions, none of the beginnings of lividity. A deputy coroner showed up at ten after one and made the official pronouncement of death, with an unofficial finding of death by unnatural causes. A Mutual Aid ambulance arrived at one-thirty and took Bobby Blasco away at one thirty-eight. Carlucci, Turner, and Dulac conferred for about two minutes about whether it made any sense to continue working the scene. They agreed it was time to take Zupanc, Seslo, and Filopovich to the Rocksburg PD station to take their statements. They also agreed it was time to see where they were, what they had, what they didn't have, what they needed next.

First thing Carlucci did after he got back to the station and separated Zupanc, Seslo, and Filopovich was to pull the paper files on the Protection From Abuse orders outstanding against "Robert Joseph Blasco, male Caucasian, age sixty, six feet one, two hundred twenty-five pounds—"

"Two twenty-five?" Turner scoffed. "Thirty, forty years ago maybe. Guaranteed he weighs two seventy-five he weighs an ounce. I don't think I could've rolled him by myself. Hey, you mind if I take some coffee out to Emrich?"

"Just don't take one of the good mugs," Carlucci said. "There's plastic cups right under there. In the cabinet. Hey, Jack, you wanna take him home, that's okay with me, go ahead. We're gonna be here for a while."

"Lemme see how he's doin', I'll let you know."

"Or check with, uh, Nowicki, the dispatcher, right there, around the corner, yeah right there—see if maybe who's ever on patrol can swing by and take him home, that'd be okay with me."

"Yeah, okay, Rugs, thanks." Turner prepared a coffee for Emrich and then went outside. In seconds he was back, talking to Nowicki, then he came around and told Carlucci that he was going to take him up on his offer of a ride for Emrich. "I'll just be outside till the car gets here, then I'll be back and we can pick this up, okay?"

"Yeah, sure," Carlucci said. "Where was I here, uh, lemme see, black graying, blue, no distinguishing marks or tattoos, last known address 205 Washington Street, Rocksburg, Pa., occupation, businessman, owner Bobby B's Brushback Bar and Grille, 567 Helen Street, Rocksburg, Pa.

"So, Dulac, what's your pleasure? You want the goofballs or you wanna go make the announcement everybody can sleep a little easier tonight?"

Dulac shrugged. "I had enough driving for one night, it's okay with you. Besides, you know where these people are, I'd be wasting time looking for them. I'll stay with the goofballs. Just point me to a room."

Carlucci led the way to his office, former chief Mario
Balzic's old office, and showed Dulac where everything was that
he might need, including a tape recorder if he didn't have one of
his own, which he did. "Don't wanna tell ya how to do your job,
Trooper, but make sure you get a good look at 'em, okay? With
Polaroids. You see one mark on 'em, I don't care how small, a
scratch, brush burn, don't matter what, hold 'em. Lockup's downstairs. Dispatcher'll take care of it for ya."

Dulac nodded and set off to start his interviews.

Carlucci went back into the duty room, gathered up the
copies of the PFAs, his notebooks, all the film he'd shot of the
scene, and went to talk to Nowicki.

"Do me a favor, Nowicki, okay? Leave a message on Per-
otta's machine, okay? Tell him I need this film developed fast as
he can do it, okay? Tell him I'm gonna put it in his box, and then,
uh, I'm goin' to see all the, uh, Missus Blascos I can find, plus this
Marlene, uh, what's this say—can you read this?"

"Looks like Donatello, Donatallo. And that looks like
Elaine to me. Don't look like Marlene. Whose writin' is this, Fischetti's? I can't make out whether that's an 'e' or an 'a' there. Fischetti write this? Man, this is some scribblin'. But that address is
definitely wrong, I can tell ya that right now. She don't live there."

"Huh? How do you know that?"

"'Cause that's where my aunt lives. Yeah. Seven zero one
Ridge Avenue, that can't be right, my Aunt Josie lives there. Bet
it's seven one zero. Man, Fischetti better get his act together. But
meanwhile, you oughta stop in see my aunt. Maybe my cousin'll
be home from work, maybe she'll answer the door. Franny? Remember? Third-place Miss Pennsylvania, huh? Ten years ago, huh?
Twelve maybe, I can never remember. But she's the one I been
tellin' ya about, the one I said I'd fix you up with if you got me
out from behind this fuckin' microphone? Don't tell me you forgot—"

"C'mon, Nowicki, not now, Jesus—"

"Hey, in the meantime, I almost forgot, you got like five calls from your mother, and is she pissed. Wow. Says you abandoned her, says she didn't think she raised a son would do that—"

"Hey! Knock it off, okay? I don't needa hear that right now, okay? Take the messages, tell her where I am, tell her it can't be helped, we both know she's in good shape, she's got the right people lockin' out for her, she don't need me right now, okay? You do that for me, I'll appreciate it."

"Uh, appreciate it enough to get me back out on the street—"

"Hey, Nowicki, what the fuck's wrong with you? We got a fuckin' homicide and you're gonna pick *now* to bust my balls about your job? Just for your information, you know how many times I talked to the mayor about switchin' to county nine-one-one? Huh? Gettin' civilian dispatchers in here? Just so you know, every fuckin' month since February, I made a special request—in writing, you hear me? And sent copies to the safety committee on council, and I bring it up in the council meetings—fuckers don't even wanna give me a straight answer about whether I'm the chief or not, you hear what I'm sayin'? It's fucking November, I'm doin' the chief's job, I'm gettin' paid sergeant's pay, so I don't need you bustin' my balls about *your* job anymore, okay? This is the last time I'm gonna tell ya about this, I mean it."

"Hey, Rugs, chill, Jesus, you know, I'm just talkin', that's all."

"Don't give me that shit, you're not just talkin'. You gotta stop this shit, Nowicki. I don't know where you learned it, I don't care, but you gotta stop bustin' people's balls about things that're none of your business. You don't needa tell me exactly what my mother said, okay? Just tell me she called, that's enough—"

"Hey, Rugs, there are times you ask me what she says—"

"If I ask you, it's 'cause I wanna know, fine, you tell me. If I don't ask you, don't tell me, simple as that. So tell me now—did we reach an understanding here or not? I need to know."

"Yeah. Sure."

"Good. Then take a look at these three addresses. This is where I'm gonna be. I'm goin' to Ridge Avenue first. I change my mind, I'll call in, okay?"

"Okay. Just one more thing about what you were just talkin' about. Okay? Don't get pissed off now. This is strictly information, okay?"

"Yeah, okay. What?"

"I ran into Bill Rascoli yesterday. He told me he was goin' nuts sittin' around the house, he said if you managed to get nine-one-one in here, you know, civilians on the mikes, like you just said you were tryin' to do? He said he was willin' to work four twelve-hour shifts like Thursday through Sunday for minimum wage, no benefits, he just really needs to get outta the house."

"That's interesting. No, really. Glad you told me that."

"That ain't all. He said he was talkin' to Stramsky and Royer—Royanovich, Royanowicz, whatever name he's goin' by now, you know? He said they were also kickin' around an idea, you know, startin' a company, the three of 'em, to hire out to the city as dispatchers. He said they'd be in to talk to you about it, you know, if you had some time. Either way, you know, by themselves or together, they're definitely interested."

Carlucci rubbed his chin and nodded. "Hey. I'm not the problem, I'd hire 'em in a minute. Fuckin' mayor's the problem. Bellotti and that fucker Joe Radio, that bowlegged prick. One-eighties me every fuckin' meeting about somethin'. Out in the hall, nobody around, he's my man, oh yeah, sure, Rugs, fine, absolutely, I'm with ya on this, all the way, down the line. Get in the fuckin' meetin', prick does a one-eighty. Then he's Bellotti's man. He's done it to me so many times now, every time—on the computers, dispatchers, promotions, reorganization—get in the meeting, it's like I'm fuckin' hallucinatin', I can't remember one thing he said to me. So tell Rascoli call me, I'll listen to him, hell yeah. It's a huge waste those guys aren't in here doin' what you're doin'. If we could work somethin' out, man, I think it'd be great. All we gotta do is convince Bellotti and Radio, they're the fuckin' roadblocks. I gotta go."

Carlucci squeezed into the only available space left on Ridge Avenue, in the part of Rocksburg known as West Park. Carlucci only half understood why it was called that. While it was true it was on the western edge of the city, as far as he knew there had never been a park there. He guessed that people might have thought of it as a park at one time because there had never been any industry located there, nothing but the businesses that supported urban life, groceries, bakeries, drugstores, cleaners, gas stations, auto repair shops, and the like. But in this part of West Park, for eight or ten blocks, there was only the occasional tavern to interrupt the monotony of single-family dwellings. Apartment houses were as rare as the taverns. Most of the houses were covered with some kind of metal or vinyl siding, and they were set so close together that usually they were separated by nothing more than a narrow walkway, shared by both houses, barely wide enough to drag a garbage can through. Only the newest houses had integral garages, and since Ridge Avenue on the north side was backed up against Norwood Hill, with no room for an alley like there was behind the houses on the south side of the street, on-street parking was a source of friction among neighbors.

Before Carlucci had closed the Chevy door, lights came on in the house on the north side of the street, and a woman clutching a robe at her throat rushed down the steps at him, waving her other hand in the air and yelling at him.

Carlucci put his portable light on his roof and turned it on and walked past the sputtering woman, saying, "Police business, ma'am, I'll be outta there shortly, okay?"

"Better not be there when my old man comes home, I don't care what kinda business you're on."

"Uh-huh, yes, ma'am, I hear ya. Shouldn't be too long. You have a nice day now."

"It's night, s'matter you, you blind?"

"Have a nice night, ma'am."

"Yeah yeah, I'm tellin' ya, you better not be there when my old man gets home."

"Yes, ma'am," Carlucci said, without breaking stride.

He was up on the porch, finger on the bell, feeling relieved that the light was on. He could hear a TV inside, and almost immediately somebody was hurrying toward the door, which started him wondering if Miss Elaine Donatello, or Donatallo, however she spelled it, might've already heard the news, especially since no news team, print or picture, had showed up in the Flats by the time the Mutual Aid ambulance had taken Bobby Blasco to the morgue in the Conemaugh General Hospital Pathology Department. And that had been at well past 1:30 A.M.

Carlucci was still wondering how they'd managed to get so lucky as to avoid the Pittsburgh TV stations' roving ghoul-squads. Blood on any street within fifty miles of downtown Pittsburgh normally attracted a camera crew faster than blood in salt water drew sharks. According to the three commercial TV stations in Pittsburgh, no bleeding body—shot, stabbed, or crushed—was too unnewsworthy to be left unphotographed. Films of the actual body were never broadcast, of course. But pools of blood? Empty cartridge casings? Smashed automobiles? Distraught witnesses? Hysterical next of kin? *Feelings* spurted across the TV screens as surely as blood spurted out of the severed arteries of the victims of violence, no matter what had caused it. And should the blood flow out of a minor celebrity like Bobby Blasco, it was nothing short of amazing, from Carlucci's point of view, that his department had managed somehow—so far—to skate clear of the problems reporters and photographers create just by their presence.

Carlucci, of course, got almost all of his information about the content of local TV news from his mother, who never missed a broadcast and tried her best to keep Carlucci abreast of all the terrible happenings despite his refusal to express any interest whatsoever in what local TV newscasters had decided was newsworthy. The rest he heard from the members of the Rocksburg PD, among whom local news was a standing joke, which invariably began: "Hey, you see that shit last night?" Followed by: "Yeah, I seen it. You know, I can remember when they used to have other stuff on there. Now, hey, all they do is the blotter. It's like if it don't involve cops or firemen it ain't news, I don't get it."

"What do you want?" came a woman's voice, bringing him back to the present.

"Rocksburg Police. Miss Donatello? It's the police, ma'am. I have to talk to you."

"Hey, Rocksburg Police, you have the wrong house. She lives at seven one oh. This is seven oh one. Sixth house on the other side."

Seven oh one? Oh-oh. Oh man, Carlucci thought. What would a shrink do with this? "Uh, I'm sorry, ma'am. Really. Uh. I knew the right address, I, uh, I mean I . . . I don't know what I'm doin' here." Yes you do, you lying bastard, you know exactly what you're doing there. "Uh, you're, uh, you're related to Nowicki, right?" Oh man, how lame can you get?

"Freddie? Is that who you mean?"

"Uh, yeah. Freddie. Oh man, we were just talkin about this address, it was, uh, honest, it was marked on a court order, and, uh, he told me it was wrong, he said his, uh, his relatives lived here, his aunt, and he told me what the right address was, and like a dummy, I, uh, I got outta the car and looked at this sheet and forgot everything he said." Oh man, shut up, you're just makin' it worse. "Sorry to bother you, ma'am, really, it was stupid. I know it's late. Hope you weren't sleepin' or anything."

The chain and locks came undone, and the door opened the width of her face. Carlucci's mouth fell open. He tried to swallow, tried several times to clear his throat, but couldn't. His mouth was suddenly full of cotton. Her black hair was short and thick and naturally curly, she had no makeup on, there were pouches under her eyes, and red flecks through the whites of her eyes as though she'd had a rough night, but her olive skin was smooth and her eyes were so brown they were almost black. She looked at him with an intensity that made him shiver.

"You Rugs?" she said. Her voice was low and liquid and he immediately thought of how different it was from his mother's. When his mother talked he heard sharp stones bouncing against the underside of a car. But when this woman said his name he thought of honey streaming into a cup of steaming tea.

"Uh . . . yeah. Rugs," he said, trying to sound like an adult man. He hated his voice. It was high and thin when he wasn't nervous. But when he was nervous, he thought he sounded like a cartoon character. And he was so nervous now his chest felt like he couldn't empty it. "That's me. Uh, how—how'd you know that?"

"Freddie's told me about you. I just took a guess."

"Wow," he said, adding a low whistle. "Some guess. Listen, I'm, uh, I'm really sorry I disturbed you . . . aw what am I sayin', I'm not sorry at all. You wanna go out with me sometime, huh? Oh man, what'm I sayin'? I shouldn'ta said that—"

"Franny?" came a voice from somewhere behind and above her. "Who is it? Is there somebody down there? I thought I heard the bell, did I hear the bell, or am I just dreamin'?"

"It's okay, Mom, you're not dreamin', go back to sleep." She'd turned away from the door to answer her mother, but when she turned back it was as though she'd never taken her eyes off him. "It is okay, isn't it? Should my mother be worryin' 'cause you show up at twenty-five after two askin' me for a date? After you already told me a lie? 'Cause you didn't get the address wrong. We both know that, right? Smart as Freddie says you are?"

Carlucci kept trying to get rid of the cotton that was clinging to the roof of his mouth. "Uh, I didn't mean to lie, honest.

I'm just not real good at this. I'm, uh, I'm . . . man, I'm practically a beginner. Jeez, I haven't done this since high school. I can't believe I'm sayin' this stupid shit—aw Jeez I'm sorry!"

"For what? For asking me? Or for saying 'stupid shit'?"

"No no, not that, not for askin'. No. The other . . . you know—"

"If that's the worst I ever hear from you I'll consider myself lucky."

"Yeah but still, I shouldn'ta said that . . . aw man—listen, I'm not usually this dumb, but, uh, I have to go, I really have to go talk to this other person, uh, at seven ten. But I hope . . . you know, you think about what I asked ya, okay? I'll get your phone number from Freddie. Is that all right—would that be okay with you?"

"Why don't you get it from me?" she said.

"Nah, that's okay, you don't have to do that now, I'll get it from him—'cause I gotta go. I don't wanna keep you."

"You don't?" She cocked her head and smiled. "That's a surprise."

"Not keep you, no, that's not what I meant, you know— keep you up, that's what I meant. But I don't mean I don't wanna keep you—oh man, I'm just makin' it worse, huh? I'm goin'. Good night. Nice to meet you. Uh, you're lots better lookin' than your picture. Really."

Carlucci nearly fell off the edge of the porch shuffling backwards and sidewards away from the door, and he stumbled again, on the last step before he reached the sidewalk, and careened into an old Ford Mustang parked at the curb, banging his knee.

Oh please don't let her be watchin', Carlucci prayed to himself, please please, and don't you turn around, you jerk, just keep movin' like nothin' happened, holy shit, she's gorgeous, way better lookin' than that picture Nowicki carries around, she don't look Polish, he looks Polish, he *is* Polish, she looks Italiano one hundred percent. And her voice, God, it's so pretty, so low, so clear, her eyes, she needsa get some sleep, her eyes were all bloodshot, she must be workin' too many hours, that ain't right, where the fuck does she work, she comes home this late . . . oh man, what's Ma gonna say, this ain't happened in twenty-three years, why is life so fucked up . . . lyin' bastard, boy was that lame, you got the address wrong, bitchin' out Nowicki and practically beggin' him to let you fall right into his trap. What a trap, ho man, what a trap you just set for yourself, like you don't have enough shit you don't know how to deal with. Man . . .

"C'mon, lady, open the door," Carlucci muttered after having rung the doorbell three times at 710. He could see night-lights in the back of the house, probably in the kitchen, and he could hear a TV.

Through the window in the wooden door, he saw the dim outline of bare feet coming hesitantly down the stairs, then the robe, then the torso. Then the light came on over his head and momentarily blinded him, and then he heard, "Better not be you, Bobby, I swear to God if that's you, I'm calling the police, I've got the phone right in my hand here, I'm not joking—hey, who are you? What do you want?" She may have been in bed moments ago, but she sounded very awake.

"Rocksburg Police, ma'am. I need to speak to Miss Elaine Donatello. Or Miss Marlene Donatallo."

"Rocksburg Police? Jesus, you scared me—you know what time it is? Hold up some ID or something—not too close, back up! I'm not openin' this door without ID. What do you want?"

Carlucci backed up half a step and held up his ID case and said, "Are you Elaine Donatello? Or Marlene Donatallo?"

"Who are you again? Tilt that up a little, lemme see that again."

"I'm Detective Sergeant Carlucci. Actin' chief, Rocksburg Police. I want to talk to you about your PFA, you know, against Robert J. Blasco?"

"You wanna talk to me about my PFA? Now?"

"Open the door, ma'am, please? I don't wanna disturb your neighbors."

She undid the locks, four of them, and pulled the door back enough to expose her face. She was probably in her forties, with dyed red hair in curlers, her face puffy, especially on the left side. Her eyes were suspicious, hard. "You come here at two-thirty in the morning to talk to me about my PFA order? What is this?"

"The man you signed out the PFA on? Robert Blasco? He's dead, ma'am. I thought you'd wanna know that."

"Oh my God." Her face went slack, her eyes suddenly soft. "Bobby's dead? You sure?"

"Yes, ma'am. May I come in, please? It's cold out here, and we're lettin' cold air in your house."

"Yeah, yeah, sure, come on," she said, clearing her throat and opening the door and backing away. After she closed the door, she backed into the living room and sank onto the arm of a couch. "My God. You know somethin'? All day I had this feeling, all day I had it, honest to God, I had this feelin' somethin' was gonna happen all day. In my chest. My heart was beatin' a little bit too fast all day long, and sometimes it was goin' ba-boom, like it was hollow in there, honest to God . . . it was scary. He's dead, I can't believe he's dead, you sure he's dead? That's so hard for me to believe. How did it happen? Somebody killed him, didn't they?"

"Yes, ma'am. Looks that way."

"When? How? Where?"

"We're not sure exactly when or how. Got a pretty good idea, but I don't wanna speculate, you know. Now the where, that was in the alley behind his place. His apartment on Washington Street?"

"Honest to God," she said, shaking her head. "I knew somethin' was gonna happen today—just had this funny feelin' all day. I took Valiums all day, every three hours, even though I'm not supposed to do that, I couldn't help it, I still couldn't make it go away. Almost came home, but I was safer at work, work was definitely safer. That was one thing about him, he never messed with me at work, thank God. But I'm gonna tell you the truth. I didn't think it'd be him. I thought it was gonna be me. I thought—I know it's crazy—I thought either he was gonna kill me today or I was gonna have a heart attack and die, honest to God. 'Cause I never went this long on this little sleep."

"Excuse me? What about sleep?"

"Oh God, Jesus—who're you again? I never talked to you about him, did I?"

"No, ma'am, who you would've talked to in my department, that would've been Patrolman Fischetti. Or you might've talked to a couple of other patrolmen, but I think Fischetti's name is on the PFA—"

"No, right, Fischetti. He's the one, that's the name, he's the only one I talked to from Rocksburg. Everybody else was from Family Court. I talked to a detective a couple times—"

"Sure it wasn't a state cop?"

"Oh no, he wasn't a state cop, I'm sure. He was connected with Family Court."

"Well, yeah, but any detective investigatin' anything for Family Court, he would've been from the DA's office. But the reason I'm here, ma'am, I mean it happened in Rocksburg, number one, and number two, Patrolman Fischetti's name is on this PFA as the investigating officer, also as the arresting officer. But you're right, ma'am, you never talked to me, not that I recall, no."

"Oh God," she said, sobbing once, shivering violently, "I can finally get some sleep. God, I thought I was never gonna sleep again as long as I lived." She scooched around on the arm of the couch, clasped her hands together, hunched over, and let out a squeal of joy. Then she looked pathetically at Carlucci and said, "Guess that didn't look too good, did it? But you know what, I don't give a damn, 'cause God, you don't know what it's been like. I haven't had one hour straight of uninterrupted sleep in like six

nights—not since I signed that." She pointed at the PFA in Carlucci's hand. "He called me all the time. All night long. Every half
hour. Sometimes every fifteen minutes. When he finally got tired
and went to sleep, he paid some guy to do it. Tonight was the first
time he didn't call me—after eleven. Then I really got scared. I
thought, Jesus God, what's he up to now?"

Carlucci laid the paper on a coffee table and asked, "Mind
if I sit down?"

"Oh please, sit sit, God—can I get you somethin'? Huh?
Name it, beer, wine, whiskey, coffee, tea, milk, water, oh God I'm
gonna have such a party—soon as I see the—this is gonna sound
terrible but I don't care, I mean it. I'm gonna have a party soon as
I see him in the casket, the second I see that, I'm comin' home and
callin' all my friends and I'm gonna throw the party of my life, I
swear, I don't care how that sounds." She blew out a long sigh of
relief and threw her arms out and then gave herself a rocking hug.
She stood and spun in a circle, thrusting her arms out, chanting.
"I can sleep, I can sleep, God, I can sleep."

Then she stopped and looked at Carlucci and said, "I'm sorry,
what did you want? Did you say, huh? I'm so spacey, God—"

"Uh, just wanted to ask you some questions, that's all.
Okay?"

"No, I mean to drink."

"No. Nothin', thanks, just some information, okay?"

"Sure," she said, going to the couch and falling backward
into it with a whoop, her head going back and her eyes closing.
"Yesssss! I can sleep!"

"These questions, uh, I gotta ask 'em, ma'am, understand? I
mean, you feared the man enough to get an order from the court,
Protection From Abuse order, you had the man arrested, it was
common knowledge the man was abusive toward women, the ones
in his life—both his ex-wives at one time or another, they did the
same thing you did—"

"And what's worse, they told me they did it! That's the worst part," she said. "Both of 'em called me up, they told me, they said, honey, you're makin' a biiiiiig mistake. And naturally, smart-ass that I am, I said what do you know, if you were so great you'd still be married to him. Yeah, honest to God, they both called me— and neither one of 'em told the other one they were gonna do it, swear to God. And naturally I'm the one thinks I'm gonna kiss him and turn him into a prince—hey, don't get me wrong here. Bobby, I mean when everything was goin' good? Bobby was the greatest. He was! Best guy I ever knew. When he was bookin' the right bands and he had Pops Fennelli runnin' his kitchen, God, Bobby was the sweetest, most generous man you ever saw—not you. Me. But when it wasn't, oh God, when he was losin' in the back room and when he booked a loser band, and when he couldn't find anybody to replace Pops, oh God, Bobby was a walking nightmare. He was the king of the pricks."

"When he was losin'? Losin' what?"

"Oh whatever. You kiddin'? Whatever he was bettin' on. Bobby was the classic degenerate gambler. Textbook case. Believe me, I know, 'cause that's where I met him. Gamblers Anonymous. But he was so bad, I didn't find out until way later, the only rea- son he ever came to a meeting—it wasn't to kick—oh man, did he push my buttons, so many warning signs, Jesus—it was to cover his trail for a while, till he could get some money together to pay his debts. They were gonna kill him. They didn't want his business, they didn't want him washin' money for 'em, they were so pissed, they didn't want anything but his money. They didn't want anything to do with him. 'Cause nobody wanted to be around him. Not when he was losin', he was so miserable, 'cause he hated himself so much for bein' a loser. I know everybody's supposed to have two sides, but I never saw it so obvious like it was in him. God, when I think of all the nights I sat up with him talkin' to him about what a good guy he was, tellin' him how he didn't need to beat up on himself like that, you know, and then I'd say somethin' he didn't like, God knows what it might be, whatever—it could be something about the way he held his spoon, you know? Not that I ever did that, I'm just givin' you an example of how crazy he could get over nothin'—somethin' he didn't like—and the bastard would turn right around and beat me up! All I had to do was say somethin' he didn't like! And you'd never know. It could be anything!"

"Uh, this 'they' you're talkin' about, how long ago was this?"

"You mean when I first met him? Three years ago—at least."

"Did he get straight with those people?"

"He said he did. But he was always behind with them. And anyway, you could never believe what he said—any gambler, you know? Not just Bobby. If they lie that they're tryin' to kick, they'll lie about anything, and they're so convincing, sooooo convincing, I mean, that's how you always know—only problem is you don't know till afterwards. Then's when you remember all the times they lied to you. You say to yourself, my God he was puttin' up billboards all over my life and I still didn't get it."

"So, far as you know, he was straight with them, right? That's what I'm askin'."

"Yeah, far as I know."

"Who are they? Were they locals?"

"Oh God, I don't know. You know, the real junkies, I mean, trust me, they bet with anybody. Until they wear it out, then they go someplace else, start the merry-go-round all over again, you know. So I don't know exactly who that was that particular time. All I know was Bobby was really scared of 'em. And Bobby wasn't scared of too many people. He was scared enough to bullshit me—and a whole lotta other people too I might add—that he was really tryin' to kick. But he wasn't. First sign was—and I should've seen this one a mile away—he got real fat. Anytime he was really hatin' himself, he'd empty the fridge. Start with the dill pickles, end with the heavenly hash. Both his wives told me that. They said watch out when he starts eatin'. I'm not kiddin', they both said that, but stupid me, did I listen? Nooooo. That was my problem. Delusions of grandeur—I was gonna be the one to help him. Talk about stupid, God.

"But just like now—the last five, six weeks, I'll bet he put on thirty pounds. I saw it all comin', all the signs were there, I mean, he'd show up here after he closed his place, you know, five-thirty, six in the morning, after he shut the games down in the back, he'd show up here and he'd have to make breakfast. Course I was still asleep, I didn't have to be at work till nine, later if I was showin' a house—he'd stand down there and pound on the door, wake me up, wake up the neighbors, I'd say, Bobby, what're you doin', are you nuts, I have to go to work, I need my sleep, and he'd push me into the kitchen and push me onto a chair and make me listen to every goddamn gory detail, like I didn't know how many different ways you could lose. If you saw what that man ate for breakfast, when you knew he was eatin' and drinkin' all night long, you couldn't believe your eyes.

"I mean, a dozen eggs, a pound of bacon, half a dozen bagels, that was nothin', that was just warmin' up. That was him just stretchin' his stomach. He'd say that. 'I'm just gettin' loose.' Yeah. 'Cause then he'd put on the sixteen-ounce New York strip. And the baked potatoes, and the bread, Jesus God, he ate a loaf of bread and a half a pound of butter—after he ate everything else. I had to sit there and toast the bread and butter it. The toast and butter was to calm his nerves—that's what he said, honest to God. Where he got these theories of nutrition, god only knows. . . .

"Oh I'm so relieved, God—isn't that awful? What I just said? I'm relieved another human being is dead. My therapist is gonna get so rich on me she's gonna retire before she's fifty."

Carlucci sniffed and cleared his throat. "Look, I wouldn't wanna guess about his weight now, but he looked pretty fat to me. You sayin' he was in the middle of another bad streak?"

"Oh God yes, I thought that's what I just said—didn't I just say that? I mean, that's how I wound up in Family Court, you know? Six weeks ago. This last one started six weeks ago. I know I said that."

"Yeah, right, I heard ya. Sorry. Go 'head."

"Okay, but see, bad streaks're all relative. Bad doesn't necessarily mean you're losin', 'cause winnin' was just as bad to him as losin'. Worse. Three weeks ago, after Pops got sick, he started winnin'. Those two things right there should've told me—"

"Who's this Pops guy?"

"Pops? Pops Fennelli. He's been workin' for Bobby I guess since Bobby opened up, when he had his first place, out in Oakland. By Forbes Field—so he told me, that was way before my time. Then when they tore Forbes Field down, he moved to the Flats. Pops is a chef—but don't call him that, he hates it. Says he's just a cook. But what he does is he ran the kitchen, hired all the help, kept everybody in line—did. Doesn't any more. He's dyin'. Lung cancer. Only surprise there is what took so long, he smoked constantly, probably since he was a kid. Wasn't for him Bobby wouldn't have stayed in business two weeks. No, really—not in that business. Bobby didn't know squirrel shit from snow peas— that's what Pops said to him once. Only time—according to Bobby—that Pops ever raised his voice at him. I don't know what got him started, but I was sittin' at the bar and Pops came out of the kitchen and he said—oh he was so mad—he said, 'Bobby, I don't tell you how to run your life, don't you ever come in my kitchen again and tell anybody how to cook anything 'cause if somebody put snow peas and squirrel shit on a plate you wouldn't know which was which.' And the whole band was standin' there— that was right after they just started their break but right before the canned music came on, and everybody who was sittin' at the bar heard him, and everything just got real quiet except for the kitchen, like everybody was waitin' for Bobby to explode. 'Cause that's what Bobby did. I mean nobody talked to Bobby like that. But he never said a word. He just hung his head, he got real close to Pops, he put his hand on Pops's shoulder and you couldn't hear

him but you knew he was apologizin' all over the place, and everybody at the bar, we were all sittin' there goin', you know, Whaaa?
Then the canned music came on and they went back in the
kitchen, Bobby and Pops."

"So this guy gettin' sick, this Pops, this was evidently a real
loss for Bobby, right? This guy was with him a long time? So when
he got sick, the place had to be gettin' messed up, right?"

"Oh absolutely. The day he found out Pops was in the hospital and what he had, that night Bobby won somethin' like seventeen hundred dollars playin' poker. And he came up here and he
gave it to me. I wouldn't take it, I told him, don't leave it, I didn't
want any part of it, believe me, 'cause there are some junkies, I
don't know whether you know this, but see, winnin' for them is
worse than losin', and believe me, Bobby was one of those. 'Cause
winnin' just puts off what they really want, just postpones it."

"What they really want?"

"You don't know? You really don't know? Serious?"

"Tell me."

"They wanna get beat up. They wanna lose. They want
somebody to show 'em they're no good. A lot of 'em now, they
love goin' through the cycle, it's all part of it, the ones that're also
partly manic-depressive? Winnin' is what they gotta go through
before they can get to the losin', it's part of the anticipation of
the losin', you know? So some of 'em love that anticipation. But
Bobby, he couldn't stand it, winnin'. I mean, he'd be doin' all the
faces and gestures and body language that winners're supposed to
do, he'd say all the words, but you didn't have to be any genius to
see how much he really hated it—oh God did he hate it. I mean
he'd give it away. If not to me, somebody else. Mostly to Pops,
and whoever Pops told him needed it in the kitchen.

" 'Cause Bobby was no dummy. That was the awful thing for
him. He knew what the game was and he hated it and he hated
himself 'cause he couldn't quit, but he knew exactly what the
game was. But God help you if you happened to be in front of

him when he was in the middle of winnin' and you knew he was supposed to be losin' and—and this is the real kick in the ass here—he was supposed to be losin' and he'd already given the money to somebody else and he thought he'd given it to you. 'Cause then it was suddenly a test of your loyalty. Which you were supposed to fail, 'cause he was pretending he'd taken the monkey off his back and put it on yours, only he'd given the money to so many different people he couldn't remember whether he'd given it to you or not. He really couldn't remember. So the only thing he had left was the belief that you'd just cheated him, took the money and you were lyin' to him. So that's when he'd give you the punishment. 'Cause there was goddamn stupid luck on his side all of a sudden, and there you were, and oh God, you can't believe how miserable it was to get caught in the middle of that. I mean you didn't have to say anything, or do anything. It was all projection with him. Whatever he hated about himself, he just threw it onto your face, whoever was in front of him.

"I knew this, believe me, I could read all the signs, I understood the way it worked, but it still caught me by surprise. 'Cause I'd see everything comin' except his hand. Thank God he was a slapper. 'Cause if he'd been a puncher? Strong as he was, he would've killed me. But Bobby didn't want to kill anybody. That's what really did it for me. When I finally saw that in him, when I finally figured out that he didn't wanna kill you? He just wanted to make you suffer as much as he was sufferin'? He didn't wanna let anybody off easy. He wanted to rub everybody's nose in it, God. Did he ever."

"Sounds to me like you've given this a lotta thought. And I'm not real sure I'm followin' it all."

"Oh God, of course I've given it a lotta thought—Jesus, that's all I did, do you think I wanted to? It was not my ambition to be an expert about Bobby, believe me. I tried tellin' myself I was backed into it, I fell all over myself tellin' that lie. They do that at the meetings, you know? One thing you can't do, you can't bullshit, so when you're first startin' out, you know, if you have any tendency at all toward playin' the mother hen, oh God, you know, you can just suck yourself right into that hole. But the old heads, they *will* tell you about it, I mean they *do* try to warn you. But you're so anxious at first, you know, to show everybody how smart you are and how this shit really didn't happen to you, it was all some cosmic mistake, and you go to enough meetings, and you drink enough coffee afterwards, and you listen, and pretty soon, whether you want to or not, you start thinkin' you're the expert and you've got this shit all figured out. Which doesn't mean necessarily you don't actually want to hear anybody else makin' sense, but eventually, you know, if you really wanna kick, you got to start payin' attention to the old heads. And I didn't have any choice. 'Cause the only two things I had left were my job and my life. Some order I just put them in, huh?

"But I mean, hey, everything else was gone. I'm ashamed to think of what everything else was. I still can't tell anybody outside the program what I actually lost. It makes me sick. I mean actually sick, I'm not just usin' words here."

"Listen," Carlucci said, "could we come back to this in a minute. Miss Donatello—is that with an 'a' or an 'e' by the way? How do you spell your name?"

"D-o-n-a-t-e-l-l-o. Why?"

"Couldn't make it out on this form here. And your first name, it's Elaine, or Marlene?"

"Oh it's Elaine. *Marlene?* God, never heard that before. And what'd you say your name was again? You didn't tell me your name. Or did you? I'm so spacey tired right now, I'm not thinkin' straight."

"Carlucci. Detective sergeant, Rocksburg PD. Right now I'm actin' chief. Since February. Uh, to get back to the people Bobby owed money to that time you were talkin' about—and now, from what you're describin', sounds to me like he was in the middle of a streak, good, bad, winnin' losin', uh, you have any names that come to mind, you know, people he mighta owed? Anybody at all?"

"Oh God, just go to his place any night. They'll all be there. Well I don't know about who's gonna be there now—now that their pigeon's gone. What'll happen to his place? Is it gonna get shut down?"

Carlucci shrugged. "He had kids, didn't he? From his first marriage?"

"Oh yeah. Two daughters."

"Musta had a will, right? If he did, you know, that goes through probate. Or maybe he had some kinda trust set up for 'em—hell, maybe he left it to you—"

"Oh right. No. When Bobby was that kind of generous with you, he wanted to be right there, so he could watch you. He ate that up. He loved watchin' you watchin' him bein' generous. No, guaranteed, he didn't leave it to me."

"Well, I don't have a clue, Miss Donatello, that's the point. I haven't even thought about lookin' into any of that yet. He have anything set up for you?"

"Oh please. If he had anything set up for me—no, Bobby didn't think like that. He could think as far as tomorrow morning, that's it."

"His kids, where're they?"

"Oh wait, I have to think. Arizona I think, but I'm not sure. If you want to know his wives' names and addresses, phone numbers, I have those. We talked a lot, really. They were nice. Good people, both of them. I really feel for his second wife. She didn't have a clue what Bobby was about. It was like livin' on the beach, lots of sunny, gorgeous days and then all of a sudden this storm'd blow in and knock your house down and all you could do was cry. That's the way she described it to me, livin' with him. She married him, she didn't understand nothin'—I mean not a thing about him! And she's a really fine person. She's a nurse, no, LPN is what she is. In Conemaugh Hospital? And works for a lotta families, in their homes—oh she's gonna be so upset. She was very confused about him, I don't know how she's gonna take this. You tell her yet, does she know?"

"No, ma'am. Not yet."

"So you don't care if I call her?"

Carlucci shrugged. "Hey, it's probably better if she heard it from somebody she knows."

"Okay if I call her now?"

"Uh, no, no, I gotta ask you some more things here. Where were you tonight?"

"Me? God, you think I did it? You gotta be kiddin'. The only way I would've ever done—not would've, could've—the only way I could've ever done anything physical to Bobby, maybe if I was in an army tank. Dependin' on whether I'm havin' a period or not, I can weigh a hundred and twenty, I can weigh a hundred and thirty-five, you kiddin'? Bobby could pick me up with one hand. He did it—more than once! Believe me. Grabbed me around the throat with his left hand and just lifted me right up! I'm not jokin'! Bobby was in pathetic shape generally, I don't know why he wasn't dead ten years ago from a heart attack or a stroke, but believe me, Bobby was strong as a bull—not his right arm. That was pretty weak—I mean compared to the other one. But there was nothin' wrong with his left arm, believe me."

"You didn't answer my question."

"Where was I you mean? I was here."

"Since when?"

"Since I got home from work."

"What time was that and where do you work?"

"Five-thirty. Demoise's Real Estate. Five thirty-five. Takes me five minutes to get here. A minute actually to get here, four minutes to park. It's on Broadway. Right on the corner of Seventh. Joe Demoise was there when I left. So was his wife, Shirley."

"Nobody else here?"

"No."

"Any nosy neighbors?"

"Every one of them. I'm the gamblin' slut of Ridge Avenue."

"So they'd tell me if they saw you leavin' tonight, right?"

"Oh God, guaranteed. Especially the Taraskys. Across the street. If she doesn't know when I'm comin' and goin', he does, believe me."

"Uh-huh," Carlucci said, adding that note to the others he'd made. "Uh, just curious. I don't usually associate gamblin' with women, you know? I mean, uh, what did you gamble on?"

"You don't associate women with gamblin'? Oh please, women don't gamble? Who do you think's in all those bingo halls? Come on. Detective, you should go to a couple meetings. Between the Catholic Church and their bingo games and all the volunteer fire departments and all the churches with their building funds, and all the Moose clubs and the Elks and the Legions and the VFWs, plus don't forget the state of Pennsylvania with all their lotteries and their horse tracks and now Ladbrooke's—God, you don't even have to go to the tracks anymore, you kiddin'? You can go to the Rocksburg Mall and there's Ladbrooke's sittin' right there waitin' for you. And I guess you think those're guys in drag on all those barstools? Huh?

"Listen, the longest you have to walk in that place to get fifteen bets down—well I never measured it but I'll bet it's not more than a hundred feet—boy, there's a sucker bet if I ever need one, hmm—oh God, listen to me. Anyway, if you want, you can be bettin' on something legal every night of the week. It's not like Vegas or Atlantic City, it shuts down here, but if you can wait a little bit, if you have just a little bit of a delayed gratification pattern, you can find all the legal action you want, not to mention the other kind.

"Couple meetings ago, somebody said the two biggest growth industries in this corner of the state are prison construction and lobbyin' for riverboat gamblin'. Everybody laughed when he said it 'cause they all knew it was true. I mean it's sick, really. Think of it, when was the last time you heard of anybody building a new school around here? I've been selling houses for twenty years, I've never seen it worse around here than it's been the last five years. There are perfectly decent houses, all they need is a new roof, new siding, new paint in a couple of rooms, they'd be cream puffs—and you can't give 'em away. Young people want 'em, God their tongues are out to here, but as soon as the bank starts checkin' their credit, they're dead. We have all these people goin' nowhere, it's pathetic. Old people have these houses, they're gettin' killed on the taxes, they're stuck, the goddamn politicians don't wanna cut 'em a break on school taxes, and the damn banks don't wanna give up a half a point to the kids, honest to God.

"That's why I knew I had to get in the program. I just couldn't keep it up, as little as I'm makin' these days. I'm serious, it's awful. I've sold seven houses this year. Five years ago I had months when I sold seven. Lotsa months. I used to make more in two months than I'm gonna make this year. Yeah. Honest to God."

"Let me back up here," Carlucci said. "Some things you said."

"Like what?"

"Like how many times Bobby used to call you at night. To harass you? You said tonight he stopped callin' after a certain time. When was that?"

"Last call he made, God, I'm not sure, 'cause I kept waitin' for the next one, you know? Had to be either eleven or eleven-thirty. I have to think what was on TV. I can't remember whether the news was still on or whether Letterman was on already. God, why can't I think when that was. I'm so spacey. God, I'm so tired, these Valiums're finally startin' to kick in."

"Why didn't you get your number changed?"

"Oh please, why do you think?" she said, sighing disgustedly. " 'Cause Bobby didn't like that. It *inconvenienced* him. And whatever *inconvenienced* him, you didn't do. Look, if you don't understand that, you need to talk to a pro, maybe they can explain it to you. Maybe *you* don't get scared when people say don't do something, but when he's big as Bobby? And strong as a horse? And you're not? And you're scared of guns—which I am? I mean, what choice do you have—why're you lookin' at me like that? Why do you think I got that PFA, huh? You know what you have to go through to get that? Huh? All the looks you get from the people fillin' it out? God, it's humiliating! I'm not talkin' humility here. I'm not talkin' about eatin' a little piece of humble pie! I'm talkin' *humiliation!* First you get it from him and then you get it from them. They can't help it! I don't care who writes the laws or what the laws say. And don't tell me about how they've all gone through all this *sensitivity* training. That's bullshit! It isn't about them. It's about you! *'Cause you are humiliated!* My mother doesn't even know about this! She *knows* about Gamblers Anonymous, she doesn't *know* about *Bobby*. And you know all that paper does? Huh? All it did to Bobby was make him stop and think how he could get around it, which in his case was use the phone, that's all. 'Cause you wanna drive somebody nuts, it's easy, just mess with their sleep, that's all. Just dial their number once, then keep hittin' the redial button, what could be easier? Kept wakin' me up all night long, that's all you have to do if you're him. He didn't have to touch me. And don't be stupid enough to try to leave it off the hook. That's just a magnet, that's all that is. 'Cause I did. And you know what he did? He parked in the alley all night and every fifteen minutes he shot at the house, at the aluminum siding, with an air pistol . . . all night long, every fifteen minutes, ping! Fifteen minutes, ping! Fifteen minutes, ping! Know what the order says? Says he has to stay fifty feet from the house. Know how far the alley is from the house? Fifty-one feet. The other side of the alley is exactly fifty-one feet from my back door. Doesn't say he has to stay fifty feet from the property line. Says fifty feet from the house. Come back when it's light, see all the dings, all the dents for yourself.

"Change my number, God. That'd just give him somethin' new to get pissed off about, that's all. He'd just think of somethin' else. One thing Bobby knows—knew—he knew the rules. You know, there are some guys—despite what you cops think about bad guys, not all bad guys are tryin' to rig the game, swear to God, not everybody's tryin' to cheat. Some guys *like* the rules. They like playin' by the rules. Makes it more interesting figurin' out what you can do inside the rules. And Bobby, he was almost a genius about stuff like that—don't ask me why he was so stupid about everything else about himself."

She yawned and scrunched up her face, ending with a weary laugh of relief. "Finally," she said, "I think vitamin V's gonna work."

"Beg pardon?"

"Vitamin V. Valium."

"Oh. Listen," Carlucci said, scratching his chin with the back of his pen. "I heard—I don't know this 'cause I was never in his place—but I heard those games in the back of his place, I heard he was rakin' those—"

"Oh he was! Absolutely."

"Well, if he was rakin' 'em, how was he losin'?"

She looked at him as if he was the most ignorant person she'd ever met. *"How was he losing?"*

"Yeah. 'Cause what I've always believed—or been led to believe by every gambler I've ever known—I mean, whoever rakes the game eventually winds up with all the money, if the game lasts long enough. Takin' somethin' out of every pot, how can you lose?"

She hunched forward, rubbed her eyes with the heels of her hands, and said, "That's how lousy he had to play to lose. That's how hard he had to work at losin'."

"Yeah, but see, that doesn't make sense to me. If you wanted to lose, why wouldn't you just go to somebody else's place, why

stay in your own place and go through all the motions of rakin'
the game—"

"And go through all the motions," she said along with him.
"Exactly. That's how hard he had to work to keep up the lie that
he wasn't participating in his own beating. See, I never found out
what was really eatin' him. Seriously. As well as I knew him. I
know it happened when he was a kid, whatever it was, but I don't
know when exactly or what exactly. He didn't talk about things
like that—which should've been the first sign he wasn't serious
about kickin'. Bobby just tried to show everybody he was still so
cool and so much in control and he had everything and everybody
else in the whole world figured out and nobody else knew shit.
That was his act. His schtick. And nobody would ever know anything was out of whack unless you had to watch him eat. Or until
you were like me, and you said somethin' stupid, somethin' so in-
consequential that nobody else in the world would've paid any attention to it but him—and he wouldn't just pay attention, he'd
explode.

"Look," she said, pointing to something over Carlucci's
shoulder. "Get up and look at the wall there, in the dining room.
See that? See that indentation? Go on, go look."

Carlucci stood and walked into the dining room, studying
the wall as he went.

"There, stop! Right there, you're lookin' right at it. Run
your hand over the wall there, go ahead. Feel that?"

"Yeah," Carlucci said, rubbing the flat of his hand gingerly
over the wall and feeling the depression.

"You know how that got there? I said to him, 'Is your coffee cold or somethin', you're not drinkin' it.' Swear to God, those
were my exact words. Next thing I knew I was on my knees and
the back of my head felt like somebody was playin' the drums inside there. And he was sayin', 'Stupid cunt, what the fuck do you
know?' Yeah. So that's what I'm sayin', I could see everything except when it was finally comin'. And I still don't know how he did

that—that particular thing you're lookin' at—I didn't see anything comin'. I don't know whether he threw me up against there,
or slapped me up against it or what, I have no memory of that.
But that was the last straw. That was seven days ago. One week
ago exactly. The next day I was in Family Court—oh, God, I have
to go to sleep, I can't talk anymore, I have to get in my bed, oh,
it's gonna feel so good, please can we talk some other time, okay?"

"Yeah, sure. Go 'head, get some sleep. You deserve it. Don't
worry, I can let myself out. I'll probably call you in a couple days,
okay?"

"Oh thank you, thank you. Really."

"Yeah, sure. Go to bed now, don't fall asleep where you are,
you wake up like that, your neck's gonna be killin' ya."

"Uh-hmm," she said, but she was already breathing heavily
and her eyelids were fluttering.

Carlucci set the door to lock behind him and went out into
the night. It was starting to rain, big, soft, cold drops, very cold.
He went to his Chevy and while he was unlocking the door and
taking the flasher off the roof, he looked back at the corner, at
701. The lights were still on. The rain fell on his lips and he
licked them and he tried to tell himself that it tasted good, but all
it tasted was wet. He couldn't remember if he'd ever been as
thirsty.

The next place Carlucci went to was dark. It was the house
of the second Mrs. Bobby Blasco, in the eastern edge of Westfield
Township where it abutted Rocksburg, in a development of mod-
est split-levels whose trees had only recently grown to the height
of the roofs. Carlucci remembered when there had been nothing
there but cornfields and pastures for a dairy farm. He couldn't remember the name of the farm, even though in elementary school
he drank the milk they packaged in half-pint paper cartons. It was
one of those things he thought he'd never forget, but he had.
Looking at the houses through the rain as he was looking for a

place to turn around, he tried to remember himself with a carton of milk in his hand, tried to visualize the carton in his hand to see if the name of the dairy would come to him. It didn't. All he could remember was that he'd always wanted chocolate milk and his mother wouldn't let him buy it because it cost two cents more a day than the white, ten cents extra per week.

Driving back to the station to compare notes with Trooper Dulac, to compare interview results, as well as evidence and observations at the scene with Jack Turner, his mind flashed on his mother in the hospital, probably still seething with her sense that she'd been betrayed once again, abandoned once again by a son who wouldn't stay home or couldn't get home. She'd never forgiven him for enlisting in the army, and then going to Vietnam, because before he'd enlisted, her husband, Rugsie's father, had been alive and healthy. On the day Rugsie was flying back from the Philippines, his father's life was ending on South Main Street not two blocks from City Hall, the victim of a combination of ice, snow, and a metal utility pole. And now here Rugsie was, driving through the wet night, thinking of the woman who lived at 701 Ridge Avenue and wishing he were going there to see her tomorrow instead of to the hospital to bring his mother home.

He wondered if she'd called Nowicki. He hoped she hadn't, because if she had, Nowicki would already be working on how he could use that. Nowicki was a promoter, famous in the department for his talents in arranging picnics and golf outings and bowling tournaments and in getting food and beverage vendors to "cooperate" in making all the outings grossly inexpensive successes. Carlucci hoped he hadn't set himself up with Nowicki, but it almost didn't matter if he had because he couldn't get her voice out of his ears or her eyes out of his eyes. Carlucci knew that if his mother was awake she was cursing him right now as surely as he sat in his Chevy and tried to keep it on the slickening streets. He also knew that if Nowicki had even a hint of what had happened he would be scheming his ass off three walls thinking how he could use it. Because Nowicki wasn't capable of believing that anything other than his own promotion had led Carlucci to make that stupid mistake with the addresses on Ridge Avenue. But it hadn't been Nowicki. It had been the picture in Nowicki's wallet. The picture had talked him into it. Her picture. The one that pervert Nowicki carried around in his wallet, the one he'd been showing Carlucci since just a couple short weeks after Balzic had retired. Carlucci tried to remember if he'd ever carried around any pictures of his cousins in his wallet, even in high school. What the hell am I thinkin' about, he said to himself. I don't even have any female cousins.

Just blurted that out, Jesus, "You wanna go out with me?" Oh man, what a fucking Danny Date I am. Danny Dogmeat, your neighborhood dorkball, hasn't had a date in so long he's probably gonna try to buy a corsage, oh God, please don't let me do anything that stupid, okay? Who do I talk to about this, holy shit . . . "you wanna go out with me?" Pul-leeze, Dorkboy. The woman is gorgeous, why would she do such a thing to herself, allow herself to be seen with Dorky Ditzoid, the walking zit for brains. What did you have in mind, Dorky? The movies? Popcorn maybe? A box of Milk Duds? Or maybe dinner? Take her to your favorite restaurant, which is, duh, your own kitchen, where your favorite personal chef, Mrs. Comito, will prepare her world-famous vegetable soup and macaroni topped with shredded Velveeta. What're you gonna do here, Dorkboy, huh? Danny Date, the Dogface Dorkboy from Norwood Hill, attempts at age forty-three to become a normal guy despite the fact that his mother's gonna bust both her guts when she hears about it. Both of them. The little one, and the big one. And she's gonna bust them all over—ta-da! Who else? Her loving son, Dorkboy . . . .

After he'd driven back to City Hall, parked and locked his Chevy, and collected his notebooks, Carlucci went inside to find Nowicki playing solitaire at the radio console and Trooper Dulac dozing in a chair. Jack Turner was nowhere to be seen.

"Anything happening?" he said to Nowicki in passing.

Nowicki barely glanced up and his face showed nothing but boredom. He shook his head and continued his game.

Oh that's good, Carlucci thought. She didn't call him. Good. Got some time now. Okay. "Hey, Dulac! Hey, Trooper? Wanna step in here a second, see what we got?"

Dulac roused himself, stretched, and lumbered after Carlucci into former chief Mario Balzic's office.

"I can tell you right now," Dulac said, putting a half dozen Polaroids on the desk before he sat opposite Carlucci. "These guys didn't do this. I mean, except for the one goin' through his pockets, there's not a mark on 'em, not any of 'em, see for yourself. Besides which, they're who flagged down your patrol car, right?"

Carlucci studied the Polaroids carefully, shots of Zupanc, Seslo, and Filopovich stripped down to the underwear, front and back, showing not the slightest evidence of participation in any kind of physical struggle. Carlucci put the pictures down and shook his head. "Looks that way. Unless they surprised him. Unless they're a buncha sickos, get their jollies thinkin' they're smarter than every cop who walks."

"No way," Dulac said. "From what I got from them and from what I've been hearing from your dispatcher and from Fischetti? This has got to be either a domestic or a gamblin' debt. These kids are a bunch of assholes, but no way—not to my way of thinkin'—are they gonna beat this guy to death with a baseball bat—and then flag down the cop? Never happen. I sent two of 'em home. The other one, the one took the seven bucks? He's downstairs in case you wanted another crack at him, but you'd be wastin' time in my opinion. He doesn't know anything. It's what it looked like far as they're concerned. They stumbled on him. End of story. So what'd you get?"

Carlucci told everything he'd learned from Elaine Donatello.

"I went to the other address, the other PFA, you know? House was dark, catch her tomorrow. I think our best angle is we check out the male relatives, plus see if Donatello was tellin' the truth about the gamblin', but soon as I start the case file, that's it for me tonight. I'm beat to shit and back. It's gonna be a long day tomorrow, and the weather's gettin' nasty. Think it's gonna freeze, you hear?"

"It's predicted. Freezin' rain."

"Terrific. So which do you want, you want the gamblers or the relatives?"

"I'll take the gamblers, just give me the address of his club. I'll talk to some people in our organized crime unit, see what they have to say, then I'll check out his place. What's the name again—the Brushback Bar and Grille? On Helen Street, right? Okay, no hitches, glitches, or mad dogs, I'll see you about noon, catch somethin' to eat and see what we have, okay?"

"Good enough," Carlucci said, nodding as Dulac left. "Wait a minute. Where's Turner?"

"Who?" Dulac stuck his head back around the door.

"The crime tech. From the county."

"Oh he left an hour ago. When we heard the ice hittin' the windows, he said he had thirty miles to go to get home—after he took the truck back. Wherever he parks that, I don't know. Said he wasn't gonna get caught on the roads if it was gonna freeze up. Don't blame him. I don't look forward to drivin' over this crap myself. Good night."

"Yeah, okay. Good night—wait wait. What'd he do with the evidence?"

"Took it with him, I don't know. I don't think he had much besides blood samples and the bat."

"He took it with him? You sure?"

"He carried something back out to the truck, I'm assumin' that's what it was. I didn't ask him about it. I had enough to do myself."

Carlucci shrugged, sighed, and waved good night to Dulac. Then he opened the drawers to see if anything had been disturbed, then locked them, and went out past Nowicki. It had been eleven months now since Balzic had sat at that desk, but Carlucci still couldn't shake the feeling that he was obliged to leave it as he found it.

"Your mother called three times. You wanna know what she said?"

"No. She calls again, I'll pick her up tomorrow morning— unless the weather gets really ugly, and it's s'posed to. So don't tell her any specific time 'cause you tell her a time and I don't make it within five minutes, that's all she'll remember. I don't know what time. Whenever I get up. Which if I'm lucky will be at least— God, it's three-thirty for crissake. Oh man, I'm so tired. Good night."

"Hey hey, wait. What about the guy downstairs? Zupanc."

"Oh Jesus, I forgot. Let him go. He's booked, right?"

"Yeah. Absolutely."

"Yeah. Okay. Unless he gives you some shit, wait fifteen minutes, then send him home. Tell him the DNA test came back positive, we got a lock on him for robbin' a corpse."

Nowicki's mouth fell open. "Test? What the fuck're you talkin' about, what DNA test?"

"Don't worry about it, it's all bullshit. I just needed to scare him, that was the first thing came to mind. I'm goin'. Good night."

He drove home over worsening streets. The cold rain that had been falling for more than an hour now was starting to freeze. Carlucci nearly fell getting out of the Chevy in front of his house. He crept up the steps and across the porch, making a mental note to bring the de-icer with him when he left the house tomorrow, both for the steps and sidewalk and for the Chevy. Inside, he fell into bed with his clothes on, sat back up to take his boots off, then fell back again and pulled the top cover around his shoul-

ders. He went to sleep thinking of the lights in the windows at
701 Ridge Avenue.

Carlucci awoke with a start from one of his Vietnam
dreams. He'd been slogging along at the end of his platoon on a
dusty road that came from nowhere and went to nowhere when
mortar shells started dropping down the center of the road toward them. He dove headlong into a ditch filled with putrid
water. The surface of the water was squirming with leeches but
the leeches didn't want anything to do with him. Every time one
of them attached itself to him, it would retch and convulse and
spit his blood out and swim away. It was always at that point that
he would awake.

Carlucci swung his feet over the side of the bed, rubbed his
eyes, and looked at his watch. It was seven-thirty.

"Dream of esteem," he muttered. "As in I have none. Dream
of esteem. As in I have none. If I could just find somebody to put
that to music, I know it'd be a fuckin' hit. All those kids love that
grunge shit? They'd eat it up. Dream of esteem, as in I have none,
even the leeches don't want my blood—how could that miss?"

He pulled off his clothes, took a shower, shaved, dressed,
went to the kitchen and put on a pot of water for instant coffee.
He phoned Mrs. Comito next door and told her she didn't have
to come over until he called her.

"I saw you takin' her out last night, Rugsie. You have to take
her to the emergency room again, huh?"

"Yeah. But she's okay. I mean she's not okay, you know, but
at least it's not her heart. I mean, lookin' at it from another way,
it probably is her heart, you know? Just what's wrong with her
heart they can't see on one of their ECG monitors. Never mind.
I'll call you when I need you, okay?"

"Okay, Rugsie. Listen, you be careful today. It's a sheet of
ice out there. I'm listenin' to the radio, they're closin' all the

schools, it's terrible, lotsa wrecks. Couple people got killed already."

"Not here I hope. Here?"

"No no, in Pittsburgh. Comin' in from Etna, I think. On the North Side."

"Well you be careful too. Anything you need? You want me to pick somethin' up for you, huh?"

"Oh no, Rugsie, no thanks, I don't need anything. I just went shoppin' yesterday. I'm good. Except there's one thing you could do for me, maybe."

"Yeah? What's 'at?"

"Oh, this is gonna sound so nuts, but, Jeez, if you would, please, you know? Tell your mother I didn't have nothin' to do with takin' Phil Donohue off Channel Four."

"She thinks you did what now? Took who off?"

"WTAE took Phil Donohue off. He used to be on four o'clock every afternoon. And they switched him to real real late, in the middle of the night. I guess he wasn't gettin' no ratings anymore or somethin'."

"She thinks you did that?"

"Yeah, Rugsie, if you would talk to her maybe, really, 'cause she's been so mad at me over this. Monday, he wasn't on there again, I told her he wasn't gonna be on, and when four o'clock come around and he wasn't on, she got so mad she started throwin' all her *Better Homes and Gardens* at me."

"You okay? She didn't hurt ya, did she?"

"No no. I can still juke around pretty good, you know, but if I couldn't, those magazines're sharp, they hit you with the corners, you know? But she's sayin' all these terrible things I did, and you know, she hurts me when she talks that way to me. I can't help it, Rugsie, I don't deserve that, I know she doesn't know what she's sayin'—"

"Hey, right, you most certainly do not. Aw I'm sorry, Missus Comito, honest to God I am. Hey, you want me to talk to her,

I'll talk to her, but you know it won't make any difference. Especially now. She's so mad at me right now 'cause I hada leave her in the hospital last night. She called the station all night, yellin' about me, how I abandoned her one more time, you know."

"Was that 'cause of Bobby what's-his-name, the pitcher? Did he get murdered? The news said he got murdered."

"Yeah. 'Fraid so."

"Oh God, what's wrong with everybody anymore, honest to God, everybody just wantsa kill each other, I don't understand it, Rugsie, every time you turn on the news, that's all that's on there anymore, what's wrong with people?"

"I don't know what's wrong with everybody, Missus Comito, I just try to deal with 'em one at a time. I gotta go now, okay? I'll let ya know when I need ya. Maybe you could have the whole day off, who knows? Sounds like you could use one, you think maybe?"

"Oh Rugsie, wow, that would be so nice. Honest. It'd be so nice not to hear how it's my fault Phil Donohue ain't on anymore, you know? She still blames me 'cause they took that Richard Dawson offa *Family Feud* and that was so long ago I can't remember when it was—"

"That's okay, Missus Comito. Take the day off, really. Fill up the tub, give yourself a hot bath. And don't worry, you'll get paid, okay?"

"Aw Rugsie, you don't have to do that—"

"Never mind about that, okay? Just take care of yourself today for a change. And don't even start believin' that stuff my mother says. You can't let her get to ya. Okay?"

She was still thanking him when he hung up.

The water was boiling. He made the instant coffee, popped a frozen raisin cinnamon bagel in the toaster, and leaned against the kitchen sink to wait for the toaster to pop up. He took 500 milligrams of vitamin C and 400 IU of vitamin E and an aspirin while he was waiting for the bagel. He got a knife to spread peanut butter and marmalade on the bagel, and he zoned out looking at the toaster.

The phone rang. He picked it up thinking it was probably going to be somebody from City Hall, either from the station or from Mayor Angelo Bellotti's office or more likely, given the weather, somebody from the streets department.

"Acting Chief Carlucci?"

"Yeah? Who's this?"

"Joe Barone. *Rocksburg Gazette?* We met last March I think it was. Last bowling outing you guys had? For that little girl needed a kidney? We got stuck on the same team? Remember? We had the two worst scores?"

"Oh yeah yeah, I remember you now. What's on your mind?"

"Well, believe me, I want you to know from the start, this was not my idea. I was given this assignment, okay? And I did my best to talk 'em out of it 'cause I really don't wanna do it. I'm supposed to do a feature on the life and hard times of Bobby Blasco."

"Feature? What's 'at mean?"

"Well, it's not the hard news story. Uh, other people're gonna be doin' that, the who, what, when, where, and how. I'm not gonna be touchin' on that much at all. Just need a few details to wrap it up with, that's all. The thing I've been given—see I've known Bobby since we were kids. And we played ball together, and, uh, this managing editor, he had this brilliant idea there's nobody but me to, uh, reveal all of Bobby B.'s demented outlook on sports and life and whatever. Believe me, it is not my idea, so the least painful I can make it for both of us, you tell me how, and I'll do it, whatever you say. 'Cause I don't look forward to annoying you any more about this than you look forward to bein' annoyed by me."

"Uh-huh. So whatta ya wanna do, exactly?"

"Talk to you for maybe a half hour."

"Well, look. You say you've known him since you were kids? And you used to play ball with him?"

"Yes."

"Well, maybe we can help each other, whatta ya think?"

"Possible. But I make no promises. 'Cause I have not kept in touch with Bobby. Before I started back with the *Gazette*, I hadn't seen him in, oh man, at least fifteen years. Longer."

"Uh-huh. Just tell me one thing. As I recall when I met you before, when we were bowlin'? You said you'd just started workin' for the *Gazette*, do I remember that right?"

"Right, right. Before that I worked for the *Pittsburgh Press*. Before it croaked out. Me and a small army of other ants, yeah."

"But you're originally from Rocksburg, right?"

"Yeah. But I live in Squirrel Hill. I have ever since I went to work for the *Press*. I may have to work here, but I'll be damned if I'm gonna live here. Livin' here the first eighteen years was bad enough."

"So then you really did grow up with him, Bobby."

"No, not really, not until high school. He went to St. Mary's grade school. Ninth grade, that's when we met. Then for the next seven years, we were pretty much inseparable. Till he went to the majors, and I went back to Triple-A, which is where I stayed until I got sick of ridin' the buses. Then I started takin' courses here and there, wherever I was, and, uh, pretty soon I was able to retire from the ultra-glamorous life of the minor-league catcher and begin the ultra-glamorous life of the minor-league reporter. And now, sixty-one years old, here I am back in the minor leagues of journalism."

"Could be worse," Carlucci said, taking his bagel out of the toaster and spreading peanut butter and orange marmalade over its halves. "Could be layin' in the pathology lab in Conemaugh General waitin' for somebody to take you apart. Find out what killed ya, see which blow was the lethal one."

"Oh man. He really was beaten to death, I mean I heard it, but it hasn't really sunk in yet. Jesus."

"Yeah. With a Ted Williams model Louisville Slugger. All the guys I heard he hit when he was pitchin'? Must be some kind of poetic justice in that, whatta ya think?"

"I don't think so. Course I never thought poetry had anything to do with justice. I mean, all the guys he hit? He never killed anybody. Broke a couple wrists, smashed up one guy's cheekbone, but nobody ever died. Whole world would've heard about it."

"He really hit that many guys?"

"Oh early on he did, yeah. When he was young he loved throwin' at people. His hero was Sal Maglie."

"Never heard of him. I'm not a fan. Now my old boss, I'm sure he would know who you're talkin' about, but I don't."

"Well, Sal Maglie pitched for the Giants and the Dodgers back in the forties and fifties. Some other teams too. He was also one of the guys who jumped to the Mexican League after the war—Big Two—when they decided they were tired of bein' slaves to the reserve clause."

"You just lost me. I don't know what you're talkin' about."

"Well, some other time maybe I'll explain it—if you're interested. Only thing you gotta know about Bobby B. and Sal Maglie was, Maglie's nickname was the Barber. For all the close shaves he gave hitters. Bobby loved that. He built his whole theory of pitchin' on that, the fact that every guy that stepped in there against him would have that thought right up in the front of his mind, you know, that Bobby couldn't wait to get the count to two strikes and nothin' just so he could throw the next one at their heads. Remember, this was in the days before helmets, and believe me, it was very effective. Not 'cause Bobby could throw that hard, 'cause he couldn't, but he had the best curveball I ever caught. Nobody could bend 'em like him. Listen, I'm beatin' your ear here, takin' up your time, when what I oughta be doin' is findin' out when would be a good time to talk about what I really need to talk about."

"You looked at the weather yet?"

"The weather? Oh yeah. I just drove in. Main roads and streets are clear, they've been salted. It's the side streets that're a skatin' rink. And you really gotta watch your step gettin' in and out of your car. I went down twice already. Matter of fact, I'm holdin' a cold can of pop on my knee right now."

"Well, uh, look. Mister Barone, I have a couple people to see and because of the way the streets look, I'm gonna have to call you back, 'cause I really don't know when I'll be able to talk to you. Unless you wanna do it right now. I can give you all the information I have in about five minutes—all the information I'm gonna give anybody is what I mean. Will that suit ya?"

Barone said it would, and so for the next few minutes, Carlucci sketched out the barest details of the who, what, where, when, and how Bobby Blasco met his death. Barone thanked Carlucci for making his job easier and gave Carlucci his phone numbers, at work, in his car, and at home, for when Carlucci wanted to pick his brain about Blasco.

Carlucci hung up, finished his bagel and coffee, and put on his parka. He collected his bag of de-icer crystals for the steps and sidewalk and two cans of de-icer spray for the Chevy and set off to meet the weather.

It was worse than he'd imagined. The steps and sidewalk were indeed a skating rink. His first step on the sidewalk away from the steps to the house, his feet shot straight out in front of him and he went down on his right buttock. He turned over and inched back up the steps on hands and knees. Inside, he rooted through the hall closet for the rubber sandals with the carbide grippers that fit over his boots. A letter carrier had told him that when the world was an ice ball, there was nothing like them for staying upright. All you had to do was remember to put them on—outside. Only other time he needed them, he'd put them on in the house and his mother had screamed at him, "Look what you're doin' to my floor!" Even now, with her in the hospital, he put them on outside before he began salting, spraying, and scraping.

The ice on the Chevy was the most troublesome. Carlucci used up both cans of spray de-icer getting the window clear and the driver-side door open, and he wouldn't have been able to do that without the aid of a wood chisel to lever the door open, after he'd wrapped a rag around the blade. It required all his strength to crack the seal of ice. When he succeeded, he could hear Mrs. Comito next door let out a cheer from inside her living room where she'd been watching him. He turned and gave her a shake of his left fist, thumb up, then got in and started up the engine. The Chevy started on the first try.

Fortunately, there was the space of a car length open along the curb behind the Chevy, otherwise he would never have gotten away from the curb. But that one car length allowed him to back out into the street and down the slight grade until he came to the intersection with McCoy Road by Mother of Sorrows Church. He touched the brakes when he was about thirty feet from the intersection—he was barely going ten miles an hour—felt the brakes grab and the tires begin their slide, so he slipped his foot off the brake pedal, opened the door, and began to steer backwards while the Chevy picked up speed as it approached the stop sign at the end of Corliss Street.

A woman was on her hands and knees in the middle of McCoy Road. Behind her, approaching slowly but weaving, was a bright red pickup truck, its horn bellowing, westbound coming directly at both the woman and Carlucci's Chevy. To Carlucci's left, a priest came flailing out of Mother of Sorrows Rectory and went down on his rump so hard his head bounced. The priest spun around and slid back-first into a utility pole at the intersection.

Carlucci shouted as the pickup careened lazily around the

woman, blocking her from his sight, its back bumper glancing off the utility pole where the priest had come to a stop and sending the priest into another slide back toward the church. As the pickup disappeared from Carlucci's vision, the woman reappeared, this time on one knee, shouting back at Carlucci as he tried to steer around her, but the Chevy went into a slow spin on its own, revolving around the woman as though she were the fixed point of his compass, so that when the Chevy finally came to a stop on its own, it was in front of Oriolo's Confectionery, where the gas pumps used to be, facing Mother of Sorrows Church.

Carlucci scrambled out and rushed to the woman, now up on both feet, her fingers touching the glazed macadam, and he could hear her repeating, "Mancini's bread . . . Mancini's bread . . . my sister has to have Mancini's bread. . . ."

"Hold it, hold it, don't move, I'm comin'," Carlucci said.

"Don't move?! You think I'm gonna move? If I could move, you think I'd be here? What the hell's the matter with you?"

"C'mon, lady, gimme your hand, gimme an arm, I got ya."

"Oh Jesus I'm gonna fall, watch out!"

Carlucci held her up, his carbide-tipped grippers giving him such purchase that he finally just put his arm around the woman's waist and lifted her up and carried her to the door of Oriolo's Confectionery.

"God, lady, you don't know how lucky you are," he said when he put her down.

"What're ya talkin' about, lucky. Lucky, schmucky, I still gotta get back across there, how'm I gonna do that, huh? You gonna carry me?"

"Lady, you almost got hit by a truck, you know that? And I spun right around you and I didn't have anything to do with it, I was just spinnin', I wasn't steerin'."

"Truck? What truck? What the hell you talkin' about, truck?"

"You didn't see that truck? You didn't hear him blowin' his horn?"

"What truck?! I didn't see no truck! I didn't hear no horn! How'm I gonna get across, that's what I wanna know. Oh the hell with it, I'm over here now, might as well get the damn bread. I'm gonna choke her, swear to God."

"You know, you look just like Missus Ciangiarullo, but you're not."

"I'm her sister, if it's any of your business, and youns people around here, I'm tellin' ya, youns don't know nothin' about takin' care of streets in the wintertime, honest to God, I never seen such streets like you got this morning. What, everybody in the street department, they all retarded or what? They never heard of salt?"

"Where you from, lady?"

"I'm from Brooklyn, buster. That's in New York, in case you never heard of it. And in Brooklyn they wouldn't allow ice like this to build up, this is a disgrace, everybody would be fired, nobody would be able to go to work or school or shoppin' or nowhere, what kinda people are youns around here? And my sister, la-de-da, she don't eat day-old bread anymore! Noooooo! When we was kids, if we would get bread two days old, she would be dancin'! Now if it's a day old she can't even toast it! Toast the bread, I'm tellin' her, but noooooo! Got to have fresh Mancini's bread. I'm outta the house, I'm on the sidewalk, one step! I'm Dorothy Hamill! I'm in the goddamn Ice Capades!"

"Listen, lady, you want some help gettin' home, better go buy your bread now, okay? Hey, Father, you okay?" Carlucci called out to the priest struggling to get his feet under him across the street.

"No . . . I'm not," the priest called back, slumping back down with a grimace and a hiss of pain.

"Well, gimme a couple minutes here, I'll be over to give ya a hand. C'mon, lady, let's go, get your bread, c'mon."

"What're you, the Good Samaritan? I didn't know the Good Samaritan was so goddamn bossy. I musta missed that part."

"I'm the actin' chief of police is who I am, and you give me any more lip I'm gonna get a whole lot bossier, c'mon, get your bread, let's go."

"Actin' chief of police?" She thought that was hilarious. "Better not say that too loud, sonny, you'll get arrested for impersonatin' a police officer."

Carlucci showed her his ID and gold detective's shield.

She wasn't impressed. "Ha! In Brooklyn, you'd be on the rubber band squad, they'd never let you out on the street, you ain't big enough."

Carlucci put his ID away and started across the street.

"Hey! Where you goin'?"

"I'm goin' to help the father," Carlucci said. "There's a pay phone in the store behind ya. When you're ready to get back across the street? After you get your bread? Call one of those big cops from Brooklyn."

"Hey you! I can't move!"

"I can," Carlucci said over his shoulder. "I'm comin', Father, hang on, I'll be right there. Anything broken, you think?"

"I'm afraid so, my hip feels like there's a knife in it. I heard something snap. Ruggiero, is that you?"

"Yeah, Father. Listen. I'm gonna get you a blanket outta my car, and I'm gonna call nine-one-one, see if they got an ambulance with chains on, but if they don't, then I'm gonna have to take you to the hospital myself, but it's gonna be a coupla minutes 'cause I'm gonna have to put chains on. I mean I got a set in the trunk, but it's gonna take a while, can you hang on?"

"Ruggiero, I don't think I have a choice."

"Okay, lemme go get the blanket, call nine-one-one. I'll be right back."

Carlucci crossed the street again. Mrs. Ciangiarullo's sister was standing where he'd left her.

"S'matter, ain't they answerin' in Brooklyn?"

She glared at him and started to say something but he cut her off by picking her up and carrying her into the confectionery. He set her down and said, "Make yourself useful. Call nine-one-one, ask 'em if they got an ambulance with chains on. You got that?"

"I think I can remember that."

"Good. If they say they got one, tell 'em about the priest across the street. You know what the name of that church is?"

"Oh get the hell outta here, do I know the name of that church. I was baptized there, I took my first communion there, go do what you gotta do, I'll get you an ambulance if they got one—"

"Yeah but the important part is to ask 'em if they got chains on, ya hear? If they have to put chains on, tell 'em forget it, I'll take him myself. That's what I'm gonna do now, put my chains on. Understand the problem, huh? We don't wanna duplicate the effort here, that's what I'm tryin' to avoid, understand?"

"Oh you're such a pain in the ass," she said. "Yoo-hoo, where's the phone? Anybody?"

"It's right behind ya," Carlucci said before going back outside. He had to use the wood chisel to pry open his trunk. It took him less then ten minutes to get the chains on, and only took that long because Mrs. Ciangiarullo's sister kept shouting out the door at him about how dense the 911 dispatcher was and how they *did* have an ambulance with chains and then they *didn't*, and she made him repeat every response to her information and commentary so he'd have to stop working on the chains and stand up. It was as though she couldn't hear him unless she could see his mouth moving.

"So which is it now, they have one with chains, or they don't?"

"They don't, I told you!"

"Okay okay."

"What?"

"Aw never mind, okay?"

"What?"

After he'd snapped the last link shut, Carlucci stood up, closed the trunk, and said, "You got your bread?"

"What?"

"Your bread! Get your bread and let's go! Get in the car, c'mon!"

"The bread, the bread, I forgot the goddamn bread, yoo hoo, where's the Mancini's bread?"

Carlucci waited outside the door until she found the bread and paid for it. He waved hello through the window at Mrs. Oriolo.

Mrs. Ciangiarullo's sister finally came out with her loaf of Mancini's, and he helped her into the Chevy. "Listen to me. I'm gonna get ya to your sister's house, but once we get there, you're on your own. That priest's in misery, understand? I'm not gonna walk ya in the house—"

"Oh shuddup and drive, you don't have to explain everything, God, you're such a pain in the ass. What'd your mother do to you, huh? Make ya explain every time she caught ya playin' with yourself? You're so defensive, Jesus. Drive! I'm in, let's go already!"

"Make me explain when I did what?"

"See? I knew I shouldn't've said that. Forget I said that, just ignore me. Just drive, c'mon c'mon, go go!"

Carlucci couldn't help himself. He stared at her, his mouth hanging open. "Make me explain every time she caught me? Lady, you're twisted, you know that? You're really bent outta shape."

"Don't be too sure which one of us is bent, buster. You sound just like my second husband, and believe me, that's what started all his problems, his mother followin' him around everywhere he went. Thirty years after she was dead, she was still sittin' right there on his shoulder sayin', 'Alex, oh Alllll-ex, you been playin' with your wee-wee again, don't try to deny it, Mommy knows. Mommy knows evvvvvverything.' And the man couldn't empty the garbage without explainin' himself, so don't give me that baloney about who's twisted around here—c'mon, drive for crissake! Look at the priest! The man's in agony over there! And close your mouth. It's very unattractive. You're probably not married either."

Carlucci closed his mouth and shook his head vigorously, trying to clear this woman's logic out of his head. He put the Chevy into the highest gear he thought it would move without stalling and crept across McCoy Road and up Corliss Street, stopping three houses up to let Mrs. Ciangiarullo's sister out.

"Oh for God's sake he's gonna say 'Be careful' yet," she said as she was getting out and as he was saying "Be careful." She used the door handle on a parked car to get out and then leaned her way around the car to get to the sidewalk.

"That's exactly what my second husband would've said," she said. "Exactly. The man spent his entire life overstating the obvious. You really should seek professional help, young man."

"You're welcome," Carlucci said. "And you should seek a book on etiquette. 'Specially the chapter on how to say thanks when people go outta their way to help ya."

He backed down the street to where the priest was, backed the Chevy into the curb, and put his red light on the roof. He hurried to the priest's side, trying to figure out how to get him into the Chevy. The priest outweighed Carlucci by forty or fifty pounds.

"Father, how ya doin', pretty crappy, huh?"

"Ruggiero, that's a considerable understatement," the priest said through clenched teeth.

"Uh, how much you weigh, Father?"

"Two fifteen about a month ago. That was the last time I got weighed. Why?"

"Well, you got me by a few pounds, sixty-five, more or less.

Listen. You think if I spread this blanket out, you can get your—which hip hurts?"

"The right one."

"Okay. Lemme get this blanket doubled up here, and, uh, if I get it down by your left side, you think you can sorta scooch over and get your left hip on it? Huh? Think you can do that? Well, no thinkin', you're just gonna have to do it, 'cause if you can't, I don't know how else I'm gonna get ya to the car, you know?"

"What do you intend to do?"

"Well if you can get on the blanket, I'm gonna pull ya over there, that's what. Then I'm hopin' I can get ya up and into the front seat."

"Oh dear God, Ruggiero, I don't know if I'll be able to do that."

"Listen, Father, Mutual Aid, all their ambulances are either makin' calls or else they don't have chains, I don't know what their story is, but I do know there's no ambulance comin' for you here, so it's either the Chevy or nothin', understand? Up to you. You ready?"

"No! Ruggiero, this bone—some bone is sticking into my thigh like a hot knife!"

"I'm sure it is, Father, I don't doubt that for a second, but you can't stay here. The hospital's not gonna come to you. So, uh, say a prayer, bite your teeth, and on three, okay? When I say three, you lift your hips best way you can and I'll slide the blanket under there, okay? You with me? Ya ready? One, two—"

"No no! Wait, wait!"

"C'mon, Father, I know it hurts, but ya gotta suck it up, c'mon, you can do it. You have to."

"Ruggiero, my God, the pain . . . it's intense." Tears were streaming down the priest's cheeks.

Carlucci nodded and patted the priest on the shoulder. "I'm sure it is. But the longer you stay here, the harder it's gonna be to move, Father. C'mon, here we go. Our Father, who art in heaven, hallowed be thy name, c'mon, Father, say it. You can say it, c'mon, you gotta help me, Father, I can't get ya there by myself, c'mon, Our Father, c'mon, say it, you can say it."

"Our Father," the priest said, grunting and hissing with the pain.

"Atta boy, Father, c'mon, here we go, one, two, three—up!"

"Ahhhhh!" the priest cried out, leaning back and heaving his hips upward so Carlucci could shove the blanket under him.

"Okay, down, down! Good, good good good, c'mon, Our Father, who art in heaven, c'mon, you can say it, atta boy."

"I can't, I can't," the priest sobbed. "I'm a coward!"

"Oh bullshit! Coward. You're a priest. Who told you that, you're a coward, where'd you get that nonsense? You deal with people sick and dyin', hurt, every day, cowards don't do that, c'mon."

"Oh, Ruggiero, easy to deal with other people's pain, believe me. I don't feel it. Consolation's just words to me. But I feel this! My God, do I feel this."

"Well, if you say so, Father. Listen, what I want you to do now is this. Take hold of both of these corners here. Grab the blanket, both sides, and don't let go, okay? 'Cause you slip off the blanket, you're gonna have to lift your hips again, you know? Understand? Gonna hurt like hell again you go off this blanket. Okay? You ready?"

"No . . . oh God, yes, I suppose," the priest said, squeezing his eyes shut and shaking his head.

"C'mon, you're ready, here we go." Carlucci gathered up the other end of the blanket and started pulling the priest across the sidewalk. The priest winced and hissed with every bump. "Hang in, Father, c'mon, you gotta hang in with me here, you can do it."

"Oh God," the priest screamed as they went over the curb and into the street.

"Just a little bit farther, couple more steps, Father, hang in there."

Carlucci put the priest's screaming out of his mind, pulling him around the front of the Chevy and down beyond the passenger door. "Okay, Father, here we are, that was good, that was good. You're a brave man. Now here's the hard part, you gotta help me out here, I can't do this alone, you're way too big for me to get ya inside by myself, you hear? You gotta grab hold of the door there somewhere, you gotta pull yourself up, I mean, I'll give it my best shot, but you gotta give it your best shot too, okay?"

"I've never felt such pain," the priest said, grunting with every word.

"Well, look at it this way, Father. Next time somebody tells you they're in pain, you'll know what they're talkin' about, whatta ya think?"

"Ruggiero, I've never known you to be a cruel person, but that was not . . . that was not a kind thing to say."

"Aw bullshit, Father. Little while ago you were sayin' how consolation's just words to you—ain't that what you said?"

"Yes. Yes I did."

"Well from now on, it won't be just words. Somebody tells ya they're hurtin', it'll mean somethin'. Believe me. That's what you guys used to tell me all the time—everything happens for a purpose. All part of God's plan. So you're part of the plan now for sure. From now on you are definitely not a coward. Okay, ya ready? Grab hold of the handle there, c'mon, let's do it, no foolin' around now, c'mon. On three. One, two, three!"

The priest let out a long sigh, took in a deep breath, grasped the door handle, and heaved himself upward as Carlucci got behind him and pulled him up by his armpits. The priest shrieked in Carlucci's ear, but together they managed to get the priest leaning against the door with all his weight on his left foot.

"Wow, way to go, Father, that was good. Okay, here we go, take another deep breath, Father, that worked pretty good. Another big breath and we turn ya around, get ya aimed toward the seat, okay?"

"Okay," the priest grunted, turning slowly, hissing with every move, until his backside was aligned with the seat.

"All you gotta do is lean back in there, Father, just hang on to the door, lemme get in front of ya, I'm gonna grab you by the lapels, okay? Ready? Don't let go of the door yet, hold it! Okay, okay, here we go. One, two, three! Go on, ease on back, go on, c'mon, you can do it."

When his rump landed on the seat, the priest was trembling from head to toe, the color in his face had drained from bright pink to pasty white, his breath was coming in short gasps, his eyes were squeezed shut, he was whimpering.

Carlucci stepped back and shook his head. There was only one thing left to do and he didn't know if they could do it. Somehow they had to get the priest's legs and feet into the car, and that would mean that bone would be stabbing him every fraction of an inch. Carlucci wiped his nose with his thumb and index finger and licked his lips.

"What's your name, Father?"

"John."

"I know it's John. I mean your last name. Long as I've known you, I never knew your last name."

"Vescio. John Joseph. Why?"

"I don't know. Just wanted to know all of a sudden. Well, Father, we gotta get you inside, and I know this is gonna hurt worse than anything else we've done so far, so since it's your pain, I'm gonna let you tell me how you wanna do it."

"I don't want to do it," Father John said, swallowing hard and breathing through his mouth.

"I'm sure you don't, but I can't drive ya to the hospital with your feet hangin' out like that. We hit a pothole or somethin', well, you figure it out. So how you wanna do it?"

The priest took two deep breaths, swung his left foot inside, grabbed his right leg with both hands and pulled it into the car with a scream that raised the hair on Carlucci's neck and caused doors and windows to open for half a block.

Carlucci made sure the priest's feet were clear, and he slammed the door and scurried around the front of the Chevy and got behind the wheel. He backed out onto McCoy Road, red light flashing, horn blowing, and said to the priest, "I don't know where you ever got that crap about you're a coward, Father, but believe me, you ain't."

The priest said nothing. His head rolled back against the seat and stayed there during the twenty-five minutes it took Carlucci to drive to Conemaugh General. The trip would normally have taken at most seven or eight minutes, ten if all the lights had been against them, but the streets were littered with cars, most of them abandoned by people who thought they were too important to stay home.

At the hospital, Carlucci let the ER pros get the priest out of the Chevy and inside, which they did after they'd given him enough morphine to start him humming "White Christmas." Carlucci stayed just long enough to complete the hospital's paperwork and call a nursing supervisor to make sure his mother was still all right, then he drove to City Hall. He filled out an incident report on the priest and then went to talk to Patrolman Robert Canoza, who was working the radio.

"Hey, Booboo, what's doin' out there?"

"Well, you know, lotta people shoulda stayed home. We're gonna have a problem sweepin' up their cars, but otherwise, there was only one bad collision—so far. Some asshole lost it on the bridge over Chartiers Creek, hit three cars before he got stopped, one lady was trapped for a while, she's in surgery, don't know how bad yet, but nobody else. I think we're pretty lucky, considerin'."

"Considerin' what?"

"Hey, when I left the house this mornin', just in the time it took me to back outta the garage, I heard three bodies hittin' the sidewalk. That was in, like, twenty seconds, the time it took me to decide to pull back in the garage and put my chains on, go hunt up my carbide sandals. I think it could've been a whole lot worse."

"So what's the total so far?"

"Ah, lemme think here. Eleven. Not includin' the four on Chartiers Bridge."

"How about falls?"

"Oh man, lotsa them. Mutual Aid's goin' nuts tryin' to keep up. All our mobiles're out. I called everybody in who could make it, figured you woulda done that you were here, right?"

"Absolutely."

"Yeah. Two guys in each car, except for one. Got three in that one. And right now they're either at the ER or they're on their way there. You were just there, right? With a priest? Didn't you see 'em?"

"Nah, I was busy with him. Yeah, Father John. Vescio. Can you imagine, I've know the guy must be twenty years, longer. Never knew his last name till today, can you imagine that?"

"You go to church once in a while, you might know his name."

"Don't get wise. Nah, I didn't see anybody else up there. Poor bastard broke his hip. God, gettin' him in the car, I never heard such a scream in my life—well, that's not true. I heard lotsa people screamin' like that in Nam. So, uh, this pretty much screws the day. I had a lotta people to talk to. How's the phones? Power? Lotta lines down?"

"Oh yeah, you kiddin'? The whole Pill Hill's out. Clear to the community college. Trees snappin' everywhere with all that ice. I heard what's-his-face on Channel Four sayin' this is the worst ice storm in twenty-five years. But that can't be right. There was one worse, but I can't remember when it was."

"You talkin' about the one, oh, when was it, back in the early eighties?"

"Oh yeah right, that's the one. Yeah, that was the one we had those three fatals that day, three separate collisions, three fatals. Man, that was some storm. Yeah, man, how could I forget that one?"

"Hey, Booboo, changin' the subject here, lemme ask you somethin', okay? How long we known each other?"

"Ah, lemme think. I followed you into the department by a month. So, uh, what, it'll be twenty-three years, right?"

"Yeah. That's what I figure, so, uh, you know me pretty good—"

"Oh wait a minute, what is this? This gonna be personal, huh? You know how I hate personal shit, Rugs, don't do this—"

"It's not that personal, c'mon—"

"What do you mean, *that* personal—see already I don't like it—"

"No, nah, c'mon, just listen, it's not gonna be like that, you're gonna be able to handle it, I'm tellin' ya—"

"Hey, Rugs, you're gettin' that look, I hate that look—"

"What look? What're you talkin' about, this isn't about you, this is about me—"

"Yeah, see that's the way it always starts, this personal shit, it's not about me, it's about you—yeah. Right. Bullshit. Next thing I know, it's all turned around on me, and the next thing, I'm the one in the waitin' room, and I'm the one with the clipboard tryin' to remember my medical history and what kinda medication I'm takin', if any. I'm warnin' ya, Rugs, this better not be about me."

"Booboo, honest to God, I start one thing about you? You can throw me out in the parkin' lot. I'm tellin' ya, this is about me, okay? Swear to God. It is not about you."

Canoza stood up, all six feet four, two hundred and sixty or seventy pounds, depending on what he had for breakfast. "Okay, Rugs, but I'm warnin' ya, I'm not kiddin' here. You turn this around on me, I *will* throw you out in the parkin' lot, actin' chief or no actin' chief. I'm still pissed about how Balzic worked a turn-around on me and I ain't never gonna forgive him for that. Much as I love that man, and you know I love him, got all the respect in the world for him, but that fucker, he started the same way you're startin'—'Hey, Booboo, lemme ask you somethin'.' If he'd've just come to me and said, 'Hey, Booboo, I think you got a problem,' hey, I would've listened to the man, but no. That ain't what he did. He started out talkin' about himself, how he had this problem with violence when he first started out, you know, and he had to work it out all by himself and he wished there was somebody around in his day who coulda helped him out, and the next fuckin' thing I know, I'm up the fuckin' mental health clinic, in the fuckin' waitin' room, fillin' out all these fuckin' forms in that fuckin' shrink's office. And for the next six fuckin' months, I'm gettin' my onions crushed 'cause I'm the department nutzoid, Booboo don't know how to handle violence, Booboo don't know his own strength, Booboo this, Booboo that, every fuckin' day I walked in here, guys were duckin' under the desks, they're goin' Booboo Booboo, oou oou oou, scratchin' their armpits, like I'm some fuckin' gorilla. That was humiliatin', Rugs. I mean it, man, that was fuckin' humiliatin'. Mario should've handled it better'n 'at, he was smarter'n 'at, I'm still pissed off about that, Rugs, you know what I mean? That was, uh, that was, uh—what's the word I want here—oh. Duplicitous. Yeah. Fuckin' duplicitous."

Duplicitous? Oh-oh. Booboo's readin' vocabulary books again. "Oh yeah, absolutely, I know exactly what you're talkin' about. I agree, man, Mario, he was wrong, he shouldn't've done that—"

"Now wait, I'm not sayin' he *shouldn't've* done it. He was the chief, that was his, uh, that was his, uh, prerogative—"

Prerogative? He knows *prerogative* too?

"—just not that way, that's what pissed me off, the way he did it, that's all."

"Yeah, right, that's what I meant too, I'm agreein' with you. Uh, Booboo, you wanna sit down now, okay?"

"Yeah, I'll sit, I'm sittin'. But I mean it, Rugs, just don't, uh, just don't try to, uh, manipulate me. Yeah. Just don't try that. I resent that. I find manipulation reprehensible."

Whoa. *Manipulation? Reprehensible?* Oh man. "Listen, on second thought, see, what I was gonna ask ya was, uh, do you think I have a tendency to explain things too much? I mean, really, you've known me longer'n anybody in the department, and since I'm actin' chief, you know, there aren't too many people I can trust to gimme a straight answer—but I don't want you thinkin' for a second I'm tryin' to manipulate you, you know? 'Cause I'm not. I wouldn't do that to you. I mean, really, man, I wouldn't."

"What's the question again? Do I think you tend to explain things too much—is that it?"

"Yeah, that's it. Whatta ya think?"

Canoza slumped down onto his chair and sprawled out and swiveled from side to side. "Uh-huh. There's no way you could three-sixty me there, 'cause my wife, she says if there's one thing wrong with me it's I don't explain anything. Not to her anyway. So you gotta be on the square here."

"Oh I am. I mean it, this is about me. But it's not three-sixty, Booboo. It's one-eighty. If it was three-sixty, that would mean it came clear back around to me."

"Yeah I know, I get that confused sometimes." He stopped swiveling the chair, leaned forward, and peered intently into Carlucci's eyes. "You're not gonna hold this against me, right? No matter what I say? Next fitness report? You know, you're not used to writin' 'em, that's gonna be a whole new thing for you—"

"Wait wait, I wrote 'em in June, the semiannuals, yours included, remember?"

"Oh yeah. Right. I forgot. But still, if I say somethin' you're maybe not gonna like here? I mean you gonna be able to put that outta your mind, huh? Next fitness report? You see my name on the sheet there? You gonna be able to put this aside, huh? I have to know that, Rugs, or I'm not sayin' nothin'. I'm not as dumb as everybody thinks, you know?"

"If I thought you were dumb, would I be askin' you? Huh? And you have my word, I don't hold nothin' over you. Absolutely. On my shield." Carlucci crossed his heart.

Canoza pondered that for a long moment. "What're you crossin' your heart for, your shield's in your back pocket probably."

"I'm crossin' it where it would be if I was in uniform, c'mon, Booboo, this is important. Somebody said somethin' to me, it's really botherin' me."

"Okay, Rugs, you asked me, I'm gonna tell ya. You always explain everything too much, man. You're not anywhere near as bad as you used to be, but from the first time I met ya, you was always explainin' every move you made. You were so scared you were gonna fuck up, and people weren't gonna like ya, you told everybody twice why you did everything. Three times. And each time it'd get more, uh, complicated. I used to look at you, I used to think, this guy's been to Nam, he was a fuckin' grunt over there, he survived that, what's he so scared of, why don't he shut up for crissake. Finally, one day I told ya."

"Told me what?"

"I told ya shut up! You were makin' everybody nuts. 'Specially me."

"You did? I don't remember that."

"Naturally you don't remember—'cause it was me. Who remembers anything I say? I'm just Booboo, the big stupe, what do I know—what knowledge do I possess? And I hate that fuckin' nickname too, man. Booboo. Fuckin' name's Robert, you know?"

"Yeah I know it's Robert."

"Well why the fuck don't you call me that?"

"I didn't know you wanted me to."

"Well how would you like to be called Booboo? What kinda fuckin' name is 'at? Hate that fuckin' name."

"You want me to call you Robert, I'll call you Robert. I didn't know, I thought you liked 'at name."

"Aw c'mon, man—Booboo? 'At's what little kids say when they get hurt. Hey, Mommy, I got a booboo. Shit."

"Hey, okay, man, it's Robert. From now on. And I'll pass the word too. No more Booboo. So, uh, back to what you told me. Remember?"

"I remember. What I told you, man, I told ya ten times, shut up, you explain too much. Then you made detective, and I said this is probably none of my business anymore. Then you made sergeant and for sure I never said anything again."

The phone rang and Canoza opened the line and spoke into his headset. "Rocksburg Police. Patrolman Canoza speakin', how may I help you? . . . Yes he is, yes, ma'am . . . About Mister Blasco? . . . Yes, ma'am, hold on, I'm sure he'll wanna talk to you."

"Who?" Carlucci said.

Canoza put the caller on hold. "Missus Blasco. Said she wants to talk to you."

"Put it in Balzic's office," Carlucci said, hurrying there. The phone was ringing when he got there. Before he picked it up, he got out the case file he'd started last night, his notebook and pens, his tape recorder, and a fresh tape.

"Detective Carlucci speakin'. Missus Blasco?" He put the fresh tape into the recorder.

"Yes. I'm the second one." Her voice was raspy and deep. Either she had a cold or she was a longtime smoker.

"You had a PFA outstanding on Mister Blasco, is that correct, ma'am?"

"Yes I do. Did, I guess."

"And you live in Westfield Township on, uh, Hartman Drive, is that correct, one three nine Hartman?"

"Yes."

"Uh, Missus Blasco, your first name—I'm tryin' to read my copy of the PFA but it's smudged. Your first name Jane or June, I can't make it out."

"No. My first name is Virginia, but nobody calls me that, not even my mother. Everybody calls me by my middle name, June. Or Juney. But it's June, not Jane."

"Uh-huh. Uh, Missus Blasco, I would like to record this interview, but, uh, I can't do that without your permission, understand? So is it all right with you if I do that?"

"Record it? I guess, sure, why not?"

"I have to ask, ma'am. I'd get in a lotta trouble I recorded it without your permission. That's a serious violation of the Crimes Code, recordin' a phone conversation without tellin' the other person that you're doin' it."

"Well it's okay with me, I guess. I don't see why not."

"Okay, ma'am, just have to ask, that's all," Carlucci said, connecting the recorder to the phone. He turned it on, and then listed the particulars of the interview. Then he asked Mrs. Blasco to repeat her acknowledgment and consent that the conversation was being recorded, which she did.

Before he could ask anything, she said, "So it's true then. About Bobby?"

"Why do you say that, ma'am?"

"Because Elaine called me this morning—Elaine Donatello? You talked to her last night, right?"

"I did, yes, ma'am."

"Well she called me about six-thirty this morning, quarter to seven, I forget when it was exactly, and she told me how you came to her house last night, and she had a PFA on him just like I did, but I didn't get a paper this morning, and the power's out, I don't have any TV or radio, I used to have a portable radio, but the batteries are all dead, turns out I don't have a good battery in the house, so I didn't have any way of checkin' what she said— not that I doubt her or anything. It's just, you know, something like this, this big, you wanna check—you have to check, you know? And I was so scared, I called your station about five times, but I kept gettin' a busy signal and the one time I did get an answer I hung up, I didn't . . ."

"Didn't what, ma'am?"

"I don't know, God, I wanted to hear, I didn't want to hear, I wanted to believe, I didn't want to believe—honest to God, you gotta believe me, I really loved Bobby. At one time, I mean, Bobby was, oh God, he was everything to me. He was, oh, I loved him so much—I still do. It's almost stupid to say it, how you could love a person like that—I mean, I feel so sad now, I've been cryin' all morning, just sittin' here cryin' and cryin', I think I'm gonna stop and then I start again . . . and sometimes it's a relief, honest to God I'm glad—I mean I hate it when I think like that—I hate myself when I even think that, but it's the truth. I'm soooo relieved, God, nobody'll ever know how relieved I am, but then I get so sad . . . 'cause Bobby was the greatest guy in the world, he was wonderful . . . but then he could be such a bastard, such a goddamn spoiled brat . . . 'cause that's what he was. The world's biggest spoiled brat . . . oh God, excuse me, I have to get more Kleenex."

It was almost two minutes before she picked up the phone again.

"You okay, ma'am?"

"No. I'm not gonna be okay for a long time—I mean I'm a lot more okay than I've been for weeks, but . . . this is terrible. Nobody should have to . . . oh shit."

"Have to what, ma'am?"

"Have to die like that."

"Like how, ma'am? How do you mean?"

"Scared to death . . . 'cause somebody's so mad at you all you can see is how much they would like to see you dead. That . . . that was the worst part for me, honest . . . to look into Bobby's eyes when he was just . . . just insane. He'd go insane, his mouth, you couldn't even see his lips, all you'd see was his teeth and he'd be making these noises, I swear to God he'd be snarling, like an animal, his eyes were just . . . so wild . . . just so awful, I tried to tell this to a judge one day and I know he didn't know what I was talkin' about—well whether he knew or not he didn't care, he just kept sayin' the law doesn't care about that, the law doesn't care about how somebody looks at you, it's just about whether they assault you, there's nothing in the law about how somebody's eyes get before they hit you. But honest to God, the way Bobby looked at me the instant before he was gonna hit me . . . and while he was hittin' me, I can't explain it, but it . . . it hurt so much more than what, you know, what his hands were doin', I swear. Nothin' hurt like the way he looked at me, the way his eyes got, like I was the most disgusting thing in the world to him. I couldn't stand that, that's what really hurt me, it hurt so much. Hitting me, hurting me, I know it doesn't make sense, but it was so much worse just seein' that he wanted to hit me, that hurt so much worse than any time he ever hit me . . . I don't know how else to say it."

"Uh-huh, yes, ma'am, I'm sure that was very painful," Carlucci said. "Uh, could you explain something to me? I'm sure you explained this to the investigating officer—that was Patrolman Reseta? You remember talkin' to him, ma'am? Patrolman James Reseta?"

"Yes I do. Several times."

"Uh-huh. Okay. So what was the complaint exactly, what and when, that prompted you to seek the PFA? I mean the date here is October fourteenth, but there's no disposition on the accompanying paperwork, ma'am—I know I'm talkin' a lotta red tape here, but do you understand what I'm askin' you?"

"No, I'm not sure—oh. You mean what happened afterwards?"

"Well yeah, that too. But no, what prompted the complaint, that's what I wanna know. All it says here is assault and spousal abuse, but there are no particulars. But I'm tryin' to find out—I mean first of all, how long had you been divorced from Mister Blasco? You were divorced at the time of this incident, correct?"

"Oh my God yes. We'd been divorced almost four years."

"Four years? And he was still comin' around?"

"Oh he never stopped comin' around."

"What, was he angry about the terms of the settlement?"

She laughed. "Terms of the settlement? You mean like what he was supposed to give me? Here's what the settlement was—I wanted him out of the house, that's what the settlement was. And he was supposed to quit takin' my money. I wanted him to quit stealin' the mortgage payments."

"So he wasn't required by the terms of the decree to give you anything?"

"Give *me*?! Jesus, all I wanted was him to quit taking what didn't belong to him, which was my pay from two jobs! God. The bank called me in three times about the mortgage payments—Bobby was waitin'—here's what he'd do. He'd wait till I put them in the envelope—I guess he could set his watch by me, I don't know, I guess that's how predictable I am. Anyway, he'd just hang around by the mailbox out at the entrance to the planned development and he'd tell the mailman, you know—when he came to pick it up? He'd say he made a mistake in the check and he'd ask the mailman to give him that envelope. And the mailman would give it to him, naturally, 'cause he knew Bobby. He did it three times before I just happened to have a conversation with the mailman one day and found out that's what he was doin'.

" 'Cause when the bank would call me up, I didn't know what they were talkin' about. I took my checkbook in and showed them the stub, and they'd just look at me, you know, like how dumb did I think they were, right? I mean God, anybody can fill out a stub and say they sent the check. God, it was embarrassing."

"I'm sure it was, ma'am."

"So then I started carrying my bills, deliverin' them myself to everybody. One day a month, I'd drive around and hand every-body their checks. And that's when Bobby started beatin' me again. And then he broke into the house, and stupid me, I left the checkbook up on my desk, in my bedroom, and he took it, and he wrote checks all over town, he took everything I had—which wasn't much, believe me, but it was what I was livin' on, Jesus!"

"So that's what your complaint was? When you finally filed a complaint, when Patrolman Reseta showed up to take the in-formation, it was because of Bobby stealin' your checkbook?"

"Oh no. I'd been callin' the police, I must've called the po-lice a dozen times. Way before that."

"This police department, ma'am? The Rocksburg PD?"

"Oh no, the state police—"

"Why were you callin' them, ma'am?"

"Huh? What do you mean, why was I callin' them—I'm out in the township here, we don't have a police department, who was I supposed to call? The state police are who we're supposed to call—"

"Yeah, sure, on paper, yes, that's correct, ma'am, but did they respond—ever?"

"Once. Yes."

"When was that?"

"Oh that was in June. Early summer. I'm not sure now."

"That's this past summer you're talkin' about, correct?"

"Yes, this past summer, right, but I'm not sure when ex-actly."

"And the trooper who responded, he didn't say anything about they don't respond to domestic disputes?"

"No, he didn't say anything like that."

"What I meant to say was they don't respond to a domestic disturbance or dispute unless there is a Protection From Abuse order on file in their barracks. He never said anything like that to you?"

"No. Jeez, I would've remembered that."

"So, uh, you're sayin' every time somethin' happened, you just continued to call the state police?"

"Yeah. Sure. Who else was I supposed to call?"

"Even though they didn't respond?"

"Well what was I supposed to do?"

"Should've called us, ma'am. We're the nearest police department, we would've responded, believe me, uh, when did all these incidents take place, what time of day, was there a pattern?"

"Well they didn't all happen at the same time, but they all happened after I came home from work, from one job or another."

"Says here you're a licensed practical nurse, is that correct? Employed at Conemaugh General Hospital?"

"Yes, that's correct."

"And what's your other job, ma'am, the other one you referred to?"

"Well I work private duty as much as I can, usually I get at least three nights a week, but a lot of times, I'll work every night for a long case, you know, somebody with cancer or paralysis from an accident. This year, when all this started with Bobby, this summer I was working for a man with bone cancer and he was, uh, oh, just hangin' on and on, I felt so sorry for him, and his wife too, but I was working six nights a week for them, for, God, seven months at least. That's how I'm able to live in this house. I mean I couldn't pay the mortgage on this house if I didn't work privately, my God, no way. That's why I was so mad at Bobby when he stole the mortgage checks. Jeez, I'd been workin' like eighty, ninety hours a week the whole time we were married and he never once made a mortgage payment, not once. And then, we're divorced, he starts stealin' 'em for God's sake, I couldn't stand it. And if that wasn't bad enough, then he'd come around and *ask* me for money. I mean he owned a bar for God's sake. And a restaurant. And when I wouldn't give it to him, he'd beat me. God, how much're you supposed to take?"

"I'm sure it was terrible, Missus Blasco, I have no doubts about that. But what I'm tryin' to get clear in my mind is what was the incident that prompted you—or was it any one particular incident? What made you call us finally, that's what I'm tryin' to determine."

"Well what difference does that make?"

"To you, ma'am, doesn't make much difference at all, but see, I have to deal with this kind of situation all the time, and it's a big mess, big confusion about who's supposed to respond, and I have to work with the state police all the time, and Family Court, and I have to know how these things work. The more I know, the better I can train my men. See? I don't wanna make you feel like you're part of a crowd here, but, uh, the fact is, this situation, you know, it happens all the time. More and more it seems like to me—well I don't know whether it's happenin' more or whether women are puttin' up with it less, that I don't know. I just know we're gettin' a lot more calls about it than we used to, say, just five years ago. So the more I know, the more my men're gonna know, the better they're gonna be able to react whenever they're called out, see? And since I've never talked to you before about this, all I'm goin' on is the paperwork I have in front of me. And I don't care how diligent people are, I don't care how careful a patrolman is, there's only so much you can fit in on these forms, you see what I'm sayin'? There's only so much you can write down here."

All of which is true, Carlucci was thinking as he was wondering whether she was buying it, but he didn't know how else he was going to ask her how bad she had it in for her ex-husband and what she was capable of doing in reaction to that, especially since he couldn't read her body language. Which was why he hated interviewing potential suspects over the phone even though most interviews were done exactly that way. But when an ice storm had locked everybody up, nobody had any choice about how interviews were done, so he had no compunction about saying whatever he had to say to get the responses he was looking for. He was resorting to a trick Balzic had taught him years ago about phone interviews, especially with a potential suspect and especially before you'd made up your mind about whether you were actually dealing with a suspect. Because once the word *suspect* was said, everything had to change.

Balzic hammered it into him: to get the person on the other end of the line to give up information before you'd committed yourself about your suspicions, you always wanted to appeal to that person's vanity about their intelligence. Balzic couldn't emphasize it enough: never underestimate how much everybody likes to be asked to tell what they know. People love showing they know something, doesn't matter what it is. And one way to elicit that was to ask him or her to become, so to speak, your teacher. And while Balzic never liked to generalize about which techniques worked best with which kinds of suspects in which kinds of cases, he insisted that the teaching angle invariably worked better with women than men. According to Balzic, women couldn't help teaching.

Carlucci agreed. But he still hated phone interviews, and he knew there was no way he wasn't going to talk to this Mrs. Blasco face-to-face eventually. The ice had to melt sooner or later. Still, there wasn't any point not getting as much as he could any way he could.

"Well, I guess it was talking to Elaine, really," she said after a long pause.

"Elaine Donatello? But your PFA's dated much earlier than hers—"

"Oh yeah. Sure. A month at least."

"Thirty days exactly, that's right," Carlucci said, comparing dates on the PFAs. "So you were talkin' to her about this and what, she told you to call us, is that it?"

"Yes. I've known Elaine since, oh God, we went to high

school together. We were both majorettes. In fact, if you can believe this, I'm who introduced her to Bobby."

"You introduced them?" That was interesting, considering
that Donatello had said she'd met him at a Gamblers Anonymous
meeting.

"Oh yes. They met—well, they didn't meet. They encoun-
tered each other, I guess is how you say it, at a GA meeting, you
know, Gamblers Anonymous? But then we were out one night—
I used to bowl with some of the nurses from the hospital, they
were in a league, it was all really very disorganized, you know,
'cause everybody works such crazy hours. So you bowled if you
had the time off, you know? And if you didn't—anyway—I mean
we weren't together, Elaine and me, I just ran into her at the
Rocksburg Bowl, you know, in the lounge."

"Uh-huh, I see."

"So I hadn't seen her in years, and we were sittin' there at the
bar, you know, talkin' over old times, renewin' our friendship
there, and here comes Bobby, out of the back room. And he sees
me and naturally he comes right over 'cause he needs money,
'cause he's been in there all day playing gin, and naturally, he lost,
dropped another bundle, I mean, what else was new? So that's
when I introduced them. But it must've been at least two years
later before she—Elaine—told me how she really met him, you
know, at GA, and like a fool, she said—she still says it, the world's
biggest sucker she calls herself, she saw all those signals he was
giving off about how he was going to meetings and the first place
she sees him outside a meeting, he's asking his ex-wife for money
to pay his losses, and she *still* gets involved with him."

"So, uh, what exactly did she say to you, do you remember?
About why you should call us?"

"Oh I can't tell you that exactly—I don't remember. I don't
think it was any one thing. It was just a whole lot of different
conversations we had, my God, we talked all the time. Misery
loves company, it's true—I guess. But she'd call me at work, she'd

come up to the hospital cafeteria for lunch or she'd pick me up and she'd have lunch she bought somewhere, especially this summer, 'cause that was practically the only time I could get free, you know, for lunch. But it was just a lot of things we talked about. And I got so mad when Bobby broke into the house and took the checkbook—well, now that I think about it, that had to be it. The checkbook. When he stole it, I know I told her about that—there's no way I wouldn't've told her about that, 'cause I'm pretty sure that was when she told me about how you guys, you know, somebody from your department—I forget who she said, Fisher or somebody—"

"Fischetti?"

"That's the one, yes. How he'd been so nice, so courteous, didn't patronize her or give her any of that stupid macho bonding baloney, you know, that boys-will-be-boys crap. She said he really listened to her and told her what to do—not that she paid any attention to him right away—later on she did, but I remember now, she did tell me everything he said, Fischetti. And so I called, and he didn't come, but this Patrolman Reseta came. And he was just as nice, and just as understanding, and he told me exactly what to do, and I did it. I went to Family Court and I filled out all the papers and I had my hearing and they gave it to me, the PFA."

"Okay, I'm startin' to understand the sequence here, the time line, but what I'm puzzled about, see, is there's nothin' happened. That's what I asked you before. You get the PFA, but there's no prosecution, no disposition. The guy stole your checkbook, he busted you out, right? Isn't that what you said? He wrote checks all over town? Emptied your account?"

"Yes."

"So then you get the PFA, but then nothin'. That's what I don't understand. So, uh, who didn't pursue this, you or Patrolman Reseta?"

"Well me—I mean who do you think?"

"Well that's exactly what I'm tryin' not to do, Missus Blasco, that's why I'm askin' you. I'm not thinkin' anything until you tell me somethin'. So what happened?"

"He beat the hell out of me, what do you think? I couldn't work for three days. I couldn't stand up for the whole next day, I had to crawl to the bathroom. He kicked me in both legs, kicked me in the ankles, I could barely walk the second day. So damn right I dropped the charges, I was scared. Bobby said if I ever called the cops on him again he'd come back and do it again worse. Reseta was really mad when I told him, but I couldn't do it, I didn't care how mad he got. I knew he wasn't gonna kick me, the cop. But there wasn't any question about Bobby, what he'd do, God."

"Uh-huh. Now see, Missus Blasco, June—okay if I call you June?"

"Sure, certainly."

"Okay. June. That's the part that bothers me."

"What part, I don't understand."

"Well, see, the fact is, it doesn't matter whether you dropped the charges—I mean, did Patrolman Reseta see your injuries? Bruises, abrasions, lacerations—it wouldn't take a doctor, would it, to determine you were the victim of a physical assault, that's what I'm askin', you follow me?"

"You mean could the patrolman see the bruises?"

"Yes, ma'am."

"Oh well sure. I showed him, yes. He took pictures. Polaroids."

"There's no doubt about that in your mind? Patrolman Reseta saw your bruises? And he photographed them? And you told him it was your ex-husband that assaulted you? That's how you came to have those bruises, is that correct, you told him that specifically, Patrolman James Reseta?"

"Well I didn't know his first name, but all the rest is right, yes."

"Well, see, that's very disturbing to me, ma'am, 'cause since 1986, police officers, we don't need a victim of spouse abuse to sign the information. The law's very clear about that. All the officer has to do is observe, uh, the exact words are, 'recent physical injury to the victim or other corroborative evidence.' In other words, ma'am, it wouldn't've made any difference—should not have made any difference whether you wanted to drop the charges or not. As far as the patrolman was concerned, by law, he should've arrested Bobby. But the paperwork I'm lookin' at right now is very clear about that. Nobody arrested him. You wanna help me out here?"

"I don't know what you mean, help you out. Help you out how?"

"Well, do you know any reason why Patrolman Reseta did not arrest Bobby for that."

"Well probably 'cause I begged him not to. Or I hope that's why, Jesus. I mean, I said, please don't do that, don't arrest Bobby 'cause if you do, he'll just come back and do it again. He said he would. And I mean, if you knew anything about Bobby, if there was one thing he didn't do, he didn't make—Bobby never, ever said anything just to hear himself talkin'. Most of the time, believe me, you never got any warning at all what he was gonna do. So maybe according to the law, the patrolman, as you say, he should've arrested Bobby, but I made him promise not to."

"You made him promise? How'd you do that, June? How could you make him promise not to do his duty, I don't get that."

"Listen. Maybe you should be askin' him about this. I'm startin' to get a real funny feeling here. A little while ago, you, uh—never mind."

"Little while ago I what?"

"No. Never mind. You ask him about this. I don't wanna talk about this anymore. You just make me . . ."

"I make you what, ma'am? I'm not tryin' to make you anything, what's the matter?"

"You're startin' to make me feel real . . . uncomfortable. Like I did something I shouldn't've, or like I didn't do something I should've, I don't know what exactly, but all of a sudden I don't like the way you sound. I don't like the way you're talkin' to me here."

"Ma'am? June? Listen, I don't know what it is you think I'm doin' here, but I don't wanna make you feel any kind of uncomfortable. If I'm doin' that, I'm sorry, I'm outta line, because I'm not tryin' to, believe me. If anything, I'm tryin' to do the exact opposite. It's just that I've known Patrolman Reseta for a long time, I've worked with him for a lotta years, and I just can't imagine him not doin' the right thing here."

"Well the right thing maybe isn't always what you think it ought to be, you know?"

"Oh I'm sure of that, ma'am. Sometimes nothin' looks like you think. Listen, tell ya what. I'll call you tomorrow maybe, how would that be? Give you some time to think about this—"

"I don't need time to think about this."

"Uh-huh. Well, you know, you decide whether you think I'm doin' what you think I'm doin', okay? 'Cause I'm not, believe me. But I'll call ya tomorrow, whatta ya think? Or maybe if the ice is gone, I'll come by and see ya, how would that be?"

"I don't know. I don't know at all." She was close to hostility. He'd screwed up, no doubt. He'd lost her. For now anyway. He just wished he knew what he'd said that had shut her down.

He told her again that he'd call her tomorrow and then said good-bye and hung up before he could compound the damage.

Shit. I explained too much, that's what I did. Should've just kept quiet about what Reseta should've done, should've just been asking her what he did. Dummy. You ever gonna learn? Fuckin' woman was right. Canoza was right. I *do* explain too much. But it sure wasn't 'cause my mother caught me pullin' my wang, that's bullshit. She never caught me. Least I don't think she did. Maybe she did. Did she? Nah. What the fuck, maybe I don't remember.

Can't remember everything. Aw bullshit, I would've never forgot that, man, that would've been embarrassin'. Mortifyin'. Christ, I would remember that. Shit, get real—forget whether I'd remember, Ma would remember. She'd never forget that. Never let me forget it either. She'd be on my ass forever she caught me jerkin' off. That lady was fulla shit, that never happened. Only thing Ma ever caught me doin' was leavin' home. Day I enlisted, that's the day all the shit started, that's the day that poison got planted. And the day Dad died, that's the day it sprouted. Man, that goofy woman had me goin' there for a while. Mrs. Ciangiarullo's sister. Needs to go back to Brooklyn, that woman. The sooner, the better. . . .

Carlucci spent the rest of the morning coordinating responses to accidents and cleaning up incident reports as they were filed—in between fending off Mayor Angelo Bellotti's sudden insistence that as chairman of city council's safety committee and as a lifelong fireman, he could coordinate the responses better than Carlucci.

Carlucci didn't argue. He saw it as an opportunity to turn every pause in the mayor's conversation into a demand for a response to his months-long pleas that the department could not continue to function organized as it was—or rather disorganized as it was.

The mayor was ecstatic. "Gets the juices goin', Rugs, you know? Days like today. I miss puttin' on the old bunker suit. I really do, no kiddin'. I was tryin' to tell my wife this mornin', but she doesn't understand. Women, they don't understand this kinda thing."

"Uh-huh. Uh, Mister Mayor, you think you're gonna reach a decision any time soon? About the department?"

"The department? What about it—oh. You mean, you. Chief."

"Not just me, sir. Whoever you appoint chief is gonna have

the same problems I do—if nobody does anything about 'em. They're not goin' away. Doesn't matter who's sittin' in this office."

"Rugs, you keep askin' me about this, and I keep tellin' you, if it was up to me, this thing would've been settled months ago."

"I know that's what you've been tellin' me, sir. But what I'm tellin' you is, it's eleven months now—"

"I know how long it is."

"Well, yes sir, I'm sure you do. But, fact is, Balzic retired New Year's Eve, which you know as well as I do, and I've been actin' chief since the middle of February, which you also know as well as I do, but, Mister Mayor, this can't continue. I'm on serious overload here. The whole department's on serious overload. There are six, seven guys workin' overtime right now, gonna be workin' double shifts—"

"Well, my God, Rugs, this is the sort of day you expect people to be working overtime, you think they shouldn't?"

"Mister Mayor, that's not what I'm talkin' about."

"I know what you're talkin' about. You don't know what I'm talkin' about. What I'm tellin' you is, things have changed around here. I'm bein' stonewalled every time I turn around. My God, I've been a volunteer fireman since I came back from Korea. Fifty-three. That's forty-one years. But these guys on council, I mean, I thought since we were all firemen, every one of us, we'd be able to get along. Cooperate. Get things done. Put the city ahead of our petty little personal disputes, especially since we got rid of the mayor, Strohn—and that goddamn woman. Julie Richards, Jesus, what a pain in the ass she was." Bellotti began to drum his fingers on the desk.

"I thought, hey, smooth sailin' now, boy, no opposition, now we can run this city the way it oughta be run. Like a business, hell, that's what it is mostly anyway, day-to-day operations. They're just business decisions, that's all. They're not philosophical decisions, political, that's baloney. I said we oughta have a city manager in here, Jesus Christ, you'da thought I said Mary wasn't a virgin. I mean, almost from the second public meeting—why, my God, it's like operatin' on somebody without an anesthetic. Suddenly the most routine decision, how much salt to order, how many light-bulbs we need, my God, it sounded like the United Nations, you know what I'm talkin' about, you've been at those meetings. You've seen me, I'm talkin' myself blue in the face," Bellotti went on, sud-denly very animated, but looking everywhere around Balzic's of-fice except at Carlucci. "We've got a goddamn split on council—hey, you'd've asked me this last November, I would've said you're nuts. Never happen. Not possible. We're all the same party, all good Democrats, we're all volunteer firemen, we've got the city's interests at heart, we're all gonna do what's right for the city—baloney!

"Every goddamn time there's a vote comes up on police ap-propriations, we got this goddamn split, three two against. I go into executive session—you know what I'm talkin' about, you're there, you know I'm tellin' the truth!"

"I didn't say you weren't, Mister Mayor."

"Well what you don't know is what goes on when the door closes and that's what I'm tryin' to tell ya, goddammit!"

"You've told me this before, Mister Mayor."

"I know I have! What you just can't seem to get it through your head is I'm not your problem! We get in my office and there they sit, these three guys, all they wanna say is, screw the police department! Screw the police, screw the police, that's all they know how to say. You know who I'm talkin' about, I don't need to name names."

"No sir, you don't."

"Damn right I don't. We both know who they are. I tell 'em, I say, look, this is ridiculous, I don't know whose nose you think you're cuttin' off to spite whose face here, but that's the city's police department. It's not mine, it's not Carlucci's, it's sure as hell not Balzic's anymore, but it's not yours either, it's the city's! And it doesn't run on air. It costs money! And you guys act like if you had it all your way, what we'd have is a goddamn volunteer police force—like volunteer firemen! And that stupid Figulli, that sonofabitch Egidio, he said—I'll never forget it, Jesus Christ Almighty—he said, 'Well, why don't we explore the possibility?' *Volunteer police, why don't we explore the possibility!* Yeah, you're lookin' at me like I'm nuts, but the sonofabitch actually said that!

"And I said, 'Egidio, for crissake, don't you think it's about time you read the code? You know? The Third Class City Code.' And he says, 'Why the hell should I read that, that's what we got a solicitor for. That's what we pay him for, to read that legal mumbo jumbo, I don't have to read that, that's not my job.'

"Now I ask you, Rugs, what do you say to a guy like that, huh? You were me, what would you say to him? And remember, he's the one I thought was gonna be my biggest ally. I've known the man all my life. We've served in the same hose house for forty-one years, number seven. I mean, Egidio, he's shrewd, he knows his way around, but nobody's ever gonna get him mixed up with Einstein. I used to be able to talk to the man, but I don't know how to get through to him anymore. So c'mon, tell me, I wanna hear, what would you say to him?"

"Well, whatever I said, it wouldn't be in public, that's for sure. I'd take him someplace very private, that's the first thing I'd do."

"And what, you think his IQ's gonna go up just 'cause there's nobody else around?"

"Mister Mayor, you asked me what I thought was a serious question, I'm tryin' to give you a serious answer—"

"All right, all right, go 'head."

"Well, look, you get him privately, first thing it does, it takes away the element of showboatin' for anybody else. It's the first rule of interrogation, separate and isolate. Takes away all their incentive to be frontin' for somebody else—"

"Rugs, I don't wanna interrogate the man, I wanna win him over."

"What you want is for the man to feel free to speak. And you do so wanna interrogate him, you just think you don't. You wanna find out what happened with him just as much as I would, I was in your place. I mean, a *paisan* for all those years? And then all of a sudden he's crackin' your walnuts every time you turn around? You don't wanna know what happened? C'mon."

"I just don't like your choice of words, that's all. Interrogation. Not in that situation."

"Okay, so forget interrogation. Think interview. You like that better?"

Bellotti shrugged. "Okay. So?"

"Okay, so, no matter what you call it, it has to be someplace where there's no question in his mind any of it was bein' recorded. So you could both say, you know, if you had to, but especially him, that the conversation never happened."

"Okay, okay, so I do all that, then what? After I get him there, wherever that is, what do I say exactly?"

"Be honest with him. Tell him how it is. Tell him he can't keep actin' like all those assholes in Harrisburg, in Washington, all they think they have to do to get elected, or reelected, is get tough on street crime. They don't like this, they don't like that, pass a law against it. Build more jails, build more prisons, mandatory sentencing, automatic five years for crime with a gun, automatic drug sentencing, DUI sentencing, it's all bullshit, Mister Mayor. Because when the police say, hey, how we s'posed to do this? How we s'posed to enforce these laws you guys pass? They put their hands in their pockets and give us the big shrug. We're supposed to figure it out. Huh? You won't give us the computers—"

"I just got you two computers, Rugs."

"I know that, Mister Mayor, I'm not talkin' now about you specifically and computers. Fact was, you got 'em, yes, you did, I'm not denyin' that. But it was after ten months of me beggin', houndin' ya everywhere you went. But now that we got 'em, who's transferrin' the records, Mr. Mayor? Who's takin' what's on paper and puttin' it on the floppy disks, huh? Me. When I don't have anything else to do. 'Cause one of those computers is still in the box. There's nobody else in the department knows how to use it—or has the time to be trained. And if I didn't know a guy teaches computers in the high school, I'd be goin' nuts tryin' to figure it out. 'Cause the manuals, they're ridiculous. I pester that teacher so much, poor guy, I'm callin' him so often, he oughta be on a retainer—which I'm sure he's thinkin' about right now, so be ready when he shows up here. I never said anything about that to you till now. But you think I'm learnin' this stuff by myself? You ever try to read one of those manuals? They drive you fucking crazy."

"C'mon, Rugs, don't get sidetracked here, Egidio, remember? What would you say to him, c'mon, not to me, him—what would you say to him?"

"First I'd tell him he has to read the code, he has to find out what the law is, he can't keep actin' like the code is what's in Eddie Sitko's head. The code's written down, it was here before Eddie Sitko, it'll be here after Eddie Sitko, and whether he wants to remember it or not, he took an oath—Egidio—to uphold the laws. All of 'em. And not Eddie Sitko's version of the laws, or just the ones Sitko likes. All of 'em—which start with the Third Class City Code. And if you can't get that in his head, you yourself? Then I'd get the solicitor, set up another meeting, the three of us. If Figulli doesn't wanna read the code himself, if he thinks that's the solicitor's job, then I'd get the solicitor. I'd get him and I'd say, hey, we gotta make this guy understand we can't keep goin' like we're goin', we got a mess here, that's what I'd do."

"Get the solicitor, huh?"

"Yessir, that's exactly what I'd do. And if that didn't work, next thing I'd do, I'd call the fire chief—"

"You'd call Sitko?" Bellotti's mouth fell open.

"Absolutely. I mean who they takin' their orders from? Figulli and Joe Radio—all of 'em for that matter? The whole goddamn council. You gonna tell me *you* don't talk to Sitko? You expect me to believe that?"

"Well whether you believe it or not, Rugs, the fact is, I haven't talked to Eddie for three months now, 'cause the last time I talked to him, we had one helluvan argument about exactly this. I told him, I said, Eddie, you can't keep playin' this silly game. You're the boss, you're the man behind the men. But this is ridiculous, what you're doin'. 'Cause everythin's goin' to hell—Balzic's retired, you're not gettin' even with Balzic, what the hell you got to get even with him for, he's gone, the man's workin' for the state—when he works, which isn't much. He sure as hell don't work for the city anymore, c'mon, what's wrong with you?

"You know what he says, exact words? 'Carlucci's his man. He picked him. Long as Carlucci's there, might as well be Balzic there.' That's exactly what he told me. I said, 'Eddie, Balzic may've been wrong about a lotta things, but he was right about one thing. You're paranoid. You think you're the only guy knows what's good for this city. You got delusions of grandeur. But without an enemy you don't know how to function. You're like George Bush when the Berlin wall came down, he didn't know whether to shit or go blind. Within a year, Bush has us in a war, fightin' a new Hitler him and his PR guys invented'—ah, what am I talkin' for, you know what I'm sayin'."

"Mister Mayor, all the more reason why you got to get 'em together. You gotta get the solicitor to explain to these guys, they can't keep actin' like just 'cause they don't like me, they can let the department go to hell. 'Cause I'm gonna tell ya what's gonna happen, Mister Mayor—"

"Oh don't tell me what's gonna happen, I know what's

gonna happen. It's already happenin'. It's been happenin'. You think I'm not gettin' the letters? The phone calls, huh?"

"The what? What letters? What phone calls—I don't know what you're talkin' about."

"Don't play dumb, Rugs, you don't know how to do it, you just look stupid—and I know you're not, so don't insult me, okay?"

"Mister Mayor, I'm not playin' dumb, I don't know what you're talkin' about, what letters?"

"Somebody's been writin' me letters since March, they started callin' me around the end of June, maybe July fourth, callin' me at home, tellin' me what's gonna happen."

Carlucci threw up his hands and slid his chair back and shook his head emphatically. "It's not me, Mister Mayor, I'm not writin' you letters, and I'm not callin' you, I don't know what you're talkin' about—"

"Oh stop, don't insult me, okay? I know it's not you. I don't know who it is, I don't recognize the voice. And they're comin' from pay phones. I had Bell security involved a week after they started, the calls. And I had every typewriter in the building checked, the letters aren't comin' from here."

"When'd you have the typewriters checked—I don't remember that."

"That guy you thought was servicin' the typewriters? You asked me about him, in April, remember? He was a state cop."

"Man, he fooled me, I didn't make him—"

"You weren't s'posed to, at that time I thought it was you."

"Well, Jesus Christ, no wonder you never made any decision about me—how long's this goin' on?"

"It's still goin' on, whatta ya think I'm tellin' you?"

"Well who else knows about this? That you suspect me? I mean, the rest of council, is this why everything's stalled? Christ, now it's makin' some sense—"

"No no no, nobody else knows about this. Just me. I'm the

only one gettin' the letters, the calls. I haven't told anybody but the state cops, the postal inspectors, and Bell's security people. If anybody on council knows, they didn't learn it from me."

"Well, Jesus, what're they sayin'? They threatenin' you?"

"You tell me, Rugs. You tell me what they're sayin'?"

"Aw c'mon, what're you tryin' to do, Mister Mayor? You just told me I wasn't a suspect anymore, now you're tryin' to game me?"

Bellotti wagged his finger in Carlucci's face. "You listen here. Don't you go gettin' paranoid on me, it's bad enough I gotta deal with that goddamn Sitko. I wanna know what you think the consequences are, I wanna know if you think the same thing this caller thinks, 'cause if you do, that's gonna tell me somethin' about who he is and where he's comin' from. Okay?"

Carlucci didn't believe him for a second. But he began to wonder whether he should, began to wonder whether he hadn't himself just been going along on worn-out prejudice about Bellotti left over from his years sitting at Balzic's feet.

"Okay," Carlucci said. "Okay. The consequences—as I see them, and I repeat, I don't know anything about these letters you're talkin' about—or the calls—"

"Yes yes yes, stop defendin' yourself and just tell me!"

"All right. The consequences are simple. If nothin' changes, if we keep goin' the way we've been goin' here, it's inevitable. Somebody's gonna get fed up. Either in the department or somebody who used to be in the department, or somebody who used to be in city government, or somebody who wants to be in city government, or county government, or maybe in state government—"

"Yeah, okay, enough theories about motivation already," Bellotti said, nodding vigorously. "This person—or persons—who wants to do his civic duty, either 'cause he's fed up with the way things are or 'cause he's got ambition, what's he gonna do, Rugs, c'mon, you tell me."

"One of two things. He's either gonna go to the attorney general, either the state or the federal. But eventually the state, 'cause if he went to the federals, they'd send him back to the state 'cause it's a state problem. Or else he goes to some reporter. That's all he can do, one or the other. And he sure as hell can't go to any reporters in this town, 'cause the paper here's nothin' but a right-wing propaganda machine, which you know better than I do. Which just goes to show, you guys don't care whether you call yourselves Democrats or Republicans."

Bellotti was frowning, but the frown sat atop a curious crooked little smile. "Huh. Coulda fooled me. Didn't know you thought about such things, Rugs."

"I wasn't tryin' to fool anybody, Mister Mayor. But I watched Balzic, you know, like he was my father. Which in a lotta ways he was. And I watched how at the end there, he kept sayin' over and over to me, how the worst mistake he ever made was tryin' to steer clear of politics, which wasn't true—far as I could see. He was a lot closer to what was goin' on politically than he liked to let on he was. But he said he wasn't close, so, uh, I didn't see any point arguin'. But he made a mistake not gettin' closer. And he knew it, and he knew it was a big one. And he's never tried to tell me how to act in that regard, but he never fails to tell me how big a mistake that was."

"So, uh, you're not gonna make that mistake, is that what you're tellin' me?"

"Mister Mayor, you asked me a specific question. Couple of 'em. And I'm tryin' to give you specific answers. Fact is, I'm gonna say it again, and I'm gonna keep on sayin' it. It doesn't make any difference who winds up in this office, who gets the scrambled eggs on his cap. Whether Sitko loves him or hates him, doesn't matter. Whoever it is, he's gonna have the same problems I've been tellin' you since January. You cannot run a police department on hope and hot air. It takes manpower, equipment, and the brains to recognize that somebody has to organize that manpower and that equipment so they can do the job they're supposed to do, and most of all that takes money, sir. And the job's spelled out very specifically. It's all right there in the codes and rules. Third Class City Code, Crimes Code, Rules of Evidence, Rules of Criminal Procedure, all the city ordinances that pertain to public order. It doesn't fucking matter, Mister Mayor, whether Eddie Sitko doesn't like me or hates me or hopes I get cancer tomorrow. He can't just say, 'Fuck the codes, fuck the rules, we're not gonna do 'em, 'cause I'm Eddie Sitko and you're not'—he can't do that, Mister Mayor, and somebody needs to spell it out for him. That's why I'm tellin' ya, get the solicitor, sit those guys down in a room someplace, absolutely private, don't tell anybody else it's gonna happen. And tell 'em, you're not gonna unlock the door till they understand they got some obligations that are bigger than they are, what they have to do."

Bellotti threw back his head and laughed. "That's funny. You actually think I can keep Eddie Sitko locked in a room until he decides to start actin' responsibly, huh? That's really comic."

"Nothin' funny about it, Mister Mayor. There're some people, Eddie Sitko's one, the publisher of the *Gazette*, he's another. These guys, they're so used to havin' people say yes to 'em all the time, they think there's nobody around can remember how to say no. I mean especially now. All those Republicans just got elected to Congress, they're tryin' to tell everybody what's wrong with this country, it's all poor people's fault. Poor people and sick people and teenage black girls. And old people. Can you imagine, Mister Mayor, the balls it takes to tell that lie? Huh? The balls it takes to believe it? The U.S. government's in financial trouble because of poor people, old people, sick people, and black girls? You believe that, Mister Mayor, next thing you gotta believe is that's who wrote the laws. I mean, Jesus, did poor people write the tax laws? Who wrote Social Security, a bunch of geezers? And I guess sick people wrote Medicare and Medicaid. And who wrote the welfare laws—illiterate black girls? Who wrote those laws? I mean, no shit, I didn't know black teenage girls got elected to Congress, did you? And people with terminal diseases? When did that happen?

"Mister Mayor, people can believe bullshit for as long as they want, but sooner or later, reality's gonna jump up in front of 'em and they're gonna have to deal with it. Nobody's gonna tell me it was homeless people shut all those steel mills down, shipped 'em to Korea and Brazil and Mexico. It wasn't people livin' in cardboard boxes wrote those defense budgets. See what kills me, Mister Mayor, is anytime those poor, sick, illiterate black girls in Congress, anytime they don't like somebody? You know, like Manny Noriega, or Saddam Hussein, man, I mean, they never talk about how the government's goin' broke when they wanna drop some bombs on somebody, do they? You hear anybody talkin' budgets and deficits when they were callin' ol' Hussein the new Hitler? Huh? I didn't hear a word about budget deficits then, did you? I mean if I'm wrong, tell me. You hear anybody say, hey, we can't be goin' over there, we can't afford it, you hear any of those illiterate black girls in Congress, you know, those teenagers can't keep their knees together, especially the ones on the foreign affairs committees and the defense appropriations committees, you hear them talkin' about how that's gonna raise financial hell for our children and our grandchildren, huh, make 'em pay taxes forever, huh?"

Bellotti was smiling in spite of himself. "Well that's a very interesting analysis, Rugs. But let me just remind you of one thing."

"Yes, sir, what's that?"

"You're not dealin' with Congress here. You're dealin' with Eddie Sitko. And Egidio Figulli. And Joe Radio. And those guys, if they were sittin' here now, they wouldn't be smilin' like I am. They wouldn't get it. Because what they'd think is you lost your marbles—illiterate black girls in Congress, Jesus, homeless people writin' defense budgets. Can't you see Egidio leanin' over, whisperin' to Eddie, 'What's he talkin' about, there's no black girls in Congress.'"

Carlucci shrugged. "All the while I was in Vietnam, Mister Mayor, I thought I had lost my marbles. The whole time I was there, every time my father used to send me the paper from here, I used to read about all those lights at the end of all those tunnels, and how we were winnin' their hearts and minds, man, I'd look around, there were tunnels all right, there were fucking tunnels everywhere, but I never saw any lights comin' outta 'em. Only thing I heard was incoming. Headed for me or the guys right around me. And I enlisted. Yeah. Guys'd look at me like I was completely fuckin' nuts. Gone. *You enlisted? You volunteered for this shit? You thought it was your duty? To serve your country? What the fuck're you smokin'?*

"And now here I am. Still doin' my duty—tryin'. Servin' my city now. Only now I'm as confused as I was over there, at the end. Nobody here is sayin' anything about lights or tunnels or winnin' anybody's hearts or minds, all I hear is nobody's made up their minds yet. That's all you been sayin' to me, we haven't decided. And so I'm just hangin' here. Just driftin'. I got work up to my eyeballs, everybody in the department has, we don't know what's goin' on, we don't know where we stand, half the guys in this department passed promotion tests, some of 'em two ranks, nobody's gettin' promoted, and all I'm hearin' is how Eddie Sitko thinks I'm Balzic's dummy and he's makin' my mouth move and doin' all the talkin', which is bullshit. Not true.

"But what gets me—I mean, I really don't understand this—we got a fire chief, and the only people elected him to anything, to any kinda office at all, is his own men. They keep on electin' him chief every coupla years or whenever, but he's got no public office directly involvin' the city. If anything, this guy is supposed to be takin' his orders from the safety committee on city council, and you're the chairman of that committee and what's really goin' on is the whole fuckin' council takes orders from him.

Un-fucking-believable. I mean it. He's got a whole fuckin' department, twenty-eight people hung up, don't know what they're doin', don't know what's gonna happen next, just 'cause he thinks I'm the former chief's talkin' dummy. And what's really incredible to me, Mister Mayor, is never once has Sitko come to me himself and said, hey, we need to talk. Uh-uh. Fucker just assumes he knows what's goin' on in my head. That just kills me. I mean it. And now you're talkin' about letters and calls you're gettin' from somebody, who's obviously pissed about what's goin' on, and believe me, if there's one guy pissed off enough to be writin' to you and callin' you, you know that's just the tip of the iceberg. I can tell ya, Mister Mayor, no question, there are a lotta guys in this department really pissed off about this. I mean, seriously pissed.

"Think of it, Mister Mayor, we have three patrolmen workin' as, uh, what's the word, oh yeah—de facto watch commanders, which is a sergeant's slot. Sergeant's pay, sergeant's rank, privileges, vacation time, all the benefits, and they're workin' the radio, and all of 'em passed the sergeant's test years ago. For crissake, Fred Nowicki passed the lieutenant's test! The man's makin' twenty-five nine as a patrolman, he should be makin' thirty-eight nine! And with time in grade, if he'd've been promoted when he should've been, he'd probably be up around forty-two five, forty-three. You think that man's happy with Sitko's bullshit, huh? Every conversation I have with Nowicki, doesn't matter what it's about, sooner or later, he starts bitchin' about how if he's doin' a sergeant's job he oughta be gettin' a sergeant's pay. And because he's passed the lieutenant's test, that's where he oughta be, sir.

"This department needs to be reorganized, somebody needs to pick a chief. I don't care if it's not me—honest to God I don't. I'll be very satisfied to go back to doin' what I was doin'. But, Mister Mayor, for about the tenth time now, I'm tellin' ya. Doin' the chief's job for almost eleven months, in addition to doin' my own jobs, while I'm gettin' paid a sergeant's pay, sir, there's only one word for that. That word is bullshit. I can't keep it up. I'm losin' weight, I can't eat right, I got this rash all over my legs and arms, I wake up bloody from scratchin' in my sleep—"

"Aw that's winter itch—"

"Winter itch? Fuck if it is!"

"Fuck if it ain't. Listen. You're gettin' older. One of the things you find out as you get older, your skin dries out. Christ, it's been years since I could pick up a piece of paper without lickin' my thumb first, that's all that is, that itchin' while you're asleep, winter itch. Go see a dermatologist, he'll tell you."

"Who's got time to see one of those? C'mon, Mister Mayor. This is not right, expectin' me to keep this up. And Sitko and his, uh, they need to be told. You have to tell 'em, Mister Mayor. You do. 'Cause it's worse than I'm tellin' ya. I don't wanna tell you what I've been hearin', but it's not good. Scares the hell outta me. Sitko thinks 'cause he got all these firemen, three hundred and fifty of 'em or whatever, you know, he thinks 'cause they love every step he takes, he thinks the people who don't like him can't touch him. He's wrong. And that's all I'm gonna say about this, Mister Mayor. Except I'm pleadin' with you, sir, you have to make him and Figulli and Joe Radio, you have to make 'em understand. There's nobody else to do this. It's you and the solicitor."

"Wait a second here, what've you been hearing? Is somebody makin' threats? Huh? In your department?" The mayor stood, and he glared at Carlucci. "You tellin' me there are people sayin' they're gonna hurt him? Is that what you're sayin'?"

Oh, Carlucci, shut the fuck up. Talk about not knowing when to stop talking. Jesus. "Uh, I'm not gonna say what I've been hearin, Mister Mayor. Fact is, I've told you and told you, so many times I've lost count, this place just can't keep goin' like this—"

"I know what you've told me. I wanna know about these threats. Are people making threats, yes or no?"

Carlucci was flustered. He'd gone too far and there was no

backing out. Not without clear insubordination. "Mister Mayor, uh, I didn't say that right. I didn't mean threats. No sir. What I meant was, uh, morale is terrible. And anytime, you know, morale gets bad people start sayin' things—"

"Listen, there was an expression when I was in the army, some NCOs I knew used to say as long as the men were bitchin' they were happy. And my response was, well, there's happy bitchin' and there's the other kind. Which kind we got here, Rugs? We got happy bitchin' here? Or we got that other kind, I want a straight answer."

"Mister Mayor, I'm bitchin', and I'm not happy. Not at all. I don't know what kind of bitchin' we have here, according to the way you see it. I'm just tryin' to tell you something. The fact is, I've put it in writing and I've presented it formally at every council meeting since March. What's that, nine times now? Yeah. I'm pleadin' with you, get council to understand the situation here. I don't care who they make chief, it won't make any difference to me I swear to you."

Carlucci stopped talking, even though what he wanted to say was that he didn't care if council made Sitko chief. In fact he'd enjoy that. 'Cause every time Sitko went walking by Nowicki, Nowicki would bitch at him just like he bitches at me. Man, if anything, Nowicki'd give it to Sitko worse! Way worse. 'Cause he hates him! And if nothing changed? Man, he wouldn't let a day go by he wasn't bustin' Sitko's balls. And Mister Prima Donna Fire Chief, I don't think he could handle that. He's not used to having subordinates talk to him that way. He's so used to walking by people, their lips all puckered up ready to kiss his ass, he couldn't handle Nowicki. But oh how I'd like to see him try. That's what ought to happen. It never will, but it ought to. Mister Sitko ought to come down here for a couple days, sit through all the watch changes, let him hear for himself what I have to listen to every day, what I've been listenin' to since right after the March council meeting, which is when I first passed the word what kind of response I got from council. That'd be real enlightening for Mister Fire Chief, you ask me. As if anybody was going to.

"Rugs, you're not answerin' my question. I'm gonna ask you again. Are you telling me that you're hearing specific threats against Sitko?"

"No sir, I'm not. I misspoke. I was outta line. I have not heard specific threats." He was lying. He'd heard more than one, but he feared from the expression on Bellotti's face that he'd just walked into a trap.

Carlucci studied the mayor's face, trying to figure him out, trying to figure out how much of what Bellotti had told him about his problems with Sitko was the truth and how much was said for effect to lay a very simple, very effective trap for Carlucci to stumble into. Balzic had said repeatedly not to underestimate any of these people, not Sitko, not Bellotti, not Egidio Figulli, not Joe Radio. Carlucci leaned back against the wall and thought, well, I've done it now. Fucker knows I'm lying. It's all over his face. Someday I'll learn to shut my mouth. Why'd I have to say that, Jesus Christ, Carlucci, why'd you say that shit about all the things you've been hearing?

"Rugs? Not gonna give me an answer?"

"Uh, sir. I already said I misspoke. I apologize for that."

"Misspoke my ass," Bellotti said under his breath as he went to the door and closed it. Then he came back and put both hands on the desk and looked at Carlucci. "I'm gonna tell you something, young man. Sayin' you heard a threat is the same as makin' a threat—"

"Aw wait a second, I was not makin' threats—"

"You wait a second! You tell me you heard threats? And then you refuse to tell me who's makin' them? You think because you put the words 'I heard' in front of it, you think that changes it, huh? It doesn't. You're just passin' it on! And if you don't tell me where it's comin' from, passin' it on is just a goddamn sign of your approval! You listen to me. Anything happens to anybody in this government while I'm mayor, paid, volunteer, elected, appointed, I don't care who. You'll be the first one interrogated, that's a promise. And another thing. You're gonna lie, you better practice. 'Cause you're a goddamn amateur. Now I'm gonna walk out that door, and I'm gonna act like this conversation didn't happen. It never happened, you hear me?"

"Yes, sir. Loud and clear. Yes sir."

" 'Cause any goddamn part of it comes back to me, I'm gonna know something else about you, won't I?" Bellotti didn't wait for an answer to that one. He splayed his hands at Carlucci, shrugged, turned down the corners of his mouth, then left.

Carlucci watched the mayor go and thought, Well, asshole. What lesson in politics did we learn from that, eh, Rugsie? Goddamn amateur liar, huh? Learn anything from that? Well, let's see. We learned about some of the mayor's frustrations—or the mayor wanted me to believe those were his frustrations. Then we learned that the mayor and the fire chief were no longer speaking—or the mayor wanted me to believe they weren't. Then we learned that some people think if you say you've heard a threat but you don't say where this threat came from that what you're really doing in their mind is giving it your sign of approval. And then we learned that some people tell you they're going to act like something they said they didn't say at all, and because why? Because if any of what they said comes back to them, they'll know something else about you. Wowsie. Why didn't I say, hey, same goes for you, pal? Oh right. 'Cause it's hard talking around your toes.

Sometimes Carlucci had the feeling it was almost as bad around City Hall, trying to deal with the mayor and council, as it was at home, trying to deal with his mother.

Canoza knocked and let himself in. "They finally got around to deliverin' the papers. I got one outta the box. You probably wanna take a look at it."

"Yeah? Why?"

"Couple stories in there about Blasco. One on the front page, and then there's another one on the first page of the sports section. Jeez, I never knew he was that good. I heard he was good, but, man. This guy, this sportswriter, Barone? He must be new, I never heard of him. He makes it sound like he was the greatest, Blasco."

Carlucci sniffed, still reeling from his fiasco with the mayor. "Yeah. If you're talkin' sports. Barone's not a sportswriter, least that's what he told me. Said he just got stuck with the job 'cause he grew up with Blasco. Used to play ball with him. But I don't think he writes sports as a rule. Yeah, lemme see it, uh, Robert."

Canoza broke into a huge grin. "Hey. Thank you, Sergeant. Sir. Actin' Chief."

"Okay okay, not too thick, I could be back in a patrol car at the next change of watch."

"Huh?"

"Never mind. By the way, we hear from the county crime lab yet? Nobody from there called, Jack Turner, anybody, right?"

"I woulda put it through, Rugs."

"Yeah. Course ya would. Coroner too, right? Okay. Thanks for the paper."

Canoza left and Carlucci settled back in his chair. He skimmed the page-one story about Blasco, saw nothing of interest there, just a couple of reporters trying hard to turn it into a celebrity whodunit. Which, of course, it was and would be until he'd gotten around to all the male relatives of all the women involved. Which he would as soon as the ice melted, when, he felt certain, it would no longer be a whodunit.

He turned to the sports section. On the front page, there was a three-column picture of Bobby Blasco in the uniform of the Boston Red Sox, posed in the follow-through of his pitching delivery. He looked incredibly young. But of course he *was* incredibly young. Twenty, twenty-one at most. The headline over the

story and picture read: "Right-Hander Finally Beaten By Bat."
Oh, man, Carlucci thought, that's cold. Somebody actually
thought that was funny?

The text, written by Joe Barone, Rocksburg Gazette Staff
Writer, began under the picture.

> Last night, a Rocksburg legend that began more
> than 50 years ago came to a stunning and ugly end
> when three young men stumbled upon the battered
> body of Robert Joseph Blasco, 61, of 205 Washing-
> ton St., in Rocksburg's Flats.
>
> Known throughout the baseball world as Bobby
> B., or Bobby Brushback, the right-handed pitcher from
> the Flats set records in every league he pitched in for
> winning percentage, lowest earned run average, fewest
> hits, fewest walks, and most hit batsmen.
>
> The last category earned him the nickname he
> relished as much as the grudging fear and contempt it
> signified, which he once flaunted by throwing at the
> head of none other than the great Ted Williams dur-
> ing batting practice in spring training 1954.
>
> Blasco was born in the Flats in 1933 and went
> to St. Francis Elementary School and Rocksburg High
> School. As a ninth grader, he accomplished a feat un-
> paralleled in the school's sports history: he was a
> starter in three varsity sports, football, basketball, and
> baseball.
>
> By graduation in 1951, during the single-wing
> era, he was a multiple-threat tailback and held football
> records in total and single-season rushing yardage,
> passing completions, touchdowns scored rushing,
> touchdowns passed for, and total yardage gained, all of
> which, except for passing touchdowns, still stand.
>
> He also punted, kicked off, and kicked extra

points, and as a defensive back led the team for three years in total tackles and in intercepted passes.

He was named to the All-WPIAL team three times, All-State twice, and rejected scholarship offers from more than 40 universities and colleges.

In basketball, he started every game for four years and led the team in scoring average every year, except for his first year. In an era when it was rare for a high school team to score more than 50 points in a game, Blasco averaged more than 20 points a game his last two years.

As in football, he was All-WPIAL for three years and All-State for two years and rejected more than 30 basketball scholarships.

But it was in baseball that Blasco truly stood out. In four years at Rocksburg High, the right-handed pitcher lost only four games, and one of those was a no-hitter he lost when teammates committed three errors in one inning, allowing the only run scored in the game.

During his senior season, Blasco not only pitched every game, but he threw an astounding total of three no-hitters, four one-hitters, and five two-hitters.

In no game did he give up more than four hits, and that happened only four times. One of them, the WPIAL championship game against Dormont his senior year, lasted 12 innings. He lost 2–1. His high school record was an incredible 39 wins and four losses.

As a professional Blasco rewrote records in three leagues. Signing with the Boston Red Sox on graduation day, he was assigned to the Elyria, Ohio, Red Sox, of the Class C Ohio-Indiana League.

From June 5, when he made his first start, until Aug. 29, his last start, Blasco started 24 games, pitched and won an amazing 20 complete games, lost only two, and led the league in fewest runs allowed, in earned run average, fewest hits, fewest walks, was second in strikeouts, but also led in hit batsmen, 30.

The next year, he was assigned to Birmingham in the Double-A Southern Association, where he made 34 starts, completed 27, won 25, and lost only six. He led the SA in winning percentage, ERA, most complete games, fewest hits, fewest walks, most strikeouts, and, once again, most hit batsmen, 36. He was also the league's most valuable player as selected by league managers.

Blasco spent the 1953 season with Louisville in the Triple-A American Association. His record there: 39 starts, 29 complete games, 30 wins, four losses, 1.78 ERA, 255 strikeouts, 32 walks, 40 hit batsmen. He was a runaway MVP.

In his first three years of organized baseball, Blasco's won-lost record was a phenomenal 75–12, with a combined earned run average of 1.98, earning him an invitation to spring training with the parent club Boston Red Sox the following year.

In 1954, Bobby Brushback achieved full blossom, generated primarily by the infamous batting practice encounter with the great Ted Williams, the last man to hit more than .400 in the major leagues. Among fans, much debate surrounds the encounter because details have always been in dispute.

Some witnesses insist that Blasco's pitch never hit Williams in the head. Batting helmets had only recently been introduced into the game, and Williams certainly wasn't wearing one.

Williams says to this day he wasn't hit, that the pitch sailed over the top of his right shoulder and past his jaw as he was falling down and backward. But this writer, who was catching, has no doubt that Williams was nicked on the top of his right shoulder and that the pitch left an unmistakable brush burn on Williams' jaw as he fell away from it.

Others say if a rookie had the gall to knock down the implacable Williams, he would have most certainly retaliated. Williams did retaliate, as this writer can attest, but not by throwing his bat or charging the mound.

Williams merely stayed in the batting cage and started hitting line drives back at Blasco, four in a row on the next four pitches, the last one hit so hard that it tore Blasco's glove off as he was falling backward to get out of its path.

Incredibly, the ball stuck in Blasco's glove as it went sailing behind the mound, and Blasco, scrambling to retrieve it and finding the ball still in the glove, shouted to Williams, "You're out, sucker!" Thus did the legend grow.

At the end of spring training, Blasco went north with the Red Sox and started the third game of the season. And the eighth. And the thirteenth. The result: three complete games, three wins, two shutouts. He surrendered a total of only two runs, neither earned, 10 hits, and only two walks, while striking out 29 and hitting three batters.

The cause of what ended that brilliant beginning has never been fully revealed. It is indisputable that Blasco broke his elbow and tore the triceps tendon in his right arm as the result of a fall in the shower after his third win.

Red Sox officials have always maintained that Blasco was engaged in horseplay, and that his fall, while ultimately ending his career, was nevertheless nothing more than an unfortunate accident.

But rumors began circulating almost immediately that Blasco's fall was caused not by horseplay but by a punch to the jaw delivered by a teammate. Blasco, these rumors went, had entered the clubhouse enraged because a throwing error on a routine double play had allowed two runs to score, thus ending his personal scoreless streak at 24 innings.

These rumors said that Blasco had been vehemently disliked since his batting practice incident with Williams and had previously been the victim of numerous pranks by teammates: his baseball shoes filled with soft drinks, street clothes smeared with foul-smelling liniments, his gloves and shoes repeatedly thrown into the garbage, etc. Red Sox management said these sorts of pranks happened in every clubhouse in professional sports.

But team officials have never explained why Blasco wore a different uniform number in each of the three games he pitched. Insiders said it was because his teammates had defaced his uniforms with shoe polish. If true, this would seem to indicate an unusually intense level of contempt for a teammate, as professional athletes generally consider it sacrilege to deface the uniform of the team that's paying them.

Whatever the cause, the fall in the shower ended Blasco's major-league career. He had two operations, the first performed immediately to fuse the ulna bone with surgical screws. The second, done much later, was one of the first attempts to transplant tendons in pitchers, then highly experimental, though now relatively routine. It failed.

Blasco tried to come back in 1956 and again in 1957, but was released in spring training by the Red Sox in '56 and the Pirates in '57. He had strengthened his arm by lifting weights, a practice then frowned upon by most ballplayers. Though he could not by his own admission throw hard enough to break a window and trying to throw a curveball caused him excruciating pain, he taught himself, with sheer courage and tenacity, to throw a knuckleball. Unfortunately, he could not throw it for strikes.

In 1957, he came home to western Pennsylvania and opened his first bar and restaurant, in Oakland, Pittsburgh, within walking distance of Forbes Field. When Forbes Field was torn down, Blasco closed his restaurant and moved back to Rocksburg, where he opened Bobby B's Brushback Bar and Grille on Helen Street in the Flats.

The restaurant will remain closed until after the funeral tomorrow, at which time it will open, according to his daughters, Patricia Wallingford, 30, and Mary Lou Heinlein, 28, both of Phoenix, Ariz., to hold a "whiskey wake," Wallingford said, as "my father wished in his will." She invited "all of Bobby's friends to join my sister and me in celebrating" their father's life.

Blasco was a complicated man, difficult to know, more difficult to like. He was one of the most intelligent people this writer has ever met, yet one of the most maddening to call a friend.

He was by turns kind, generous, mean, cheap, thoughtful, thoughtless, utterly self-absorbed, and yet capable of vast understanding of the games he was involved in and their place in our culture.

He could turn on you in an instant for the most minor infraction of his rules, of which there were many and known mostly only to him. This writer saw him jump into a rain-swollen creek in Alabama to save a cat. And three months later saw him shoot a bird dog to death that had bitten down too hard on a quail. Witnessed him supporting his mother through her long and painful terminal illness, and read news accounts of his assaults on his wives.

One final irony envelops Blasco. The bat his assailant used had once been used by Ted Williams. It bore not only Williams' autograph but also ball marks made most certainly by the great Williams himself. Blasco told this writer that Williams had given him the bat after his second shutout in 1955.

Williams, when phoned yesterday, said that since his stroke, his memory is poor. "I've given so many bats to so many people, sold so many of them, I just don't remember who has them," he said. "I don't even remember this Blasco guy you're talking about, but if he's who I think he is, he probably stole it."

This writer does remember. He caught every game Bobby Blasco pitched in high school, in the sandlots around Rocksburg, and in the minor leagues, as well as every game in spring training in 1954. Before Blasco got hurt, he had the best curveball this writer ever saw. And the best control. Would that he had had more control over his life.

Carlucci put the paper down, thinking, man, there's a pile that man left unsaid. "This writer this, this writer that," why couldn't he just say I? Me? I saw this, I did that, what's so tough about sayin' that? But I have to talk to this guy again—oh shit! Ma! Oh man. She's still in the hospital, oh Jesus Christ, I'll never hear the end of this, she's gonna bitch for the rest of her life, oh God. . . .

On his way out of City Hall, Carlucci stopped in the city administrator's office to inquire about which streets had been salted to find out whether it was safe to remove his chains.

"Salt trucks get up to Norwood Hill yet? When I left there this morning, Corliss Street was glass."

The administrator shrugged. "Lotta streets out there, Rugs, and we only have two trucks."

"How about around the hospital?"

"Oh hell, that's the first place they went."

Carlucci went back to the duty room and called Mrs. Comito and told her that he was sorry but she'd have to go on standby despite what he'd said earlier about her taking the whole day off. "I'm on my way to pick Ma up at the hospital. If she's still speakin' to me when I get there."

"That's okay, Rugsie, I couldn't go nowhere anyhow. I ran outta salt, I couldn't've made it off my porch if I wanted to. I was gonna buy some but I forgot. So if you need me to watch your mother, you're gonna have to walk me over, okay? Unless you could pick me up some salt, you know. You know how scared I am of fallin'."

Carlucci promised to buy a bag of salt and said he would help her get from her house to his if he needed her.

"Should I call Missus Viola? Tell her she's gonna have to work tonight?"

"Let's just wait and see, okay? I have no idea how Ma's gonna be when I get there." Carlucci hung up and trotted out of the building.

Ten minutes later, after stopping to buy gas for the Chevy and a ten-pound bag of de-icer for Mrs. Comito, he was hurrying down the corridor to his mother's room. She was waiting for him in a wheelchair just inside the door, looking up at him under her brows, her arms folded, her ankles crossed, her right foot going back and forth.

"Where you been? Jesus Christ, I been ready to get outta this place since I woke up this morning, seven o'clock. Since seven I been waitin' for you. I been callin' your station all day, where the hell you been? Don't they give you my messages, huh? What the hell's wrong with those guys?"

"Ma, I know you don't care about this, but there was a guy murdered last night, and there was an ice storm, started about two, two-thirty this mornin'. There were a pile of accidents, sixteen so far, moving cars hittin' other moving cars, hittin' parked cars, hittin' utility poles, people fallin', some of 'em hurt real bad, you know? And I had to supervise all that. My job, remember?"

"That's how your father died. My husband. That's exactly how he died. Slid on the ice and hit a telephone pole. Which you wouldn't know about. Since you was someplace else."

Oh God, here we go again. Carlucci slipped between the door to the john and the chair and started to push her out into the hall, but stopped. "Hey, Ma, before I go anywhere, you have been discharged, right?"

"Oh just go! Push! Get me the hell outta this place, gives me the willies."

"Listen, just hold it a second, okay? Till I make sure you been discharged?"

"Oh for God's sake, how you think I got this wheelchair?"

"You coulda gone out in the hall and just grabbed it, you know?"

"Oh right, so now I'm a wheelchair thief. Well you're a cop, arrest me, why don'tcha? Jesus."

"C'mon, Ma, okay? I'll be right back."

"Sure, run off, why don'tcha? That's what you're good at."

Aw shit. Run off, why don't I. That's me, that's what I'm good at, you betcha. Jesus.

Carlucci hustled around until he'd located the nursing supervisor and cleared it with her that his mother had indeed been
discharged. He hurried back and started pushing the wheelchair
toward the bank of elevators without a word, while his mother
continued to berate him for leaving her last night and for not
being there to pick her up at 9 A.M. when she'd been discharged,
even though she'd been ready to leave at 7, and now here it was
the middle of the afternoon.

In the elevator, crowded with people in hospital clothes,
Mrs. Carlucci announced: "This is my son. Youns people might
not recognize him, but he's the chief of police. He got time for
everybody but me. And all I am is his mother, that's all, just the
person who gave him life, that's all. He dumps me off here last
night 'cause I got chest pains, and then he leaves me here all day
'cause he gotta supervise all the people writin' accident reports,
like as if they don't know how to do it unless he's lookin' over
their shoulder. How many times's a cop have to write out an accident report before you think he knew what he was doin'?"

"Ma, cut it out, okay? Please?"

"Oho! Listen to him now. Don't want nobody to know how
he treats his mother, so he's all fulla *please*s now, you hear that?"

Finally, mercifully, the elevator reached the floor to the tun-
nel leading to the parking garage, and they got off.

In the Chevy going home, she complained about the noise
and how bumpy the ride was. "All you gotta do is stop and take
the goddamn chains off, how much trouble could that be? You
put 'em on, didn't ya?"

"Yeah I put 'em on. But I don't know if the salt trucks made
it up Norwood yet, and when I left this mornin', it was nothin'
but ice on our street, okay? That's why I'm not takin' 'em off."

"Jesus, feels like we're ridin' in a tank in here."

Carlucci sighed and counted to ten. Then to twenty. He
could've counted to a thousand. He was so angry he wanted to

pull over and ask her if she'd rather walk. Or call a cab. But he kept on driving, the chains clanking away.

"Guess you think you got them chains on nothin's gonna happen, huh?"

"Things can always happen, Ma. That's what life is, somebody told me once, things happenin'. Some of 'em good, some of 'em bad, most of 'em just routine, stuff you gotta do every day."

"Oh brother, ain't we philosophical. Sounds like something your father woulda said. After he had a snoot fulla wine."

"After he had a what? That's the way you talk about him now?"

She clenched her teeth and threw up her chin and fell silent for the first time since he'd seen her today.

"Maybe Dad did say that, I don't remember. But it sounds like somethin' he woulda said. Maybe. Yeah."

"Well for your information, Mister Philosopher, chains didn't stop what happened to him from happenin'."

"What? What're you talkin' about?"

"Oh, listen to you. I say somethin' about your father and you're all of a sudden interested in what I have to say for a change. Well loo-dee-doo and la-dee-da, smell me."

Carlucci turned up McCoy Road from Island Avenue and found that the salt trucks had been over it. At the top of the hill he turned left around Mother of Sorrows Church in time to see the salt truck coming back down Corliss Street. He'd come this far, no point in stopping to take the chains off now.

"Ain't you gonna take the chains off? There's the goddamn salt truck right there."

"We're half a block from home, Ma. I'll take 'em off when I get there. Anyway, what're you sayin' now—chains didn't stop what happened from happenin' to him?"

"To us, to us! Not just him! I was in the car too, remember? Jesus Christ he coulda killed me too you know!"

"Wait wait, what're you talkin' about, coulda killed you too? You're makin' it sound like he, uh, like he, uh . . ."

"Like he what, huh? C'mon Ruggiero, spit it out! Say it! Like he what?"

Carlucci pulled in to the curb in front of their house, pushed on the emergency brake pedal, put it in neutral, and turned off the ignition, all the while staring at his mother.

"Hey, Ma, why're you sayin' he had chains on, huh?"

"That's exactly what I'm sayin'. And they didn't keep nothin' from happenin'!"

"Ma, I don't know why you're sayin' this now, about the chains, except I know you're really pissed off at me for what you think I did to you last night—"

"Don't use that kinda language with me—and this mornin'! Don't forget this mornin'! All day! All day I hada wait for you to show up. But that's you. Ohhh, is that ever you. When I need you, you ain't there."

Carlucci tried to clear his throat. It felt like it was closing from the inside. He got slightly dizzy, and forced himself to exhale hard through his nose to expel all the air until he was compelled to inhale.

"What're you doin' now, huh? That goofy breathin' thing? Huh? That breathin' thing your hero taught you, you're always braggin' how Balzic taught you this, he taught you that, is that what you're doin' now?"

"When did I ever brag about this, c'mon."

"Well if you could see how you look when you're doin' it, if you could see your face, I'm not kiddin' now, your face gets all red—quit it! Makes me nervous, honest to God. Sometimes I'd like to get my hands on that bastard."

"What bastard? Who're you talkin' about now?"

"Balzic! Who do ya think?"

Carlucci sighed, got out, went around the front of the car, helped her get out and up the steps and into the house where she collapsed with a great sigh on the couch. She started to unbutton her coat, then stopped to search frantically for the TV remote control.

"Where the hell's that thing? I know it was here before you made me go to the goddamn emergency room. Last thing I did last night, I stuck it down between the pillows here, what'd you do with it?"

"I didn't do anything with it. Ma? Listen, forget about that thing, I wanna ask you somethin'. And I didn't make you go anyplace last night. That was you wanted to go to the hospital, not me."

"Oh I knew I shouldn'ta said that about your father. That's all I have to do to get you started, just say somethin' about him and away you go, bing, bam, boom, start makin' him out to be the guy never did nothin' wrong."

"Hey! Ma? Listen to me! I've read that accident report a thousand times—"

"A thousand times," she said, snorting. "Why do you have to exaggerate like that?"

"I'm not exaggeratin', Ma, I have a copy in my desk. Every once in a while I take it out and I read it and there is not one word in there about Dad havin' chains on. Just the opposite. 'Cause the investigating officer wrote exactly that—"

"That drunk? You're gonna tell me what that boozie wrote?"

"He said, in his opinion, if the vehicle had been equipped with chains, the accident would most likely not've happened. That's down there in black on white, besides which, Ma, the man told me that himself—"

"Oh what the hell did he know? Drunk half the time that guy, everybody knew that."

"The man drank, Ma, that's for sure. Not on duty, I never saw him drunk on duty, and everybody I ever talked to who knew him or worked with him, they all said the same thing—"

"Hoo hoo hoo—cops coverin' up for cops."

"I'm not coverin' anything up for anybody, Ma. I'm tellin' you, I investigated it. As thoroughly as I know how. It was my father, you know? I wanted to make sure. And I made sure. There were no chains on Dad's car, and the investigating officer was not drunk, and you were in the backseat. A cop said so, he told me so himself—"

"Oh here we go with all that old baloney again—"

"A cop said you were in the backseat, Ma, and so did three EMTs, and so did the firemen who cut you outta the car, I interviewed every one of 'em myself! Everybody who was at that scene, Ma, every single person who was there, who cut you out of the car, who put you in the ambulance, who took you to the hospital, I interviewed 'em, I talked to every single one of 'em and they all said the same thing: the investigating officer was not drunk, there were no chains on the back tires, and you were in the backseat. Okay? You got that? That's the way it was. And what you're talkin' now, this, uh, this—I don't know what this is you're talkin'. This, uh, this crap, that's all I can call it—this crap about you coulda been killed too, like you're implyin' that—man, I can't even get the words out—you're implyin' Dad had chains on and he, uh, you're implyin' somethin' like he drove the goddamn thing into the pole, and that's bullshit, Ma! That's pure bullshit, that did not happen!"

"And of course you were there, so you would know I guess—and I told ya don't use that kinda language with me—"

"C'mon, Ma, Jesus, you know exactly where I was. In a C-147 flyin' back from Nam. Ma, I've told you and told you and told you, you don't have to be someplace to know what happened. All you have to do is know how to ask the right questions and know what to look for and you can wind up knowin' a whole lot more than the people who were there, the people who were involved. It's what I do, Ma, you know?"

"Well if you know so much, if you're so smart, Sherlock, then why don't you tell me why I was in the backseat?"

"Huh?"

"Yeah, right, huh. Huh huh huh!"

"Ma? You sayin' what I think you're sayin'?"

"Am I sayin' somethin'? What'm I sayin'? You tell me, you're so smart."

"Oh you're sayin' somethin' alright. I just can't believe you're finally sayin' it. This is the first time you ever said it—the first time you ever *admitted* you *were* in the backseat."

"So okay, so whoop-dee-do, so now I admitted it, smell me. So you know so much, you know how to investigate everything, so you tell me, Fearless Fosdick, why was I back there, huh? Why wasn't I in the front seat beside my husband, you know so much, huh?"

Carlucci slumped into the worn Windsor chair beside the couch. "I don't know, Ma. Not without askin' you a lotta questions. All I been doin' for years and years now is speculatin' and surmisin' and guessin'. And goin' nutso. 'Cause till this moment you never even admitted you were back there—"

"Oh Jesus you sound like a busted record, quit talkin' about it already and tell me why, c'mon, you're the Fearless Fosdick here."

"I wish you wouldn't call me that, okay? It's really, uh, it's really—never mind."

"Oh stop feelin' sorry for yourself and tell me who dunit, c'mon. Fearless investigator you, c'mon!"

"Hey, Ma, I told you already, I can't figure nothin' out unless you answer some questions—"

"Nah, I'm not answerin' no questions. I'm gonna ask some. You're the one's gonna answer the questions. Maybe then you'll figure it out. C'mon, hotshot, you ready?"

Carlucci didn't know what to say. In twenty-three years of his asking her about the accident in which his father was killed, she had never once done what she was doing now. Carlucci didn't know what to make of it. He stuttered some inane response that she took to mean he was ready, so she launched a barrage of questions at him.

"You remember the letters, huh? The letters you got the whole time you were in the goddamn army, huh? Whose did you keep? Who wrote to ya every day? Who wrote to ya every six months if he was lucky? Whose did you keep? Which ones you take out and read, huh? His or mine?

"And what did I write to you about, huh? How much I loved ya? What I was cookin'? Was I cookin' all your favorite foods? Was I seein' all the things you used to look at when you were a little boy and woke up every mornin' and the world was all so goddamn brand-new to you? And beautiful? Who made ya rigatonis every Friday, huh? Who wrote ya about 'em every Saturday, huh?" Tears were streaming down her cheeks. She was quivering, trembling, her whole body shaking.

Carlucci didn't know what to do or say. He was stunned.

"And what'd your father write to you about, huh? Duty, didn't he? Duty, huh? And patriotism, huh? And servin' your country? And how you had to be a man, huh? And how young men, how they have to serve, do their duty when their country calls. Didn't he write you all that stuff, huh? 'Cause you have to fight evil, right? Just like he did. Right? Ain't that what he wrote? How you have to fight evil just like he did?"

Carlucci couldn't help himself. His eyes were filling up. He looked at his hands in his lap and then at his shoes and the floor. He felt sadness sweeping over him like a cold wind, making him shiver.

"Fight evil just like he did, Jesus Christ. What a crock. You know where he fought evil, huh? Where did he meet me? Where were you born? Why you lookin' so surprised, don't you think one thing has nothin' to do with the other? Huh? You were born in New Jersey. You don't remember 'cause you were a baby! But that's where you were born, Buster Brown. In 1951, in the base hospital, Fort Dix, New Jersey. Which is where your father was fightin' evil, fightin' the communist menace. Collectin' utility bills from all the married personnel livin' on the base, that's how he fought the commies! That's what your hero father did durin' the Korean War he was always talkin' about."

"Oh Ma, cut it out, please? Just stop, okay?"

"You think I should stop, huh? I don't think I should stop. I think it's about time you heard some things. I think it's about goddamn time you heard the truth!"

"Ma? Ma, please, okay? I know the truth."

"You know the truth, ha! Double ha! You don't know nothin'! For twenty-three years now I been keepin' my mouth shut, I'm not gonna keep it shut no more, I'm sicka this crap. Your father ain't no hero, he was *never* in Korea, he was *never* outta the United States, he was *never* outta New Jersey, he spent the whole time he was drafted—that's another thing, *he was drafted*, he *never* volunteered, he *never* enlisted, he was drafted! And the whole time he was in the army, the whole three years, he was stationed at Fort Dix, New Jersey—which is where he met me, which is where we was married, which is where you were born—and the whole time he was askin' me to marry him I had the feelin' the only reason he was doin' it was so he wouldn't have to go overseas, so they wouldn't ship him to Korea.

"Which I put up with. 'Cause I didn't care. 'Cause I had my reasons too—I ain't innocent in all this. I had my own reasons for wantin' to get married, so I married him—and whether anybody knows this or not, I don't care. I loved him. In my own way, yeah, I loved him. Right up until he started fillin' your head with all that bullshit about how you gotta do your duty, when your country calls you gotta go—"

"C'mon, Ma, don't do this, please? I mean it—"

"Don't do what, huh? What, you think I'm makin' this up? Huh?"

"I know you're not makin' it up, but I remember all those arguments, you know? You think I'd forget them? You think I don't remember how you two used to argue about me enlistin', you think I'd forget any of that—"

"And I suppose you want me to think you didn't, huh? The hell you didn't. 'Cause if you did, you'd remember me tellin' him, huh? Beggin' him, huh? Tell him the truth, I said! Tell him the truth, he's your son for crissakes! He deserves the truth! You remember me sayin' that? Hell no you don't remember! 'Cause you say you remember but you don't! All you wanna remember is what he used to tell you! About how he was in the infantry in Korea, how he served under MacArthur, how he went in at Inchon—you think I don't remember the names of all those places, huh?

"You wanna know where he got those names, huh? He got 'em outta the goddamn papers, Ruggiero! Outta the newspapers! You don't believe me, I'll show ya, I'll prove it to ya, I'll get his goddamn discharge papers. Says right on 'em where he was, where he served, from when to when, how he got drafted, what his job was, you'll see for yourself—"

"Ma, you don't have to do that, okay? Stay there, it's alright. Ma, don't bother, okay?"

Too late. She had heaved herself off the couch and scurried to her bedroom. He could hear her rooting through the chest of drawers, hunting for her husband's discharge papers.

"I don't know what the hell's goin' on here, goddamn thing was right here, been here ever since we moved into this goddamn house, somebody's playing games on me, somebody's tryin' to trick me! Ruggiero! Ruggiero, get in here! What's goin' on here? Where the hell's his papers, d'you take 'em, huh?"

Carlucci ran his tongue around the inside of his lips and sighed. He rolled his neck from side to side, stood, and slowly made his way into her bedroom. His feet felt like they were mired in mud up to his ankles.

"Ma, listen to me, okay? Nobody's playin' games on you. I took 'em. I have 'em."

"What? Speak up, don't mumble, I can't hear you."

"I said it's okay, okay? I have 'em. Nobody took 'em. I took 'em. I've had 'em for about, hell, you know, ever since like, six months after I got home."

Her mouth fell open, her eyes blinked heavily, her hands went up and out and then fell back to her sides as she scooched around on her bottom to face him. "You got 'em? When'd you get 'em? I didn't give 'em to you."

"No no, you didn't give 'em to me. I took 'em. I got 'em. First time I took ya to the hospital and you hada stay overnight, it was when you were gettin' those headaches, when you first started gettin' 'em. So you were in there, and then I came home, and I was sittin' around, you know, nothin' to do, I started nosin' around, lookin' for somethin' that was his, somethin' I'd never seen before. What can I tell ya, I don't know, I wanted to see somethin' that was his. Somethin' he had his hands on, that's all."

"You went snoopin' through my things?"

"I wasn't snoopin', Ma, I was lookin'—never mind. I found 'em, that's the important thing, and then I made copies of 'em, you know, and then I called the VA and I checked his against theirs, and, uh, that's what I did. And then I put the originals back. And then, I don't know, coupla months ago, I don't know why, for some reason, I wanted the originals again. Don't ask me why. I don't know. But I took 'em again. Which was the second time. And I still have 'em, I haven't done anything to 'em, they're still in good shape, you want 'em, I'll go get 'em—you want 'em? I can get 'em right now."

She shook her head furiously. "What I don't understand, this is . . . this is what I don't—why the hell'd you let me go on like this? If you knew it, goddamn you, why didn't you say somethin'? I kept it from you for Jesus Christ twenty-five years and you knew all the time?! And every time I told you I didn't know why I was in the backseat and you knew—"

"Hey, Ma, slow down, okay? I didn't know any such thing, I don't know. All I knew was everything he was tellin' me about what he did, that he, uh, you know, he, uh, he made it all up, I mean that's all I knew, that's all I know, how'm I s'posed to know what you were doin' in the backseat, I don't know everything!"

"After all this? After you know? You still can't figure out why I was in the back? You don't understand why I didn't wanna sit in the front? Next to the sonofabitch! Bad enough I hada stay in the same house with him! The same bed! Jesus. He thought I was supposed to just keep on sleepin' with him! Anytime he wanted to do somethin', huh? I was supposed to just roll over and keep my mouth shut! He puts you in a war, God knows what it was about, you sure as hell didn't know, I didn't know, but . . . but your father! He knows! He understands! Oh goddamn right! He knows everything about dominoes and Kissinger and all them bastards! And he filled your head with all this bullshit about what a hero he was, fightin' the commies in Korea! It was all a lie, every goddamn thing he told you—"

"I know, Ma, I know. Enough already, okay? It's history, I'm back, I been back for twenty-three years, it's time to stop—"

"You coulda been killed! You coulda been maimed! You coulda had your legs blown off, every goddamn night on the TV there it was! I had to watch! You understand? I couldn't help it, I had to watch! You think he watched? Never! He couldn't even look at the TV, where his lies put you! He'd leave the room. Just like you! Explain that to me, Dick Tracy, huh? He couldn't watch the news either! His phony baloney lies, all his bullshit about duty and patriotism and honor and courage, all that bullshit! The man collected utility bills, gas bills, water bills, electric bills, phone bills, that's how he fought the commies! That's how he fought evil! But you! *You were there.*

"And every letter you wrote, you wrote to me! You didn't write to him, you wrote to me! And what were you doin'? Huh? I'll tell you what you were doin', you were tellin' me more lies! How you were fine, no problems, everything was fine, you were fine, the army was fine, Vietnam was fine, you hadn't even seen a

Viet Cong, wouldn't know one if you saw one and every night I'm watchin' it on the TV! Where the hell do men learn to lie like that, huh? Can you tell me, Ruggiero? Where do you learn to lie like that?"

Carlucci sank to the floor on his knees in front of her. "Ma, listen to me. You can't tell the truth about that. Maybe some guys can, but not me. I can't. I couldn't. I don't know why Dad couldn't. I've thought and thought and thought until my head hurts, and the only thing I can come up with, is for some reason he thought he should be ashamed 'cause he wasn't there, I don't know. I don't know what else to think. Maybe he knew some guys that got shipped over and got killed or got wounded, I don't know. But whatever it was, it wasn't somethin' he could tell me, don't ask me why, but I know it—I knew it soon as I saw his discharge."

"Well, why'd you have to believe it? That's what I don't understand, why'd you have to believe it? What was so goddamn important, you had to give up everything, every goddamn thing you had here, you threw it all away and went and enlisted and wound up in a place where any goddamn second you coulda been blown to bits, Jesus Christ, I had to watch it every night on TV, night after night, thirteen months, thirteen goddamn months you were there, thirteen goddamn months I hada look at it on TV every night, every morning, three times a day, every goddamn news show, I hada look at people bein' blown to bits and it was 'cause of my husband's lies that my only son was there! You two made me crazy. You think a crazy woman sleeps with the man who made her crazy? You think she sits beside him in the car when they have to go shoppin'? You think they eat together? Huh? If anything happened to you, I swear to God, as God is my witness, I woulda killed him myself. . . ." She was sobbing, her whole body shaking.

"Ma, stop, okay, please? Don't talk like that. Please don't talk like that. And don't cry, please, don't, it ain't worth it, I'm home, it's over, it's history. It's been history for years and years, it's done. It's finished."

"No it ain't. It ain't finished. I'm crazy. I'm not a normal person. You two made me crazy. I talk to the TV. I keep records of what kinda clothes the people on TV wear. What normal person does that? I'm nuts!"

"Ma, you're not nuts, stop it."

"Oh yes I am. I don't know what's up anymore. I love you, I hate you, sometimes I could kill you, sometimes I wish I woulda killed him. How many times I asked you to kill me, huh? How many times I said get your gun and shoot me right here?" She jabbed herself between the eyes with her thumbs.

"Stop it, Ma, okay? I'm not shootin' ya, not now, not ever, okay? Time . . . time, man . . . it's time you gave him a break. Time you gave me a break—"

"Oh sure! Give him a break! You, give you a break! What about me? Who gives me a break? Huh? My head's dizzy all day long—"

"I was gonna say that, Ma, honest to God I was comin' to that. Time to give yourself a break, you're the one needs it more'n anybody, I mean it."

"Ah sure. Just like that. Poof. Snap my fingers, poof. Everything's fine. Yeah."

"No, not just like that, not just snappin' your fingers. I know it ain't gonna be easy, Jesus, I been doin' this as long as you have—"

"Oh bullshit, long as I have! You didn't have to sit here night after night and watch it and pray—"

Carlucci clapped his hands over his ears, jumped up, and walked in circles, fuming. He wanted to grab her shoulders and shake her, just once. "Hey, Ma, you think it was tough here, huh? Watchin' it on TV, you think that was tough? It was a little bit tougher there, Ma, I guarantee ya. And don't ever say that to me again, 'cause if you think that's true, you are nuts. You never zipped up a body bag in your life, don't ever tell me you did, don't ever tell me 'cause you saw it on TV you know what it was like 'cause you don't."

"Ruggiero, don't talk to me like that, you're scarin' me."

"Maybe you need to be scared, Ma. Maybe that's what it's gonna take for you to know the difference between what's real and what's TV—ah shit, what am I sayin' here, this is—God this is terrible, let's just stop this, okay? Let's just give this a break. Everybody. You, me, Dad, everybody, let's just give it a break. I can't handle this any more today, I thought if I ever got you to talk about it, I thought I could handle it, but turns out I can't. I'm gonna call Missus Comito, okay?"

Without waiting for her reply, he went to the kitchen and dialed Mrs. Comito's number. When Mrs. Comito answered, she said that it was almost four o'clock, didn't he know that? And didn't he want to call Mrs. Viola instead, since that was when she usually started.

Oh man, he thought, was it that late? Damn. He had a ton of things to do, he was so hungry he could eat a dirt sandwich, all he needed was ketchup. He told Mrs. Comito to forget about it, that he'd call Mrs. Viola. "But you're gonna be here tomorrow, right?"

"Oh sure, Rugsie, I'll be there. But you don't have to call Vi, I can see her comin' down the street right now. I'm lookin' through my front window."

He hung up and went to the front door and opened it and saw for himself Mrs. Viola making her way gingerly down the sidewalk, using parked cars and utility poles to keep her footing on the icy sidewalks.

His mother said behind him, "Ruggiero, don't go to work no more today, okay? Stay here, talk to me, we need to talk."

"Ma, listen, soon as Missus Viola gets here, I gotta go. I got a pile of stuff to do, I was supposed to meet a state cop for lunch,

Jesus, I didn't even call him, oh man. I'm gettin' way behind here, I can't stay. I'm gonna be gone all night."

"You're never here, you're always workin', that goddamn Balzic, he never cuts you any slack—"

"Ma, Balzic ain't my boss anymore, I'm the boss. At least for a little while longer. I'm the one sets my hours, not anybody else—and boy they're gonna love me tryin' to collect overtime for today, they find out where I been. Gotta go, Ma, here she comes. Bye. Just one thing. There's one thing I wish you would think about, okay? You remember that doctor last night? You remember he gave you a prescription to go see somebody? You remember that?"

"I remember," she said, leaning against the doorjamb, eyes downcast.

"I wish you'd give that some thought, okay? Just think about it, that's all. Maybe we should both think about that, okay? I gotta go."

"I don't wanna talk to no strangers," she said, turning and going back into the living room. "I got strangers in my house every day."

"They're not strangers, Ma. You know these two people, man, c'mon—"

"They're here to watch me! They're cops! Just like you! "

Aw shit, here we go again. He grabbed his parka and put it on while holding the door with his hip for Mrs. Viola, telling her that he was sorry he couldn't help her with her coat but he was late and he'd call as soon as he got the chance.

He walked carefully down the steps, avoiding patches of ice the salt he'd spread this morning hadn't touched. He could hear his mother protesting to Mrs. Viola that she didn't want her there, she wanted her Rugsie, didn't Mrs. Viola have her own home, why was she always coming to this house every night, for crissake, she was sick of looking at her, but as long as she was there, would she find the goddamn remote, it was somewhere in the couch pillows. "Rugsie hid it, he's always doin' that."

Carlucci took the chains off, put them in the trunk, and drove to City Hall, stewing, on the way, over everything his mother had said. What baffled him was why, if she was still so furious with her husband for lying about what he did when he was in the army and for lying to me, which she thinks influenced me to enlist—which it didn't, or which it only partly did, 'cause there was a lot of other stuff happening with me then—the thing I don't get is why she's always blaming me for not being there. If she's as pissed at him as she says she is—or was—then why's she always on my case for not being there—I wasn't there, I'm not where I'm supposed to be, I wasn't there when he got killed, I didn't get home till the next day, and from then till now, that's all I've been hearing, "If you were where you were supposed to be, if you were a good son like the Bible says, honoring your mother and father, then my husband wouldn't be dead." Now she tells me she was in the backseat 'cause she couldn't stand to sit next to him in the car, bad enough she had to sleep in the same bed with him. Makes no fucking sense. She's talking out of both sides of her mouth at the same time, I don't get it. God, we ought to be seein' somebody, whoever that ER guy prescribed. I have to check those people out, those two people he recommended. Who knows, maybe she'll go for it, maybe I'll even go for it. Maybe I'll go by myself. Maybe I'll go and won't even tell her I'm going. Aw shit, why's everything so fucking hard sometimes? Why can't it ever be easy? And Franny, good God, you're the best-looking woman I think I ever saw. Why ain't she married? Why's nobody ever scooped her up? Woman looks that good, there must've been a thousand guys taking shots at her, why's she still living with her mother? Oh, God, listen to me—why is *she* still living with her mother? Like who'm I living with? See? See there, asshole? Just more complications. It's never fucking easy, I swear to God, why

you keep thinking it's ever going to be easy? Who said it was supposed to be easy? . . .

On his way into the duty room, he picked up all his phone
messages from Patrolman Fischetti, acting sergeant, acting watch
commander, duty dispatcher. There were three calls from state
police Trooper Dulac, all between 12:30 and 1 P.M., one from the
coroner at 2:16, and one from somebody named Lazzaro.

"Who's this Lazzaro? Man, woman, what?"

"Attorney. From someplace out in the boonies. That's a
Westfield Township number. Wouldn't say what he wants, just
wants to talk to you. Never heard of him."

"What'd he want?"

"Hey, Rugs, I just told ya he wouldn't say what he wants,
what do I know?"

"Okay, okay, take it easy. Wait a minute, what're you doin'
here?"

"What'm I doin' here? What's it look like?"

"I know what you're doin' here. I mean what're you doin'
here—you were out there all day, I know you were, I saw ya about
three times. How come you're working a double shift? Who's
sick?"

"Canoza broke his wrist."

"He broke his wrist? How'd he do that? When, where?"

"Fell down up in the hospital parkin' lot. Comin' outta the
ER. And he's happier'n shit, he thinks he's gonna sue the hospital, make a pile of money, can you imagine? What the fuck's
wrong with him, he's so stupid sometimes I can't believe it."

"He's not as dumb as everybody thinks."

"Well, he called me, told me he's gonna sue? I told him, I
said, what's wrong with you, which one did you break? He says
the left. So I says, hey asshole, how you gonna get any money for
that? What're you gonna claim, huh? You're right-handed, you can
still write tickets, you can still use a fork, you can still open a beer
can, you can still pick your nose, you can still wipe your ass. So

you had a little pain, so what's your loss, where's the suffering? Your insurance is gonna cover it, and whatever time you're gonna lose you got sick days for that. So what's your loss? Don't make sense. You know what he says? 'I'm callin' this lawyer I know.' I says yeah, right. F. Lee, uh, what the fuck's his name, Bailer there I guess you're gonna call."

"Bailey."

"Huh? Bailer, Bailey, what the fuck, Booboo ain't gettin' a penny outta that hospital, I don't give a fuck Moses files his petition. You better talk to him, all he's gonna do is piss some judge off."

"What do you want me to talk to him for? You think any lawyer ain't gonna say the same things you just said?"

"C'mon, Rugs, there's some hungry fucks out there."

"Forget about it. What's wrong with you? Somethin' wrong with you? Every time you move you're wincin'. You get hurt today?"

"Ah it's nothin'. I fell at home this mornin'. Thought I got the steps, you know, with the salt. Missed a spot. I'll be alright, just need a couple aspirin in about an hour—course we had some fuckin' civilians in here doin' this job, I wouldn't have to be doublin' up now, would I? Meanwhile, I don't wanna say nothin', Actin' Chief, sir, but I doubled up yesterday, too, you know?"

"Hey, don't start, okay? I talked to Bellotti all mornin' about this, the whole time he was in here, between calls, that's all we talked about. Wait, you doubled up yesterday?"

"Yeah? So what? I wanna hear what Bellotti had to say."

"Whatta ya mean so what? You're doublin' up two days in a row, what the fuck, you crazy? How long you gonna keep this up?"

"Don't worry about it, okay? Just tell me what Mister Potato Head had to say, c'mon, I wanna hear this."

"Hey, don't do this again, you hear me? No more doublin'

up two days in a row. You do it again, the next two days are gonna be vacation, understand?"

"Hey, Rugs, get off my ass, you score more overtime than anybody in this fuckin' department and you been doin' it for as long as I can remember—"

"Hey! I'm a detective. When I'm workin' a major crime, I got no hours. Been that way since I made detective, gonna be that way as long as I am a detective, or until the next chief, whoever that is, tells me otherwise. But until we get a new chief, I'm gonna decide whether I'm workin' a major crime or not. Me. Okay? The actin' chief? 'Cause far as I can see, overtime's the only perk I get for this fucking job. We straight about this? Or you want me to remind you about policy on double shifts? No double shifts two days in a row unless council declares an emergency. Now if they declared that ice storm was an emergency nobody told me about it. Am I wrong?"

"No, uh-uh, you're not wrong. And you made your point, okay? So, you gonna tell me what he said or not?"

"What who said? Oh. Bellotti. Only thing I heard new was, uh, he's beefin' with the fire chief."

"Get outta here, I ain't buyin' that shit."

"I'm just tellin' you what he told me. Said Sitko hasn't talked to him in weeks—three months, he said. But one thing for sure I know now, Sitko's who doesn't want me for chief—"

"Oh right, you didn't know that before." Fischetti shook his head in mock disgust.

"Listen to you—course I knew it. All I'm sayin' is now I know why, that's all. Says I'm Balzic's pupil, or protégé or some shit like that. So don't be surprised you walk in here, you find somebody you don't know in Balzic's office. I got a feelin' it's not gonna be anybody we know."

"C'mon, Rugs, you serious? You done a hell of a job, you ask me. I mean, for doin' it like the rest of us? For doin' it and not gettin' paid for it? Shit, whatta they expect? I'm tellin' ya, we oughta sue the fuckers, if this ain't an unfair labor practice I don't know what one is. The way they been fuckin' us around? I mean it, man, I'm for gettin' the FOP shysters in here, I'm tellin' ya. I'm gettin' ready to circulate a petition, I'm not jokin'."

"Hey, Fish, go easy, man. I mean, do what you have to do, but you start puttin' names on paper, watch out. Especially for the ones who don't sign it."

"Would you sign it? I'm serious. Be straight with me now."

Carlucci shrugged and chewed his lips. "See, I'm gettin' so paranoid, my first reaction is, you know, why put it on paper? Why don't you just ask around? Get enough reactions to what you wanna do, then if it looks like you got some bodies behind you, okay, do it. But if it doesn't? You don't have anything on paper. I'm tellin' ya, man, I don't trust this fuckin' council—I mean, politicians are politicians, they're mostly all nuts, but this bunch, man, I wouldn't put anything past this bunch.

"Bellotti told me that fuckin' asshole Figulli, that asshole actually said—according to Bellotti now, remember—he said they oughta explore the possibility of havin' volunteer cops. Like volunteer firemen?"

"Get outta here, you're shittin' me."

"No. Honest to God, that's what Bellotti said. Said Figulli said it in executive session one night. Yeah. He couldn't understand why if we had a volunteer fire department, why we couldn't have volunteer police, save all kindsa money. Imagine that, if you can. I mean, unless Bellotti's a lot better actor than I think he is, he sounded really frustrated today. He sounded like Sitko was playin' with him, and he knew it, and he didn't know what the fuck to do about it. I almost felt sorry for him, no shit."

"So what'd you tell him?"

"Same thing I been tellin' him for months—all of 'em, every council meeting. Somebody gotta do somethin', we can't keep operatin' like this. I told him set up a meeting with the solicitor. Just the solicitor and council and invite Sitko, don't announce it, don't publicize it, make sure it's private, maybe the solicitor could get through that fuckin' concrete around their brains. I told him I didn't care who they picked for chief, I'd be perfectly happy doin' what I used to do before I got stuck with all this other shit—which I told him again they're not payin' me for."

"D'you talk to him about switchin' over to nine-one-one? And civilians on the mikes in here? Nowicki tell you he talked to Bill Rascoli? And Stramsky, and what they wanna do? He tell you—"

"Yeah, he told me. I'm tellin' ya, Fish, Bellotti's not the problem. I'm convinced the guy's in a bind. He gets elected, all those guys get elected, they're all firemen, so he thinks, hey, smooth sailin', you know, all for one, one for all, Musketeers shit, but it ain't workin' out that way. Man, I don't know what's gonna happen—hey, meanwhile, I got people to talk to, Jesus Christ, look what time it is, aw man, Christ, I forgot to give Missus Comito her salt. Hey, do me a favor. Get whoever's free in a mobile, okay? Swing by here and get that bag of salt outta my car and take it up my next-door neighbor, Missus Comito, okay?"

Fischetti said he'd take care of it and waved him away, and Carlucci hurried into Balzic's office and called the coroner. Dr. Wallace Grimes didn't have any surprises. The facts were almost self-evident. The cause and manner of Bobby Blasco's death were exactly what Carlucci had known almost from the moment Fischetti pointed out the body and Dulac found the baseball bat. What Carlucci didn't know was the mechanism, which was the coroner's turf: "Deceased's skull fractured in several places, including one eggshell break indicative of a severe blow with a round oblong instrument, a bat, a sledgehammer handle, something of that sort, causing extensive lacerations of the brain, causing hemorrhaging and eventual death within probably ten, fifteen minutes of the first fracture. Manner of death, clearly homicide. I'll get it to you on paper in a couple of days if I'm lucky. Five, if not. Any questions?"

Carlucci said no, thanked Grimes, and hung up. Then he called Trooper Dulac at Troop A Barracks. Dulac said he'd just finished working out and he'd call back after he showered and changed clothes. When he called back, Dulac started running down all the information he'd gathered over the course of the day, starting with his interview of several members of the organized crime unit familiar with the gambling in the back room of Bobby Blasco's Brushback Bar and Grille.

"This was apparently no big deal, a regular occurrence, uh, not any great shakes as to volume of money, but a steady thing. But not worth bustin', which apparently you people didn't think either, 'cause nobody I talked to mentioned anything about a bust by your guys—"

"Lemme tell you right now, Trooper, I got way better things to do than bust card games—"

"Take it easy, that's not what I'm sayin', I'm just statin' the facts, that's all. OCU didn't bust it either, that's all I'm sayin', the games there weren't worth anybody's time, that's all, don't get defensive, Sergeant, we're on the same team here."

"Okay, okay. Agreed. I just had a long talk with my boss, I'm a little touchy. So what else?"

"Well, the place was closed, out of, uh, deference isn't the word I want, neither is respect, uh, I guess the best thing I can say is, the place was closed 'cause his daughters told 'em to close it until they opened it up for the, uh, whiskey wake, is what they're callin' it. What I'm sayin' is, this Blasco, I mean, he was so universally disliked by everybody—Jesus, I have never in all my years as a cop heard mob guys talk about how they didn't want a piece of a guy's business because they couldn't stand the guy, but I swear to you, that's what I heard today. I heard—I know you're not gonna believe me, but it's true, so help me, I head a mob guy from New Kensington, a known snake, loan shark, doper, pimp—I think you've heard of him, Lenny Masciolo, right?"

"I've heard of him, yeah, but I don't know him, no."

"You're pretty near the bottom of the water with Lenny. Among other lowlights, he's been busted for dealin' horse-and-doggie porn, you know? And one time he was busted for, uh, he had this woman, she was in her seventies for crissake, he had her doin' a sex show with a German shepherd, that gives you some idea about Lenny, okay?"

"Oh yeah, now I place him, yeah, I remember that. That was a long time ago, right?"

"Oh at least fifteen years. Twenty maybe. Anyway, I thought, what the hell, I'll take a ride up and talk to those guys, see what's goin' on. So I went to Sonny C.'s place, you know? By the river?"

"No, I'm not familiar with those people. Never had any reason to be—not yet anyway."

"Well, Lorenzo Chianutto, you know, Sonny C.?"

"I know."

"Right. Well, he has this club, I used to stop there all the time when I was workin' the turnpike, it's right by the Harmarville exit. So anyway I go in there, there's Sonny and two guys I don't know, but also Lenny Masciolo, who's now gotta be, hell, at least seventy-five himself. I bought 'em all a drink, told 'em I have a problem, and when I say what the problem is, you know, that Robert Blasco was murdered, honest to God, Lenny Masciolo got up and started doin' the twist. Not only dancin' it, he was singin' it, if you can believe that. 'I'm gonna twist again, like I did last summer,' yeah. And the rest of those guys were sittin' there clappin', yeah, applaudin'. They're laughin' at Lenny and cheerin' him on and they were applaudin' 'cause Blasco was dead and somebody murdered him. And for twenty-five minutes they beat my ears with what a miserable sonofabitch Bobby Blasco was.

"Listen to this. You're not gonna believe this. Sonny C. looked me straight in the eye and said words to this effect—I can't imitate him, so I'm not gonna try, but it was hilarious, I'm serious. I couldn't keep a straight face. He bitched for ten minutes uninterrupted about all the guys he put in Blasco's bar 'to keep an eye on things'—you know, skim the gross and rake the games in the back—and he said, within weeks, they all came beggin' him to put 'em someplace else, they couldn't stand Blasco, they all wanted to kill him but they knew if they did they'd be in deep shit, 'cause it was Sonny's loan they were watchin'.

"So the last guy Sonny put in there, he said he didn't care how mad Sonny got, if Sonny didn't give him another job he was gonna put Blasco's head in the hot oil in the french fryer and then he was gonna burn the place down and then he was gonna shoot himself so Sonny would lose three ways. So Sonny said he was close to gettin' his vig back on the loan, and he just pulled out, just took a walk, said fuckit, it wasn't worth the kind of grief he was gettin'. You ever hear anything as wild as that?"

"No, can't say that I have," Carlucci said, making a mental note that Trooper Dulac was having too much fun retelling this story, either because he was too cozy with the bent-noses in New Kensington or because he wanted to be. Either way, this phone call was worth remembering.

"So you think, uh, what—these guys're clean?"

"If they aren't, they're the greatest actors I ever saw."

"So you're sayin' Blasco was square with those guys? On his loans?"

"Not square, no. But close enough that Sonny didn't want to bother with it anymore. And when was the last time you heard a shark give up on his vig?"

"Tell ya the truth, I never heard of it. Until now. So you're convinced they're not worth followin' up, right?"

"Right. Listen, my opinion? This is domestic."

"Uh-huh. So, uh, who else you talk to? Anybody works in his place?"

"Nobody there, I told you. I'll get to them tomorrow. After the funeral."

"Okay. Oh—just talked to the coroner. No surprises. I'll

get you a copy of his report soon as I get it, okay? Couple, five days. Anything else?"

"Not that I can think of. Where were you today? Called you three or four times around lunch, couldn't find you."

Carlucci briefly recapped how and where he'd spent the afternoon and got off the phone as quickly as possible. All of Dulac's "Sonny this" and "Sonny that" had put him on edge. When he'd first met Dulac, he got the impression that Dulac was solid, self-contained almost to the point of being bored by the routine of a homicide investigation. But over the phone, talking about talking to mob guys, he was suddenly no longer bored. Suddenly his words were riding on laughter, and what made Carlucci nervous was the laughter had no ironic edge to it.

He'd known about Balzic's association with Dom Muscotti for almost as long as he'd been a cop, but there was never any question whose side Balzic was on. Some things about Balzic and Muscotti had set bells off when Carlucci had first heard about them, but Balzic had always been able to explain what he'd done and why, to Carlucci's satisfaction if to no one else's. But over the last twenty years or so, Carlucci had known too many other cops, local, county, state, and federal, who had slipped, tripped, or backflipped over the line after they'd gotten close enough to smell dirty money. Even Dulac's manner of speaking had changed since last night. Last night he'd pronounced all his words clearly, even the *g*'s on the ends, but today he sounded like he was practicing for an audition in a bad gangster movie. And then there was what he'd said about stopping in Sonny C.'s "all the time" when he was working the turnpike.

Don't dwell on this, Carlucci, he thought, just file it. Call this Lazzaro, whoever the hell it is, get that out of the way so you can move on. He dialed Lazzaro's number and waited through four rings before he got the answering machine. He left his name and number, hung up, and started through his notebook to go over yet again what he'd seen and heard last night. Within a minute the phone rang.

"Sergeant Carlucci? Attorney John Lazzaro. Thank you for calling." His voice was trembling.

"You're welcome, Mister Lazzaro. What can I do for you?"

"You're investigating the homicide of Robert Blasco?"

"Yes."

"My client, uh, he wishes to surrender and to, uh, to confess."

"Beg pardon?"

"My client wishes to surrender—do we have a bad connection? I can call you back. I mean I can hear you fine, are you not hearing me?"

"No no, I heard ya. I just, you know, it sorta took me back, that's all, what you said. Your client is, uh, who now?"

"In due time, sir," Lazzaro said, stuttering and stammering. "Certain conditions have to be met. That's why I'm calling. And before I go any further, I want to alert you that I'm recording this conversation and I suggest you do the same. I urge you to do the same—you do have that capability, don't you?"

Carlucci said he did and got a fresh tape, identified it with permanent ink, slipped it into his recorder, and connected it to the phone. "I'm ready. Go."

"Well, number one, my client is an elderly man and in very poor health. Very poor. I want it understood that every consideration will be given to him."

Elderly man in poor health? An elderly man in poor health works over Bobby Blasco with a baseball bat? "Such as what considerations?"

"Well first and foremost that he won't be taken from where he is and put in some cold, damp cell with a steel bed until I can arrange bail, that's my primary concern."

"Wait, Mister Lazzaro, you have things a little out of sequence here. I can't make any commitments like that. That's for the DJ when I file the information, that's up to him, what he'll agree to, what he won't, I can't make—"

"Yes, of course, Sergeant, I understand. I just want your assurance that you or nobody else investigating this case is going to come on, you know, like some hard-charging jerk, that's all, and put this very frail, very ill, elderly man in handcuffs and haul him off to jail."

"If the man's how you say he is, you know, I'm not a prick, but, uh, Mister Lazzaro, the county jail doesn't have any cold, damp cells. That place is barely a year old, and their central heating works, believe me. Sounds like he's in bed—"

"Well in fact he's in Conemaugh General Hospital, and no matter how new the jail is, it's still not a hospital and my client is having serious heart problems. *Serious* heart problems. *Very* serious."

"Uh-huh. Okay. Listen, if he's in a bad way, you know, maybe the DJ'll come to him. It's been done before. They're not thrilled about it, but hey, that's life. So what else?"

"Well, okay, but do I have your assurance—your personal assurance, aside from how the district justice is going to rule—I want to know that you're not going to behave like some John Wayne character just because of the celebrity of the victim—"

"You don't have to worry about that," Carlucci said.

"You didn't let me finish. Just because of the celebrity of the victim, do I have your assurance you're not going to do something, let's say, utterly irrational if, as is almost certain, my client is unable to furnish property or bond to meet the terms of the bail, that's what I'm asking you, Sergeant."

Utterly irrational? "I thought I already answered that. What do you want me to say? I mean, I'm not gonna go pullin' an old man out of a hospital bed if his doctor tells me he can't be moved, or shouldn't be moved, I mean, that's not gonna happen."

"Well fine. Good. That's what I wanted to hear. And I will take you at your word."

"Okay, so what else? Anything else?"

"The man has relatives who were involved. He doesn't want them prosecuted—"

"Oh whoa, wait a minute. Wait wait wait. They in the hospital too?"

"No."

Carlucci shook his head and threw up his free hand. "I don't know where this is goin', Mister Lazzaro, but I'm not makin' any commitments about, uh, coconspirators, that's out. And furthermore—"

"No commitment about the relatives, no confession—"

"And furthermore, what're you, new at this? This stuff you're askin', there's no cop in the world can make you promises like this. You need to be talkin' to somebody in the DA's office, not me, c'mon. What're you sayin'—these relatives, they're not willing to surrender and confess? Huh? But I'm supposed to look the other way forever just 'cause why? 'Cause of the batter, huh? This old guy, he wantsa play this part of the game by himself, otherwise he takes his bat and goes home? Hey, Mr. Lazzaro, you already told me where the man is. How hard you think it's gonna be to eliminate the rest of the patients up there?"

There was a long silence. Then Lazzaro said, "I'll get back to you."

"When? I'm not gonna wait very long. Gimme a time, you know?"

"Soon. I will get back to you very soon. Just give me a few minutes here, thank you very much, I appreciate your cooperation."

"I will give you five minutes, that's all, understand?"

"Understood. Yes. Five minutes. Yes."

"Good," Carlucci said, depressing the button, then calling Fischetti. "Hey, Fish, call Mutual Aid Ambulance, ask 'em for the names of all adult males transported to Conemaugh General between, say, midnight, or no, make it twenty-three hundred yesterday and, uh, let's say up until within the last hour today, okay? Got that?"

"All of 'em?"

"Yeah all of 'em—no no, not accidents, not traffic, nothin' ice related. Everything else, heart attacks, strokes, that kinda stuff. Shouldn't be too many. And see if you can find Dulac. When I talked to him coupla minutes ago he was still up Troop A Barracks. Tell him get here soon as he can."

"Anything else?"

"Yeah. Find the duty assistant DA, get him down here. Tell him I got some rookie shyster wants to negotiate an arrest with me."

"With you?"

"Yeah. Don't ask. I don't know where they come from. I'd do this stuff myself Fish, except this guy's supposed to be callin' me back in a coupla minutes, okay? So this Lazzaro calls, put him through, okay? Oh, wait a second. Anybody call from the county crime lab?"

"I would've told you, Rugs. No."

"Okay. If you get time, you know, pull their chain, okay? Ask 'em if they got anything about Blasco I could use right now."

"Hey, Rugs, what, you can't make some of these calls yourself? Jesus."

"Hey, Fish, soon as this jaboney calls me, we'll see where we are, okay? If you stopped talkin' to me and started dialin', we'd both be a little bit further ahead, you know?"

Fischetti grumbled something unintelligible and hung up. Carlucci sat and waited, wondering who this Lazzaro was, but not able to tie up the line with calls to find out since he was who had set the time limit on Lazzaro.

Carlucci brought his notes up to date. Then he removed the tape from his recorder, ID'd it further in anticipation of Lazzaro's next call, and replaced it in his recorder. Then he sat and waited, breathing slowly and evenly, thinking that if this former whodunit was cleared with a confession he might be able to pay attention to someone else he found himself thinking about every time his mind was not otherwise occupied. He could still see her face framed in the door, that shiny black hair, that olive skin, those brown eyes. . . .

Three minutes later, Fischetti called back and said there was only one adult male transported by Mutual Aid Ambulance between twenty-three hundred yesterday and zero three hundred today. "Name's Philip E. Randa, uh, male, Caucasian, seventy-four, two eight one Horace Road, Westfield Township. Transported zero four hundred ten hours, chest pain, dizziness, sweating."

"That's my man, Fish, way to go," Carlucci said, writing fast. "Now, if you could call the courthouse, find out the maiden names of Bobby Blasco's two wives, I would really really appreciate that."

"Hey, Rugs, what the fuck, gimme a break, huh? I only got one phone line here, you know?"

"At ease, Fish, I was just playin' with ya, that's all."

"Fuck you were. Sell that bullshit to somebody else."

"Man oh man, you ever talk to Balzic like that?"

"Hey, Balzic was the chief. You're the actin' chief. Big difference. You want me to make these calls, lemme go do it, okay?"

Carlucci hung up, sighed, rolled his neck five times from shoulder to chest to shoulder and stared at the phone. A minute and a half later, Fischetti put Attorney Lazzaro's call through.

"Yessir, Mister Lazzaro, what can we do for each other?"

"Well, Sergeant, after discussing this with my client, I don't think we can do anything for each other. It's been decided that we should take your advice and speak directly to the district attorney—"

"Uh, no sir, that was not advice I was giving you, that was strictly information, that's all. And, uh, I'm gonna give you some more information. We're also lookin' for the duty DA, and we haven't found him yet, so, uh, if your client, uh, Mister Randa is it? If he wants to talk to me, tell him I can be up there in less than ten minutes from the time I hang up, he has anything he wants to get off his conscience."

There was a long moment of silence. "How do you know, uh, how did you, uh—where did you get that name?"

Carlucci couldn't resist. "Ah, Mister Lazzaro, I shoulda told ya, I trained at the North Pole. Believe me, you wanna find out who's naughty or nice, that's the place to train. There's a fat guy up there knows everything."

"Oh. Very funny."

"C'mon, Mister Lazzaro, you don't want people to know where your client is, don't tell 'em. That wasn't Santa Claus told me what hospital he was in, that was you."

"Good-bye, Sergeant—"

"Hold it, don't hang up!"

"Why not?"

"Why not? Look, Mister Lazzaro, until you called a little while ago I had sort of a whodunit. I mean I would've got Mister Randa eventually, but it would've taken a whole lot more work and time and sweat, instead of which, thanks to you, what I have now is a cherry in my hands, it's that simple. And when somebody drops a cherry in my hands, man, I scarf it up, I don't ask questions. I eat it before anybody knows it's there, that's the best way I know to make sure it doesn't spoil, understand?"

"No. No, I'm not sure I do. If there's a message in there somewhere for me, I'm not getting it."

"Well there sure is a message. You owe it to your client to tell him to get himself a lawyer who's got some experience in criminal court 'cause the one he's got is gonna get him and his relatives locked up for a long time, guaranteed. What's wrong with you, man? Your first duty to your client—I can't believe you, man—I mean, for crissake it oughta be tattooed backwards on your forehead so you see it every time you brush your teeth, you know? Tell your client to shut up!"

"Oh for God's sake this isn't my idea! The man's dying, he's Catholic, he wants to confess, I—"

"Hey, the man wants to confess, Jesus, call a priest, what the fuck's wrong with you?"

"What? What's going on here? Call a priest?! I'm, uh, I'm apparently either very ignorant or very confused, I don't think I could say at this point which I am, I mean, for God's sake, the man said explicitly he wanted to clear his conscience—"

"Yo, Lazzaro! Anybody home there? You're not the man's priest, you're not his psychiatrist, you're the man's lawyer. Your duty is to defend the man, it ain't to help him feel better about himself, where the fuck did you go to law school?"

Lazzaro cleared his throat several times. "I'm not sure I like this at all—and I certainly don't understand what's going on. I, uh, I . . . a few moments ago you were laughing at me, making jokes about me telling you where my client was—is—and now you're lecturing me about my legal duty? Is that what you're doing? You lecturing me?"

"Goddamn right I am. Listen. A man, huh? Some sonofabitch is beatin' his daughter, stealin' her money, abusin' the shit out of her, terrorizin' her, he can't take it anymore—and who can blame him? The man thought 'cause she divorced this creep, all that crap was history, but it turns out it ain't, the sonofabitch just keeps it up. And the old guy cracks. Perfectly natural. Can't do it himself—which wife was it by the way? First Mrs. Blasco, or the second?"

"The second."

"Oh. Yeah, uh-huh. I met her. Gutsy lady. Virginia. Virginia June. Yeah, woman works hard, busts her buns workin' all those hours, tryin' to make a decent life, nurse, helpin' other people, that prick comes around, steals her mortgage payments, steals her checkbook, beats her up, she calls the state cops, whatta they do, huh? Nothin'. Old man snaps out, has to do somethin', he can't do it alone. So he gets some *paisans*. Or relatives. Who'd he get? Brothers, sons, who?"

"Sons."

"Sons, huh? Sure. If I had sons, been in his place, that's what I woulda done. Bet your ass. Put up with that crap all those years, watched his daughter put up with that crap. I woulda done the same thing, Mister Lazzaro. Believe it. Me? I woulda had two guys hold the sonofabitch while I slipped a garbage bag over his head, watched the bastard flop around like a fish, woulda enjoyed every second of it too, believe me. And then what happens, huh? When it's over, he knows he shouldn'ta done it, his conscience starts gettin' him, so what's he do? He gets the family lawyer— that's who you are, right? You searched the titles on their houses probably, right?"

"No. No. I didn't do any title searches. Just his will, that's all I did. Well, I helped her with the Protection From Abuse order a little bit, just advised her, that's all. That's all I did."

"Sure, right. And you did your best. But, Mister Lazzaro, this is intentional killing here. This is first-degree murder here. This is a death penalty crime. On top of which this is conspiracy to commit murder, which is another felony—and this is the important part—your client solicited other persons to act with him, which makes them coconspirators in first-degree murder, Mr. Lazzaro, no matter whose fingerprints we find on the bat. You tell me, you think anybody in the DA's office is gonna make a deal with your client about his sons, huh? No matter how much you or me might think they're justified—how many are there—two, three?"

"Three."

"Tell me the truth, Mister Lazzaro, you think anybody in the DA's office is gonna let three guys walk—just to get one dying man's confession, you really believe that? How ya think that's gonna look on his résumé, you know, when he starts runnin' for higher office, you know what I mean? He gave up three to get one—who's not gonna do any time if he's as sick as you say he is—you did say he's in bad shape, right?"

"Yes, very bad shape. His heart. Doctors here aren't sure they can do anything for him. They're still debating, last I heard."

"Well, see, that really makes it tough for the DA. I mean, if you believe he's gonna let the three sons walk just to get the old man's confession, I mean, whatta you think his opponent would do with that kinda information next time the guy runs for office, huh? I know the man, believe me, he wants to be a judge, and he's one shrewd monkey. All the more reason, sir, you should do the right thing and advise your client he really needs to get a lawyer with some criminal experience—no shame in that. I mean you owe him that much, Mister Lazzaro, especially since it was you dropped the cherry in my hands, you know? Don't you think that's the right thing to do? What are his sons gonna think when they find out what you did for their father? When they're lookin' at the same charges?"

"I wasn't thinking about them—not at that time!"

"'Course you weren't."

"Listen, Sergeant, I was thinking about him, and that's what he said he wants to do, and he's insisting on it, he doesn't want to hear anything else from me—he wants to confess, period. He wants to go with a clear conscience, I mean, what's so hard to understand—"

"There's nothin' hard to understand, Mister Lazzaro, but you're still not gettin' my point. He wants to confess, get him a priest. Let him confess to God, not to me. Listen, how hard did you try to talk him out of it, sir? I mean, really? How hard did you try to tell him that confessin' to me was not in his best interest—d'you really try? Did you really explain all his options? For example, did you explain the difference between confessing to first-degree murder and havin' the DA try to prove voluntary manslaughter, you know?"

"I don't know what you're talking about."

"I know you don't. Which is exactly my point, John—all right if I call you John?"

"Yes. Of course."

"Well, John, hey, clearly you don't know about clause b, unreasonable belief killing justifiable, see? All the more reason why you should not be the man's attorney in this."

"Unreasonable belief what? Killing justifiable—is that what you said?"

"That's what I said, John. Been so long since you passed the bar exam, you don't remember anything about clause b, do ya? Lemme tell ya, John, very important distinction here, which, if you don't mind my sayin' so, really, I think it applies. Here, lemme read it to you. It'll only take a second, let me get my copy of the Crimes Code here. Here, right here, John, listen. Section 2503, clause b—you listenin'?"

"Oh God, yes of course I'm listening."

"Right, good. Here. Quote, 'A person who intentionally or knowingly kills an individual commits voluntary manslaughter if at the time of the killing he believes the circumstances to be such that, if they existed, would justify the killing under Chapter 5 of this title,' parenthesis, 'relating to general principles of justification,' end parenthesis, 'but his belief is unreasonable.' John, you got that? And remember now, voluntary manslaughter is a second-degree felony, you know? Big difference between that and murder first degree, right?"

"Of course."

"So whatta ya think, John? Can you argue principles of justification and unreasonable belief, huh? In your client's behalf? Especially when he got three accomplices? And the DA's gonna be arguin' lethal injection for somebody? I mean he's gonna want somebody on death row for this, John, c'mon, man, think it through. How's it gonna look, huh? You're the DA, what kinda scalp would you wanna hang on your next job application—a dyin' man's confession? Or somebody on death row for killin' the local hero, whatta ya think'd look better in the papers, huh? TV? Next election campaign? Nothin' personal here, John, really, but I think you're outta your league. 'Cause if it was my father, I'd want a lawyer who didn't have to have some police sergeant explainin' the law to him, you know? And, John, I gotta be honest with you. That's what I'm gonna say to his sons when I arrest 'em. I'm gonna explain to 'em about clause b, voluntary manslaughter. This may be hard for you to understand, John, but, uh, I really wanna see 'em get good representation."

After a long moment, Lazzaro said, "This is the strangest conversation I think I've ever had."

"Aw don't worry about it, John. Believe me, I've had stranger ones. Listen, go look out for your client. Nice talkin' to you."

"Yes. Same here—I think."

Carlucci hung up, then rushed out to talk to Fischetti, who was just depressing the button on the phone. He took his head-set off, scratched his scalp hard, and put it back on. He screwed up his face and shook his head at Carlucci.

"That was the duty DA," Fischetti said, still shaking his head. "I don't know where they found that one. Sounds like a lit-tle kid, I'm not jokin'. Like a little boy."

"Yeah, well right now I don't care what he sounds like, all I wanna know is where the fuck is he."

Fischetti pointed over his shoulder with his thumb at the window facing the south parking lot. "Right out there."

"What?"

"Yeah. I guess the DA hires you now, one of the perks is, uh, you know, you get a cell phone, and he's so excited he's callin' his mommy and all his little playmates. So when he finally gets around to answerin' me, he's drivin' right down Main Street here apparently, right in front of the building, you know, and so he turns into the parkin' lot, and he sits there the whole time I'm talkin' to him. Yeah. He sits out there in the parkin' lot talkin' to me on the goddamn cell phone instead of comin' in here and talkin' face-to-face—look at him, he's talkin' to somebody else now. Look, I'm not shittin' ya—oh now he's hangin' up. Finally, he's gonna come inside now. Jesus, look at him—he looks like he's fuckin' fourteen for crissake. Guaranteed, this kid don't own a razor, he don't shave yet."

"Hey, everybody gotta start somewhere, Fish," Carlucci said under his breath. To the very young man who came through the door, "Yo, sir? You the duty DA?"

"Yep. That's who I am. Yes!" the duty DA chirped, smiling brightly.

Carlucci waved the duty DA through the counter door and held out his hand. "Sergeant Carlucci, actin' chief, Rocksburg PD. That's Patrolman Fischetti behind the mike, actin' watch commander, actin' sergeant, actin' dispatcher."

"Wow. Lotta acting going on here," the duty DA said, giggling at his joke.

"And, uh, you're, uh?"

"The deputy district attorney of Conemaugh County—well, one of them. There are seven others. But right now, I'm the only one. As of now, today, I'm the duty DA."

"Hey, that even rhymes," Fischetti said, nodding appreciatively at Carlucci. "I definitely think we got the answer to gangsta rap here."

Carlucci made a face at Fischetti to knock it off, this was going to be tough enough without the comedy. "Uh, yeah, but what I mean is, what's your name?"

"Oh. I'm Lloyd. Uh, Merwin. Well, S. Lloyd Merwin actually. Esquire." He gave Carlucci his most character-revealing handshake, firm, but not too firm, full of conviction but not intended to dominate. He'd been working on his handshake, that much was clear. After he withdrew his hand, he produced a flat leather case from his inside coat pocket, took out two business cards, and gave one to Carlucci and the other to Fischetti.

Carlucci shot a glance at Fischetti, whose brows were up and jaw was down.

"So, uh, how long you been with the DA's office now, uh, Mister Merwin?"

"Oh. Last Monday was my first day."

Carlucci cleared his throat and swallowed and fought to keep his eyelids from drooping. "Uh-huh. Okay. So, uh, lemme tell you what's goin' on here today, okay?"

"Sure. Fine. Uh, do I need to take notes or, uh, something?"

"Well see, I don't think it's gonna be that complicated, but, if you think you need to, hey, that's up to you."

"Well, I should wait, probably. See what you say, first, and then, you know, I'll decide."

"Okay. Sure. Well what I'm gonna do now, now that you're here I mean, uh, based on my belief that I have probable cause, I'm gonna make what's called a warrantless arrest—"

"Oh. Warrantless arrest, sure, I'm familiar with those, yes, I can handle those."

"Uh-ha," Carlucci said, clearing his throat. He could hear Fischetti's chair squeaking from Fischetti shaking with silent laughter. "Well, the man I'm gonna arrest is in the hospital, okay? And my information is, uh, he conspired with at least three other persons to commit a murder. They may not have thought, when they started out, it was gonna be a murder—I don't know that yet—but a murder is what resulted from what they did, I mean, the coroner's already ruled on that—not in writing but to me on the phone. So what I'd like you to do, I mean because the suspect is supposedly in bad shape physically, I want you to go along with me in case the man makes a statement, alright? I mean a state trooper was supposed to be on his way here, and it's his case but I don't know where he is—"

"It's his case? The state trooper's?"

"Yes. Homicide cases are always theirs officially, theirs

meaning the state police, uh, in third-class cities, which this is, Rocksburg here—you with me?"

"Yes. So far, anyway."

"Okay. They're theirs unless they can't handle it or don't wanna handle it, but I wanna get the wheels turnin' as soon as I can, so, uh, since he's not here, the investigating state trooper, uh, I need somebody to accompany me, you know, to observe that I've Mirandized the suspect, that I'm recording the interrogation, that I'm not badgering him or bullying him, you know, like that. Nobody better to do that from my point of view than somebody from the DA's office, you with me?"

"Oh yes. I'm with you. Sure."

"Okay. Then one other thing. Now this part gets a little tricky, so, uh, I want you to stay with me on this, okay?"

"Well, I think I've stayed with you so far." Merwin turned from Carlucci to Fischetti and back, smiling and nodding several times.

"Uh-huh. See, the thing is, most of the information I got about this suspect, I got, uh, well I got it from his attorney."

"You got it from his attorney?" Even S. Lloyd Merwin, Esquire, a deputy district attorney for less than a week, recognized something amiss here.

"Yeah. See, I sorta chiseled it out of him. Uh, it's not that I actually deceived him, understand. It's just I sorta played on his ignorance, uh, his inexperience. See, he called me and he tried to tell me the man he was representing wanted to confess, but I told him—the attorney—I said, man, you should tell your client he should get another attorney—"

"You told him what now?"

"I told him tell his client to get another attorney. 'Cause it was obvious to me that the attorney he had—the guy I'm gettin' the information from—I mean, 'cause, face it, that klutz kept goin' the way he was goin' he was gonna get the whole family on death row, understand?"

S. Lloyd Merwin, Esquire, shook his head, pursed his lips, and twisted his mouth from side to side. "Umm, I don't think so, no, I don't understand. Could you explain, I mean, if the man you want to arrest, he's the one in the hospital, right?"

"Yes."

"And you learned this from his attorney?"

"Yes."

"Well what I mean is, why was *his* attorney telling *you* this, I don't understand that—at all. Not at all."

"Well, see, that's why I told him he should tell his client get another attorney. I mean, this attorney should *not* have been tellin' me any of that, you know? Which is why I told him what I told him. Go back to his client and tell him to shut up, you know? Listen, Mister Merwin, let's get in the car, we'll go the hospital, on the way, I'll explain it to you, how's that?"

"Well, see, I hope you do, because . . . it's not that I'm confused or anything, it's just, uh, I don't understand."

"No shit," Fischetti said under his breath but loud enough for Carlucci to hear.

Carlucci put his hand on Merwin's back and gently steered him through the counter door toward the door to the parking lot. "Nice coat, Mister Merwin. Man, camel-hair topcoats, I always thought they were pretty cool."

"Oh, this?" Merwin lifted his arm and looked at his sleeve as though he'd never noticed it before. "This was a Christmas present from my mother to replace one that was stolen at my bar exam party. When I passed? Mother said it had to be one of the waiters, but I told her since the insurance covered it, it would do way more harm than good to sue the club. Club doesn't background waiters, for God's sake."

"Oh I don't think anybody does that, no. Patrolman Fischetti, you ever hear of anybody backgroundin' a waiter?" Carlucci said, rolling his eyes at Fischetti, whose brows were starting to come down but whose mouth was still open as he leaned forward to watch them leave the building.

In Conemaugh General Hospital, Carlucci and Assistant DA Merwin found many people milling about in the hall outside the cardiac intensive-care unit, most of them bleary-eyed, all somber, in various states of dress. The woman Carlucci guessed was Mrs. Randa was wearing a wool coat over a flannel robe and was blowing her nose into a faded red and white dish towel. A man half her age wearing a red plaid mackinaw over his red flannel pajamas whispered into her right ear, while on her left a man in the full uniform of a private detective agency rubbed her back and stared at the floor.

Carlucci glanced around until he saw the only three-piece business suit and approached the wearer, S. Lloyd Merwin in tow.

"John Lazzaro?" Carlucci said softly, leaning close.

"Yes? Sergeant Carlucci? Let's go find us a little privacy somewhere, okay?"

Lazzaro shook Carlucci's hand and nodded for him to come along down the hall away from the ICU. "There's an empty room down here I've been using, nobody's objected so far. Really surprising how many empty rooms there are up here, though I don't know why I should be surprised about that, given the way the insurance companies are behaving these days."

They went in, closed the door, and stood around the end of an empty bed, one of two in the room. It was a general purpose room, not connected to the cardic ICU. Carlucci introduced Assistant District Attorney Merwin. The attorneys shook hands and talked over each other nervously until they both grew quiet.

"So how's he doin'?" Carlucci said.

"Not good. Slipping in and out of consciousness, losing it more often than not, or that's the consensus. I've only been allowed in to see him a total of fifteen minutes since I got here, which was a little over three hours ago. And, uh, the eldest son is talking right now with the cardiologist and a surgeon about whether to fly him to Pittsburgh because apparently they don't have either the staff or the facilities here to do what needs to be done surgically—assuming something can be done, but I'm assuming a lot of things, so don't hold me to any of this. When I first got here, for instance, they were saying nothing could be done, but that was before the surgeon got here and now the debate is about what can be done. But then I heard one of the other sons saying he didn't think Medicare would pay for the helicopter, and for a while there that seemed to be the issue, so, uh, to be perfectly honest, at this point, I really can't tell you what's going on. I think there's a lot of confusion between the mother and the sons over the kind of insurance they have—the parents I mean, whether they've been keeping up their supplemental or not and apparently nobody knows and they're arguing about whether, you know, she can handle what Medicare won't cover—as if they don't have enough other problems.

"I don't mean this in any way disrespectfully," Lazzaro went on, "but the mother's none too bright and neither are two of the sons. The only one who seems to know what's going, the oldest one, Frankie, he apparently doesn't get along with the other brothers, and not too well with his mother either. As near as I can get it figured out, he was against the, uh, the, uh, you know what I'm talking about, Sergeant. Don't you?"

"I can guess. So he's the one talkin' to the doctors right now, is that it? What's his name again?"

"Frankie. Francis. He's the oldest and he, uh, he sells office furniture in Pittsburgh someplace. Seems a fairly intelligent, fairly reasonable person, but the youngest one, George, the one in the security uniform? Uh, he also drives a school bus. Used to be a machinist, uh, apparently very skilled mechanically, but, uh, ever since he was laid off from Westinghouse, he's become, uh—this is according to Frankie now—a very angry, very rigid man. I don't know him well enough to say whether it's because of that or he's just so angry at his older brother for some reason, he just, uh, he just is not open to a whole lot, if you know what I mean. The middle one now, Ronald, they call him Rennie for some reason, well, he's just very obviously retarded, I mean you can tell to look at him there's not a whole lot going on behind those eyes. But he is intensely loyal to his family, especially his father, so I'd be very careful what I said to him, I'm not trying to tell you how to do your job, I'm just letting you know.

"Again, I'm not speaking disrespectfully, but I'm just letting you know what I've been trying to deal with up here, and what you yourselves are going to have to deal with. I mean, I don't care which attorney they get. I, uh, in all honesty, Sergeant, you know, since I've had some time to reflect on what you said, I think maybe you're right. I *am* out of my league here. 'Cause it's true— I have never been involved, not in my whole career, in a criminal defense above a summary level. So, uh, I really do think I should step aside—but regardless, whoever steps in here is going to have certain problems with this family, and I thought I should alert you to those, I thought that was the least I could do."

"Well I appreciate that, Mister Lazzaro. John, I really do," Carlucci said.

"So, what now—aren't we going to get a confession?" Merwin said, his eyes alternately almost closing and then going wide.

"You all right?" Carlucci said. "Somethin' wrong with your eyes?"

"Oh it's just my contacts. I should just take them out and put my glasses on, but my mother insists I don't look good in glasses, but I really hate these contacts, they just irritate me sooner or later. So are you going to arrest somebody or not?"

"Well, see, that's what I'm wonderin'. I mean these people aren't goin' anywhere. The kids'll stay with him, don't matter whether it's here, Pittsburgh, wherever, long as he's alive. When he dies—if he dies, they'll stay with him till he's in the ground.

Those two younger ones, Christ, they're practically glued to the mother, they're not goin' anywhere."

"So what's your point, Sergeant?" Merwin asked, suddenly annoyed.

"What's my point? My point is what I just said—these people aren't goin' anywhere, so I'm thinkin', you know, what's the point of hasslin' somebody when they're already in the middle of a hassle. I mean just to make an arrest? I arrest 'em today, I arrest 'em next week, what's the difference? There is no difference."

"Well," Merwin said, tossing his head from side to side impatiently, "coming up here you were acting like it was a really primo deal. Rush rush. FedEx. So if you're not going to arrest anybody, what are we doing here, let's go! I don't want to stand around here any longer than I have to, I hate hospitals. Smells terrible in here, I'm going to be sick, I stay here much longer. Ouuu." Merwin shivered his disgust.

Carlucci shrugged at Lazzaro and said to him, "C'mon, let's see if we can talk to the old man. Maybe they'll let us in, see if he has anything he wants to say."

"Meanwhile, what am I supposed to do?" Merwin said. "Stand here, or what? Am I supposed to come or not?"

Carlucci leaned close to Merwin and whispered, "What's with you? All of a sudden you're gettin' real testy here—"

"I told you, I can't stand hospitals! I hate the way they smell! If all I'm going to do is stand around I'm going to be sick, so let's get out of here, okay?"

"No, I wanna see if I can talk to the man here, okay? You're gonna be sick, you better go find a john someplace, so if you do get sick, nobody else'll have to mop it up, you know? Have a little consideration—"

"Oh consideration, isn't that cool, Jesus." Merwin rushed out of the room, muttering "Asshole," and hurried importantly up to the first nurse he saw.

Been on the job a week, Carlucci thought, he meets me less

than a half hour ago, already he's callin' me asshole. And he thinks either I'm deaf or nothin's gonna happen. Right.

Lazzaro, for his part, tried to act as though he hadn't heard what Merwin had said. He quickly set off back to the ICU, where he pointed out the nursing supervisor. They approached her, and Carlucci identified himself and asked if they could have a few minutes alone with Mr. Randa.

The nurse shook her head. "Five minutes, every hour on the hour, no more than two members of the immediate family, those are the rules, they're posted all over the place, you can read them as well as I can say them. If the attending physician says otherwise, fine. You want to get around the rules, find him, otherwise get in line with the family, okay?"

"Look, I know the rules, but this man's a suspect in a homicide, and this is his attorney, and his attorney has told me the man wants to confess—"

"I don't care what anybody's told you—"

Over both their voices, blaring repeatedly, an alarm started sounding every half second, and over that came a nurse's unhurried voice, "Three-oh-two-A is arresting! Three-oh-two-A is arresting! Three-oh-two-A—"

"My God," Lazzaro said. "That's him."

"Excuse me!" the nursing supervisor said, grabbing a table with a piece of equipment on it, backing out between Carlucci and Lazzaro, bumping them aside with her hips while other nurses and at least two doctors came bounding into the unit from several directions. Within moments seven persons had converged on the bed nearest the door of 302-A. Arms and hands were hooking up IVs, ripping open blister packs and sending them flying. Shiny debris fluttered to the floor behind them as they surrounded Philip Randa, blocking him from view, their backs rising and falling in what seemed a chaotic dance to the unmistakable music of an ECG monitor's flat line.

What surprised Carlucci was not how quickly they had arrived but how quietly they worked. He was standing no more than twenty feet from them but he never heard a voice louder than a normal tone.

Fifteen minutes later, however, when they started coming out, their voices couldn't be heard at all over the wailing that had begun to Carlucci's right, where Philip Randa's wife and daughter and three sons and one daughter-in-law and six grandchildren were embracing each other, one by one and two by two. Carlucci tried to distract himself from that by concentrating for a moment on the faces coming out of the room, to see if he could tell how they were taking it. Some of them were taking it very hard indeed, especially a young nurse whose eyes were filling as she carried a clipboard to the nurses' station. But then the voices from the family crowded back into his consciousness, compelling him to turn away as the grief, the anger, the loss, the mourning began in earnest.

And then somebody was touching him on the shoulder. He turned and nearly bumped foreheads with John Lazzaro, who was crying very hard and trying even harder to suppress it, pushing his hands into his face and eyes. But he couldn't suppress it. Carlucci turned slightly and put his arm around Lazzaro, a short, roundish man with coarse black hair streaked with gray. As he leaned his head forward, nearly touching Carlucci's shoulder, Lazzaro's bald spot on the top of his head revealed itself. Carlucci didn't know why he did it, but he put his right hand over the bald spot. "It's okay," he said.

"No it isn't," Lazzaro said between sobs. "He never got to confess . . . it's my fault . . . couldn't make up my mind . . . what to do."

"Aw sure he did. He confessed to you. If somebody else was supposed to hear that and didn't, then, hey, too bad for them. But he confessed. No question. No judge I know would say he didn't. It was heard, believe me."

"You don't understand, I'm . . . I take my religion very seriously, I strongly considered a religious life . . . I had a chance to participate in a holy sacrament . . . I dropped the ball . . . it was handed to me and I dropped it."

"Listen, Mister Lazzaro, when he left, I'm tellin' ya, he was straight, don't give it another thought. You wanna do somethin' for him, huh? Get the kids another lawyer, I mean it, 'cause soon as the funeral's over, I'm gonna bust 'em, all three of 'em."

Then Carlucci took his arm and hand away and said, "C'mon. Soon as I offer my condolence to the missus there, I'll buy ya a beer, whatta ya say? You could use one I think."

"Don't like beer. Especially in cold weather."

"Well somethin', you know? Little wine maybe. My old boss got me drinkin' wine about a year ago. I'm really startin' to like it. Never used to. C'mon, let's pay our respects and get outta here, let these people alone."

They had to wait until the sons calmed down enough to let them approach their mother, but they finally got to say what needed to be said, and then they went their separate ways in the parking lot promising to meet at Muscotti's.

Waiting beside Carlucci's Chevy, pacing and fuming, smoking furiously, was Assistant District Attorney S. Lloyd Merwin, Esquire.

"What're you doin' here?" Carlucci said, opening the driver-side door.

"What do you mean what am I doing here—waiting for you, what's it look like? You brought me up here, remember?"

"Yeah? So?"

"What do you mean, yeah so? My car's back at your station."

"Oh. So it is," Carlucci said, getting in and turning the ignition key.

Merwin skipped and slid around the car and rapped on the window with his bare knuckles. There was a wide smear of dirt across the front of his camel's-hair topcoat where he'd brushed against the bumper.

Carlucci rolled the window down a couple of inches. " Now what?"

"What do you mean, now what?! I don't believe you! My car's at your place, you bring me up here, you make me stand around smelling that place until I get sick, then you just walk off and leave me?! And now you won't take me back?!"

"How do you expect me to know what you're talkin' about, I'm an asshole, remember?"

"What is this, this some kind of initiation? Huh? This supposed to be some kind of hazing on the new guy or something? My mother said I'd have to watch out for you, uh, for you, uh . . ."

"For you what? What you?"

"Never mind. Listen you, you brought me up here, you take me back! I insist you take me back to my car! I don't have any overshoes, my gloves and my scarf are back in my car, I'm cold, I'm supposed to be back in the office, my phone's in the car, I can't even call anybody!"

"Oh man, this is too complicated for an asshole like me to figure out, my head's startin' to ache, I gotta go." Carlucci glanced around to make sure no one was coming, then backed out of the slot, and drove slowly toward the exit ramp.

"You're leaving me here? You're really leaving me here?!" Merwin shouted, running after the Chevy for about ten steps before giving up.

Carlucci decided that anybody who gave up that quickly wasn't going to get the message unless it was explained in very clear terms. Even then, there was no guarantee. So Carlucci stopped, backed up, and unlocked the passenger door as Merwin started running toward the Chevy and then slowed to a walk and finally a saunter, taking his time getting in. This would be a humongous waste of breath, Carlucci thought. Only question is, do I wanna waste it or not? Nah. Fuckim. Guys like this never get it.

He drove in silence past City Hall to let Merwin out. Merwin fumed the whole way, and when he got out he slammed the door so hard it rocked the Chevy. Carlucci reached over and depressed the lock, then drove to Muscotti's without a backward glance. He could see Merwin in the rearview mirror shouting something like, "Fucking greaseball." At least that's what it looked like. The "fucking" and the "ball" were pretty easy to read. He wasn't too sure about the "grease" part. Carlucci filed it with the rest, thinking, hey, next time we'll know who we both are, won't we? Camel's-hair coat and all.

At around three o'clock on the afternoon of Philip Randa's funeral, after the few friends had left and there was just the family and several women neighbors to put away the leftovers and clean up the kitchen, Carlucci was sitting in the cellar at a picnic table nibbling on cold, gluey rigatonis, drinking a lukewarm cola, and listening to Virginia June Randa Blasco talk about how much her father had hated Bobby.

Carlucci had been watching her and the rest of her family at the Sanavita Funeral Home in Westfield Township every chance he could get away from the station over the last three days, watching to see who was crying, how hard, what about, and how long. What he'd noticed foremost was that Virginia June and her brother Francis, Frankie, had apparently done their crying in private, because neither shed a tear in public. The mother and Rennie, the retarded son, provoked each other into long crying jags that sometimes went on for almost ten minutes without interruption. Brother George had abrupt swings of temper and mood, loud grief over almost as quickly as it started, followed by sullen anger that seemed to last for hours, shattered suddenly by enraged shouts at one or both of his brothers. The first night his father's body was laid out, George got into it with Rennie over a wreath. Rennie said the wreath "stunk like cat piss" and started to carry it outside. George jerked it out of his hands and moved it closer to the casket, where Rennie kicked it over as soon as George put it down. George then kicked Rennie in the shin and butted him on the chin, knocking him into a rolling-eyed stagger. Mrs. Randa began to shriek at them to stop, but when they continued to menace each other and call each other shit-face and dog shit, Frankie stepped between them grudgingly, calling both of them jerks. After he got them separated, he put the wreath on the far side of the room opposite the main entrance and told Rennie to hold his nose or sit on the other side of the room. He told George to grow up for once.

When Carlucci got a chance to read the card on the wreath, it said, "Sympathy to the Randa family from Sentinel Security." Carlucci recalled seeing George in a private security uniform and guessed that George was hoping hard that one of his supervisors was going to show up eventually. When Frank left the room a few minutes later, George returned the wreath to a place near where Rennie had kicked it over and started the whole ruckus. Nobody mentioned the wreath again.

Here in the cellar, June sat opposite Carlucci, drinking coffee, smoking, talking softly about her father. Carlucci picked at his food and watched her keep refilling her cup and lighting one cigarette after another.

"He just could never understand what I saw in him. All he saw was the blowhard—and the gambler of course, he saw that right away, or maybe he knew about it from somebody else, I don't know. My father didn't talk about it, you know, he never discussed it with me. He'd just walk around making statements, you know, how he absolutely refused to believe I could marry such a jerk. Kept telling me I must be blind, or he didn't know who I was, 'cause no daughter of his would've done anything as stupid as that all on her own. I told him I had plenty of help, but naturally he didn't know what I was talkin' about.

"He really never forgave me for marryin' him. Neither did Frankie. Frankie still doesn't talk to me. Quit talkin' to me two

weeks before the wedding, only time he talks to me is when he
wants me to get him something—God forbid we should ever happen to sit down at the same table to eat or something. Pass me the
bread, that's all he says. Otherwise, forget Frankie. Like I could.

"You were there, you saw how he was in the funeral home.
Ignored me the whole time, three days, walked right by me like
I'm a ghost. Course for him I am a ghost. But for a completely
different reason. Totally. Totally different reason."

Carlucci was following only about half of what she was saying, but he said nothing; he just nodded and continued to listen
and study her. This was the first time he'd talked to her since she'd
called the station to find out if what she'd learned from Elaine
Donatello about Bobby's death had been true.

"What was I supposed to say to them, you know? My family. Any of them? I thought I was in love with him. Every stupid
thing you ever heard anybody say about love, it's all true, believe
me. Love is blind? That kinda stuff? Believe me, you're blind, period. All you see is whatever you need to see to feed whatever you
think you need to keep on living, that's what you see. And nothin'
else. Nothing. Only thing is, you don't know what you wanna see
or why you wanna see it. And the people who tell ya they do
know? They're fulla crap, you ask me. You see what you wanna see,
only you don't know what you're lookin' for and you don't know
why.

"All I remember is what I saw. This tall, good-lookin' guy
with shoulders out to there, had this great laugh, man, if there
was a room fulla people and Bobby laughed, you could pick his
laugh out from all the rest, he laughed great. He liked to laugh,
and he liked to make me laugh—at first. Easy to think, you know,
'cause somebody laughs great they think lotsa things're funny.
Know what I think now?"

"No, what?"

"I think like a lotta other things about Bobby, he laughed a
lot 'cause he had a great laugh, didn't have anything to do with

whether he had a great sense of humor or anything. It was almost just like how he liked to dance, God, did he like to dance—he *loved* to dance, he was a really great dancer, did you know that? Everybody told me what a great jock he was, but I never saw him play anything so what do I know, but all these people that say what a great jock he was, I never heard any one of 'em talk about him dancin'. The people that never saw him dance, they didn't know what I was talkin' about when I told 'em what a great dancer he was. Maybe 'cause they didn't wanna believe that, you know? That this big fat guy—can you imagine?—that he was so graceful, and he knew so many different dances? Most people I talked to about that, they never knew that about him, or if they did, they wouldn't talk about it. I could never figure that out. Like it was fantastic he was coordinated enough to be a great baseball pitcher, but if he used his coordination on the dance floor it was kinda like he was a little bit fruity, if you know what I mean. It was stupid. Course I'm probably wrong about that."

Carlucci shook his head and shrugged.

"Well he was one great dancer, believe me. And you know how many guys there are who don't like to dance? Who won't dance? Not even if you strapped a bomb to their buns and told 'em it would go off if they quit dancin'? Or else if you do get 'em out on the floor, they're apologizing for steppin' on your feet when you know all they're tryin' to do is get back to the bar where they can pretend they're listenin' to you while they're watchin' some game? Huh? Bobby didn't do that. When we went out, we went out, you know? If he said dinner and dancin', we ate and we danced, you know? We ate and drank and then we danced our buns off, didn't matter whether it was kolbasi and kraut and polkas or burritos and salsa and mambos, Bobby really loved to dance. I never once saw him watch sports on TV, or heard him say, you know, Hey, I can't dance now, I gotta watch this game.

"Only thing I didn't know was, I mean, what took me so

long to learn was, when he was dancin', that's all that was dancin'—just him. It was just him showin' how good he was at somethin'. And it took me, God, forever to wise up to the fact that all I was—I may as well've been a clothes dummy, only instead of him hangin' clothes on me, he was hangin' his moves on me. 'Cause, you know, when we started, he'd be lookin' right into my eyes, and God, you know, I would just melt. Nobody had ever looked at me like that. But then eventually, pretty soon really, when I had to work all the hours 'cause he wouldn't help me with the mortgage? Pretty fast actually, he wasn't lookin' at me anymore, he'd be lookin' around, lookin' over my shoulder, you know, he'd be pretendin' he was lookin' into my eyes, but I could tell. He was usin' his, uh, peripheral vision, you know, to scout other chicks.

"But hey, I didn't care, I was still dancin', at least on my nights off, you know? By that time, I got to be pretty good myself. Not as good as him, you know, but good enough to keep up with him. And I also found out somethin' I never knew before. I found out I could attract some attention if I wanted to. Yeah. Not that I wanted to. Most of the time I didn't. Tell ya the truth, till I met Bobby, I hated it when men looked at me. I still hate it. I can't stand to have men lookin' at me like they wanna do somethin'. Almost makes me sick. But for some reason it was okay if they were doin' it when I was dancin' with him. I guess I felt safe, you know?" She was working on her third cup of coffee and third cigarette that Carlucci had counted and looked ready to start bouncing off the ceiling.

"Yeah, I imagine you could," Carlucci said. "Attract some attention I mean. If you wanted to."

"God, please help me make it through this," she said, resting her forehead in her left hand and shaking it. Her fingers were shaking when she stubbed out her cigarette and lit another. "You know what's stupid? I quit smokin' ten years ago. Two months ago I started again, Jesus."

Carlucci rubbed his mouth for a moment and said, "Listen, try not to get carried away—I know, I know, easy for me to say, but try, uh, you know, I mean, I'd hate for you to lose it over this, you know? You work so hard, you know, to make a life for yourself, get a house, you know, then this happens. I know it's gotta be tough. Is there somebody you could call maybe?"

"Oh what, do I look like I'm gonna run out and do something? Huh? To myself? No way. If I didn't do it before now, I'm not doin' it now, brother, believe me. Besides, she's here, I don't have to call her. Right over there, talkin' to my Aunt Elvira. The tall one with the gray hair and no makeup? Black dress, black sweater?"

Carlucci dragged out one of his standard lines. "You think you maybe should be talkin' to her instead of me?"

"Oh she's only heard my story about a hundred times, that's all. It's gettin' tough for either one of us to stay interested anymore—or to fake lookin' interested. I said it so many times it's startin' to sound like it's about somebody else. But Jesus, how do I get through this? I mean my whole family's a wreck 'cause I found a guy who didn't need to be coaxed to dance, Jesus Christ, what kinda stupid reason is that to get involved with somebody?"

"Well, you said it yourself, all the clichés about love're true. You were in love," Carlucci said, as though he knew. He was thinking of a face looking through a partly opened door and wishing he knew what he was talking about.

"I didn't say I was in love. Did I? I said I *thought* I was in love. But God, that wasn't love. *That* was love? God, that wasn't love, that was sick. That—Jesus, my whole family's ruined now. And why? 'Cause my first husband was a bump on the couch, it was all he could do to sit up and take nourishment, like as soon as the honeymoon was over, his brain turned to yogurt. So I waited six years to find out whether he was ever gonna have an intelligent thought again, and then, when I admit finally all he's ever gonna want to do is watch football, I said see ya later.

"And then who do I find? I find a guy who hates even the idea of sittin' around, I mean if he's sittin' it's cause he's either eatin' or playin' cards, he sure isn't watchin' TV. And I think, you know, 'cause he was always movin', cha-cha-cha, mambo, tango, polka, whooptie do, drinkin', goin' to the tracks—I think *that's* love? I think *that's* a basis for marriage?"

"How long were you married to your first husband?"

"Oh God, six years. About five years and eleven months too long. He went into a coma about a month after we got back from Ocean City. Well, there's one thing I have to say for him. He sure never interfered with me studyin' for my LPN license, that much I gotta give him."

"Then Bobby comes along?"

"Oh not while I was married, uh-uh, you kiddin'? I'm a good little Catholic girl. I had to wake my first husband up to serve him the papers. Didn't have a thing to do with Bobby—I didn't even know Bobby then. Now look—God, just look at 'em, my family. Look like a buncha zombies—and why? 'Cause I found a guy couldn't sit still, and I thought that meant he loved to dance as much as I did. It's really funny—I wanted to dance with somebody, he wanted to dance to show off, and we're both dancin' and I couldn't really tell any difference for the longest time. I mean I thought we were both doin' what I thought we were doin'. Just shows ya.

"And then there's my father, honest to God, who never understood. Anything. Right under his nose, he wouldn't even listen to me when I tried to tell him. It wasn't Bobby, I must've told him ten times. It was me! Understand? It was me! Me! I'm the one. Long before I met Bobby, before I ever heard of Bobby. Bobby just showed me some different ways to get abused, that's all. But my father would just sit there and listen to me and his eyes would just go, you know, like somebody was unrollin' a sheet of wax paper over them, hey, Daddy, hello? Anybody in there? I mean, he wouldn't get it or couldn't get it, I don't know which, I guess mostly he didn't wanna get it, and finally he'd just get up and walk away, go out and play with his precious rosebushes. And my mother? Forget it, she didn't have a clue—doesn't have one to this day. And now for sure they're all gonna hate me for the rest of my life over this—as if they didn't before.

"Look at 'em! They can't wait for me to get outta this house so they can say why it shoulda happened to me—or what they'd like to do to me. Especially Rennie. God. I mean, I don't even understand this myself, but I actually feel sorry for Rennie, can you believe that? He gave me all that shit—well George too, but Rennie, Jesus Christ, he's just a big dumb dog, he never knew what was goin' on—and I'm feelin' sorry for him now. For sure I must have screws loose, I must've been born with screws loose, I don't understand, I swear."

Carlucci chewed the inside of his lip and said, "You're not the only one, June, you're all over the place here. What I'm hearin', I mean it sounds like somethin' was goin' on with you and your family long before Bobby, but I'm guessin'. I mean listenin' to you, lookin' at you, knowin' what you do, I mean, you're a smart person, you're a kind person, you're a nurse—"

"LPN, big difference, Detective, I'm no nurse."

"Okay, LPN. Maybe a big difference technically, according to the licensing boards, but what I'm sayin' is, no matter what, that means you have to have a lotta kindness in you otherwise you wouldn't be doin' that kind of work, but the way you're talkin', the way you're lookin' now, I'm gettin' the impression you think you deserved all this crap that's happenin' to you, and that doesn't fit with what you do—"

"Really?" She pursed her lips, took in a deep breath through her nose and then expelled it the same way, looking at him without blinking for a long time. She took another long drag on her cigarette, exhaled that, stubbed it out and said, "I'm just gonna say this once. I was the youngest. I was the only girl. When we first moved out here, you couldn't see another house, that's how

alone we were out here. I have three brothers and one of 'em's retarded, and the other two're pricks. You figure it out. And that's
all I'm ever gonna say about it, and now I gotta get out of here,
'cause I'm startin' to choke on the memories here. Just do me one
favor, okay? I know you're gonna arrest them. Just wait till tomorrow, please? 'Cause it's not my mother's fault, okay? She can't
help it, she's just . . . she's just not a very smart person, that's all.
I really can't stand to hurt her, so for her sake, okay? Give her at
least the rest of this day with them, okay? Please?"

"Sure, yeah, no problem," Carlucci said. "Wait a minute, I'll
walk out with ya. Just lemme say good-bye to your mother."

"I don't wanna talk about it anymore, okay? I'm sick of
talkin' about it, so don't think you're gonna walk me out and I'm
gonna answer everything you think you wanna know, okay? Don't
ask me anything else, just do what you gotta do and let me alone,
okay? Please?"

Carlucci stumbled getting his legs out from under the picnic bench. He said nothing, just splayed his hands and shrugged
at her. He watched her walk up to the gray-haired woman with no
makeup and whisper in her ear. The gray-haired woman touched
the arm of the woman she'd been talking to, then gave a little wave
to everyone in the room, and followed June Blasco up the stairs.

Carlucci located Mrs. Randa in the kitchen upstairs, again
expressed his sympathy for her loss, and hurried outside where
the air was cold and damp, and getting colder and damper. The
sky was purplish black on the northwest horizon, the kind of sky
you'd expect to see in July or August at the beginning of an elec-
trical storm, except this sky was bringing wind, snow, and dropping temperatures.

For a moment, Carlucci tried not to think about what June
Blasco had just told him. He tried to think about the weather and
how the city street crews had finally plowed and salted the city
out from under the ice and now they were about to get hit again
with another blast of forced overtime. But thinking that didn't

work because what compelled his thoughts was what June Blasco had said about being the youngest child and only daughter. There had been cold emotion in her voice when she'd said it, but nothing much that Carlucci could tell in her eyes, neither hot nor cold. So then she grew up and married a guy who turned out to be a lump on the couch. And then she dumped him, and found a man who wanted to dance as much as she did. And now her family was ruined. Her words.

Carlucci wished he'd been taping the conversation. He'd like to have it to play back a couple dozen times just to see if he'd heard what he thought he'd heard. So was she looking for somebody that wasn't a bump on the couch? Somebody who was just a dancing partner? Or was she looking for a lot more? 'Cause at the end it sure sounded like she was looking for something else. Sure sounded like she was looking for an accomplice—whoa, I'm getting way ahead of myself here, this is gettin' way too complicated for me, Carlucci thought. S. Lloyd Merwin, Esquire, might be right, maybe. I might be an asshole, maybe. Whatever, I'm thinkin' things that are way over my head.

Wait a second, who was that woman she left with? Carlucci went bounding back into the house, into the kitchen, and started asking the women doing the dishes if they knew who the woman was that June had just left with.

Juney's friend from work, somebody said. Lisa something. "She works in the mental health," one of the women said, tapping her temple with her finger. "With the crazies."

"Well Juney always said she was crazy. Since she was a little girl—"

"Oh she did not, what're you talkin' about, you don't know what you're talkin' about, she never said that, what a thing to say."

"Oh yes she did. Lotsa times. So now I think maybe she found somebody finally believes her."

"Oh shuddup, Mary, you don't know what you're talkin' about."

"That makes two of us then," Mary said, laughing. "That's why we're here. Everybody who don't know nothin', we have to clean up the mess, clean the kitchen after everybody eats."

Carlucci darted forward and kissed Mary on the cheek provoking howls of laughter from the others. "Ouu, Mary, look out, he'll be comin' around at night, you don't watch out."

"Let him come, she wouldn't know what to do."

"How would you know what she knows to do, you been watching her?"

"Get outta here, watchin' her. I got a VCR! I don't need to watch her, for God's sake."

"Oh listen to her, she's gonna tell us she rents *those* movies!"

"So what if I do? Ain't too old to learn."

"She might take one off the shelf, but she takes it up to the counter, some cute little boy wantsa take her money? Hoo, I bet she runs right back where she got it!"

"Maybe not too old to learn, but too old to do nothin' about it."

"Only time you're too old to learn is when you're dead and when you stop learnin' you might as well be dead and I ain't dead—yet."

"You have a Lisa somebody workin' here?" Carlucci said to the receptionist, holding his ID and shield up for her examination.

"Yes we do. Lisa Sonner."

"What's she do here?"

"She's a psychiatric social worker."

"Does that mean she sees patients?"

"Clients. We call them clients. But yeah, she sees some of them. Depends, of course, what their problem is."

"Any chance I could see her now?"

"I could call her and ask. You want me to do that?"

"I'd appreciate it."

"Do you want me to tell her this is official police business?"

"Yeah, you can tell her that."

"Should I say it's about one of the clients here now?"

"No. Not that I know of anyway."

"Well, let me see if she'll answer her page." The reception-ist punched some buttons, said that a detective was there, and rang off. "She'll be out in a moment."

Carlucci went back to the foyer and stared out at the street, at the snow still falling steadily as it had since yesterday when he'd left the Randas' house after they'd buried their father. Since then, he'd been ducking everybody, his mother, the mayor, Trooper Dulac. The only person he'd actively been seeking was Patrolman James Reseta, but Reseta had been ducking Carlucci as profi-ciently as Carlucci had been ducking everyone else. Reseta knew that Carlucci was looking for him and knew, furthermore, what Carlucci wanted to know: why hadn't Reseta arrested Bobby Blasco after Reseta had observed the results of Bobby's assault on June? And Reseta also had to know that Carlucci wanted to know what had happened to the Polaroids Reseta had taken of June, the ones she'd said Reseta took. They weren't in the case file.

Carlucci was reasonably sure he knew what Reseta had done, and reasonably sure of the motive behind it, but he was still pissed because had it gone the other way, had it been June dead instead of Bobby, Reseta's failure to follow the law would have left him wide open for suspension and dismissal if anyone came forward with information that June Blasco had been pho-tographed after an assault and no arrest had been made. Reseta would claim that since all the pictures had been Polaroids and that only he knew what had happened to them, there would be no hard evidence to corroborate that information, should anybody come forward. But what Carlucci wanted to reinforce in Reseta's mind was that hard evidence wasn't necessary to end a police ca-reer, that even the dumbest investigator from Family Court would be asking about the Polaroids, and there would go another police career, sucking wind for a stupid reason, despite the good motive behind it.

So Carlucci and Reseta both knew Reseta was up for an ass-chewing and both knew the longer Reseta ducked Carlucci the lower Carlucci's temperature would be when they finally fronted each other. They also both knew, given their respective ranks, that Reseta would have to give in sooner than Carlucci. But Carlucci admired and respected Reseta's effort. It showed determination, tenacity, courage, and guile, in addition, of course, to empathy for the bind June Blasco had been in. Carlucci thought that since Reseta had passed his sergeant's test at least five years ago, he probably ought to be a detective, and he will be—if anybody ever gets around to making me chief. If I ever find Reseta to give him the ass-chewin' he deserves.

"Excuse me? You the detective who wanted to see me?"

Carlucci turned around and saw the tall, gray-haired woman he'd seen yesterday in the Randa family cellar.

"You Lisa Sonner?"

"Yes. Is there something I can do for you?"

"Someplace we can talk?"

"Certainly," she said, and turned and led him down a corridor and into an office jammed with two desks pushed back-to-back and crammed full of file cabinets and shelves bulging with books and periodicals. She closed the door and motioned for him to take a seat behind one desk while she slipped into the chair behind the other.

"Just push that stuff around, make a place for your elbows, that's my desk, it's okay. Now. What's this about?"

"June Blasco. She told me some things yesterday at the house, just puzzled the hell outta me. Thought maybe you could help me out."

"Yes. I saw you talking to her."

"She was the one doin' the talkin', I was just listenin'. Tryin' to. Think you can help me out?"

"Well, depends, I guess. I'm not sure I know what you want."

"Well, like, uh, are you two just friends, or you, uh, you counselin' her, or what?"

"Mostly I'm just a good pair of ears. Big ears anyway," she said, smiling and tugging on her left earlobe.

"Yeah, well, what I'm gettin' at, you know, is whether you're gonna get all defensive and outta joint about talkin' to me about her. 'Cause see, right now, I'm not sure whether you got any privilege about this, you know? You're a what now? Psychiatric social worker, is that it?"

"Mmm-hm, yes. And I'm sure if I wanted to make a big deal out of it, I could get the hospital's solicitor to tell me why I don't have to be talking to you, but who wants that? I don't. But I think I ought to warn you, I'm not going to tell you a whole lot. Not, you know, out of any claim to, uh, privilege. Just 'cause she's a friend."

"Hey, that's okay, you don't have to tell me anything. Just nod or shake your head, or hold up one finger for yes, two for no, however you wanna do it."

"Oh I don't think we'll have to go through that, do you?"

"I don't know. There's somethin' really botherin' me about this. I mean I thought it was a straight-up revenge thing, you know? And maybe that's what it's still gonna turn out to be, you know, the old man sees his daughter gettin' abused by her husband, he calls his sons, and they go kill the bastard, end of story. But after listenin' to June yesterday, I got all kinds of strange sensations. Like, for instance, how old was she when she got married? First husband. You know?"

"Yes. Eighteen. Married him the day after she graduated from high school."

"So, uh, she was makin' a run for it, right?"

"Mmm, yes, that would probably be a fair way to say it."

"She have a job? Or did she have to depend on him for room and board?"

"Yes and no. She had a job. Right here, on the switchboard."

"But she wasn't makin' enough to support herself, right?"

"No, I would sorta doubt that. Probably not, no, I don't think she would've been able to support herself on what she was making then."

"So, uh, in one sense, it was outta the fryin' pan into the fire, right?"

"Mmm, I suppose you could say that. But I think her husband was not very, uh, oh, let's say, not very aggressive. Much more passive."

"Hell, from what she said, I got the impression he barely had ambition enough to breathe. Or do you mean as aggressive as what she was runnin' from, is that what you're sayin'?"

"Yes, that's probably more what I mean."

"Well, see, I got the distinct impression yesterday, June's brothers, you know, uh, they messed with her. You know what I'm sayin'?"

"I think I do."

"Does that mean it's true?"

"I didn't say that. I said I think I know what you meant."

"Well is it true?"

"Well, why do you think it's true, again?"

"She said—and I don't have this on tape, I'm goin' strictly on memory now, but it's close—she said she was the youngest child, the only daughter, she had a brother who wasn't smart enough to understand, and she had two brothers who were pricks. Sound right so far?"

"Mmm, yes. More or less."

"And when they moved out to that house—she didn't say from where, which doesn't matter—apparently it was very isolated. No neighbors close by, and to top it off, her mother wasn't very smart and her father didn't wanna hear anything. Which to me, sounded, you know, like she'd been tryin' to tell 'em, but nothin' doin', one of 'em was deaf and the other one couldn't hear. So what it sounds like to me, and I don't wanna pretend I'm in your business, but what it sounds like is, and I want you to correct me if I get any part of this wrong, I mean it sounds like, her brothers started messin' with her when she was very young and she tried to tell her mother, but her mother couldn't understand, and she tried to tell her father and he didn't wanna understand. So she married the first guy who would ask her right out of high school so she could get the hell outta there. How'm I doin' so far?"

"Mmm, pretty, uh, pretty good, I'd say, yes."

"Uh-ha. So now here's the thing. I don't know how to say this exactly 'cause I can't remember exactly what she said. I mean it wasn't any one thing she said, just a lot of things that add up to something else—might add up to something, you know? But maybe I'm tryin' to turn it into something else, maybe I'm tryin' to make a bigger deal than it is, you know?"

"Um-hmm."

"That's all you're gonna say, um-hmm?"

"Well, you're the one who's, uh, what do I wanna say, theorizing? Isn't that what you're doing? And I certainly don't want to put words into your mouth—since it's your theorizing. And I don't think you've actually said anything yet, but maybe you have and I just missed it."

"Well, okay, listen to this. I got the distinct impression—not at first, but the more I thought about it—see, the thing is, somehow or other, she got a police officer to, uh, what words do I want here? Lemme put it this way: she got a police officer I've known for a lotta years to fall asleep on a case. Now I know it can happen in domestic cases, all kindsa situations and circumstances, no two of 'em alike, and the first guy on the scene, man, he can get so hung up tryin' to figure out what was goin' on and who did what and everybody's upset and maybe somebody's bleedin' and what's he supposed to do, God, you can get such a headache tryin' to figure it out, but the fact is, see, I mean, my problem is, there's evidence missin' here. I'm not gonna tell ya what kind or how it came to be missin', 'cause I don't know exactly, I just know it's not there and this officer's been duckin' me. And those two things bother the hell outta me. So what I'm wonderin', you know, hey, is this lady what she seems? Or was she doin' somethin', you know what I'm sayin'?"

"Mmm, yes, I think so. But, uh, I don't know," Lisa Sonner said, sighing. "I think what you're talking about, if I understand you right, I mean, I think what you're suggesting is, uh, well, what are you suggesting? I'm not sure."

"I'm not suggesting anything, I'm askin'. And what I'm askin' is, is this woman somethin' other than what she seems? 'Cause she told me herself she got this officer to not do what he was supposed to do, and I've known this officer for a long time, and I've never known him to not do what he was supposed to do. The man's a professional in every way. If the law says if A, do B and C, and if this officer responds to a call and finds A, he will do B and C, no question. But in this instance, he found A when he responded to the call but he didn't do B and C. And June Blasco told me herself, she got him to do that—or to not do that, which is what I mean. So what I'm thinkin' is, if she got him to not do somethin' I woulda bet my life he woulda done, I'm wonderin' what she had to do, if anything, with her family, you know, what they did to her ex-husband, you followin' me now?"

"Well, mmm, yes, I'm following you, but I don't know, I mean, that, uh, that would take some sort of calculation, don't you think? And I just don't think, I mean the person I know, the person you're talking about, at least not from my point of view, I mean I don't think she would be capable of that."

"Yeah? Well what I'm askin' you is, what is she capable of?"

Lisa Sonner shook her head, licked her upper lip, and closed her eyes in long thought. "Mmm, I don't think she's capable of a whole lot, really. I just think, you know, really, if you want my opinion, and please don't forget this, I'm speaking as a

friend, really, certainly not as a counselor. I mean the most serious counseling I ever gave her was that she should get herself into
counseling."

"Did she?"

"Well she's in a group, that much I know. But if she's gotten into an individual situation, you know, one-on-one therapy,
really, she hasn't discussed that with me."

"She discuss everything with you?"

"Mmm, really, Detective, do you think anybody discusses
everything with any other person? I mean, maybe there are some
people who like to think they do, but I seriously doubt the reality of that. I just don't think that much intimacy is humanly possible, do you? Or desirable? What do you think?"

"You ever gonna give me a straight answer?"

She smiled and looked at her hands in her lap. "I know you
don't think so, but I have been giving you straight answers."

"Excuse me, but you're the world's greatest hedger, or the
greatest one I ever met. Man, everything you say is a maybe, a
probably, a possibly."

"Well, I'm sure from your point of view, it may sound like
that. But I warned you. At the beginning? Remember? I said I
wasn't going to tell you much. Didn't I? Or did I? I think I did,
maybe I didn't."

"Shit, there ya go again—oh, sorry, didn't mean to say that."

"That's okay," she said, smiling with her lips together. "Gee,
I mean, I promise you, that won't be the worst I hear today."

"Well, okay, but gettin' back to her, okay? You don't think
there was any calculation on her part maybe, none?"

"To do what, exactly? Use her husband? Is that what you're
getting at? Her ex-husband I mean—use him to provoke the men
in her family? Incite them in some way to physically attack him?
To commit murder? Is that what you're getting at?"

"Well, yeah. 'Cause somehow she finessed a real professional
police officer into withholding evidence—like I said I haven't

talked to him yet so I don't really know all the facts, but I do know the evidence that should be in the case file is not there. And she told me herself the first time I ever talked to her that she talked him out of doin' what he knows very well the law says he's supposed to do. But now, see, according to you, that would not— I mean you're sayin' she's not capable of that kind of calculation, but from where I sit, I mean, knowin' that police officer, I'm sayin' it shows, if nothin' else, she's persuasive as hell in gettin' what she wants, you know what I'm sayin'? From a man, remember. A very competent, professional officer."

Lisa Sonner yawned and scratched her cheek. "But, mmm, aren't you making some large assumptions here? I mean I certainly don't know the officer you're talking about, but you, mmm, you've said several times I think that you haven't talked to him because, why did you say? Because he's ducking you? He may not be ducking you at all, isn't that possible? And there may be perfectly reasonable explanations why the evidence is not where you say it should be, isn't that possible? And isn't it possible that she didn't persuade him to do anything, I mean, since you haven't talked to him yourself, isn't it possible he may have decided for reasons of his own not to pursue what you think he was supposed to do, I mean, all of that's possible, wouldn't you agree?"

Carlucci folded his hands on the desk and leaned forward over them. "You ever gonna tell me anything, huh? That isn't fulla possiblys?"

"Okay, if that's what you want, certainly I can do that. I can tell you without one iota of equivocation that June is severely conflicted about men."

"Aw shit," Carlucci said, shaking with silent laughter.

"Why are you laughing? That was a very positive statement, Detective. Made with great conviction and great certitude."

"Conflicted, huh? She's mixed up about men, right? And you're absolutely sure about that, right?"

"Mmm, yes. Yes, I am."

"Oh right, and I'm conflicted about women too—how, that's what I wanna know, conflicted how? In what ways is she conflicted? What would these conflicts about men she's walkin' around with, how would they cause her to behave, huh?"

"Well I certainly don't think they would cause her to plan, at least not in my thinking, I doubt seriously that June is capable of planning to avenge herself on any one particular man or group of men because of her conflicts about that particular group of men. I just don't think she's reached the point where she'd be able to think in those terms. Because really, Detective, think about what you're saying. I mean, because one police officer does or does not do something he should or should not have done, and because it involved her, I mean that presupposes, what you're suggesting, that would mean he had no will of his own. I mean, I think that's highly dubious, because, really, June is simply not that strong a personality. Completely opposite. She's not a person who uses men. Men use her. And they have since she was a child. And up until a very short time ago, she was not even able to admit that she was aware of these conflicts."

"Short time ago? Like how short?"

"Oh, I'm speaking relatively, of course. I mean within the last couple of years. I mean, when I met her, oh, I'd say at least five years ago, she really had no idea what was going on. It was as though she was aware of all the sides and top and bottom of a box, but she had no idea all those sides formed a single unit, something called a box, and that the box was a container, and that things could be put in it and carried around in it. She couldn't conceive that all those sides were related and that if you took off the top, it could still be used as a box, but if you took away something else, it wouldn't function as a box anymore, the parts that were left were just pieces of cardboard and they could not stand, that's how unaware she was—just my opinion, of course, and, uh, was that helpful? Am I making myself clear?"

"Yeah, perfectly. You ain't gonna tell me anything," Carlucci

said, standing. He reached out and shook hands with Lisa Sonner. "Thanks for your time. Really, I mean it. No probablys. But
I think what I probably oughta do is go find my patrolman."

"I'm sorry you think I haven't helped you, I really am, but,
mmm, yes, I think maybe you should talk to your officer, that
would probably be good, or better."

Carlucci said he could find his way out, said good-bye, and
went outside into an almost blinding snowfall. It suited his mood
perfectly.

It was before the beginning of the 1500-to-2300 watch.
Carlucci told Nowicki, "No matter what my mother says, got it?
I don't care if the house is on fire, I need to talk to Reseta. The
only way you interrupt me if she calls is if *she's* on fire, okay?"

"What about my cousin? What if she calls?"

"What? What're you talkin' about?"

"My cousin told me she's been callin' you, you don't return
her calls, she asked me what's goin' on. What'm I supposed to tell
her?"

Carlucci canted his head and squinted at Nowicki for a long
moment. "You're fulla shit. She didn't call me, uh-uh, no way she
called me."

Nowicki grinned and started to chuckle. "Had ya goin'
there for a second, didn't I?"

"Hey. Knock it off, man, that ain't funny."

"Ouu, I believe I may have touched a raw one there," Nowicki said, rocking his head from side to side, making grunting
noises.

"Hey, Nowicki, how'd you like a walkin' beat, huh? Oh
twenty-three hundred to oh seven hundred, down in the Flats,
huh? Where the wind comes whippin' off that river, how'd you
like that? Wind chill's supposed to go to fifteen below
tonight—"

"Oh please, please," Nowicki howled, sliding off his chair

and dropping to his knees and folding his hands in mock prayer. "Oh praise Jesus, don't toy with me, Sergeant, sir. Restore my legs, touch my feet, make me walk again, I'll do anything to walk again, I have open wounds on my ass from sittin' by this fucking radio, please, sir—"

"Aw fuck you, Nowicki, get up! Reseta? James? Wanna see you now, James, in Balzic's office, and don't even think about makin' a run for it!"

Carlucci hustled toward Balzic's office amidst laughter, ouu-ing, booing, and catcalls at himself as well as at Nowicki and Reseta from both watches as they changed.

Patrolman Reseta followed Carlucci into Balzic's office by a couple of seconds. He waited, polished, creased, and oiled, his jaw bluish and square, eyes front, heels together, as Carlucci fussed with the key in the office drawer to get the June Blasco file.

"Aw sit down, James, Jesus Christ, don't make this any tougher than it is."

Reseta pulled out the chair on the opposite side of Balzic's desk and settled into it, as close to attention as one could be said to sit at attention, heels together, back straight, head up, eyes front.

Carlucci opened the file and turned it around and pushed it toward Reseta, who didn't bother to look at it. "I got no excuse," he said. "I did it, I shouldn't've done it, and I'll never do it again. But I did it, and I can't make that go away."

Carlucci sighed. He leaned forward over his forearms on the desk and said, "I hear ya. And I don't think I have to say this but I'm gonna say it anyway, okay? If this winds up on a tape, it's on a tape I don't know anything about, okay?"

"I know that, Sergeant. But thanks for sayin' it. I appreciate that."

"Okay, you're welcome. But. I still have a problem. I wanna know, did you fail to act according to statute and department pol-icy because of her, or because of you?"

Reseta didn't hesitate. "Because of me."

"Okay. Okay. I'll accept that. Now why?"

"Because I knew what she was sayin' was the truth. I mean, from the start, you know, she was sayin', don't arrest him, don't arrest him, he's just gonna get out and come back and do it again. Which, naturally, I'm listenin' to. I mean, from the time I got there, till I got her to the ER, from the time I took her statement till the time I took the pictures, that's all she was sayin', don't do it, don't arrest him, you do that he's just gonna come back and do it all over again.

"So I listened to her, you know, but I knew this jaboney's history. And I'm not gonna lie to ya, I mean, seein' her, Jesus—I thought somebody, not me necessarily, but somebody could do everybody a favor they just apply a little discipline to this asshole, you know? I mean, what he did to that woman, fuck, that shouldn't happen to skinheads. Fucker kicked her in both her Achilles tendons, you believe that? She couldn't stand up. Never mind that he's stealin' from her, and now he fixes it so she can't go to work, she can't even walk to the toilet, she has to crawl? What kinda prick does that, huh? Jesus."

Carlucci leaned farther forward. "I wanna hear it from your own mouth—you did not apply a little discipline, is that right? You did not do that yourself, correct?"

"Absolutely not. No way. I wanted to, I'm not gonna deny that, 'cause I mean if ever an asshole deserved to take a beatin', he did. But I did not. No."

"So you took the pictures at the hospital?"

"No, I took a couple at the scene, two or three, I can't remember, but the rest, yeah, I took those in the ER."

"You still have 'em?"

"Of course I still have 'em. Yeah. At home. You want 'em, I'll go get 'em."

"Nah, not now. But tomorrow. Bring 'em in, for sure now, okay?"

"Okay."

"So, again, I wanna know your thought process, okay? She was talkin' the whole time, from the time you arrived till you left her in the ER, right? Correct?"

"Correct."

"But you've heard this story before, right?"

"Many times."

"Ever stop you before—I mean since '86 now, since the statute changed—"

"Oh sure, plenty of times."

"But you always talked to the guy, right?"

"Course I talked to 'em. Except couple times it was women."

"Daisy Johnson? You ever catch her doin' her number? Man, I had her one night, holy Christ, I'll never forget it, kitchen looked like somebody was killin' chickens—"

"She use that little cast-iron fryin' pan? That seven-incher?"

"Yeah. Fucked old Joe up somethin' awful, poor bastard, God, split his scalp three places—"

"Yeah, I had her the night she died, you know, when she had that stroke. She fucked him up pretty bad that night too. I really felt for him, poor guy, sittin' there, holdin' his head, wailin', you know, 'Daithy, Daithy, don't die, pleathe don't die,' remember, he had that little lisp? It was sad, poor fucker."

"Yeah it was. I asked him one time, I said, 'Joe, how many stitches she give you?' He said, 'Oh man, I quit countin' after three hundred, that's all the numbers I know.' Sad. Remember, he died about a month after she did?"

"Yeah, I went to his funeral. Hers too."

"You did? I didn't know that. Why'd you go?"

"Christ, I was in their house so many times, you know, I felt, I don't know, I know it's goofy, but I had to go pay my respects. I mean they never hurt anybody else. And they were always real polite with me, she'd always be apologizin'—so would he. I said to him one time, Hey, Joe, what're you apologizin' for, and he looked at me, blood's all over the place, man, his entire shirt is soaked, bloody ice cubes all over the place, she hit him with two full trays of ice cubes that time, and then she picked 'em up, wrapped 'em in a towel, and she was whackin' him with that when I got there, so I ask him, you know, and he looks up at me, he says, with that lisp, ' 'Cauthe I know you got more important polithe buthineth than me,' and I couldn't help it, I just broke up. Had to go outside for a minute, I was laughin' so hard."

"So all these times you didn't react the way you were supposed to, it never came back on you?"

Reseta shook his head. "Nah. Not that I know of. Course, remember now, I had some serious conversations with every one of those people—not Daisy now, that was hopeless. No amount of talkin' in the world was gonna change that pair. But the rest? Oh yeah. I threatened the shit out of 'em, every one of 'em. Oh yeah. Put the fear of God in 'em. What'm I tellin' you for, you know what I do."

"Yeah, yeah, I know. So, James, back to the other thing here. Once again, run it down for me."

"Look, Rugs, you know this as well as I do, some people you can talk nice to, they listen, and some people you can scare, and they listen, but some people, it doesn't matter what you say or how you say it, they're not gonna hear anything. I consider myself real lucky, honest to God, that it's never come back on me. But I knew, man, I know—if she'd wound up dead? Jesus, I'd've been in deep shit, and I would've belonged there, I know that, Christ, I know it better than anybody. I swear to you, when I heard he was dead? My heart doubled its beat in, like, ten seconds. One second I'm sittin' there watchin' TV, the next I hear Fish callin' in, honest to God, my pulse went from sixty-five to about one-forty in less than ten seconds, 'cause I knew where those Polaroids were and how easy it could've gone the other way. I was shakin', I'm tellin' ya. I didn't sleep that night, man."

"So tell me again how she didn't talk you into it."

"Aw, hell, it was him, Rugs, you kiddin'? Anybody with half a brain knows what kinda lowlife he was—same kind he'd been all his life. Christ, how many PFAs were outstanding? Fuckin' sociopath—if that word has any meaning at all, it applies to him, applied. So what, you know? There wasn't a judge in this county was gonna put him away. So what's that mean? Take him to the duty DJ, he turns him out on recognizance, then what? The bastard goes right back there, beats her again and this time no way in the world she's gonna call. Why in the fuck would she—the only reason she called in the first place was 'cause she needed help 'cause she couldn't walk, couldn't stand up, that's the only reason she called. I just happened to get there before the EMTs, that was pure accident I happened to be closer to her address than they were, that's how that went. But I knew as soon as I heard the address I wasn't gonna arrest him. And if somebody wants to bring me up on charges, hey, let 'em. I did what I knew was right, and fuck the law. That law, with some women, all it's gonna do is get 'em two beatings in two days, guaranteed. I'm just real real glad he's the one still waitin' for a coffin. I heard nobody wants to bury him, is that what you hear?"

"That's the word I'm gettin'," Carlucci said, standing and stretching. "Okay, so here's the drill. You bring me the Polaroids, I put 'em in the file, and we all act like the fucking incompetents we are and we hope nobody asks us to prove it, okay?"

"Okay, Sergeant. Yes, sir, I will do that. Thank you. I appreciate it, I mean it."

Carlucci nodded, shrugged, and said, "This stays here, okay?"

Reseta nodded, put his cap on, and left.

Pennsylvania State Police Trooper Dulac was on his way to Pittsburgh with a warrant to arrest Francis James Randa when he arrived for work at Roberts Office Decor Inc. on Baum Boulevard. The plan was for Dulac to have backup from the Washing-

ton Boulevard Barracks waiting for him at Francis Randa's office
and to take him as soon as he got out of his car and turned
around to lock it. Dulac had learned from Randa's co-workers
that every time he parked in the lot behind the office, he wouldn't
walk away from his Toyota Corolla without bending down to look
at every lock button to make sure it was down and then recheck-
ing the driver door by pulling on the handle twice, a routine that
would keep him occupied long enough to allow four state police
troopers to approach him and place him in custody without un-
duly wrinkling anybody's uniform.

While the simplicity of Dulac's plan would've pleased any
police officer, it unfortunately left Carlucci to deal with the question of why the Rocksburg PD was stuck with the annoying little detail of serving arrest warrants on the two remaining Randa
brothers, George and Ronald, considering that they lived in
Kennedy Township, officially part of the state police Troop A patrol area. Carlucci was standing at the chalkboard in the weight-
lifting room in the City Hall basement, trying to re-create from
memory the Randa house and grounds including approaches,
when Booboo Canoza brought up that annoying little detail
again.

"How come we gotta bust these two when the state guys got
all the manpower and it's their turf? I don't understand that."

"Oh-oh," Fischetti said, "Booboo's thinkin' again. I can tell
the way his forehead's all scrunched up. Read about this once in
one of those supermarket tabloids, how some guy was thinkin' so
hard his head exploded."

"That ain't funny, Fish," Booboo said. " 'Cause every time
somebody hands me a shotgun and a Kevlar vest, it feels like my
head's gonna do somethin'—I don't know what—'cause I figure
it's been about at least eight years since I had any practice takin'
down two guys—"

"Don't figure, okay?" Reseta said. "Just pay attention. This

is gonna be complicated enough without you standing around fig-
uring—"

"Okay, that's enough," Carlucci said. "To answer your question, Robert, only thing I can say, you guys all know how the state
guys are, if they decide they wanna do somethin', then we ride last
in the parade, and if they don't, then, hey, we go to the front. And
today's no different from any other time apparently, 'cause they
decided their best move was Pittsburgh and that means we're goin'
to the front out here, so, uh, Robert, fuckit, forget about it, time
to start thinkin' about other things now."

"Yeah," Canoza said, "but, man, I hope there's more cover
out there than what you're drawin', 'cause unless you're leavin' a lot
out, I mean, it doesn't look like there's anything around three sides
of that house."

"Well, actually," Carlucci said, "there isn't. Three sides is
open—are open. Behind the house is just an open field, that's
north, then east and south, hey, they're pretty much wide open
too. Nearest neighbor on the other side, west, is, I don't know,
maybe four house lots over. That's a lotta space. The road in front
of the house turns west off Township Road Six, then we have
maybe twenty-five yards to their driveway, and, uh, much as I
would like to say otherwise, that's all open too. So that's why we're
all in civvies and, uh, that's also why we're gonna take our own
cars—"

"Aw man," Canoza groaned, "you didn't say anything about
my car! My Camaro's gonna be out there? Huh? What if one of
those assholes starts shootin', there ain't enough Kevlar in this
building to cover my car—"

"Aw Canoza," Fischetti said, "give it a break, Jesus, okay? We
only need two cars, nobody asked you to take your precious
fuckin' Camaro."

"Hey man, my car's my entire estate, you know? It's all I got
left—not like you, man, you got your house and you got that

cabin up in Crawford County and you're always talkin' about your
bonds—that Camaro's it for me."

"Rugs? C'mon, make him stop, okay?" Fischetti said, walking disgustedly in circles away from the chalkboard until he
bonked his ankle on a barbell. Then he started hopping on one
foot, swearing under his breath.

"See what ya get?" Booboo said.

"Okay, Robert, that's enough, all right?"

"Hey, Rugs, I'm not clownin' around here, Fish thinks I'm
jokin' around or somethin', but I'm not. You know me, man, I get
nervous when I'm outta uniform. I don't like plain clothes. Never
did. And when I gotta put the Kevlar on, man? On top of civvies?
And start humpin' this goddamn shotgun around, man, I really
don't like it. And for a second there, maybe I was gonna have to
take my car? Fuck! I really really didn't like it."

"Hey, Robert, listen to my words, okay? Nobody's askin'
you to take your car, okay? You can ride with Fish, or you can ride
with me, I don't care. Just know I don't like it either, okay? But
somebody gotta collar these two, and the state guys just—hey,
that lieutenant I talked to yesterday and this mornin', he swore up
and down they don't have as many people to do this as we do.
Now that's what the man said. Said they had only three troopers
to patrol the whole fuckin' county last night, now you want me to
argue with him? Am I supposed to tell him he has more people
than that? Hey. Enough. No more, Robert, okay? We got things
to talk about here, we need to get with it, so, uh, listen up, okay?

"We got arrest warrants, general charge of murder, for
George Joseph Randa, age forty-four, male, Caucasian, last known
address, Box Seven, Township Road Six, Rocksburg RD Ten,
that's this house I've sketched out on the board here. Also, Ronald
John Randa, age forty-six, male, Caucasian, same address. Both of
'em built very similar, five-nine, five-ten, one seventy to one
eighty, except Ronald has a pronounced potbelly. George looks to
be in pretty good shape. Both of 'em have black hair, starting to

gray, balding in front, brown eyes, no obvious scars, tattoos, skin blemishes, distinguishing features. Since I'm obviously gonna be there, I will tell you whether we have the right people or not.

"Now what I'm thinkin' is, we get there right after George gets home with the school bus, okay? I wanna be there waitin' for him, as soon as he turns into the driveway, I want both cars to seal the bus off in the driveway, okay? If he tries to back out, I want him backin' it out over us, okay?"

"Well let's hope not," Reseta said, shaking his head and looking quizzically at Carlucci.

"Thank you Jesus I ain't takin' my Camaro."

"Look, George is the, uh, I mean, he's the one in the family with the obvious rage. But more important, he's also the one with the weapons clearance. Carries a nine on the job, baton, four-cell Mag-Lite, cuffs, Mace, only thing he doesn't have is a shotgun, but I'm reasonably sure, from talkin' with his employers both at the bus garage and at Sentinel Security, that he is not supposed to be carryin' when he's on that bus. The fact is, however, and despite what his supervisors say, every morning he gets on that bus, he has just come from his security job at Riverside Industrial Park, he gets right on the bus, he doesn't change clothes, starts drivin' his routes. In other words, nobody's sure what he does with his duty belt. He could drop it off in the house, he could drop it on the floor of the bus, put it under the seat, nobody knows, nobody's willing to say, and I'm not gonna predict how antsy he is, but he's gotta be antsy, I mean the man knows he just murdered somebody."

"Plus, far as I'm concerned, what would make him a lot more antsy is he just buried his old man," Fischetti said.

"Right, exactly. So there's a lot of emotion spinnin' through this guy, and I'm also guessin' he's real good at rationalizin' it. From talkin' to his sister, that's, uh, Blasco's second wife, and also talkin' with her counselor friend, I got good reason to believe that this guy and his two brothers molested their sister probably for eight or ten years, and what I'm thinkin' is, Bobby Blasco, lowlife bastard that he was, I mean all that aside, he was probably also a real convenient scapegoat for these guys. I think he made it real easy for them to get rid of a load of guilt about their sister—assumin' they have any capacity to feel guilt."

"Uh, Rugs, I'm havin' a big problem with this, I really am," Reseta said.

"Okay. What's the problem?"

"The other brother, that's the problem. The retard? Where's he? Is he in the house?"

"Oh shit," Carlucci said, dropping his head. "Yes. Holy fuck, if he isn't in the house I don't know where else he'd be. Aw man, I'm not thinkin' right, fuck yeah he's in the house, where else would he be?"

"So he's in the house," Fischetti said. "So we take him first, so what? We just do it real fast, park the vehicles wherever, two front, two back, use the ram, we can be in and outta there in thirty seconds. Shit that ain't any problem. Guy's retarded ain't he? And didn't you say there was a road behind the house?"

"No, no road, just flat open field, no impediments, no ditches, no fences."

"So? One car there, the other one around the front, hit the ground runnin', shoutin' as we're runnin', hit that fuckin' door with the ram—"

"Okay, fine, suppose he locks himself in the bathroom, or in the cellar? Suppose we take more than a minute gettin' him out, George sees the cars from the road as soon as he makes the corner from Township Road Six."

"Rugs, we got the ram. Bust one door, bust two, what's the difference?" Fischetti said.

"Fish, I told you last night, there's deer heads and racks on the walls, which means somewhere in that house there's rifles or shotguns or both. I just never saw a gun cabinet. They might have the damn things leanin' up in the corners in the front hall closet for all I know, I just never saw 'em, and I was lookin', believe me, but there's only so many places you can look on your way to the john, and you can only go so many times."

"Shoulda told 'em you had the runs," Canoza said.

"There was only one bathroom in the house upstairs, plus the toilet in the cellar and some fat guy was sittin' on that—forget that. Fact is, I don't know where the guns are, that's the fact. Oh man. Okay, listen up. We take Ronald first. Okay. Then we're gonna move everything up fifteen minutes at least. We park in the field behind the house, Canoza takes the back, Reseta got the whistle and a shotgun, Fish got the ram, and I got the warrant and a shotgun. You hear that whistle, Robert? He's comin' your way, take him off at the knees, do not fucking hesitate, got that?"

"Aw man, don't say that," Canoza groaned. "You guys better get him, I don't wanna shoot him. Fuck."

"Robert? Do not fucking hesitate, understand? You hear that whistle, he's comin' your way."

"Yeah yeah, I hear ya. Shit. Shootin' a fuckin' retard."

"Hey, you don't wanna shoot him, fine, I don't give a fuck how you stop him, just stop him, okay? Do it any way you want, trip him, tackle him, just make sure he doesn't get past you, only you better assume he's gonna have something, okay? Rifle, shotgun—oh, man, I hate this shit. We have no training for this.

"Okay, once we get him, handcuffs, leg irons, in the back of Fish's car, then we go back out to wait for George. Soon as he turns into the driveway, both cars pinch him in, then we're out, Canoza stays by the right rear of the bus, Reseta goes down the left side of the bus to the left front, Fish moves right flank of the bus, I go down the right side of the bus to the door with the warrant, okay? James and I hit the ground runnin', no hesitation. Then, okay? First shots, if necessary? First shots take out the back tires, that's Fish and Robert. Next shots, if necessary, from James into the radiator, okay? Don't wanna fuck the bus up any more than we have to, 'cause that MacAnulty? You guys have any history with him? Bastard owns that bus fleet? World's biggest pain in the ass, always suin' everybody. But whatever we have to do, we do, okay? George comes outta that bus with anything but his hands, which I'm prayin' and hopin' he does not, he's goin' down 'cause I don't wanna get hurt and I don't want any of you guys gettin' hurt, okay?"

"What happens if he don't come out?"

"Aw no, no way, he'll come out. 'Cause he doesn't give any evidence of bein' a thinker. But if I'm wrong, at least we've got him boxed. Least we know he's not goin' anywhere."

"What if he's got a kid on there?"

"Nah. No way, never. Guy lives across the road says he comes home empty. His mother said that at least twice at the wake. Second time she said it to me. I asked her specifically to re-peat it. So. Anything else—aw shit!"

"What'samatter now?"

"Their mother! Aw fuck! She wound up in the hospital after the wake, keeled over. I gotta call up there, make sure she's still there. If she's home we can't go bustin' in that house with a ram! Shit, how'd I forget that? God, we're not trained—*I am not trained for this shit!*" Carlucci bolted up the stairs, ducked into Balzic's of-fice, and hit the memory dial button for Conemaugh Hospital in-formation.

A minute later he was calling the MacAnulty school bus garage. Two minutes later he was downstairs, pulling off his Kevlar vest. "It's off," he said, sighing. "Thank God. Hospital said George took her home zero seven-thirty over everybody's objections. Never drove his routes this mornin', called in, said he was goin' to pick up his mother, said she wanted to die at home with her children and he was gonna stay with her till she did. So somebody from the garage went out and picked up his bus."

"Oh thank you, Mary, Mother of God, I will say twelve Hail Marys this Sunday," Canoza said, rolling his eyes toward the ceiling. "Lemme get outta these clothes. I don't care what you guys say, I just don't feel like I got any authority in civvies, I don't care what kinda gun I'm carryin'."

"Aw will you shut the fuck up, okay?" Fischetti said.

"Now what?" Reseta said.

"I gotta sit down and think this out. And I gotta tell ya, I'm really glad—God am I glad! 'Cause, oh shit, I can't tell ya how little I thought of that plan I had. I mean, takin' down two relatives? At the same time? At the same address? Jesus, just the thought of that, man, I mean, I had nerves jumpin' in both my cheeks. Shit."

"Well, you're gonna have to do somethin', Rugs," Reseta said. "Soon as they hear about the other brother, I mean, what're they gonna do? They're in there with their mother? Think about it, man, this could get really hairy."

"I am thinkin' about it," Carlucci said, sighing heavily and rubbing his forehead. "I'll tell you what I'm gonna do, I'm gonna talk to the sister. Maybe I can get in there with her, talk 'em out."

"With their mother in there? Don't bet on that, Rugs. Shit, I wouldn't," Reseta said.

"Listen, James, believe me, I'm as relieved as Canoza this thing didn't go down. 'Cause I had like zero confidence in my tactics. I mean, when was the last time we had any training in this kinda thing? Hell, I can't even remember—eight years? And anyway, Balzic told me a thousand times, anytime you got a choice between talkin' or fightin', go with the talkin' every day of the world. And that's what I'm gonna do.

"The thing that bothers me is, you know, George is in there with those guns, I know they're in there somewhere. Not that that nine of his isn't enough. But those deer up on those plaques, they didn't commit suicide. But I'm damn sure not gonna go out there, guns drawn, no fucking way I'm doin' that with their mother in the house. Shit, you know what I did this morning, huh? Six-thirty? Know how my day started today?"

"How? What?"

"Took my mother to the hospital again."

"What's wrong this time?"

"Another anxiety attack. But neither one of us knows the difference between one of them and a heart attack, and naturally we're both thinkin' it's the worst, and she starts screamin' at me— aw, fuck, just what I need. Anyway, these guys, only thing left for me is talkin', I'm no good at this Rambo bullshit. But I gotta know what to talk about. Okay, what the fuck, everybody, listen up. Back to regular duty till otherwise ordered. Thank you, guys. I mean it. Fish, James, Robert, appreciate your attention. And for not fallin' down laughin' either."

"Laughin'?" Canoza whispered to Fischetti. "Did I miss somethin'?"

"Oh will you shut up? Just gimme the vest, okay? You didn't load that fuckin' thing, did ya? Did you load that? Gimme that thing!"

"Whatta you think I am, stupid?"

"I know you're stupid, what I don't know is whether you loaded the fuckin' shotgun—will you point that at the ceilin' and clear the fuckin' piece, huh, will ya do that, please?"

Carlucci watched Fischetti and Canoza go up the steps, quibbling all the way, to the duty room upstairs. He was going to say something to Reseta but found Reseta looking dejected and disheartened.

"Rugs," Reseta said, "don't take this wrong, okay? But somebody has to do something, man, get this department organized. I swear to God, sometimes I look around, we look like a bunch of monkeys tryin' to fuck a football."

"Yeah. Why would I take it wrong? I know. Little while ago, hell, it looked like I was the one holdin' the football." Carlucci looked at Reseta for a long moment and said, "You know, James, come to think of it, I shouldn't be runnin' this department. You should be runnin' this department."

"Me? I haven't even made sergeant yet."

"Hey, that's not your fault. That's beside the point anyway. 'Cause, I mean it. Your head works right for chief, it's always worked right. Mine doesn't work right. I'm a detective, I'm no fuckin' chief. I've been stumblin' around here for almost a year now waitin' for council to make up their minds, and if they wanted me they would've told me so a long time ago. I don't know why they can't make up their minds about who they want, but I do know they don't want me. I mean, that is so fucking obvi- ous . . . then somethin' like this comes up, and, man, it's just even more obvious I don't have the kind of mind you need to be plan- nin' and organizin' this kinda bust. Right off, man, you saw where we should be startin', and I'm still fuckin' around collectin' details about how to get Georgie boy and you saw the problem with the other brother right away and I hadn't even thought of it. How the fuck am I supposed to get the big picture, you know? I'm thinkin' one detail at a time. That's too slow, man. Way too slow."

"Hey, Rugs, no details, no big picture. You were the guy got the details, I didn't get 'em. I just pointed out a really obvious problem we were gonna have we didn't get the retard first, that's all. That doesn't make me chief material."

"Maybe you're not, I don't know. But I do know that I'm not, and I've just been shittin' myself about this. God knows what would've happened if George would've driven his routes this mornin' and we'd've gone out there, huh? With my half-ass plan? Shit, I could've got somebody hurt. Man, I couldn't live with that. Uh-uh, James, fuckit, I'm not ready for this job. I don't think I'm ever gonna be ready."

Rennie slipped out the back door of his parents' house as soon as it got dark. June Blasco had called the house from Balzic's office; Carlucci was listening on another phone in the duty room. She had pulled the phone out as far as it could reach so she and Carlucci could see each other if they just leaned back a bit. Naturally, George answered. She spent a couple of minutes asking about their mother, then she asked to talk to Rennie, said she was worried about him. George didn't want to let her at first. He said Rennie was too scared and worried about his mother to talk to anybody. "Least of all you. You know how he gets when he talks to you."

"I'm havin' those dreams again," she said. "I need to talk to Rennie, put him on, George, c'mon."

"Aw take a sleepin' pill, that's what everybody else does. That's what I do. You think you're any better'n me? That's your problem, you think you're better'n the rest of us in this family 'cause you're a nurseypoo."

"Listen, Georgie Porgie—"

"If you was here you wouldn't call me that. Don't call me that, I'm warnin' ya."

"I know you hate it and that's exactly why I'm callin' you that—put Rennie on I said, I need him to help me 'cause I'm havin' those dreams—"

"If you was here you wouldn't be talkin' to me like 'at, you know you wouldn't, 'cause you know what would happen, don'tcha, huh?"

"Put Rennie on, George, c'mon, I'm serious. Please? I need to talk to him."

"Aw stop your whinin', Christ. Rennie? C'mere, somebody wantsa talk to you."

"Who?"

"Just take the phone, moron, you'll find out. But don't talk too long, you gotta go back'n watch Ma, you hear?"

"I hear. Hello? Hello? Who's 'is?"

"It's me, Rennie. Juney. You okay?"

"I'm okay. Why you callin' me up? George said you didn't wanna talk to me no more. Said you hate my guts. How come you're callin' me up?"

"I talked to you in the funeral home, didn't I? We talked a

lot, didn't we? And at the house? Afterwards? Huh? Don't you remember how much we talked?"

"George said that was 'cause Daddy died. He said you was
feelin' all guilty 'cause Daddy died. Said it was your fault, you
made him die. George said you was just bein' nice to me 'cause
you're a witch-bitch. Tryin' to trick me. Said you're goin' to hell."

"Rennie, listen, okay? We're talking now, right? Isn't this me
talking to you? Who cares what George thinks?"

"Me. I care."

"Well I don't care what he thinks, you sure you do?"

"Sure I'm sure. George is the boss now. He's daddy now.
He's the oldest one."

"No, Rennie, uh-uh, you're older'n George, don't let George
tell you he's older'n you 'cause he isn't. You're older. You're two
years older than he is."

" 'At ain't what George says. Says he's older, he's the daddy
now, 'cause Daddy ain't here to tell me what to do, I gotta listen
to George now 'cause George knows what to do."

"Listen, Rennie, I have to talk to you, I don't care what
George says. I have to. I'm havin' those dreams, you know? I can't
sleep. You have to tell me what they mean."

"George don't want me to do that no more. He told me he's
gonna beat the shit outta me I do that anymore."

"Oh that was a long time ago, Rennie, that's not now. He
wasn't talkin' about now, honest. He doesn't mean now." She covered the mouthpiece and called out to Carlucci, "You want me to
get him out of there, you have to get off the line now. 'Cause I
can tell, I mean right now, he's not goin' for it, not so far, and if
he makes up his mind like that, he can't change it, he's too scared
of George. So you have to get off the line if you want me to get
him out, I don't want you to hear what I say to him. You have to
get off and you have to promise you won't listen, or I won't do it.
If I hear you get back on I'll hang up, I swear to God."

"Okay, okay," Carlucci said, taking the headphone off.

"No. You have to promise. I want you to swear you won't listen. I won't be able to do it if I think you're listenin'. And if you want me to do it, the only way I can do it, I don't want you to hear that. He's real close to havin' his mind made up. But you can't listen to what I'm gonna say to him."

"Okay," Carlucci said, showing himself to her so she could see he no longer had the phone on or in his hand. "I promise. I won't listen to the rest of your conversation with Rennie. Okay?"

"Okay," she said.

As promised, he didn't listen.

A half hour later, Carlucci, Fischetti, Reseta, and Canoza collared Rennie on Township Road Six out of sight of the house, after he'd slipped out. He was standing by the side of the road, tugging on his penis, blowing on his hands and rubbing it when they pulled up.

"What're you guys doin'? Hey, I'm waitin' for my sister. Who're you guys? I'm gonna tell George, he's gonna be really pissed off if I don't come home. I'm gonna tell him, I'm gonna tell George. Let me go! You guys better not've done nothin' with my sister, I'll tell George, he'll beat the shit outta ya, all of youns, he'll kill ya. He'll get a fuckin' baseball bat and kill youns fuckers, every one of youns!"

"Aw shut up and put your hands behind ya," Fischetti said.

"Maybe you oughta tell him put his dick away first," Canoza said.

Five minutes later, after Fischetti had driven Rennie out of sight and chained him to the grille between the seats, he came trotting back across the snow-dusted field behind the house. June waited to ring the bell at the front door of her parents' home until Carlucci told her that Fischetti was back and had taken a position at the northwest corner of the house. Reseta was standing at the southwest corner of the house, Canoza at the northeast corner.

Six minutes later, June rang the bell and George opened the door. Carlucci started talking immediately, asking about his mother, saying he'd just come from the hospital, guiding June ahead of him into the house, gently forcing June into George and causing him to back up in spite of himself.

"I was just up there checkin' on my mother, you know? She had a heart attack this morning. Not real bad, just a mild one, not like your mother, and then here comes June when I'm on my way out. Says she needed a ride, so I brought her out here. How is she, your mother? Any better? She must be or you wouldn't have brought her home. Must be gettin' along pretty good, right? Okay if I see her? Pay my respects? I really didn't get a chance to say everything I wanted to say, you know, after the funeral."

In a matter of seconds, they were across the living room, George scowling suspiciously but not able to get a word in edge-wise because when Carlucci wasn't talking Juney was and between them they'd more or less forced him into the makeshift bedroom where the dining room had been. Then, after they'd all stood around and looked at Mrs. Randa wheezing and gasping in her bed, and after Carlucci had learned from George that he'd been calling his brother Frankie all day and nobody at work knew where he was and he was getting the same stupid response from his answering machine, Carlucci nodded for George to step out into the kitchen. George followed Carlucci into the kitchen and immediately changed his tone and attitude.

He'd been fuming quietly while they were all standing around his mother's bed, whispering yes and no to their questions but now he was furious and shaking his finger in Carlucci's face and straining to keep his voice down, sputtering and spitting, "Who the fuck're you to come into this house at a time like this, you scrawny little motherfucker, I oughta throw you through that fuckin' door!"

His tone took another abrupt change when Carlucci put the Smith & Wesson .22 against his nose and backed him against the refrigerator and told him to turn around, kneel, put his hands on top of his head and his nose against the refrigerator door, and not to make another sound. Carlucci then put the handcuffs on him, right wrist first, while reading two small square samplers, red letters on a green background, held to the freezer door with a magnet that said, "Mothrs Cook with Lov" and "My Mothrs Kichen."

Then George began to bleat, "Ma! Ma! Ma! Ma!" He sounded like a goat.

Carlucci parked in the alley, went to the side door of Rocksburg Bowl, headed for the lounge, and found Joe Barone sitting in the booth nearest the kitchen talking to a waitress. Carlucci sat down in time to hear the waitress telling Barone that he'd had too much and how was he getting home and maybe she ought to be calling a cab for him.

Barone caught sight of Carlucci and said to the waitress, "Aw c'mon, you wanna sleep at my place, you're gonna have to do better'n playin' to my best interests. I'm not that easy—"

"Oh shut up, Barone, Jesus," the waitress said, whacking him across the shoulder with the back of her hand.

"Yo, Sergeant Carlucci, of the Unroyal Rocksburg Unmounted Police, who goes there? Sit down and gimme the password. You say failure, you win an all-expense-paid trip for two for the weekend to Rocksburg. You say toilet, you win two weeks in Rocksburg. You say nothing, you convince our judges you're incapable of human speech, the audience here in the studio and our viewers at home will know you were born here, you're gonna die here, you have the intelligence of a barstool. Vinyl. Patched up with duct tape."

Carlucci looked at the waitress. "You know what he's talkin' about?"

"Oh don't ask her, she doesn't know. I'm who knows—"

"Only thing you better know, Barone, is somebody else better be drivin' when you leave."

"I'm who knows," Barone said. "And I'm tellin' ya, I'm

drunk and I'm in Rocksburg and the only thing worse would be if it was rainin' and I was in a bowling alley."

The waitress rolled her eyes at Carlucci. "Hey, genius, you are in a bowlin' alley. And it's snowin'—still snowin'?"

Carlucci nodded.

"I'm in a bowling alley? Oh man. I must not've said nothin'."

"Huh?"

"Nothing, you know? If you say nothing, you already know you're doin' life in Rocksburg. No chance for parole."

"Uh, you said you had some information? About Blasco?"

"Ah. Yes. And now, this. This just in. These are just some of the stories we're working on here in the newsroom . . . Barone continues to hold himself hostage in a bowling alley . . . Barone continues to bore the silly shit out of readers everywhere—"

"Uh, excuse me? Information? You called me? About Blasco? So far all I'm hearin' is you're drunk and feelin' sorry for yourself."

"Me? Oh, say not so. No. I have far more important things to say than that—"

"Well say 'em."

"Huh? Oh. First thing I wanna say is, uh, those words about Bobby that appeared in the *Rocksburg Gazette*? Remember them? Well, those were the most stilted, boring, inaccurate bullshit that have ever appeared under my name. Or my name isn't Daffy Duck."

"Uh, I think we should do this some other time, okay?" Carlucci started to get up.

"No, no, no. Sit down, sit. Don't leave, please. C'mon."

Carlucci slipped back into the booth again and asked for a Diet Pepsi when the waitress wanted to know if she could bring him anything.

"And you're shut off, Barone," the waitress said, "so don't even try, okay?"

"Hey. I already had one mother, you know? And if you work it right, one mother's more than enough to drive anybody nuts." Barone looked at Carlucci and said, "We still in Rocks-burg?"

"I still think we oughta do this some other time."

"No no, no. No, fuck, you're here now, stick around, I got things to say. Hey, Trish, hey, Dolly, hey—what the hell's her name, you know what her name is? You see her, okay? Give her a wave and a holler, tell her bring me a cupa coffee and a glassa ice water, 'kay?"

Carlucci stared again into Barone's bleary eyes and wondered again what he was supposed to be doing here.

"You know," Barone said, peering intently into Carlucci's eyes, "if somebody put a gun to my head and said, bet—which father-in-law would it have been, I'da bet two all the way. One was not the one."

"Huh?"

"Only reason one was ever pissed at Bobby, believe me, was 'cause he broke his elbow and wrecked his career. Only reason. Bobby coulda beat the shit outta his daughter every night of the week and a doubleheader on Sundays and holidays and number one wouldn'ta give a shit. Not one drop a sweat off his balls would he'd've given."

"And this is interesting because?"

" 'Cause he was a prick groupie. He was a groupie before there were groupies. Twenty years before anybody outside of *Rolling Stone* thought of the word."

"Hey, Mister Barone, is there a point to this?"

"Absolutely. I wanna tell you 'bout Bobby. Not that shit was in the paper. I'm 'shamed of that. That wasn't Bobby. That was PR bullshit for the tourists. Wasn't me either. Some boring ass-hole wrote that shit. Shit's embarrassing. Gotta live with that shit forever—or till people throw the paper away. Which they already did. But my stomach's been pumpin' acid ever since I let myself be talked into writin' that shit. So I'm gonna tell you."

"Tell me what?"

"About Bobby, what the fuck, what's it—too loud in here or somethin'? You want me to talk louder?"

"No no, there's nothin' wrong with your volume, it's your content I'm havin' trouble with."

"Hey, Dolly! How 'bout some coffee over here, 'kay? Some water too? Lotsa ice, 'kay?"

The waitress rolled her eyes as she walked by. "Darlene, Barone, okay? Darlene?"

"Dolly, Darlene, what the hell. Go to bed with a woman a couple times, next thing you know, expects you to know her name—no no, that's a joke. That's a very ancient joke, joke's got arthritis, you know, honest, man, I've never been to bed with this woman, I was just tryin', you know, lighten things up. I mean, Christ, your face, you look like you'd have to warm up ten degrees to die. You always so serious?"

"I, uh, I just arrested two of the three brothers, you know? For Blasco?"

"You did? When? I didn't hear anything on the scanner. Today?"

"Yeah, today. Spent most of the day plannin' and replannin', organizin', reorganizin', dealin' with one thing after another I'm not really capable of dealin' with. Finally got 'em booked and arraigned, and every step of the way I'm thinkin' their mother could be having a heart attack over what I was doin'. I mean, at one point, while I was in the middle of arrestin' her number three son, he starts callin' for her, sounded like a goddamn goat, he's goin', Ma, Ma, and she gets outta her bed, comes out in the kitchen, her daughter's tryin' to tell her to get back in bed, I got her son on the floor on his knees, just finished handcuffin' him, here she comes, into the kitchen, her lips're blue, her fingers're blue, she starts askin' me what am I doin', am I crazy? Am I a son of a bitch? Am I the son of the devil? Don't I understand God just took her husband away, now I'm puttin' handcuffs on her son, who the hell am

I anyway, what kind of dog shit am I? Yeah. She actually said those words, yeah—'What kind of dog shit are you?'

"Remember now, she's already had one heart attack, and she checks herself out of the hospital about seven-thirty this morning, and there I am in her house, like eighteen forty-five approximately, six forty-five, I'm arrestin' her son. What she didn't know was I'd already arrested her other son, and the state cops had collared her oldest son in Pittsburgh about the same time she was checkin' herself outta the hospital.

"So when you called me little while ago tonight, I'd just come back from the hospital for the second time today—'cause the first time was with my own mother, that was like about six-thirty this morning. My mother had an anxiety attack, six o'clock this morning, that's how my day started, debatin' whether my mother's havin' a heart attack or not. So then, uh, Missus Randa, after I arrested her middle son, and she was askin' me whether I was the son of the devil, naturally, I mean what else, right? Her heart attacks her again, which naturally causes her son to turn around and start kickin' me 'cause naturally I'm the one who caused her to have this latest heart attack, 'cause naturally her son didn't have anything to do with anything, none of her sons, 'cause all her sons are all good little boys, fuckin' bunch of perverts, they raped their sister for years, her daughter you know, which she refused to believe when her daughter tried to tell her about it, so, uh, no, in answer to your question, Mister Barone, it hasn't been one of my favorite days so far, and, uh, here I am with you, c'mon up, c'mon up, gotta talk, got all this information about Bobby Blasco. And so here I am and so far, all I've heard is a drunk runnin' his mouth. So, uh, yeah, you could say I'm kinda serious right now. Although I might use a different word. Serious doesn't really cover it somehow, you know?"

"Here's your coffee, Anthony, okay? And your ice water? Giorgio?"

"Huh? Anthony? Giorgio? What the hell, what're you callin' me that for—"

"Oh. That's not your name? Imagine that. Well mine isn't Dolly either. And if you're screwin' somebody for six weeks, the least you could do, you oughta be able to remember their name. I mean one night I could understand, but six weeks?"

Barone sniffed and ran his tongue over his teeth and stared glumly at the coffee. "Right. Darlene. Right."

"Oh. Now you remember. Too late, buddy boy. You won't have to worry about rememberin' it ever again, okay? And you stiff me on the check I'll call the cops, swear to God."

"You won't have to call 'em, he's sittin' right there," Barone said, gesturing weakly toward Carlucci.

Carlucci shrugged at Darlene, who brushed her cheek with the back of her hand and hurried into the kitchen.

After a long moment during which Barone stirred half-and-half and a half-spoon of sugar into his coffee and continued to stare at it, he finally said, "There was a movie I saw long time ago, wasn't great, but fair, you know. Better than fair. But it had one of the saddest lines in it I ever heard. *Requiem for a Heavyweight.* Rod Serling wrote it. Remember him? *Twilight Zone?* The character, whose name I can't remember right now, Jackie Gleason played him in the movie. There's a scene, he's on this cobblestone street, it's rainin', and it's at night, real late, and he says, to himself he says this, he was just talkin' to somebody and they leave and he says, 'I'm in Pittsburgh, and it's rainin'.' So here I am. I'm in Rocksburg, and it's snowin' and I'm in a bowlin' alley, and the woman I been goin' to bed with, I can't remember her name, and I just lied about that, tried to make a joke about it. To impress a cop. Ah, fuck . . . where was I?"

"Still in Rocksburg I think."

Barone drank the coffee and the ice water, alternating sips, first the coffee, then the water, until he'd finished both, drinking them fast. He asked Darlene if she'd please bring him one more of each and then he gave her a twenty-dollar bill when she brought the refills and told her to keep the change. Darlene shot him a look that said, you think all it's gonna take to straighten this out is change from a twenty, if you weren't so drunk, buster, I'd dump the coffee in your lap. She brought him the change on the run and was gone before he could try to force it on her.

Barone shrugged and screwed up his face. "Some things are so embarrassing, there aren't any words for how embarrassing they are, especially when you caused another person to be embarrassed." He was talking slowly, pronouncing all the words carefully. "Sometimes, just knowing that you caused that kind of embarrassment, nothing sobers you up faster than that. Lots faster than coffee or ice water, believe me."

"Yeah," Carlucci said. "You're probably right."

"No probably about it. I'm gettin' sober real fast right now."

"I still wouldn't try drivin'."

"I'll get a ride. Hey, Darlene? Refills please?" Barone rubbed his face hard with both hands and shook his shoulders and yawned. "Where was I—oh. Yeah, father-in-law number one. Uh, he would not've blinked twice if Bobby beat his daughter. All he cared about was for a while there he was related to a major-leaguer ballplayer. He was like all those old dags you know, wanted their boy kids to grow up to be Joe DiMaggio? Ever know any of them?"

Carlucci shook his head.

"Well. Unfortunately I did. And that guy, man, he was a true fanatic. Came to all the games, high school, Boys Club, all the mill teams, you know, in the old merchants leagues they used to have around here. Used to drag a folding chair around with him. And he would've traded his daughter even up for Bobby.

" 'Cause he loved the way Bobby pitched, loved it that Bobby used to throw at guys' heads. Showed 'em who was boss, took command of the inside part of the plate, it's a pitcher's right to take the inside, that's his, it don't belong to the batter, the inside belongs to the pitcher—shit, he knew all the stupid clichés. Like Moses wrote 'em. Thou shalt take command of the inside part of the plate."

Darlene brought more refills, and Barone looked at her as apologetically as anyone Carlucci had ever seen, but Darlene wasn't having any. She slid the money for the coffee off the table without a glance at Barone.

Barone looked at Carlucci and said, after she'd left, "Why do you think it is that people who need affection the most are the clumsiest at getting it, huh?"

"No idea," Carlucci said. He wondered about that himself. Many times. Especially in the last couple of days.

"Me neither—obviously. Anyway. All those people? Huh? Those people thought they knew Bobby? Didn't have a clue. He was the most contrary bastard I've ever known. He was thoughtful, intelligent, ignorant, stubborn, two-faced, hypocritical, self-centered in the extreme, one minute the stingiest fucker I ever saw, the next minute the most generous. Whatever you thought about him, whenever you thought you knew what he was gonna say or do, you didn't. One night, we were in Birmingham, second year in OB—"

"In what?"

"OB, Organized Ball. Don't ask, I don't know, that's just what everybody connected with professional baseball used to call professional baseball. Probably still do. Like every other kind isn't organized the way it's supposed to be or something, I never did figure it out. Anyway, we were in this roadhouse somewhere, and he starts speechin'—Bobby was always speechin' about something, he had a fucking contrary opinion about everything—but this night, there was just him and me. Usually he needed a lot bigger audience than that. But this night, he took off on what a joke sports was—not sports. Professional sports. And his definition was, if you had uniforms, somebody was making money on it. If somebody made money on the manufacture, distribution, and sale of the uniforms, piss on the arbitrary status of the people wearing them. If money changed hands before the game started, the name of the game wasn't baseball, it was commerce. Period.

"He bitched for about a half hour about what a fraud the whole thing was, professional sports. This big joke on everybody. The fans were all idiots full of bogus loyalty to a bunch of mercenary jocks, the whole charade based on some phoney competition manufactured by a bunch of rich pricks who couldn't get it up anymore.

"Remember now, up to then, all we ever talked about was how we were goin' to the major leagues, that was the only life for us. Only life worth living. From the time we were in ninth grade. Bobby said one time if he didn't make it to the majors, he'd sooner do a swan dive off the Rocksburg Bridge than know he was gonna have to wake up like all the dagos and hunkies in Rocksburg. Every day of their lives all they knew was they were either goin' into the mill or down a mine shaft. There was no fucking way on this planet Bobby B. was gonna get up in the morning and know that's all he was gonna do with his life, no way he was gonna wind up like his father and all his uncles. Had four uncles, hated every one of 'em almost as much as he hated his father. Course, that was before everything shut down around here."

"Hated his father, huh?"

"Intensely. Only way he'd talk about his father was with contempt, hatred, anger, resentment, bitterness, you name the kind of animus there is, that's what he had for his father. And it never went away. Never went to his father's funeral. Went to his father's grave once. Know what he did?"

"I'm not gonna guess."

"Took a six-pack out there, sat on the grave, drank all six cans, and then he stood up and let it flow. His words. 'I let it flow.'

"So back to this barbecue in Alabama. He's carrying on about all this artificial aggression and fabricated emotion and sublimated war, he was throwing words and phrases like that around for a half hour. Finally I said what the fuck's with you, where'd you get all this, this artificial aggression, sublimated war? He said he'd been thinking, that's all, he didn't get it from anybody, got it himself, just lookin' at things one at a time, rollin' 'em over in his mind, and the only thing that surprised him was, was why I hadn't thought of any of that stuff myself, smart as he thought I was.

"He said the last time we played baseball, true baseball, not that shit we were playin' then, but the true game, was when we were playing for the Herrington Hill Hawks against the Race Street Roadrunners. No uniforms. T-shirts, jeans, sneakers, no umpires, no fans. Just us. Callin' balls and strikes on ourselves. Did I understand that was the absolute last time we—the players—were in control of the game, the last time we were true amateurs, nobody was makin' money off us, we were playin' strictly for the game? Just us and the ball and the bats and the bases and the foul lines. Playing 'cause we loved it. Did I understand that?

"Looking back on it, I mean, I wish I had a tape of that speech. I mean, it was the most impassioned speech about the corruption of sports I'm ever gonna hear. But then the next time he pitched? You know what happened? This guy who was carrying on about all this artificial aggression, this manufactured emotion, this sublimated war? So a bunch of fat pricks with spongy dicks could make money off us? Him? Hey. About the second inning, somebody hit one out foul on him, and man, he starts hollering at the ump, 'Gimme a ball, gimme the fuckin' ball, c'mon, we gonna play this fuckin' game for three hours or you wanna go home sometime tonight, little boy blue, gimme the fuckin' ball.' Smoke was coming out of his ears over a fucking loud foul ball, and this was like two days after he'd made this speech about what a joke professional sports was. And the next pitch, man, he buzzed one off that guy's chin, and I thought, yeah, well, so much for artificial aggression. Let's hear it for manufactured emotion.

"And then there was the time some clown was tryin' to imitate Marlon Brando, you know, in that scene in the backseat of the car in *On the Waterfront?* Where Terry Malloy's talkin' with his brother, Charlie the Gent? Brando's talkin' with Rod Steiger, remember? That contender speech everybody loves, where he's saying, 'I coulda been somebody, I coulda been a contender,' somethin' like that, I can never remember it myself. So anyway, Bobby hears this guy, and man he goes off on him, he says, 'What, you think Brando wrote those words? Brando just said 'em, he didn't write 'em. Terry Malloy is who says 'em. And Budd Schulberg is the guy who wrote 'em—try to get it straight, asshole.' And I'm sittin' there goin', Huh? This is the guy slept through every history class we were ever in? Would've flunked every test in high school if it wasn't for me and three or four other people helpin' him cheat? Including coaches? And teachers? He's now carryin' on about the difference between fiction and fact? Between who wrote something and who said it? Where's this shit come from? Know what he said?

"He said, 'Listen, I'm not talkin' fiction and fact. I'm talkin' fantasy and reality. 'Cause we're in the fantasy business, you and me. But trust me, fantasy is not reality. On the field, that's reality. Up in the stands, that's fantasy. You don't know the difference, those fuckers'll eat you alive.'

"And then another time, we were in some other roadhouse waiting for somebody to fix a flat on the bus, and he starts telling this bartender about how he was in Korea, you know, in combat, in the Korean War, how he was over in Korea with the Marines. And I'm looking at him, like, what the hell're you talking about now? When the fuck were you ever in the Marines, number one, and when the fuck were you ever out of the country, number two? But he was telling this redneck bartender the most convincing story you ever heard about when he was in Korea in the Marines. He's going on and on about which outfit he was in and where they were and how cold it was and what it was like to see all your friends killed and wounded, and I'm thinking, this is the same guy who was talking fantasy and reality?

"Now he had a brother in the Marines, was in Korea. Aldo. That was true. I knew that. And he got seriously fucked up over there, but Bobby, I mean Bobby had been in school with me—he'd been practically everywhere with me since the ninth grade."

"He had a brother named Aldo?"

"Yeah. Died about ten years ago, longer maybe. Spent his life in a vets hospital. Was never right after he got home. I don't think he was hurt physically, but mentally, you know, he was never right. Bobby used to write to him, call him, go see him a lot, and then, you know, after we lost touch, Bobby and me I mean, I don't know what happened. Yeah. Poor Aldo. Bobby called him Odo. When he was a kid, couldn't pronounce the 'A' and the 'l' together."

"And this is interesting because, uh, why now?"

"Because of what Bobby was telling this bartender. The most convincing goddamn lies you ever heard. I said what was all that about, you were never in the Marines, you were never even in California, forget Korea. And he said assholes'll believe anything. I said I'm not talking about him, I'm talking about you. 'Cause who was the guy made that speech about knowin' the difference between fantasy and reality, who was that?

"And he gave me this big goofy smile, and said don't worry about it. What you have to worry about is how to make your feet go faster, you're the slowest guy in the Red Sox organization, and your bat's almost as slow as your feet, you don't pick up some speed, man, you ain't gonna go to the majors with me, and I would hate that 'cause you're the only person understands me.

"And I said, wrong, man, wrong, 'cause there's nobody on this planet understands you. And he put his arm around my shoulder and gave me the kind of look I used to see between the Boyle brothers, on Chestnut Avenue, sometimes I'd catch 'em lookin' at each other. They'd give each other this look like they knew something and nobody else did. And I didn't understand that when I was a kid, but later on I started to understand it, or I thought I did—I think I do, I mean—corny as it sounds—that was love, man. Love like you don't get from anybody but your brother if you know he's looking out for you and you're looking out for him.

"Course, I'm making a huge supposition because I never had a brother. And Bobby knew that, and so anytime he wanted to shut me up, all he had to do was give me this look like I was his brother, and I was done for. I was easy. Go 'head, Bobby, whatever you say, man, okay with me. Just let me keep on believing this fucking delusion I'm your brother, what do I know?

"So what do you think, couple weeks ago in the *Sunday Post-Gazette*, there was this story, 'In Closing' was the headline, about how the O.J. Simpson trial is the latest courtroom drama to hold a nation spellbound and test a lawyer's power to move a jury, and I'm reading it, I mean, it was uncanny. Story's about four trials, and they ran four pictures. There's one of a bunch of Nazis at the war crimes trial at Nuremberg after World War II; there's one of Mohandas Gandhi; there's another one of Clarence Darrow and William Jennings Bryan, and the last one's fucking Gregory Peck! A fucking actor! From the movie *To Kill a Mockingbird*. And the story's about four trials. The trial of Mohandas Gandhi in 1922, when the British put him on trial in India for sedition. And then there's the war crimes trial in Germany after World War II. And then there's the Scopes monkey trial in Tennessee in 1925. And the last trial they put in this story is one straight out of a fucking novel! For which the only picture they can provide is of one of the actors after Hollywood takes the novel and turns it into a movie."

"And this relates to Blasco, how, exactly?"

"How? Hey, what you have at the *Post-Gazette* is you have at least one writer and at least one editor who think there's nothing wrong with putting a fictional trial in the same story with all these factual trials and it's like, hey, don't anybody worry about this confusion, this blurring between fact and fiction.

"Remember what I said about Bobby? Going nuts over this guy saying it was Marlon Brando who said those words? In that scene in the movie, remember? I can hear him now—"

Carlucci held up his hands and said, "I remember, I remember, but, uh, why're you tellin' me this again? What's the relevance here?"

"What's the relevance? Come on, you hear all these people complaining about the violence on TV? They're complaining about how much is on there, but far as I can see, no way they're complainin' about the right thing. They're missin' the point entirely. I mean, imagine how hard it is for kids to tell the difference between what's real on TV and what isn't? Imagine you're three years old, you're trying to figure out whether what you're watching is reruns of *Police Story* or *Cops* or *Stories of the Highway Patrol* or the six o'clock news? Imagine that TV's your baby-sitter and you're trying to separate what's real from what isn't. You're a cop—I mean, just think of that."

"I have thought about it. Lots."

"Well what I'm saying is, the first person I ever heard complain about this was Bobby. That's what he was talking about, this huge confusion about what's fiction, what's fact, I never heard those things at that time. This was back in the early fifties, there wasn't anybody talking about things like that then—not to my knowledge. Not that I was doing all that much reading back then. But Bobby?

"Like it was supposed to make some huge fucking difference to him whether he was wearing the uniform of the Elyria Red Sox or the Birmingham Barons or the Louisville Colonels or the Boston Red Sox. Sometimes at the start of the game after he'd warm up, he'd look up in the stands and start laughing. I'd go out there and ask him what was so funny, he'd say, 'I was just thinkin' about high school, all those stupid-ass pep rallies, all that bullshit about school spirit and community spirit and how we gotta win it for dear old Rocksburg High? These bozos actually think I'm out here makin' bone chips in my elbow for dear ol' Birmingham. I could be in Caracas, Venezuela, for all I give a shit, but those fuckheads think I'm doin' this for them.' And then he'd look at me, and that fast, I mean, in an instant, you could see his whole body changing, his eyes getting hard, sometime I swore his eyes would actually change color. That fast he wasn't thinking about the fans anymore, he was looking over my shoulder at the next guy up to bat, man, and his eyes'd turn almost black, and from that second on, he was somebody else, I swear, everything he'd just said about the fuckheads in the stands, that was history. 'Cause now he was no longer in Birmingham, or Louisville, or wherever. Now he was on the mound, he was Bobby B., the Brushback Kid, and there was some asshole with a piece of wood in his hands trying to take his balls off, and he'd be thinking, just lemme get the first two over and then I'm gonna put dirt on this clown's ass. And he'd say to me, tell him don't dig in, and I'd be sayin', 'Forget that, huh? You got seven guys behind ya, and I'm behind him, you don't need to knock him down.' And he'd say, 'Go catch, I decide who stands and who falls. I'm the Brushback Kid, I fly with the birds of prey'—he actually said those words once, 'I fly with the birds of prey.' Man, I laughed out loud. He got so pissed, he didn't talk to me for two days.

"On the other hand, I can't tell you how happy I was just to be catchin' him, how glad I was I didn't have to drag a bat up there and pretend I was gonna try to hit him. 'Cause I knew from the first time I ever caught him, this was not a guy I ever wanted to bat against. 'Cause Bobby, somebody hit the ball hard off him? I don't mean they got a hit. They just had to hit it hard, you know? Solid? I mean I never met a pitcher who was real casual about gettin' hit hard, but most of them, as long as it's an out, they don't care how hard it was hit. Not Bobby. With him, man, it was life or death. You hit me hard, fucker, you think you're gonna get away with that? You're tryin' to butcher me, you're tryin' to cut a piece of me off while I'm still alive, you wait, fucker. It might take me two innings, or two games, or two weeks, but you'll come up there again. And I'll remember the day you sliced off a piece of me, you miserable piss ant. And he'd nail him. Bigger'n shit. Soon as he got two strikes on him, man, here come the fastball, right at their front shoulder and movin' inside.

"God, some of 'em, you could hear 'em whimperin'. It was awful. Really. Sickening. He didn't even look at 'em. All he wanted was the ball. Soon as they went down, he'd start asking for the ball. 'Yo, Mister Umpire, gimme the ball, man, let's get this game movin' here. Get him outta there. He can't move any faster'n that, tell him go home play softball with the fat boys, what's he doin' tryin' to play with us men?' And he'd have this smirk on his face, honest to God, sometimes I'd swear even the umps'd wanna hit him."

Carlucci tried to make sense of what he was hearing, but he'd never played baseball. It had never attracted his attention. He'd seen a few games; he'd gone to see the Pittsburgh Pirates play at Three Rivers Stadium with his father, but they were distant memories, mostly of his father trying to act like a father taking a son to a ball game. Carlucci's most vivid, most intense memory was that his father's heart hadn't been in it, that the whole thing had been something his father had thought he ought to be doing. Mostly what Carlucci remembered was his father's expression when he'd learned the price of hot dogs and soft drinks and fresh roasted peanuts.

Barone's head was dropping now. His eyelids were drooping, his mouth was slack, he was looking weary. Then his eyes filled up and spilled over. He snatched up a wet paper napkin that had been under his drink and covered his eyes. He held it there for a long moment and when he took it away, he said, "Last game he pitched in Louisville, we were making a beer run afterwards, he was all gunned up, he'd pitched a hell of a game, two-hitter, both of 'em little bloopers, barely made it to the outfield. Otherwise,

he stuck the bats up their asses. No runs, two hits, no walks, fourteen K's, but he just had to hit this one guy—"

"Excuse me? Fourteen what? K's did you say?"

"Yeah. Strikeouts. K is the symbol for strikeout, you know,
when you're scorin' the game—man, you really don't know anything about the game, do you?"

"I don't recall sayin' that I did."

"Okay, never mind, fourteen strikeouts. But he just had to
hit this one guy. Little fucker. Number eight hitter, guy was hittin' maybe one-ninety tops. Only place he was goin' was home,
you know? But in the third inning, he got the first hit off Bobby,
little dinky rainbow just over the glove of the third baseman, ball's
hit so weak, it hit the outfield grass, took maybe two hops and
stopped. But in the ninth inning he comes up again, we're up five-
zip, Bobby's just toyin' with these guys, he's tormentin' 'em, makin'
'em look foolish, but this guy comes up, man, first fucking pitch,
Bobby drills him, right where his jaw hinged. Right below his ear.
Guy was rollin' around in the dirt, he's cryin', man, I heard the
bone crunch, God, it was sickening. Bobby comes in maybe
twenty feet toward the plate, he's got this smirk on his face, hollerin' for the ball, just like always.

"I didn't say a word till way after the game. We were in the
parking lot of this joint. And I just let it out. I mean, since the
ninth grade, I'd never said ten words about him hitting guys, but
I couldn't stand it, man, to hit that guy? I mean that was the fucking lowest man. I said, 'You think you're so hard, you think you're
so tough, you think you could bowl ten pins with your balls, but
you're not a man. When you hit that guy tonight, you were a gutless bastard lowlife prick and I'm ashamed I'm your catcher. I'm
ashamed all those guys you hit think I was the one was callin' all
those knockdown pitches, man, all those brushbacks. That's what
gets me. 'Cause that's bullshit. But that's what people're gonna
think of me, 'cause I'm done. The Red Sox ain't gonna carry my
slow ass just to catch you, that's not gonna happen. You're goin' to

the major leagues and I'm goin' to spring trainin' maybe but I'll be comin' right back down here, but I want you to know what I think of you, man.

" 'Fucking odds for the defense at worst at nine to four, most of the time they're nine to one, and you know what you're throwin', straight ball, curveball, change-ups, and you know where you're throwin' 'em, but they're just guessin' what you're gonna throw, but those fucking odds ain't good enough for you, you gutless fuck, you gotta hit people. But you can't just throw at their backs or the thighs, you can't just throw it at their heads, man, you gotta terrorize people, you gotta throw it at their front shoulder, behind 'em, man, so when they're droppin' and divin', they're droppin' and divin' right down into it. You terrorize people, you rub their noses in their fear. There ain't a guy comes up there ain't scared of you, and you fucking love it, you eat it up'—oh man, I went on and on, 'cause I was really pissed he hit that guy.

"So naturally he smacked me. Punched me right on the point of my chin. Snapped my teeth together, man, fuckin' electricity went off in my mouth. And while I'm stumblin' around, my head's fulla bees, what's he do? He drags me inside, sits me down, gives me this speech. I'll never forget it. He said, 'Barone, don't ever talk to me about fear, 'cause you don't know anything about fear. You've never seen fear till you see your big brother so scared of your old man he runs away and enlists in the fuckin' Marines. And then the next time you see him, all you can see is he's so scared he's not right and he's never gonna be right, no matter if he lives to be a thousand. But now he doesn't only gotta deal with his fear, every time he looks at his father, he gotta deal with his father's contempt. 'Cause his father goes to see him and drags me along and torments him. Laughs at him, calls him names. Called him what you just called me. Gutless. Until you've ever seen that, don't you ever talk to me about fear. 'Cause you think it's all about this stupid fuckin' game. That's why you ain't goin' to the majors with me. It ain't 'cause your ass is slow, it's 'cause you think what it's about is this fuckin' game. It ain't about this fuckin' game. It's about feedin' the fantasy machine. Everybody thinks fan is short for fanatic, but it ain't. Fan is short for fantasy, the fanatics' fantastic fantasy machine. That's what it's about. Every time I hit somebody they think they could do it. Every time I make somebody look stupid chasin' a curveball, they think they could do it. But those fuckin' clowns ever walked out on that mound, looked up and saw all those other clowns sittin' there watchin' 'em, they'd puke their guts out. But they see me do it, in that fantastic machine they think is their mind, they think they can do it. That's what professional sports is, asshole, keepin' the Wally Wannabes in the seats, payin' for the parkin' spaces, buyin' all that shit food, that's all it is, it don't have one fucking thing in the world to do with what you do behind the plate or what I do out on the mound, they wouldn't have a clue what we were talkin' about, huh? When we're up? When we're talkin' about who's comin' up for them? You know as well as I do they wouldn't know what the fuck we were talkin' about. But don't you ever talk to me about fear again. I've seen fear. It don't look nothin' like those guys look draggin' those bats up there tryin' to hit me.'

"Then he put his arm around me, and he kept buying me beer till I got sloppy drunk, and I didn't say another goddamn word about him hittin' anybody. Me or anybody else. I just sat there and listened to him tell me how sad he was 'cause I didn't have balls of steel like him. But you know what the truth was, Detective? Truth was, man, Bobby B. was as close to the major leagues as I was ever gonna get. And I didn't have the guts to let go of that delusion. So he could've told me anything and I would've sat there and ate it up. Just like I always did. 'Cause the truth was, I was the biggest fan Bobby B. ever had. 'Cause Bobby was as close to greatness as I was ever gonna get. When he was on, man, which was most of the time, catchin' him was the easiest thing I ever did in my life. The easiest and the most fun. You know what they call a perfect game in baseball?"

Carlucci shrugged. "No runs, hits, walks, or errors. Right?"

"Right. But it's perfect because it's defensive perfection. You achieve perfection by preventing the other team from gettin' into the game offensively. Nobody talks about perfection in any other sport. There's no perfect game in football or basketball or hockey or golf or tennis or darts or horseshoes. Only game anybody ever uses that word, perfect, man, that's baseball.

"And nobody else ever let me get close to perfect, man. Only Bobby. The only one. Before he hurt his elbow, the only three regular season games in his entire pitching career that I didn't catch were the three he pitched for the Red Sox. I caught all the rest. All the no-hitters, all the one-hitters, all the two-hitters, all the three-hitters, all the shutouts, all the strikeouts, man, for seven fucking years I was allowed to participate in greatness. And—this is the important part—three perfect games, man. Three! One in high school, one in Birmingham, and one in Louisville. You show me a catcher was ever lucky enough to catch one perfect game, man."

Carlucci called the waitress over and asked for more coffee and more ice water for Barone. He shook his head when Darlene asked if he wanted another Diet Pepsi. All he wanted to do was leave. Because all the "information" Joe Barone just could not wait to tell him wasn't about anything except Joe Barone. It certainly wasn't going to be of any use legally about Bobby Blasco.

Barone sighed heavily and wistfully and said, "You know, I kept telling myself, one day I was gonna write a book about him. Bobby B., the Brushback Kid. I have notebooks filled with stuff about him. Most of 'em my scribbling's so boozy incoherent I can't make sense out of it. But when I heard about him, you know, when I heard what happened, I said, Jesus, of course, how else would you expect Bobby B. to die? There couldn't be any other end to his story, man. But then I thought about tryin' to write it?

That he got killed with a bat he probably stole from Ted Williams? Christ, who'd believe that? That's too fucking corny.

"But that's not why I can't write it. That's bullshit. Truth is, I don't have the guts. That's the truth. I couldn't write—you know, what I just told you about me gettin' up after he knocked me down in the parkin' lot, and goin' inside with him and sittin' there, listenin' to him tell me why I was never goin' to the majors. I mean, Jesus Christ, everybody's got a limit, you know?

"But, hell, man, here I am, livin' my own nightmare, my own bad movie. I'm in Rocksburg, I'm sixty-one years old, I'm back in the minor leagues of journalism, I'm drunk in a bowlin' alley . . . how could I write that? No way. Can't."

"C'mon," Carlucci said, standing, "I'll give ya a ride home."

"Nah, that's okay. Darlene'll take me."

"Don't bet on that," Carlucci said. "Looks pretty pissed to me."

"Pissed is what she's good at. And what I'm good at apparently, is, uh, you know, findin' people who're good at that. 'Cause, uh, what the fuck? I've been pissed at myself for havin' slow feet for, hell, must be at least forty years now. See ya around, Detective. Go 'head, I won't drive. Promise."

"Suit yourself. Good night," Carlucci said. On the way out he told Darlene that if she had anything left in her to care about Barone, she should call the cops to keep him from driving. She said she would. None too happily, but she did.

Carlucci fumbled with the buttons on his shirt. He kept ducking back into the bathroom to look at himself in the mirror, hoping each time to see something other than the wide-eyed frightened face gawking back at him. God, he thought, I wasn't this scared when I collared George Randa.

"Where you goin' again?" his mother called to him from the kitchen. "If you ain't workin', where you goin' now? How'm I s'posed to find you if I want you?"

"You're gonna be all right, Ma, you're not gonna have to find me."

"Now how the hell do you know that? What're you, psychic now?"

"No, Ma. Just don't forget to take your pill, okay? Next one's at eight, okay? Don't forget to take it, please?"

"Turn me into a goddamn drug addict, these pills. How do I know these pills ain't gonna turn me into some kinda goddamn drug addict? Huh? Would you care? I think you'd be happy I was in some kinda stupor somewhere."

Oh Jesus, Mary, and fucking Joseph, please. "Ma, those pills were prescribed for you by a doctor you said you liked—"

"Just 'cause I liked him doesn't mean he knows what he's doin'."

"A doctor you liked and trusted, you trusted him, you told me you trusted him, you said you believed the man was not capable of givin' you somethin' that was gonna turn you into an addict, those were your exact words—"

"Hoo, boy, tell me another one. You ever hear of Valium? I saw Diane Sawyer, somebody, maybe it was Connie Chung—see already my memory's bein' affected—one of them did a program about—Jane Pauley, that's who it was—oh Christ I can't remember now. See there? Anyway, whoever it was, she did a whole program about how many people was addicted to Valiums. So what's this I'm takin' now?"

"Ma, I gotta go, I'm late already. Please, okay? Eight o'clock, take your pill, okay? Promise me you'll take it. Missus Viola can't be here tonight, okay? She hurt her foot or somethin', steppin' off a curb this mornin', she's limpin' around, so you're gonna have to take care of yourself, okay? I know you haven't done this for a long long time, but I'm not gonna be out too late, okay? And I'll call ya soon as I get where I'm goin'."

"Why you gotta call me after you get there? Don't you know where you're goin'? Why can't you give me the number now?"

" 'Cause I don't know where I'm goin'. Exactly. It'll depend."

"Depend on what?"

"On where we decide. I didn't plan anything specific—"

"Who's we? What the hell's that I'm smellin'?" She walked by him sniffing and then spun around. "That's you I'm smellin'. That's you, ain't it? What is that? Why ya smell like that? You don't smell like that, that's not the way you smell."

"Ma, I been tellin' ya for three days, I got a date, okay? That's aftershave. I found it in the bathroom closet. You bought it for me long time ago. One Christmas I think. Okay? C'mon, Ma, let go of my arm. You're gonna be all right, I promise."

"You got a date? You mean like with a girl? That's the kinda date you're talkin' about? Since when, you don't go on dates. You never been out with a girl in your life."

"Yes. That kinda date. I told you. I've been telling you for three days. I have a date with a woman. Not a girl. A woman."

"A date with a woman? What woman? Who? You never told me about this."

"Ma, let go of my arm, please? I've been tellin' you for three days now, you don't wanna listen, every time I tried to tell ya, you tuned me out. This is Saturday, I started tellin' you Thursday. Which is when I got the date, okay? Now don't tell me I didn't tell ya, Ma, 'cause I told ya."

"You never told me! What're you talkin' about you told me, you never told me!"

"Aw, Ma, Jesus Christ, don't do this, okay? I'm jumpin' outta my skin as it is, don't . . . oh man."

She scowled and shoved his arm away from her as though he had been forcing it into her hands. "Fine. Perfect. You're gonna do it again. What you always do. When I need you the most, whatta you do? Huh? You walk. My son, the walker. Get a situation, get a predicament, get a condition, what's my son do? He walks. My son walks. That's what he does. He walks away. He's the best walker-awayer in the world. I get a condition like I never had before in my life and you pick now to start havin' dates. I don't believe you."

"Ma, listen to me. There's nothin' wrong with your heart—"

"There's somethin' wrong with me! I been in the hospital how many times now? You know there's somethin' wrong with me! Why you picked now to leave me, that's what I can't understand—"

"Ma, there's somethin' wrong with you, I'm not arguin' that—"

"Well that's nice of ya, least you admit there's somethin' wrong with me—"

"But it's not your heart, Ma. You've had four ECGs in the last two weeks—"

"EC what?"

"ECG—electrocardiogram. Remember, that's where they put those things on ya, all over your chest, your arms, your legs, okay?"

"Oh like that thing's gonna tell ya anything—"

"Ma, that's what they use. That's the first piece of diagnostic equipment they put on ya, I don't care what hospital you go to in the world, you walk in complainin' your chest hurts, you can't breathe, they're gonna hook ya up to one of those, okay? You've been examined by at least four doctors, one of 'em a cardiologist, the best one in Conemaugh General, everybody I talked to says so—"

"If he's so good how's come he's in this dinky little hospital? How come he ain't in Pittsburgh, one of those good hospitals. That's where they got the good doctors. The ones make all the money."

Oh shit. "Ma, listen to me. I checked that guy out, he got his training in Pittsburgh. Allegheny General Hospital. North Side, Pittsburgh. That's where the man was trained, okay? He did his internship there, he did his residency there, everything he knows about the human heart he learned right there in Pittsburgh, right there in Allegheny General, which has the reputation of bein' one of the best teachin' hospitals in the whole state. Probably in the whole goddamn country. The whole world probably—"

"If he was so smart they woulda kept him. Why didn't they keep him? Why'd he have to get a job in Rocksburg, he knows so goddamn much, huh? Answer me that, go 'head."

Carlucci looked at his watch for perhaps the third time in the last minute. "Ma, I don't know why the man decided to come to Rocksburg, I didn't ask him. But the man told me, hey, if he doesn't know what to do, he picks up the phone, he calls Allegheny General, he talks to the people who taught him, they will answer any question he has. So it's like bein' in Pittsburgh, just one phone call away that's all—"

"Don't give me that baloney, one phone call away. I talked to some people too, you know? You're not the only one knows how to investigate something. Know how many of those, uh, oh whattayacallit, where they put that thing up your leg, that camera, takes pictures inside your heart—"

"Catheterization."

"Yeah. You know how many of them they do in Allegheny General, huh? Every year, huh? Tell me, smart guy, big shot detective, bet you don't know."

"Nine thousand a year, give or take a couple hundred," Carlucci said. "And they only do about six hundred a year in Conemaugh."

"Right. Exactly. How'd you know that?"

"Same way you know, Ma, I asked—is it all right if I leave now?"

"Aw go for crissake, you're in such a goddamn hurry, go! I know how to dial nine-one-one, I don't need you for that. I don't want you doin' nothin' for me you don't wanna do, nothin' you don't think you're supposed to do . . . what any son would do."

Carlucci squeezed his eyelids shut and swallowed hard, then inhaled deeply and let it all out slowly before he reached for his parka. He opened the door and said, "Soon as I get where I'm goin', I'll call ya, okay?"

"Oh yeah, like if I need ya, you'd be right here. Don't bother. If I'm in the bathroom croakin' and you're callin' me, how'm I s'posed to answer it, huh?"

"Eight o'clock, take your pill, okay?"

"What for? Can't feel nothin'. They're s'posed to be makin' me all tranquilized, I don't feel a goddamn thing."

"The man said it would take a couple days maybe to get the full effect. He said you gotta keep takin' 'em, you can't miss a dose, okay? In addition to which, you slept eight hours straight through last night. You didn't wake up once, that's a first—"

"How do you know how much I slept? Whatta ya, watchin' me? You keepin' tabs on me?"

"Yeah, Ma, that's what I do. Listen. You didn't wake me up last night. If those pills weren't doin' anything for ya, you'da been up at least twice. But you weren't. So I'm goin' now. I'll call ya."

"My son watches me," she said, shaking her head and padding toward the living room. "My son watches me, how I sleep. I don't believe this. In my own house, my son counts how many times I get up. My son watches me!"

Carlucci stepped out onto the porch, closed his eyes, folded his hands, and tilted his head back. He whispered, "Hey, anybody. If you're up there, if you're out there, if you're any-fucking-where, if you're one, if you're two, if you're a fucking committee, if you're male, if you're female, if you're a flying fucking saucer, please, listen to me, please, this is all I'm askin'—just give me a couple hours, okay? Two fucking hours, that's all. Thank you."

On his way into the duty room, Carlucci decided he couldn't face Nowicki. Nowicki would want to know how it went last night with his cousin. Perfectly natural. He'd been promoting this get-together for months now, almost a year. Almost from the first time he'd seen Carlucci occupying the former chief's office Nowicki had been trying to manipulate Carlucci by talking up his cousin Franny. And now that it had happened, now that Carlucci had finally gathered up his nerve and done what Nowicki had been promoting all along, the last thing in the world Carlucci wanted to do was give Nowicki a description and analysis of the event. He wouldn't have wanted to do that if everything had gone smoothly.

Carlucci had been so nervous, so uncomfortable, so concerned with what kind of impression he was making, he'd drunk four beers, two more than his limit. Then he blabbered like an idiot after the third beer because up until then all he'd been able to do was give one- or two-word answers in reply to her questions. Her questions. God. He couldn't even think of her name. He was humiliated. Franny. Yes.

So he tried to slip into the duty room by coming through the front door of City Hall, then using a phone in the tax collector's office to lure Nowicki out from behind the radio with the lie that he'd left his headlights on.

"No they ain't," Nowicki said. "I can see my car from right here. You're seein' somebody else's car—who is this? This you, Rugs? This is you, Rugs, don't kid me. S'matter, you don't wanna talk to me? You better talk to me, man. I got news. I mean it, we need to talk."

"I know what you wanna talk about, Nowicki, and I don't wanna talk about it, okay? That's personal—"

"This is not about that, are you kiddin'? This is serious, honest."

"Nowicki, I'm warnin' you. You ask me one question about how it went—"

"Hey, Rugs, Jesus, man, I'm tellin' ya, I heard somethin' you need to hear. Meet ya in Balzic's office."

Carlucci hung up and tried to saunter into the station through the door from the city manager's office, muttering suspicions about Nowicki's motives every step of the way.

Nowicki was in Balzic's office, pacing and chewing a hangnail on his left thumb, looking way more agitated than Carlucci ever remembered seeing him. Nowicki quickly shut the door behind him and gave him a nudge toward the chair on the other side of the desk.

"Okay, Nowicki, don't forget what I said—what're you pushin' me for, what's with you?"

Nowicki backed Carlucci into Balzic's old chair, dragged another chair close to the desk and sat and hunched forward so that his face was only inches from Carlucci's. He whispered, "You ever find out whether they bugged this office or not?"

Carlucci shook his head and said in a normal voice, "I never had it swept. I figured, screw 'em, I wasn't gonna say anything I didn't want 'em to hear. Anyway, I couldn't figure out how to get a requisition past 'em—"

Nowicki held his finger to his lips and motioned for Carlucci to give him something to write with and on. Carlucci handed over a pen and his notebook.

Nowicki printed something quickly and turned it around for Carlucci to read. "Hired chief. Last night."

Carlucci felt his eyes going wide and his jaw going slack. His voice dropped to a whisper and he said, "There was no meeting scheduled last night. Council's not meetin' till next Thursday."

Nowicki nodded several times. "Not here. Hose Company Number One. Eddie Sitko called it. He was sittin' in the middle chair."

"Who told you this?"

"Never mind. It's true, Rugs. You're out."

"Whattya mean I'm out, what the fuck, I was never in."

"You know what I mean."

"Yeah, yeah." Carlucci licked his lips. He felt an odd fluttering sensation in his chest, along both sides of his sternum. Relief? Disappointment? Weight falling away? Rejection? He didn't know. It was just there, that fluttering, like winged insects trapped between his sternum and his heart.

"Who?"

Nowicki shrugged. "I can't say."

"Well is he from this department?"

Nowicki shrugged again. "Uh, would that make a difference to you, do you think?"

"Hell yes, you kiddin'? I can talk to anybody if they're from here."

"Maybe you could, maybe you couldn't. Maybe you'd think the guy fucked ya around behind your back. That might be a bitch to deal with, huh? Maybe you thought the guy fucked ya around behind your back, maybe you couldn't work with him."

"Shit. I can work with anybody. Your source was there?"

Nowicki shook his head.

"He wasn't, or you don't wanna say?"

"Wasn't."

"So how the fuck'd he hear about it then?"

"He heard. Guy's never been wrong before, not about what's goin' on in Number One. Remember when all that shit went down about how much money they had in mutual funds, the firemen, huh? He confirmed all that, right? Remember? I'm who told you you were right."

"I remember. No clue about who it is?"

"Me? Or him?"

"Whatta you mean, you? Him!"

Nowicki shrugged. "I know but I don't wanna say—I mean I don't wanna speculate. When it comes out I'll tell you who I was thinkin'."

"You're talkin' in circles, man, you know but you don't wanna say, you don't wanna speculate. You're tryin' to bullshit me."

"No I'm not, honest. I am not tryin' to bullshit you, I just don't wanna say what I'm thinkin', that's all."

Carlucci stared at the space beside Nowicki's head. "If it's not somebody from here, fuck, there goes my overtime."

"Maybe not. Never know. Maybe the guy'll understand. Then again, you know, maybe he'll tell you you work too much, need to get a life, time for you to start a family, you know? Maybe, I don't know, I'm just talkin' here."

"What the fuck're you, a marriage broker now?"

"I'm just sayin' maybe he'll say you work too much, that's all. Nobody should work as much as you. Maybe he'll say you need some help. All this extra shit they put on you, nobody needs that."

" 'Extra shit'? Hey. I always worked a lotta hours. And you know why I do it—no overtime, how'm I gonna pay the people to watch my mother?"

"There's always the county home."

Carlucci snorted. "Hey, that's how Bellotti got my nose open in the first place. Told me I took the job, he'd get my mother moved to the top of the list out there."

"Well she's not in there—"

"Course she ain't. I told you how that went—didn't I?"

"No. You maybe told somebody else, you never told me. You try to get her in?"

"No, uh-uh, I just asked her about it once and she freaked. Called me names, man, really hurt. Ah. So. Anyway, I talked Bellotti into goin' home with me—Balzic told me, take him home, make him ask her, you know, since it's his idea. That way he'll see I'm takin' his offer seriously, and she'll see I wasn't makin' this up on my own."

"When was this?"

"Last March sometime, I forget when exactly."

"And he went?"

"Yeah he went. So he gets in the kitchen, tries to charm her, ya-ta-ta ya-ta-ta, finally gets around to it, what would she think, you know, 'bout goin' in the county home. She was wipin' a cup or somethin', man, Jesus, she whipped that towel at him, snatched up a parin' knife, started divin' for him, man, I never moved that fast in my life. Got the knife away from her before he got the towel off his face, that's how fast I was movin'. Then she started callin' names, both of us, man, she called us names I didn't know she knew."

"Shoulda known right then, Rugs, you were never gettin' this job."

"I think I did. Soon as that towel landed I think I knew. But I didn't wanna admit it. Just kept stringin' myself along, you know? But hey, some real sharp con told me once everybody needs a con to keep movin'. You don't know how to give yourself a reason for doin' what you're doin', you can't do it. Difference in people is who believes what. Said the marks were the ones who couldn't do it without believin' it. Or to put it another way, they didn't know how not to believe it and still do it. Course he was doin' three to seven when he told me that. Come to think of it, I just heard about somebody, guy was able to do somethin' better'n most of the people who tried to do it, and all the while he was doin' it, he claimed it was all bullshit. All manufactured aggression, all fabricated emotion, top to bottom. That's what that reporter? Barone? That's what he said about Blasco. I thought I didn't know what he was talkin' about, but it turns out I do. I also guess we could probably stop whisperin' now."

"Yeah. Meantime, I better get back to the radio."

"Hey, uh, Nowicki, wait a second."

"What?"

"Uh, can I ask you somethin'?"

"Yeah? So? What?"

"You gonna be talkin', uh, you know, to your cousin, you think? Any chance you might be, uh, talkin' to her, you know, like, uh, soon?"

"Oh man, what a piece of work you are."

"Yeah yeah, I know. But I'm afraid—I mean I think I really fucked up last night. I was so nervous, honest to God, I had less nerves collarin' those two brothers, I'm not jokin'. I drank four beers, man, I got such a headache now you can't believe it. Made a total ass of myself. First I didn't know what to say, then when the beer kicked in, I couldn't shut up, and I have no idea what I said. For all I know I mighta proposed."

"So, am I supposed to take that to mean you liked her, huh?" Nowicki was grinning triumphantly.

"Oh Christ, what's not to like, you kiddin'? No, man, really, I mean, pretty, built, smart, got a great voice, aw man, like if honey could talk that's the way she sounds. But really smart, man, that's what got me. I didn't know she was a psychiatric social worker. The way you kept talkin' about her, I thought she was gonna be some bimbo. She knows a lotta shit, man. That's a smart woman."

"If you were as beered up as you say, how would you know?"

"Well you don't get drunk instantly, for crissake. I heard what she was sayin' before I got all googly. So, uh, you gonna be talkin' to her you think?"

"Hey, Rugs, I got a better idea. Why don't you talk to her?"

"Aw man, just do a little recon for me, that's all, okay? I don't wanna go blastin' in there by myself again, just pick up the phone, you know? That's scary just pickin' up the phone. I hate not knowin' what to talk about. Especially 'cause I made such an ass outta myself. C'mon, man, I'll owe ya one, I mean it."

"Hey, Rugs, consider this, okay? She talks to goofies for a livin', you know? That's her job. Believe me, you're the closest thing she's been to normal in ten years, so don't worry about it. She'll know how to talk to ya. And believe me, if you fucked up, she'll be the first one to tell you. Nothin' shy about that girl."

"Well how come she works mostly at night? I meant to ask her that but I didn't get around to it—"

"I don't know why. Last time I talked to her about it, she

said mostly what she does is group stuff. Why else—'cause most of 'em work days, I don't know. Ask her. There's somethin' you could talk about. There you go, interview her! You know how to do that, you're good at that. You're the best I know at that. Treat her like the most important witness you're ever gonna have. She's gonna be the witness to your love—"

"Aw will you get the fuck outta here, witness to my love. Nowicki, swear to God, you're the king of bullshit, man. Jesus, where do you get it?"

"The king of bullshit, huh?" Nowicki said, backing out of the room. "I better be. I hope you're right."

"Now what the fuck's that mean?"

Nowicki shrugged. "Just talkin', that's all. Call her, man. I'm not callin' her. You call her. I think you'll be surprised."

Mayor Angelo Bellotti, smiling, making tiny chatter, waved Carlucci into his office. Carlucci had a flashback: it was the 1980s, he was in Bellotti's appliance store, pricing microwave ovens because he'd seen a TV show about how convenient it was to spend a Sunday afternoon making pasta sauces, stews, chili in large quantities, freezing them in individual serving sizes, and defrosting them in minutes in the microwave just before mealtime. It was touted as the workingwoman's answer to a week's meal preparations. Carlucci saw it as the way to have the kind of pasta sauces he wanted, because, much as he appreciated Mrs. Comito otherwise, he couldn't stand her marinara sauce. She insisted on putting a large hunk of really fatty beef into it and never skimmed the fat after it had simmered for half the day. A microwave seemed like the perfect defense against that. And it was. Ever since, Carlucci had spent at least two Sundays every month cooking large pots of food and freezing them in portions for himself and his mother. Only problem with that was that every time his mother was annoyed or angry with him, she stood by the sink and poured his food down the drain while looking at him.

Which, while it diminished him, didn't diminish the value of the microwave.

But what Carlucci was hearing now in Bellotti's tone was a flashback of his tone the day he sold Carlucci the microwave oven. Bellotti hadn't wanted to talk about the oven; all he'd wanted to talk about was how convenient it would be to make a week's worth of pasta sauces or stews or chili and freeze them in individual serving sizes. Bellotti had seen the same TV show Carlucci had. But no matter how many times Carlucci told Bellotti they'd watched the same program and he didn't need to hear about that anymore and what he really wanted to hear was how to work the damn thing, Bellotti had just droned on in his best imitation of Dale Carnegie. He'd continued to sell the sizzle and not the steak, until finally Carlucci bought the best oven he could afford, after he'd figured that the only way he could get Bellotti to shut up was to buy the damned thing and learn how to operate it by reading the manual himself.

Now, here he was again, and Bellotti was once again selling sizzle instead of steak. How else could it be, Carlucci thought. The man believes that Dale Carnegie crap with every shred of his shopkeeper's soul.

Bellotti was telling him what a great job he'd done since Balzic had retired. "Just great, Rugs. I mean it. Your work has been exemplary. Fine police work, fine, fine. Broke some really big cases. Put old Rocksburg right on the TV there a couple of times, yessir, my wife said, isn't that something, made those TV people in Pittsburgh sit up and take notice. And I said, that's Carlucci. That's Rugs. That's a policeman's policeman. Outstanding investigator, exceptional detective, a man anybody, any mayor anywhere—not just myself—you bet, any mayor, hell, there isn't a mayor in any third-class city in this state wouldn't be proud to have you as a member of the police department."

Bellotti went on like that for some minutes. Carlucci sat and watched him, watched his mouth moving, watched his large gestures of approval and appreciation, the nods, the upraised palms, the sweeping arms embracing the air between them. It was one of Bellotti's better performances. Carlucci was so intent on tuning out the words and watching the expressions and gestures that he almost missed it. In fact it was only after he'd heard the name the second time that he snapped back.

" . . . he's been a fine officer for many years, as you well know. Now there was a question of course, you know, there was some discussion, you know, some people said there might be a problem because he's a patrolman, but, hell, we have to deal with these problems in perception all the time. With some things, you know very well, you have just as big a problem with the appearance of a problem as you do if you have an actual problem. It's the perception, see? The public's perception. I mean, if they perceive one thing, it won't matter what we try to tell them. That's what I learned in sellin', Rugs. Used to make all my salesmen, if he lasted thirty days with me, if I saw the potential there, off he went, made him sign up for the next Carnegie course. Absolutely, you have to learn how to recognize what the customer wants. That's the whole thing. You learn to spot what the customer's lookin' for, you can sell him. That's what Carnegie meant—"

"Excuse me. Did you say Nowicki? Is that who you said? Nowicki's gonna be chief?"

"What? Didn't I make that clear? I thought I made that very clear. I thought I said that twice. Didn't I say that twice?"

"Uh, yes sir, you did, yes. It just, uh, you know, just took a minute to sink in—I guess."

"Now, Rugs, this is strictly confidential, this is strictly between you and me, I don't want this leavin' this office in advance of our next public meeting, I want to be very clear about that. I know there's been rumors flyin' around for months now. God, seems like forever we been tryin' to get this worked out. Anyway. It's settled now. So I hope you understand why I wanted to tell you now, ahead of time. Didn't want you walkin' into that meeting next Thursday, you know, gettin' clobbered so to speak, gettin' hit with it—and I sure as hell didn't want you readin' it in the paper. I mean, you've done great work here, many years now, you've performed above and beyond, yessir, way above and beyond, and I said, I told them all, I said, listen, you have to let me tell Carlucci myself well in advance, I mean the man deserves to be treated with all the consideration and respect any man deserves. I just wish there was some way we could've actually compensated you for the work you did. Now I tried, Rugs, but, uh, just too much resistance to that. You know, just wasn't possible with, I mean, given the budget problems we have, I just couldn't, uh, muster up a consensus for that.

"But, be that as it may, uh, you think you'll be able to work with, uh, Chief Nowicki? You see any problems there? There won't be any problems, there, huh, will there?"

"Uh, no sir. I don't see any problems at all. I'm, uh, I mean, actually, now that I think about it, I'm actually, uh, yeah. I'm, uh, relieved. I can go back to doin' what I think I do best. Yes sir. I can deal with this."

"Oh good, Rugs. Good good, glad to hear that. There was some thought, you know, some discussion about how you might, you know, take it wrong, him bein' a patrolman, not havin' nearly the time in service that you have—but you know he has passed the sergeant's test."

"Passed the lieutenant's test too."

"Oh—he has? Oh hell, that's even better," Bellotti said, beaming. He stood up and came around the desk and held up his left arm for Carlucci to walk under. He gave Carlucci's right shoulder his best professional squeeze.

"Listen, how's your mother? How's she doin' these days?"

"Aw, fine. She's fine. Doin' real good, yes sir."

"Ah good. That's the main thing. Everybody healthy. Without your health, you know, what the hell. All the rest, huh?"

They were at the door. "Yes sir. Without your health, all the rest? Doesn't mean a thing."

"Listen, wanna see ya Thursday night, Rugs. Wear your dress uniform. Wanna stress continuity. That's what we wanna emphasize. Continuity. Smooth shift in power. That's the main thing. Stability. Stability, continuity. That's what the people want. That's what we think Nowicki's gonna provide. That's what it came down to, all the discussions. We thought the man had stability."

"Yes, sir. I'm sure you're right. I'm sure he does."

"Good. Good. Glad you appreciate that. As always, Rugs, good talkin' to you. Always appreciate your candor. Yes sir. Fine man, outstanding police work, really glad you're on my side, Rugs. Really glad you're on the team."

Carlucci was swallowing hard. He'd drained the first Pepsi in two gulps, but his throat felt like he'd just drunk a glass of sand. He kept turning to look at the door, then looking at his watch, then back at the door. He was trying to pay attention to what Dom Muscotti was saying, but Muscotti was drunk and rattling on about his grandchildren. Carlucci wouldn't have cared about Muscotti's grandchildren even if he wasn't waiting for Franny Perfetti. He was trying to puzzle out again how she was related to Nowicki, but he didn't care about that any more than he cared about Muscotti's grandchildren. Mostly he couldn't wait to see her, he didn't care how she was related to anybody. He just wanted her to be related to him, but he had this terrible empty feeling he didn't know how to make that happen. Dream of esteem, dream of esteem, as in I have none, even the leeches don't want my blood. . . .

Interview her, Nowicki had said. " . . . interview her! You know how to do that, you're good at that. You're the best I know at that."

Yeah, Nowicki, and you're the king of bullshit. And what

did he say when I said that? "I better be. I hope you're right."
Fucker tried to tell me, didn't he? Tried every way he knew to let
me down easy and I'm sitting there looking right at him and trying to figure out who it might be. Jesus. . . .

"Hi," she said. "Sorry I'm late." There it was. That voice.
Honey pouring into steaming tea.

"Hey, you're not late. No, honest, I'm early."

"That's right, it's late," Muscotti said, squinting at first one
clock and then another until he'd swept all six of them around his
saloon with his wobbly glance. "What're you doin' in here, young
lady? Anybody pretty as you oughta be home. You too, Carlucci,
what the hell're you doin' here? Go home. Not 'cause you're pretty.
You ain't. You also can't tell time, apparently. Don't you know how
late it is? What the hell's wrong with you? Get outta here, hit the
bricks, go home. I'm closed."

"C'mon Mister Muscotti, one drink, okay?"

"No! Get outta here, I'm closed. You pay for that drink?"

"Yessir I did," Carlucci said, standing, shrugging at Franny,
mugging like he didn't know what was going on but when Muscotti wanted to go home, it didn't matter what time it was. He
closed when he felt like it. It didn't matter that it was ten till ten;
if he wanted to go home, that was where he was going, so Carlucci had to think of something fast. Especially since Franny had
said she'd never been in Muscotti's and wanted to go there because
she'd remembered hearing her father talking about it while he was
still alive. And though that had been years ago, it seemed like yesterday to her, and she'd jumped at it when Carlucci had suggested
it on the phone.

"What now?" she said.

"I was, uh, you know, hopin' maybe you had someplace else,
uh, you wanted to see. You know, uh, fallback joint your father
went to, I guess."

"Go home for crissake," Muscotti growled. "I had this girl
here I wouldn't be lookin' for no joint to go to."

"We could always go to Ronnie's," she said.

Carlucci was so grateful he could've kissed her right there in front of Muscotti. Just the thought of kissing her made him shiver.

So they drove in separate cars to Ronnie's, with Franny leading. All the way, Carlucci was rehearsing questions, practicing his interview. He kept telling himself what Balzic had always said: the best interviews never sounded like interviews. They sounded like normal conversations between regular people, plain folks passing the time of day. They were not, of course. Ridiculous to think you could sound like you were passing the time of day asking people to explain the sequence of events leading up to a crime, then the crime itself, then the immediate aftermath. But what Balzic had meant, and what Carlucci had come to learn, was that it was tough enough with one person in the interview reeling under emotional waves; the interviewer had to act as though he was no more disturbed by or interested in the answers than he would've been if he'd been asking for directions to the nearest gas station.

But this was different. Carlucci really wanted to know how to get to this gas station. And he was the one reeling with emotion.

Inside Ronnie's, after they'd found a booth, she threw him when she said, "You okay?"

"Yeah. Me? Why? I'm okay."

"Right before we left Muscotti's, you were shivering. You're not getting the flu, are you? Lots of people I work with have it."

Christ, she noticed that? Saw me shiver? Oh man. "No. No I'm fine. Just, you know, must've been some nerve thing, you know. Twitch, somethin', tic. Goofy shit's always happenin' like that to me—goofy stuff. Sorry. Stuff. Goofy stuff. Uh, come here a lot?" Ohhhh, man, is that lame or what—come here a lot, Jesus, Carlucci, wake the fuck up!

"No, not a lot." She caught her smile before it got bigger. "But some nights, I mean, if I've had groups all night, and they won't leave me alone during the breaks, you know I just get so hungry and I can't go home at this time of night and start banging around the kitchen. My mom has enough trouble sleeping. So, yeah, nights like that, I come here. This is one of the few places you can order a vegetarian pizza and you don't get that look, you know?"

"You like vegetarian pizza?"

"I love vegetables period. That's mostly all I eat. Love 'em."

"I don't eat as many as I should, you know, s'posed to eat five a day, least that's what I read, but, uh, I got turned on to veggie pizza, I don't know where it was, but I really like 'em. Gino's makes good ones, you ever had theirs?" Oh man, now that's really probing and intelligent. Fucking Nowicki should be hearing this, great interviewer that I am.

"Yeah, I've had theirs. They're good. But I think here's better."

"Ah. You do, huh? Well. We shall see what we shall see, right? Uh, so you had groups all day today, huh? What kinda groups? Jeez, all day, man, I don't know if I could handle talkin' to groups all day. You know. Groups of people. I get nervous talkin' to groups of people—not that I do it that much, you know."

"Well, I mean, I don't do it all day. I have to leave myself time to do the paperwork. Anyway, mostly I don't talk, mostly I just listen. I only jump in when they start goin' off the wall, or, you know, when it lags. Then whenever we get new people—and we're always getting new people, you know, they come, they go. And they're shy at first, or edgy or belligerent, sometimes they're real belligerent—who am I kiddin', I mean a lot of them are really belligerent, so, uh, you have to know when to push them, you know, without seeming to."

"Get a lot of 'em from the courts?"

"Ouu," she said, rolling her eyes. "All of them are from the courts. I work for the adult probation office."

"You mean none of this is voluntary—they're all on pro?"

"Ouu no. Not voluntary, none of it's voluntary. Wish it were. Might be able to make a lot more sense sometimes."

"If every one of 'em's on pro, Jesus, how you make any sense with any of 'em at all?"

"Well, that's how they skated. God, there aren't enough jail cells in the world to put them all in, you know that. You do know that, right?"

"Yeah. Of course. But I mean, I don't deal that much with, uh, hell, I don't even know what to call 'em. What are they?"

"People."

"No I mean I know they're people. But, you know, like what—what are they, they get to do this instead of time?"

"Oh they're doing time, believe me. But, uh, mostly they're people with addictive personality disorder if you want the technical term."

"You mean junkies."

"Yeah. Right. Either alcohol or illegal drugs or gambling. Other addictions I don't deal with."

"God, what other kinds are there?"

"Oh, food, sex, violence, you name it. Anything you get a jones about. Exercise. Anything you do to the exclusion of the rest of what might pass for a normal life. Course, some people say normal is the psychopathology of the average. Listen, I'm for broccoli, peppers, onions, tomatoes, olives, mushrooms, how's that sound to you? Okay if I order—you ready?"

"Hey. Fine. Sounds good to me. Garlic, huh? No garlic?"

"No garlic?" she said, mugging at him as she stood to go to the bar. "Your name's Carlucci? And you want a pizza without garlic?"

"No, I didn't mean I wanted one with no garlic, I meant weren't you gonna order garlic on it—you know, you didn't say garlic, that's what I meant, you said everything else."

She leaned down so close to him, he could smell her breath. His neck stiffened and he knew he was blushing. He tried not to back up, but she was so pretty, her skin was so smooth, her eyes dancing with such open invitation, he thought if she didn't back away soon he'd slip right off the chair onto the floor. He felt his hips sliding forward. He grabbed the edges of the seat to hang on.

"That better be the truth, Carlucci," she said, grinning down at him. " 'Cause if I find out you're not a real dago, if I find out you don't eat garlic, I'm gonna drop a dime on you to the garlic police."

Then she swung around, tossing her shiny black hair, took four steps to the bar, and looked back over her shoulder at him. And if he hadn't known it before, he knew it now. He was lost. For as long as time would allow.

When Carlucci walked into the station the following morning, he was humming. Fischetti eyed him warily while handing over a phone message from the district attorney's office. When Carlucci asked what the DA wanted, Fischetti answered by asking if Carlucci had been humming. Carlucci said he had not. He didn't hum, he said, what was Fischetti talking about? Fischetti had said Carlucci could lie if he wanted to, but he'd been humming. Carlucci said Fischetti sounded like he was trying to start something. Fischetti said he wasn't trying to start anything, but humming was humming and Carlucci was humming.

"DA say when he wanted to see me?"

"Now. If not sooner. And you were hummin', fuck you weren't, I heard ya."

"Fish, I never hummed in my life, why would I start now?"

"How should I know? But you were hummin', bigger'n shit, you can deny it all you want. You know what I think of hummers, don'tcha? Same thing I think of whistlers. You know? Those guys that warble? That don't whistle any tune anybody ever heard? And just go on and on and on and on? Fuckers oughta be shot. Never met one yet didn't deserve to be shot. I'd sooner have a guy next door to me liked to play with a chain saw than one of those whistlers."

Carlucci was thinking about that as he went up on the elevator to the DA's office in the Conemaugh County Courthouse. *I wasn't hummin'. I don't hum. Fischetti needs to get away from that radio, he's crackin' up, I never hummed in my life.*

The DA's receptionist waved him right in. She wasn't smiling, she wasn't frowning, she wasn't doing anything with her face that Carlucci could read, and when he asked what this was about, she gave him a noncommittal shrug.

Inside the office, DA Howard Failan was sitting behind his large walnut desk, stirring coffee in his green mug with the white shamrocks on it with what looked like a heavy sterling-silver spoon, scowling at some distant thought, his eyes focused on a spot on the floor at Carlucci's feet as he came in and closed the door. Failan was definitely scowling, definitely deep in thought, but definitely scowling. Carlucci had been in the room for almost two seconds before Failan looked up and acknowledged his presence.

"Rugs," Failan said, coming forward a half-step, extending his hand. He was not smiling.

Carlucci shook hands and took a seat at the side of the desk.

"What's up?"

"I'm trying to decide whether I have a problem."

"Well, for what it's worth, my rule is, if you have to try to decide, you probably don't have one," Carlucci said, smiling.

"Yeah? Think so, huh? Read this. And observe the dates, both letters, okay?" Failan handed over an envelope. It was an unstamped, unpostmarked envelope containing two letters, one a letter to the DA on the stationery of John A. Lazzaro, Attorney-at-Law. The other was a typed transcript, certified to be a true copy of the handwritten letter on notebook paper that was stapled to it.

"That was hand-delivered about five minutes after I got here this morning. By the attorney's, uh, Mister Lazzaro's personal assistant. Seems Mister Lazzaro has taken to his bed, I think that's the expression that applies here. But read it. I wanna know what you think."

Carlucci read the letter on Lazzaro's stationery first.

Dear Mr. Failan:

In re the homicide of Robert J. Blasco:

As you may know, I was the attorney of record for Philip E. Randa at the time of Mr. Randa's death in Conemaugh General Hospital on Saturday, Nov. 4, 1995. He had been admitted to the hospital at approximately 4:30 A.M. that day and I was summoned at his request to the hospital within minutes of his admission there.

When I arrived at approximately 5:15 A.M., I had no idea why I had been summoned. I can't say with any certainty which of the sons made the phone call to me, though I think it was Mr. Randa's eldest son, Francis.

In any event, I was not told prior to my arrival in the hospital why my presence had been so urgently requested by Mr. Randa. Upon my arrival, however, and upon being ushered to his bedside, I soon learned that Mr. Randa was about to put me in a very difficult position.

Up to then, I was not acquainted with Mr. Randa in any way except professionally, and very briefly at that, i.e., I had drawn up a will for him in the spring of this year. Aside from two meetings, the first on March 1, 1995, for him to express the particulars of his will, and again on March 8, 1995, when he read, approved, and signed all copies of the will I'd drawn, I had no other contact with him or any other member of his family. I had not, until Nov. 4, 1995, ever seen any other member of his family, not his wife, sons, daughter, in-laws, or grandchildren.

So it is a gross understatement to say I was shocked when I

discovered the reason from his own lips about why he had requested my presence. He wanted to confess to the proper author-
ities to the murder of Robert Blasco, and he wanted me to
arrange that confession. He was at first verbally emphatic that he
and he alone was responsible for the beating of Mr. Blasco which
caused Mr. Blasco's death. But it became obvious in a matter of
minutes that Mr. Randa had not acted alone.

Furthermore, when Mr. Randa gave me the letter which is
enclosed, it was plainly evident that Mr. Randa was of two minds:
one, he wanted to claim sole responsibility for a premeditated
murder, but two, he also wanted to bring to a just resolution a
crime which he did not commit but for which he felt equally responsible.

However, when I tried to arrange for Mr. Randa to confess
to the proper authority, i.e., to the chief of police in the jurisdic-
tion where the homicide occurred, I was taken aback to learn
from the acting chief of police, one Detective Sgt. Ruggiero Carlucci, that one, I was not acting in the best interest of my client,
that two, I should resign the case, and that three, I should advise
my client to secure counsel more experienced in criminal law than
I was. Sergeant Carlucci specifically called my attention to the difference between murder and voluntary manslaughter as disassoci-
ated in Title 18, Section 2502 Murder and Section 2503(b)
Voluntary manslaughter unreasonable belief killing justifiable.

I considered Sgt. Carlucci's advice very carefully, and con-
cluded that he was right. I won't go into my reasoning here, except
to say that two factors weighed heavily in my deliberations. One,
I have had no criminal work at all beyond the summary level. Two,
I was overwhelmed by emotion when Mr. Randa died without
confessing, which is why I had been called to his bedside, i.e., to
effectuate his confession. It is pertinent for me to add here that I
am, like Mr. Randa was, a member of the Roman Catholic
Church, and I take the sacrament of confession very seriously.
When I knew that Mr. Randa had indeed died without my per-

forming the very service I had been asked to perform, I broke down. I felt not only that I had betrayed Mr. Randa but that I had somehow betrayed my faith. It was for these reasons that I came to agree with Sgt. Carlucci that I should resign from the case.

However, I must now reveal this other factor in the case, which further complicates my position in it. I submit the following letter, handwritten as you can see by Mr. Randa himself, transcribed to type by myself, which I vouch is a certified true copy of the handwritten letter. I have willfully and knowingly withheld this letter from you, as well as from Sgt. Carlucci, since it came into my possession hours before Mr. Randa's death. I cannot justify my failure to produce this letter for your inspection and consideration in your prosecution of Mr. Randa's sons, Francis, Ronald, and George. I cannot justify why I have held this letter until now, other than to say I found its contents so disturbing I didn't know what to do with it or about it. I'm afraid I have used very poor judgment in this regard.

I can only hope that by turning this letter over to you, I will have begun the process of absolution for myself that I find I cannot live without. My faith is apparently much more deeply ingrained in me than I'd ever imagined.

I sincerely hope you will not think that I had another motive for retaining this letter, but I will be available to answer any questions you may have. If you believe that I have acted in any way to bring ill repute or disrespect upon our honorable profession, I will understand completely if you pursue your beliefs.

Sincerely,
John A. Lazzaro
Attorney-at-Law

Carlucci stopped reading long enough to shoot a puzzled glance at Failan, who shrugged back at him.

"Keep reading," Failan said. "It gets better—or worse."

Carlucci turned to the certified true copy of Philip Randa's letter. It was dated 3 A.M., November, 4, 1995.

To whom it may concern,

I been carrying this grief with me for more than thirty-five years now. I can't carry it anymore. I did wrong to my family. Especially my daughter Virginia June. But all of them my wife my sons. Since Virginia June was a little girl she tried to tell me what was going on but I would not listen to her. I would not listen because I did not want to listen. I did not want to believe what she was telling me. I did not want to believe she was telling the truth. I puniched her for lying to me. I was terrible wrong. I did not do anything to protect her or to help her or to teach my sons the right proper way to behave. I am ashamed. I am sick. I am going to die. I can feel it. I had to do something to help my daughter. I finally thought of a way to help her and to punich my sons for what they did to her. Her husband was a no good bastard. But no worse than my own sons. But still he beat Virginia June and she did not deserve that. She is such a good person always trying to help people nursing them and caring for them. I don't know how she became such a good person. I wish I could say she learned it from me but I know in my sick heart she did not. So I talked my sons into doing right. Beating Bobby was right. He beat Virginia June he should be beat. I talked my sons into holding him while I beat him. I beat him with the damn bat he was so proud of. But my sons held him. Till he pass out. Then I made them take turns. We all wore gloves. And we burnt the clothes and shoes after words. I did not have the guts to punich my sons for what they did to Virginia June. All I'm hoping is the law puniches them as they deserve to be puniched. Now I can die. Now I know God forgives me. I hope Virginia June some day maybe forgives me.

As God is my witness.
Philip E. Randa, 72

Carlucci couldn't speak. All he could do was shake his head.

"Well, Rugs," Failan said after some moments had passed. "What do you think, do I have a problem or not?"

Carlucci blew out a sigh until his cheeks puffed. "Oh man, all I know is, Jesus, if you do, I'm glad you're the one who has it and not me."

"You are, huh? Wanna tell me what you think it is?"

"I don't know, Mister Failan, and, uh, I don't know why you're askin' me, but I'm startin' to get a funny feelin' here. Which I can't honestly say I'm thrilled about. 'Cause I'm not."

"Well let me put you at ease. You don't have anything to worry about—at least not from me. But my problem—one of my problems—is what to do if anything about our friend Mister Lazzaro. But I am very curious. Why the hell'd you tell him to re-sign?"

"Well, I mean, why else? At the time I thought it was a straight-up revenge and, uh, to be perfectly honest, I thought it was time that lowlife got dusted. You know how many times we collared him for beatin' women? I'd have to get his sheet and count 'em, but I'll bet it's at least twenty. Twenty for sure. Fucker never did more than a day. Skated every time—and that's just our department. Everybody was cuttin' that bastard slack from before he had hair on his ass, all because he could do tricks with balls. Imagine that. Everybody let him do anything he wanted just because he could throw or spin or kick some kinda ball better'n everybody else, all the other kids. Wasn't enough people stood around cheerin' for this dirtbag, clappin' for him, they looked the other way when he was beatin' women, robbin' 'em, rapin' 'em, God only knows whether he killed one someplace, we'll never know that.

"There's a photograph in this courthouse, at least one that I know of, of a judge with his arm around that prick after he skated on a rape charge in a nonjury trial. The judge let him go for a fucking autographed baseball and a photograph of the two of them with the judge holdin' the ball."

"I know the photograph very well," Failan said. "You're not answering my question."

"Sure I am—I did. It was obvious to me Lazzaro didn't know how to defend these guys, I mean, he was pushin' a confession. At that time I thought they deserved not just the best defense they could get but they deserved a fuckin' commendation, a medal, so that's why I told him resign. I didn't find out until after the funeral that there might've been the incest. That was three days after I'd told Lazzaro what I told him, you know, quit, get outta the way, you're gonna put the whole family on death row—how did I know that's what the old man was shootin' for the whole time? Shit. Would you? I mean, given what I knew at the time? I mean, I didn't know—really really know—till she made me get off the phone when I asked her to talk her brother outta the house, the retarded one. And I still didn't wanna believe it even after we found him on the side of the road, with his wang out, you know, sayin' he was waitin' for his sister. Jesus Christ. I mean, I know exactly how the old man must've felt—well I don't *know* know, but I think I know.

"Look, Mr. Failan, there are some things, I don't care how long I'm a cop, I'm never gonna get used to. I mean, I don't think I'm ever gonna get used to the idea that she knew how to tempt her brother outta the house and tempt is the wrong word 'cause it gives the completely wrong idea but I don't know what else to call it. I mean she tempted him outta the house, she was the carrot got that donkey outta that house for us. I mean I know that's how she kept herself together, how she protected herself, 'cause you don't have to be any genius to imagine what kinda shit she had to put up with when she didn't pretend she was goin' along with it. So does that answer suit you any better? I wanted them to have good representation, that's why I told him. But now that I think about it, I mean, what is your problem? That letter, Jesus.

That's better'n a wet towel or a phone book or a week in isolation. If you can't get a confession outta the retarded one, that Rennie, with that letter, I mean, Christ, whatta ya want?"

"I just wanted to know what you were thinking, that's all. I mean, uh, Rugs, you can see my point here, can't you? You? Telling a lawyer to resign because his client wants to confess? You have to admit, right? I mean, even for me, it's a bit much, don't you think?"

"Well, when you put it that way, yes, sir, I guess it is. But at the time, you know, uh, it looked like a good idea."

It took Carlucci less than a minute to clean out Balzic's desk. In the eleven months he'd been using the desk, all he'd managed to put in the drawers were some rollerball pens, the notebooks for the cases he was working, his Rolodex, his tape recorder, half a dozen double-A rechargeable batteries, and his battery recharger. All of that barely covered the bottom of one cardboard box that he'd brought up from the weight room downstairs. It seemed a paltry collection for a would-be chief, and since he'd started calling himself Wally Wannabe since his last conversation with Joe Barone, he thought even the most pitiful Wally Wannabe would've accumulated more stuff to do the job than he had. Any job.

He carried the box out to the duty room to his own desk, which was bulging with the rest of his stuff, so much so that he had trouble getting the drawers open. He sat down and started going through it, drawer by drawer, looking at all the reports, photographs, and notebooks that he'd never seemed to have time to file. He was so far behind in filing these hard files, and so far behind in transferring what was on the department's paper files to floppy disks that for a brief moment he just hung his head and shook it. Then he roused himself, went to get a couple more boxes he was always collecting at the state store and storing in the weight room, and came back up in time to see Nowicki coming through the door from the parking lot and Canoza doing stretches at the radio console.

The zero-seven-hundred watch was about to begin, and for the briefest moment Carlucci found himself worrying about who was going to man the radio. Nowicki's name had been written in for it, but last night's council meeting had changed that.

Canoza snapped to attention out of a hamstring stretch as soon as he became aware that Nowicki had arrived. Then Canoza did a grossly exaggerated salute, clicked his heels together, and immediately began to sing, "Dun dun ta-dah dun ta-da ta-da ta-dah da." Before he finished croaking out the song, Nowicki and Carlucci were both laughing, groaning, holding up their hands in protest, and saying, "Stop, stop!"

"Oh yeah, stop, huh? If my singin's so lousy, what was I singin'?"

" 'Hail to the Chief,' " they both said.

"Well how bad could I be if you knew what it was?"

"That would take more time to explain than it's worth," Nowicki said.

"Yeah?" Canoza said. "Well, O mighty Chief, maybe you can explain who's up for the radio this watch 'cause my ass has been in this chair for sixteen hours, thank you very much, thank you, thank you."

"What're you talkin' about?" Carlucci said, jumping up to look at the rosters on the chalkboard. "Says Fish was s'posed to be here—"

"He hada take one of his girls to the hospital. Appendicitis."

"She okay?" Nowicki said.

Canoza shrugged. "Last time he called he said they'd probably operate on her around six, that woulda been about an hour ago. I think if somethin' didn't go right he woulda called. He said he couldn't leave her last night 'cause she was scared and his wife hada stay home with the rest of the kids. So I told him, hey, no problem, I can use the overtime. But I'm not pullin' three watches in a row. That's out. So, Chief, welcome to your first personnel crisis. I'm outta here."

Nowicki looked at Carlucci. Carlucci looked at Canoza. Canoza looked at them both on his way to the chalkboard where he erased his name. Then he went to his locker and collected his Thermos and his parka. He put the parka on, shouldered the Thermos like a rifle, snapped off a mock salute to Nowicki, and carried on a conversation with himself on his way out.

"Sir. Patrolman Canoza requests permission to abandon his post, sir."

"Permission granted, Patrolman. And once again a grateful city thanks you for a job well done."

"Thank you, sir. Does that mean I can look forward to a merit bonus, sir?"

"Are you some kind of asshole comedian, Patrolman? Nobody's got a merit bonus in this department in ten years."

"No sir, not an asshole comedian, sir. Just an asshole patrolman, sir. Thank you, sir, and good morning." Then, after another mock salute at the door, he was gone.

Nowicki looked at Carlucci again. "You think Booboo's maybe ready for therapy again?"

"I think your more pressing problem is who's gonna work the radio. And for a couple seconds there, I thought it was my problem. But, I'm happy to say, it's not only not my problem, I haven't worked a radio since before we got that Motorola, so don't look at me."

"Some job this is," Nowicki said. "Haven't even been into my office yet and already I got people tellin' me what they're not gonna do and it's not their problem and they don't care."

"That, my friend, is why the big bucks stop in your pocket."

"Speakin' of which, as my first unofficial duty, I'm advisin' you, Sergeant Carlucci, to contact the FOP and see what they can do about gettin' chief's pay for all the time you were actin' chief.

If that results in a civil suit against the city, I'm goin' on the un-official record here that I will testify in your behalf."

"You serious?"

"Absolutely serious. Already talked to Fischetti, Dvorsky, and Havlichek, and I'm gonna talk to Canoza and everybody else who ever worked as actin' watch commanders while workin' dispatch. That's a sergeant's job, it rates sergeant's pay, and they screwed us all outta that, man, every one of us. And I'm prepared to take legal action to get the money that's rightfully owed to me and everybody else. Only reason I'm not askin' you to join with us is 'cause I think you had a special situation and counsel's probably gonna wanna split you off. But I'm for gettin' our money one way or another. They think I'm gonna get amnesia 'cause they're givin' me the office and the scrambled eggs, they got another think comin'.'"

Carlucci looked at Nowicki again. Nowicki was wearing a white shirt. Department colors were black: hat, shirt, trousers, tie, jacket. In Carlucci's memory, the only person in the department to wear a white shirt was the chief, but Balzic had always preferred civvies to his uniform, so seeing Nowicki in a white shirt was somewhat unsettling.

"Uh, don't take this wrong, uh, Chief, but, uh—"

"Already I'm takin' it wrong—not that it doesn't sound right, it just, I don't know, sounds funny."

"You didn't even give me a chance to say it yet—"

"Chief. You said, 'Chief.' It doesn't sound right comin' from you."

"Well what I wanna know—you gonna let me ask this time or you gonna interrupt me again?"

"Ask. Go 'head."

"Well, it's obvious you got the shirt, you got the brass, you got the cap with the eggs, but, uh, I mean, you didn't get all that stuff between the time the meeting ended last night and this morning. There were no stores open for you to get all that stuff."

"So, uh, you wanna know when I bought it?"

"Not when so much. More like, you know, when'd you start promotin' yourself, when'd you start campaignin' for the job? It's not I'm not glad you got it, understand? 'Cause I am glad you got it. I was surprised when Bellotti told me, I'm not gonna tell ya I wasn't. But the more I thought about it, the more I thought—and I still think—I mean I think you're gonna be all right. I think you're gonna be good at this—especially if you pull this thing off about the pay, shit, that'll be fantastic."

"But what? I mean what do you wanna know? You wanna know whether I was doin' a number behind your back? Or whether you didn't pick up on it?"

Carlucci thought that over and nodded. "Yeah. Pretty much."

"What do you think?"

"Probably a little of both."

"I think you're probably right. That gonna be a problem?"

"For you and me? Fuck no. You know me, I know you. I'm glad. Really. I'm a fuckin' bloodhound. You? You were the best promoter in this department—best one I ever saw. Just gonna have different priorities, that's all." Carlucci stood up and walked toward Nowicki with his right hand out. "Said it last night, and I'll say it again today. Congratulations, Chief. I look forward to working with you."

"Thanks, Rugs—Sergeant. Comin' from you, that means a lot, man. No shit. Really. Thanks."

"You're welcome. Now. About this fuckin' computer that's still in the box—"

"Oh Christ, will you at least let me go sit in my office first? For at least a minute? Huh? See how the chair feels?"

Carlucci shrugged and held up his hands, palms up. "Hey, you wanna feel warm and fuzzy, I can wait. But, uh, don't get too comfortable. Believe me, there's gonna be days when that chair's gonna feel like a thousand frozen razor blades. . . ."